THE
SEASCAPE TATTOO

THE
SEASCAPE TATTOO

LARRY NIVEN

AND STEVEN BARNES

TOR

A TOM DOHERTY ASSOCIATES BOOK

New York

THE SEASCAPE TATTOO

Copyright © 2016 by Larry Niven and Steven Barnes

A Tor Book
Published by Tom Doherty Associates, LLC
175 Fifth Avenue
New York, NY 10010

www.tor-forge.com

Tor® is a registered trademark of Tom Doherty Associates, LLC.

The Library of Congress Cataloging-in-Publication Data is available upon request.

ISBN 978-0-7653-7873-6 (hardcover)
ISBN 978-1-4668-6335-4 (e-book)

Our books may be purchased in bulk for promotional, educational, or business use. Please contact your local bookseller or the Macmillan Corporate and Premium Sales Department at 1-800-221-7945, extension 5442, or by e-mail at MacmillanSpecialMarkets@macmillan.com.

First Edition: June 2016

Printed in the United States of America

0 9 8 7 6 5 4 3 2 I

THE
SEASCAPE TATTOO

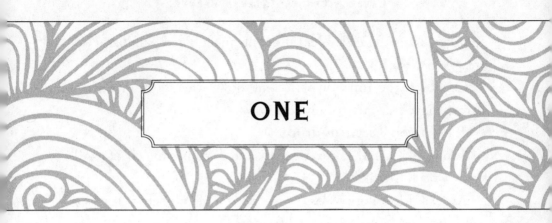

ONE

The Taxman

Because their city sprawled out along a desert coastline, Manaheimians always seemed surprised and unprepared when water fell from the sky. They rarely cobbled their side streets and seemed not to know how to control their carts and horses in muddy thoroughfares.

Aros's men grumbled in low voices as they struggled through the muck. Near the Happy Mermaid they gathered in little clumps, then one big clump. Each carried a bulging sack on his back or shoulders, each leaving a weapon hand free. They moved inside, found an empty table in the kitchen, and began dumping what they had. Fat Mal had a goat. Tor One-Eye had three kinds of potatoes. Aros the Aztec had brought finger-sized bananas, two great bunches.

Carpotet, the inn's owner, came down the stairs grinning. "Aros! More free fare for my folk?"

"Free if you'll serve us drink."

"Your first round is free, taxman, and of course my clients will know who to thank."

Aros nodded more or less happily. He'd get no better. It was a good exchange: taxmen needed friends.

Tor had picked them a table, a big one. Aros's dozen men took benches and proceedings, for the accounting and dispersal of tax money.

Aros, once a thief, had become one of the five major tax collectors in the kingdom of Quillia. He was Azteca by birth. His bloodline had gifted him with swarthy skin, straight black hair, and piercingly direct black eyes. He was a tall, broad man, whose size and strength were often underestimated until it was too late to retreat. He was too obtrusive to pick a pocket, but when he scowled, more than one citizen had simply handed him their purse from an instinctive wish to avoid trouble. It was helpful in his new role.

He looked around once, as men left off drinking to raid Aros's bananas. They'd know where those came from, and when Carpotet baked the potatoes and bell peppers and the goat, they'd know to thank the taxmen. A good bargain. You couldn't always collect coins; some families had to pay in kind, and Aros's men let them get away with that. He'd seen to it.

Aros crouched on one of the Happy Mermaid's rough-hewn benches, rubbing his muddied boots against a table leg. Damn boots were only a week old, and already filthy. As he drank, wondering which of several boot makers might clean his footwear without scalping him, he considered the bawdy conversation between the three rascals sharing his table and strove to conceal his annoyance.

In Aros's educated opinion, the role of tax collector was more profitable than outright brigandry had ever been. So long as he and his men turned in the expected minima from each district, they were left pretty much to their own devices, and their devices were endless.

But while it would be dishonest to plead total virtue on his own part, his personal code prescribed limits his men often ignored. As a result he sometimes felt more lion tamer than leader of the pride.

"Pretty widows need comfortin'," Tor One-Eye said in his weasel's voice, continuing his discourse on a woman in the capital's outskirts. He pounded his knife into the table and dragged the point an inch or two, raising a curl of wood. "I say I'm doing a public duty. A kindness, if you please. In exchange for . . . company, I ease her tax burden a coin or two."

The others hooted agreement and seemed ready to begin their own tales of fiscally enabled debauchery. But they kept an eye on Aros, knowing the barbarian disapproved of such things, for reasons they did not entirely understand.

"No widows, even if they look like pigs," he said, voice low and hard. "What you do with others is your business. But virgins and righteous widows are out of bounds, damn you."

Tor glared at him from his one useful orb. "The dice are downright unfriendly these days. I got debts," he said. "Some of us can't afford to be so pure and pristine-like." The others agreed, muttering. They were afraid of Aros, just enough to accept his odd rules. But sufficient greed would overcome caution one day—he knew it. And on that day, they would try him. While his back was turned of course.

Safely tucked into his leather tax purse was slightly more than the fifty gold pieces his employers demanded of him. When he combined that with the funds harvested by his associates, that would bring the total to just over a hundred. He'd had his heart set on a new suit of armor. But it could wait.

"Here," he said, and threw a gold coin to each of them. "Just a little inducement to remember your jobs, not your diversions."

They snatched the coins either from the air or as they rolled along the tabletop. Tor One-Eye bit his, as if uncertain it was genuine, then nodded. "Sure, Captain. We'll be good boys." And they laughed, as much at the barbarian's odd ways as anything else.

No love was lost here: they'd cosh him, rob him, and frame him for the theft the first chance they got, and everyone knew it. It was up to him not to give them a chance.

Then it was down to business, dividing up the portion of the loot that might reasonably be considered "discretionary." Five coins to Fat Mal the hairy one, five to Sailor Cree, the tall and skinny one. And five to Tor One-Eye, the small one who dressed in leather and spun his knife point-first on the table like a child's toy.

They drank, jeering at a woman singing about the days when Merfolk swam off Quillian shores. Back when there was magic in the world.

Aros snorted to himself. These inbred city folk thought they were so much more sophisticated than Outlanders like him. They told themselves that there were no gods to judge them and that the magic was gone. They wouldn't, if they'd seen what he'd seen.

Arto finished his drink just as five soldiers crowded through the swinging doors. A flying squad, sent to collect the taxes. The sergeant was a sloppy man with a quick blade, Arturo C'Vall, who sneered behind his smile and fancied that Aros wouldn't notice.

He noticed it, and also the fact that C'Vall's loathsome appetites and habits made Tor One-Eye seem like a celibate monk.

C'Vall plopped into the chair heavily. "Damned rain," he said. C'Vall always seemed to choose weather as his opening conversational gambit.

"Court's in an uproar," he said. "Big doings in the castle. Big doings." He reached into the tray at the center of the table, popping a greasy bacon confection into his mouth. "The princess is traveling far, far away," he whispered, as if he had been personally entrusted with her safety.

Aros swallowed a mouthful of grog. "What's that to me?"

"Not a thing, not a thing. The only way you're goin' to the palace is gettin' thrown in the dungeon! Har har!" The soldiers behind him chuckled to themselves, perhaps hoping that if they did, he might buy them drinks.

Aros's men, even Tor One-Eye, cracked no smiles. Aros slid his bag across the table. "Count it."

C'Vall nodded and opened the bag, pouring a flood of gold, silver, and copper coins out into a tidy pile. At nearby tables, patrons tried to avoid being caught gawking. As Aros and his men watched, C'Vall counted the gold twice and the silver once. "I'll trust you with the copper," he said.

He scrawled matching notes on two scraps of parchment and signed them both. Aros signed them both with a symbol like a split heart. Then each man took one. Taxes were taken very seriously. "I'll see you next month," C'Vall said.

Aros nodded. The entire pub seemed to exhale as C'Vall and his men left the room, degrading the atmosphere no small degree.

"Well," Tor One-Eye said. "Amusin' as always." They chuckled and commenced dividing up the copper coins, as well as the small sack of silver.

"Let's have the rest," Aros said. Accompanied by grumbles, a few more silver and gold coins hit the table. They divided those as well, Aros sweeping the last into his pouch with the side of his hand. He knew damned well that they'd held back a few jingles for themselves, but so had he—probably more than any of them.

"Well, then," he said. "Stay, get drunk and laid, or take it back to your luckless wives and get drunk and laid there. Mal and Sailor Cree—I'll see you again in two days. We're off for Isney province."

They hoisted their drinks to him, Tor One-Eye made an obscene toast, and they parted ways. As the others left the table, Aros felt a wind behind him, as if the door had opened and closed. He turned and scanned the room. No new faces had entered; someone must have left.

There had been twelve . . . fourteen people in the tavern, not counting his own crew. A clutch of sailors and their two girlfriends, all groping and whispering as if they were going to have an octopus evening. An old man in his cups. A pair of young lovers who looked as if they might be planning a getaway. A . . .

Wait.

The corner table, where the oldster had been seated, was empty now. Old man, in a hood, face shadowed. But Aros had had the clear impression of age. The ancient one hadn't glanced up at the clink of gold. Aros hadn't thought a thing about him before, but his instinct warned him that he had missed something.

Aros swept his coins into his bag and stood, the wisps of mead fog dissipated. Whence had come his sense of alarm? And why? Because an old man had vanished? Because C'Vall had irritated him, or Tor One-Eye? Because he had an intuition?

Irritated with himself, and more irritated that he couldn't nail down the *source* of his irritation, Aros ordered another mead and smashed it down without lifting the flagon from his lips.

Then, cursing fluidly, he departed.

The old man, having spent the last hour nursing a drink and watching the barbarian in the clouded mirror behind the bar, had indeed just scuttled from the Happy Mermaid so that Aros would not pass him on the way out. And his old adversary's damnably keen senses might have upset the game.

He hurried down the street, careful not to slip in the muck, to the alleyway where three hired brigands crouched waiting in the shadows.

"Well?" the largest of them breathed. He was the size of a redwood, with a rubbery, ruddy face, as if he was frostbit or sunburned.

"It was him," the old man said. "He'll be leaving soon, I think."

The smallest of them was so broad as to be almost round. "Payment," he said, extending his hand.

The old man emptied a small purse into the waiting paw and waited as they counted the pile of gold and silver coins. Not one had even pretended to trust. What was the world coming to?

The skinniest of the three looked like a skeleton wrapped in patchy, hairy skin. "It's good. His skull's as good as cracked, C'Vall." And the three oddly matched rogues set off down the street.

Neoloth-Pteor leaned back against the wall, shedding his cloak, then peeling away the false beard. Just a little gum, some llama hair, and a cloak . . . and his identity was safe. Not that any of the thugs he had just hired were likely to survive the evening, but if they did, they still couldn't describe him properly.

But if one lived long enough to pass on a name, that would be even better.

It had been a long game, with several distinct phases over the years. In the most recent, he was certain that Aros had thought him dead, entombed with a colony of giant spiders on an island on the far side of the world. "What is it?" he whispered. Neoloth closed his eyes and leaned back against the wall. "What is it that draws us together, my old enemy?"

For a decade, he and the appalling Aros had crossed paths and often attempted to cause each other's destruction. He had been shocked when here, in Quillia, the name had arisen on the foul breath of C'Vall, tax collector and blackmailer. C'Vall knew certain of Neoloth's secrets and had incriminating documents, even though Neoloth's sins had been committed far afield. He also knew where witnesses could be recruited. It would be inconvenient for them to come to light just now, when everything was going so well.

He had tried paying the man off, but the blackmail had grown onerous, and when Neoloth attempted to employ an agent of his own to acquire the documents, the nimble-fingered little elf had ended up floating in the river, his rear end pointing true north, as elf bottoms tended to do.

Well . . . C'Vall had named the stakes. Far be it from Neoloth-Pteor to deny him. C'Vall would expect a magical attack, of course, and there was no way to kill C'Vall with magic without leaving clues that another magician might use to impeach and supplant him at court.

He would try something so mundane that it would catch C'Vall by surprise. The fact that his old enemy Aros would be the instrument of his deliverance was a happy accident.

A carriage arrived, its wheels throwing off specks of mud from the recent rains. Neoloth flinched: in days not too long past, mud flecks used to veer past him. The cadaverous coachman stopped the vehicle, and Neoloth mounted the steps and swung in.

A belt-high, rounded elf crouched on the seat opposite. Fandy was a loyal follower, and, more important, he and the deceased elf had been more than friends.

"Was he there?" Fandy squeaked.

"He was," Neoloth said. "He conducted his business and then left."

They jounced down the streets a bit, wheels thumping in muddy potholes. From time to time, through gaps between houses, shops, and taverns, they could glimpse the castle, perched high on a hill. Symbol of power . . . and, in an unexpected and unaccustomed fashion, hope.

"And you did what you had to do?"

"Yes," Neoloth said. "And my hired swords will do what they have to do. And Aros will do what *he* has to do. And, one way or the other, at least one old problem will be gone by morning."

And if all went well, both might be gone. But all things going well was rare in this world, or any world he knew.

Barbarian's instinct.

Aros knew he was being followed. The back of his neck had itched since shortly after he left the tavern. Had known something was wrong, something was . . . off. He had drained that last flagon of mead largely to make himself a more tempting target. If someone was going to try to kill or rob him, Aros would prefer to meet him while he had sense enough to act clearly, rather than in his sleep or encumbered by a frisky companion.

The streets were narrow here, and dark, but the ground was

sturdier underfoot. Drier. And that would work very well for a man with confidence in his footwork.

Like Aros.

Who had that old man in the tavern been? The Aztec still couldn't place him, and in fact the struggle to place the man might well get him killed. Your mind couldn't be in the past and the future at the same time.

The sword that kills you isn't yesterday's, or tomorrow's. It is the weapon at your throat right now. *Now.* Now was all that mattered, and his mind, while not as foggy as his lurching gait implied, was not focused on Now. He was starting to think of bed, and that could get him killed.

Well, one principle he'd learned long ago: when you are less than your best, it is even more critical that your opponents underestimate you. Blurry vision? Trick your opponents into thinking you are blind. Weakened? Make them think you are unconscious, or already dead.

What did they want? The tax money? He had to admit that there was a part of him that gave not a damn. He tried to be civilized, to constrain his savage heart. But even before Flaygod, his trusty *Macuahuitl,* left its sheath, he felt the battle madness stir within him. The *Macuahuitl* balanced in his hand sweetly, a hybrid based on his people's ancient bat-shaped, glass-toothed battle-ax, rendered not in hardwood but in lethal, razor-edged steel.

As he wound through the streets, the way narrowed, and that was for the good. While it was annoying to lose side-to-side motion, he moved backward better than most and attacked on a straight line before him with devastating speed and power.

Someone emptied the fetid contents of a chamber pot out of a window overhead, almost hitting him. He cursed up at the window, receiving a similar obscenity in reply. Then perhaps seeing the size of the man who was walking beneath his window, or the flat, ugly demi-sword in his hand, the thrower mumbled what might have been a half-hearted apology and retreated.

There. The full moon above them shone its light into an alley just to his right, but the back of the alley was still deep shadow. He liked that.

Glancing back over his shoulder to be certain that his stalkers were still close enough to see him slip into the side street, Aros slid into the shadows and waited, Flaygod hungry in his hand.

He waited. For a time he began to wonder if he was wrong, if the men behind him had merely been out for a stroll. Along dark streets. With drawn swords.

Lovely evening for a stroll, he thought.

And then they were in the alleyway. Three of them, bulky but not clumsy, each with a fistful of sharp steel. One was cloaked, one wore partial armor of some kind, and one was one-handed, with a cleaver-like blade welded to the stump.

For a time they just looked at him, their outlines reduced to darkness, eyes burning in their faces. No one spoke.

"How did you lose your hand?" Aros asked. He was genuinely interested in such things, and, after all, in a few seconds either he'd be unable to ask the question, or Stumpy would be incapable of answering.

But that really didn't matter, because Stumpy didn't answer. Instead, two of the three split off, walking down the alley side by side. The one with the armor cocked his head a little to the side, as if trying to determine where Aros was.

The shadows were doing their job. Which was nice, because his enemies also didn't notice when his left hand slipped the throwing knife from his belt, and the shadows were apparently too dark to see him hurl it underhand, such that none of the three had any idea what was happening until the knife sprouted from the armored man's throat like a rose crafted entirely of thorns. Armored Man gave a wet groan and collapsed onto his side.

Stumpy turned to look at his friend and turned back just in time to avoid being beheaded by a lightning-fast swing, catching it on the cleaver welded to the stump of his left hand.

That was fine, because Aros was taking a step, setting his weight. He swung his left foot up in a short arc, planting it directly in Stumpy's groin.

To his credit, the brigand made hardly any sound as he slid against the wall. Aros would have loved to gut him, but the third man was moving in, and this one was no slouch.

He was slightly shorter than Aros, but stocky, one of those rare, dangerous men who seemed constructed of bouncy muscle and lightning nerves. Fast! If they hadn't stepped into the light, the blade would have disappeared entirely. As it was, dim moonlight still required careful attention to the swordsman's shoulders and instinctive reaction to the sound of his footwork, music on the slimy tiles.

Fierce, rat-like eyes locked with his, and he knew his opponent had survived a dozen back-alley skirmishes. Dangerous.

But that was all right. Aros had survived a hundred. He backed up until even with Stumpy, and took a moment for Flaygod to hack down into the man's right leg. Stumpy groaned and crumbled to the ground.

The tallest swordsman was, predictably, leaping forward. Aros slid back, found what he was looking for and then retreated again.

The swordsman came forward, into shadow . . .

And tripped over the armored guy, lying there in the shadows bleeding. To his credit, the swordsman recovered quickly, or would have, if Aros had not struck hard in his moment of unbalance.

The head tumbled one way, the body another.

Stumpy had lost his sword, but the cleaver on his left was still a threat. Aros looked into the man's small, pig-like eyes. "I can cut off your right hand, and then see how your pet blacksmith will correct it. Would you like to see how that goes?"

Stumpy shook his head.

"Who hired you?" he asked.

To his credit, the man seemed to possess a smidgeon of loyalty. Aros swept his leg out from under him and planted his own foot on the cleaver. For some reason he didn't want to kill the man. Perhaps he admired Stumpy's fortitude in continuing to work after a debilitating injury, not resorting to begging or simple theft. Certainly there was something admirable to be found in that.

Stumpy tried to move, but when he did Aros did a little hop and planted his left foot on the wounded leg. Stumpy squealed, which was no surprise. That had to hurt.

"Tell me who hired you," Aros said.

"C'Vall!" Stumpy hissed.

He should have known. "All right," he said. "Don't ever let me see you again." Stumpy nodded emphatically, and Aros turned and walked away.

He heard the slither of steel against cobblestone, and turned just in time to deflect Stumpy's blade and riposte, his sawtooth *Macuahuitl* cleaving Stumpy to the spine. The workman-like part of his mind appreciated the precision and economy of the motion. The animal part, the part he ordinarily sheathed when among city dwellers, bared its teeth. Blood had been spilled, awakening the barbarian's ancient and feral hunger. There would be more.

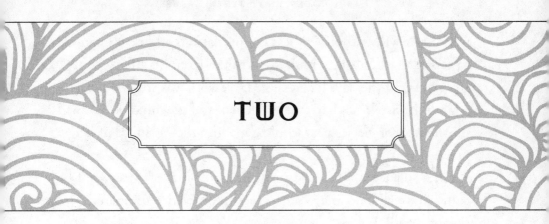

TWO

The Talisman

Like light reflected from a silver shield, the moon's rippling twin shimmered on breaking waves.

Neoloth-Pteor had walked out onto the beach, leaving his elfish assistant Fandy and the coachman on the road behind, around a curve. Down the beach a mile or two south nestled a small fishing village, and north an hour's ride was a commercial fishery. But here, and now, there was privacy.

The wizard spread his arms and began his incantation, his voice drifting out along the waves as they rolled inward toward him and then out again. They were words of power, but he remembered when they had been more powerful still. In boyhood, ages before, magic had been magic, and magicians were able to work their will without endless manipulations and machinations to separate a single miserable swordsman from his life.

But even if the days had changed, Neoloth was still the greatest wizard the Strellines had ever produced, and he would be damned if memories of glories past would deny him the workings of magic present.

The surface of the ocean roiled, as if plucked by a wind he could not feel. The image of the moon dimpled, shimmered, and then was still.

He stood on the beach feeling something of a fool, wondering if he had misjudged his spell, or the time, or place. A seagull "skawed" above him, wheeling in the night sky. Neoloth perched on the rock, and felt his foot slip a bit to one side. Righted himself, and waited.

And then . . . there they were. Five silvered wakes against the blackness of the waves, snaking toward the shore. Three bearded faces, two smooth. A family pod of Merfolk, males and females. He caught his breath: never so many at a single time, in all his long experience. Instinct told him it was important, somehow, spoke of a changing world even if he did not fully comprehend all the changes.

The males approached the rock, the two females a little farther back. He saw gray in the largest female's flowing locks, and reckoned that she was a grandmere, that perhaps the younger was a daughter, with other children and grandchildren hidden beneath the waves.

"Come," the largest of the mermen said. His voice was very clear, even with that slight gargling quality common to his people. They were coiled in the shallows, the waves washing over their scaled torsos. Neoloth clambered over a boulder and slid down to stand just above a tide pool where they could reach each other, human and Mer, each without leaving the comfort of his native environment.

"I am here, M'thrilli," Neoloth said. "As always, you call, I come."

"We have what you seek," the merman said. "Do you have what we agreed to?"

"Yes."

"Then . . . see," M'thrilli said. As if he had made an invisible gesture, one of the other males swam forward and held out his hands. The object was no larger than an infant's forearm, a cylinder of brass sealed with threaded caps. It was covered with glyphs Neoloth had seen before on one of the great Mayan time wheels. He held his breath.

The fabled device was a reality . . . at least real in that it conformed to descriptions in whispered myth. It was a talisman, *the* talisman in fact, an object of fabulous value that had not, as feared, disappeared forever beneath the waves.

If the legends were true, it was a relic of Azteca, used to store mana from the bodies of the sacrificed. What was it doing here, half a world from its origins? Again, if the legends were true, then it was simply a matter of a wizard who had outstayed his welcome, seeking to flee north when his vessel was caught in a storm.

Or was it pirates? Or sudden illness? True, a mighty enough wizard should have been able to deal with any of those things . . . but perhaps not several at a time. Looking at it, Neoloth understood that he might have been grasping at straws, but in times like these, one grasped at whatever floated.

The merman saw the hunger in his eyes. "Your part," he said.

Neoloth opened his pouch, presenting M'thrilli with a variety of tempered steel spearheads. Their eyes were now the ones burning with hunger. Craft the Merfolk possessed in plenty, and strength, and clever hands. But the workings of fire were known only to those on the land, and that was a good thing for those who spoke the Mer-tongue.

It gave such men something to trade. What did they want with spear points? Hunting? Protection? Fighting over territory? Now that the magic was dwindling, did the surviving Merfolk find themselves battling over good hunting currents?

"We fight not with each other," M'thrilli said. And, again, Neoloth was not certain if his mind was being read or they simply anticipated his chain of thought. It was not the first time he'd had that impression.

"The magic wanes. Our numbers wane. There is fish for all," he said.

"Then why?" Neoloth asked, sorry as soon as the words left his mouth.

"Our bones have power," M'thrilli said solemnly. "We must protect ourselves from those who hunt us."

The merman's eyes were sad. "Soon. Today, or in ten thousand years, we will be nothing but myth. But for now, we stay in the deeps, where the mana is still strong."

The mermen to either side took the tools and deposited the talisman in its stead. Fearing even to breathe, Neoloth bent and gathered it into his hands. Even with the precious thing in his possession, he could barely believe it.

"Why?" he asked. "Why would you trade this to me?"

"We have no need for it," M'thrilli said. "It requires spells our tongues have never shaped. We *are* magic. We do not wish to be a part of men's workings of it. Perversions of it. We could have lived for eons. It was your spells that used up the world's mana too rapidly."

Neoloth-Pteor considered. "Then why don't you destroy it. Why sell it to me?"

M'thrilli's expression was not pleasant. "The sooner the mana is used up on the land, the sooner men will forget magic. And if you forget magic, you may leave us alone, in the depths. We know you of the old days, Neoloth. There are better men than you. But there are also worse."

The slight, sad smile thinned. "Be well in the last days. We have served each other before. Likely, this is the final time."

And with that, the Merfolk slipped back into the waves and were gone, leaving Neoloth on the shore, alone with the dancing light of the moon.

Neoloth-Pteor slipped back into the coach without looking back at the ocean, holding the oilcloth in both hands. He did not unwrap it again until he was safely behind the coach's wooden door. The coachman cracked his whip, and their conveyance was on its way.

"Master?" his elf asked. Neoloth gave Fandy a single look: *do not ask.* And then leaned back against the back wall and closed his eyes. Everything was working.

Two hours later they were still in the thick of the night but drawing near to the castle. Quillia's grandest dwelling perched on a low hill, surrounded by gardens and hedge mazes, smaller mansions, and an army barracks whose soldiers doubled as emergency bodyguards. The coach bounced up the final cobbles to a small castle—or a large stylized house—just east of the main dwelling. Neoloth's own personal lodgings.

A dwelling worthy of Quillia's chief wizard.

He felt a deep sense of satisfaction as the coach drew into a tunnel formed by sculpted hedges, into a shadowed arbor. "I will want you in the morning," he said to Fandy.

Neoloth carried his package into his study, which was lined with scrolls and books and odd memorabilia, detritus of a life lived more in the shadows than in the light. He swept scrolls cluttering his desktop into a pile and laid down the oilskin. Peeled it away. Then for the second time, he beheld the talisman.

A little water had leaked out of the cracks in machining. The joining edges were so precise and delicate that they almost eluded the naked eye. Still, water had seeped into the works.

He wondered if that would damage the workings. If workings there were.

Neoloth turned the cylinder over and over again, until he saw something that looked like an entry point. He rummaged in his desk until he found a magnifying glass. He inspected the cylinder carefully. Could it be booby-trapped?

He had not been to Azteca, but in visions had seen the pyramids and sacrificial pyres, the lines of war captives and criminals, the rivers of blood running in the shadows of Quetzalquatl's titanic wings. Part of him hungered to witness that spectacle, while another part was glad that he never had, or would. There were ways that his soul was too close to a tipping point, and Neoloth knew that just as there were deeds that could not be undone, there were sights that could not be unseen, changes in the composition of the soul that could not be healed or reversed.

Yes. There was something daunting about the cylinder. The Merfolk had been wise to rid themselves of it.

Neoloth's nails were long, tapered and blackened by tarry substances beneath it, either extruded from or growing into the quick.

He wiggled his fingers to get the stiffness out and then drew up his sleeves. Neoloth's arm was covered by tattoos, mostly in dark primary colors, many faded by time. With one fingernail, he drew a cut in his skin, just over a tattoo of a spider.

Blood welled and then . . . was absorbed into the spider. The inking swelled and shook itself to wakefulness and crawled off his arm. It seemed confused and sleepy but gained confidence and purpose as it crawled across the desk and to the cylinder.

For a minute the tattoo had been rounded and corporeal, but, as it crawled up on the cylinder, it lost dimension again, became flat, and slipped into a crack through which no earthly insect could have passed.

Neoloth pressed his ear against the cylinder. He heard soft scraping sounds, as if someone was drawing a pen against the inside, scratching it about. Then . . . something that might have been a gasp or cry of dismay, on the tiniest possible scale.

Then . . . a tiny click, and a door opened on the smooth part of the cylinder. The entire machine seemed to blossom.

The spider tattoo was waiting as patiently as a trained dog. It crawled out of the cylinder and back onto his arm, where it sank into his skin again, sinking into a well-deserved rest.

Neoloth peered into the workings. Yes, there had been a trap. The inside of the cylinder was covered with engravings, miniature hieroglyphs. One of them had peeled away, a brass equivalent of the tattoo. Something poisonous no doubt, and native to the jungles of Azteca. The battle between it, and the spider, must have been exciting, and he was sorry to have missed it.

But now he wanted to look at the workings. Other than a few small gears, the compartment was largely occupied by a scroll constructed of beaten gold, gold so fine it was almost translucent. Never had he seen gold beaten that finely. And like the interior of the talisman it was covered by minute, hand-graven glyphs. The result might have taken an army of miniature artisans months to produce. The scroll was wound onto a spindle. How long was the entire thing? A hundred feet, perhaps. And the thing was designed so that it wound from one spindle to another, perhaps at the movement of the tiny gears.

"Brilliant," he whispered. A watchmaker's precision in service to a sorcerer's secrets. He bowed his head in respect to the unknown Aztec craftsman, and the wizard who must have paid dearly for the device.

Two important questions remained: Was there still power in it? And if not, could it be charged up once again?

Neoloth carefully folded the device back together again into its cylinder form and ran his fingers along the outside edge. Closed his eyes. Yes, a slight sensation of warmth.

He held his arm next to the device, slowing his breathing so that he contributed no mana to the process to come. Neoloth's right arm was inscribed with countless tattoos, symbolic of adventures, or memories, or simple magical designs ... but hidden among them were patterns of greater significance. And two of them were small butterfly-like creatures the size of gnats, tattoos that could only have been created by the smallest of hands. Fairy tats, earned in a far-off land, performing favors to a dying kingdom of the little people.

He could withdraw his own mana, his own natural life force, but by placing his arm close, if there was anything left at all ...

He held his breath.

There.

The slightest twitch of a wing. Oh, yes. The little creatures, sealed to his flesh, were stirring to life. Rousing from long slumber and death-like dream. They seemed to yawn, scratch themselves, and pull up away from his skin like little inchworms, thin as hairs, fragile as cobwebs.

He pulled his arm away. The butterflies sank back into his flesh and were still.

So. Even after decades beneath the waves, magic remained. Not much, but enough to convince him the device still worked . . .

A knock at his door.

Neoloth looked up at once. Sunlight streamed through his window. His contemplations had lasted hours longer than he had intended.

"Yes?" he asked, opening the door.

A red-bearded member of the royal guard stood there, head high, quite appropriately respectful of the court's grand vizier. The guard clicked his heels. "Her majesty the queen requests your presence."

"Tell her that I will be there quickly," Neoloth answered. Damnation! He had been up all night. His clothes would be ruffled, his hair a mess, his breath like something that had crawled out of a swamp and died.

"I will wait," Redbeard replied.

Neoloth closed the door. Well. Magic might be in short supply, but a simple spell . . . another test of the talisman, he told himself.

Neoloth held the cylinder at arm's length and passed it over his body, chanting an incantation as he did. He felt the tingle as dirt and sand fell from his body and clothes. His hair straightened itself. Fatigue, collected in his joints like sand in a watch, just . . . dissolved.

Neoloth scrubbed his teeth with a scented mint stick. Once upon a time he had used spells for such things, but why waste even a smidgeon of power in these milk-and-water days?

He examined himself in the mirror. From elegantly forked beard to the fall of his clothes (and they had made small adjustments, were no longer as tight about the waist, where his recent weight gain was more noticeable than he wished), he looked . . . perfect.

Excellent. His investment in the cylinder had been a good one.

He opened the door and was privately pleased that the guard's eyes widened at his transformation. "Please," Neoloth said. "Take me to the queen."

THREE

The Princess Tahlia

Neoloth's private minipalace was connected to the main dwelling by both a public path and a hidden tunnel. They took the tunnel. Whatever purpose Queen Quilla had in mind must be something clandestine.

The air in the tunnel was pleasantly cool and dry, cooler than it would have been in the streets above. Quillia, wealthiest of the Eight Kingdoms, was built on a desert, and the incantations that had once brought water to her streets had been largely replaced with aqueducts and reservoirs.

A series of torches cast overlapping circles of yellow light along the way. Once, magical golden plates had illuminated the walls. Now, such excess was too wasteful by far. The tunnel ended in a set of stairs carved into the rock. Neoloth mounted them, climbing up into the castle. The stairs emptied out into the back of the throne room walled with marble and veined with gold.

Queen Quilla was present, all angularity and calm command. Just to her right was an unexpected surprise and pleasure... Princess Tahlia, her golden hair brighter than the golden throne on which she sat, its seat a hand width lower than the queen's.

He bowed again, relieved that he had spent a little magic to tidy himself up before making an appearance. The queen was reason enough... but this situation went beyond logic. Neoloth was older than he appeared, a testimony to the herbs and magics that sustained him in his seventh decade of life. There were times when, despite those spells, he felt old, a sensation like frost at the core of his spine.

But that feeling vanished when the princess was near.

Princess Tahlia combined the refined beauty of her queen mother and the strength and intelligence of her deceased father, a warrior and scholar who had inherited much but expanded his holdings with conquest and crafty negotiation. Tahlia moved with such grace she seemed almost to be suspended by strings from above.

He held his breath when he saw her, afraid that her protective mother might know what he was thinking and feeling.

Then again, any woman smart enough to keep a throne could probably guess how he felt, how every man who didn't favor buggery would feel in her presence. On the other hand, he sincerely hoped she didn't know what he *might* have done to gain advantage.

Every wizard knew love spells.

"Good morning, Neoloth," said the queen.

"Your majesty." He bowed deeply. "How may I serve you?"

"I am advised to bring you into my confidence," she said. "The royal daughter will be traveling to her cousin's wedding, and I wish to know portents for fortune and weather."

Neoloth's mind whirled. "Travel . . . north to Nandia?" The northern kingdom was linked to Quillia by blood and custom, as well as by a shared language. It was a prosperous trading and shipping community clustered around a glittering bay.

"Yes. We've tried to keep it secret until now, but she departs day after tomorrow. Please, I ask that you pierce time's veil." For all her years and burdens, the queen was still a stunning beauty, still possessing much of the charm and vitality she had held in her youth, now tempered with the strength of judgment and experience that had accompanied her office.

If Neoloth did not have the younger woman to compare with, he might have been entranced. But Tahlia was alive, and present, and it was all he could do not to stare at her.

And she knew it.

Tahlia smiled at him, with the sort of impish confidence only young women of supreme beauty and status ever seemed to know.

"I will need as much information as you feel safe sharing with me," he asked. "And also . . . I request a moment alone with the princess herself."

The queen's eyebrow raised, and she looked at her daughter, who leaned back in her golden throne, smiling speculatively. Tahlia nodded.

"Good," the queen said. "Good. It is best that this was in the open."

"May I ask," he said. "What the fear might be?"

The queen's lips curled downward. "Since childhood," she said, "I have been able to see small signs and portents. I knew the dress I needed to wear when I met Tahlia's father." That thought seemed to summon an old and fond memory. "I knew we would be wed.

But also that we would not have many years together." Tahlia's father had died of a brain fever. Their court magician had not been able to stave it off, and that had been the beginning of Neoloth's tenure. If only they had called him sooner . . .

Well, it would have made little difference in an age when a wizard had to depend upon roots and herbs and leeches to effect his healings. And no mere medicines would have sufficed against the king's ailment.

Needless to say, he hadn't mentioned *that* to the grieving widow. On the contrary, he had sworn that he would have saved her beloved, if only he had been called and trusted. The former royal witch had been fortunate to escape with her life. If he was not mistaken, she had sheltered in Shrike, north of Nandia.

The queen exited accompanied by her maids in waiting, leaving the princess and Neoloth alone in the room, save for her guards. When the door closed behind the royal mother, the princess nodded to the guards, and they retreated as well, giving them privacy.

The door clicked. As Neoloth approached the princess, she rose. He dropped to one knee and took her hand.

It was warm and soft, and something inside him cried out for the beauty of it. "My princess," he said, and touched his forehead to her hand. Odd how her skin was warm against his hand, but cool against his forehead. He knew not what to make of that, but felt just a little as if he were drowning.

"Walk with me," Tahlia said, and, taking his arm lightly, allowed him to escort her to the parapet.

From there, they could look out over Quillia's capital city. The morning shadows were long now, as the city shook off the cobwebs of slumber. Thousands of tradesmen, laborers, slaves attending to the business of their masters, young ones off to teachers or mentors to learn a trade.

The scent of fresh bread wafted in the air, mingling with the clean scent of the western ocean. That ocean lay beyond the maze of roofs, just beyond his sight, and its ancient, endless rhythms would soon carry her away.

Neoloth lowered his eyes.

"I look forward to Zatch's wedding," she said. "Soon it will be my own time. Already, my suitors will grow more insistent." The princess scowled. "Since father's death, Quillia is perceived as weak. My mother is not weak!" Her eyes flashed fire.

"She is the very strength of Quillia," Neoloth said, attempting to sooth her.

"Mother adored Father," she said. "Even though their marriage was one of state, there was great love between them. Tell me, wizard. Can your glass tell me if I will find the same?"

Her smile was not cruel. There was, in truth, no spot of cruelty in her, although she had her mother's strength. Yes, that was one of the paradoxes of power: to be able to do cruel, necessary things without poisoning your own heart.

"I will look deeply, Princess," he said.

Suddenly she asked, "Can you see your own future?"

"No, Princess. It's like trying to tickle yourself or see through a mirror."

She nodded. "They say that."

He stood by her side, watched the new sun play on the fine, strong cheekbones, the gentle curve of her lips. Her pale, lovely, intelligent eyes.

He had sworn fealty to her mother, to the kingdom, and he would keep those oaths—for unexpected reasons. But it was a strange feeling, to be as bound as any of the slaves and servants scurrying in the streets below them.

But then . . . the princess too was bound, by her obligations of birth. She might be traded to a handsome prince (oh, Nandians were usually blue-eyed and square-jawed, damn it) in exchange for improved trade relations or reciprocal defense treaties.

On the other hand, her mother had been just as bound. And her father had been bound to ride into battle at the head of his army. Even protected by magical armor, in battle he had suffered the head wound that had eventually cost him his life.

And the peasants were bound to each other. Everything bound together, the entire universe, and the wizard who had once thought himself special, unique, apart from the forces he had resolved to control . . . was just another human cog in the whole clockwork design.

Was anyone, anywhere, really free?

"If I was free," she said, as if reading his mind (and who was to say she could not?), "there might be different choices."

"But you are not," he said. "And we all have our obligations, Princess."

She gazed out at the kingdom below her, the morning sun playing on her jawline. What was it, when you began to think of someone in terms of separate body parts? The swift intake of breath, the sway of a hip beneath silk . . .

He shuddered. *Neoloth . . . you're in trouble.*

"If you could make your own choice?" She turned and gazed at him, eyes steady but lashes fluttering.

Yes, she was about to say it, the words trembled at her lips . . .

Then Drasilljah, her maid in waiting, stepped onto the porch. An older woman of Celtic extraction, her red hair faded with gray. Drasilljah had the mark of a magic user about her, even if she had never displayed such skills in his presence. Retainer? Mentor? Bodyguard was more like it, and her attitude toward Neoloth reeked of suspicion.

"My lady," Draz said. She was tall and almost elementally thin, as if there was nothing of her but bones and magic. "You must make choices for the presentation gown."

The princess sighed, as if a spell had broken. She smiled at Neoloth and touched his hand. "We will speak again when I return."

"Ever at your service, m'lady," he said, inclining his head as she walked past him and out.

Neoloth stood on the balcony for a time, staring toward the east, across the roofs and gardens. The kingdom. It would belong to whoever married the princess, the sole heir. Why not him?

Magic had kept him looking forty for, oh, almost thirty years. He had served the kingdom well . . .

But that wasn't enough, and he knew it. The princess was both amused and impressed by him . . . and if he wasn't mistaken, there was attraction there. If he had helped things along a bit . . .

"Excuse me?" Draz said.

Damn it! He hadn't realized she was still behind him, and he turned, composing himself.

"It is a wonderful view," she said. "But it is not yours."

"Yes," he said. "Yes, of course." She was smiling at him, as if she had read his thoughts. And, curse it, as had been the case with the princess, once again he wasn't sure that she couldn't.

He backed out of the room and returned down the long, dark tunnel to his quarters.

Once there, Neoloth cast off his disappointment and buried himself in the books and spells needed to generate a vision of the future. A great bowl filled with water, and then a handful of eggs from a Vox, a salamander-like creature that lived on the edge between magic and flesh. Vox eggs were thin, transparent, almost fluid, just enough solid matter to feel sticky against his palm.

Once stirred together, the mixture began to spin, as if a plug had been pulled from the bottom of the pan. Good. It was working. A dim light flickered within. He gazed. This was a tricky part: he had to look at it from the right angle, with his eyes partially closed, and in the right trance state. If everything was just right, it was sometimes possible to . . .

He saw the princess boarding her ship, and the ship taking sail. The weather looked good. The ship dwindled to a dot on the ocean, sailing north. Good . . . that would take it perhaps three days hence, if they sailed on the morning tide. It would take five days to reach their destination, he reckoned, and . . .

But then the clouds came. The bowl darkened, the whirlpool diminished. He could see nothing. He had seen, nothing, except a calm voyage, followed by . . .

A storm? Misfortune, or the simple failure of his spell, perhaps. Something that happened more and more often these days . . .

He didn't know. And that was the hardest part of it all. *He didn't know.* Once upon a time, such knowledge had come readily. And now . . .

What was he going to tell the queen?

A headache was brewing. And that, at least, he still possessed the power to heal.

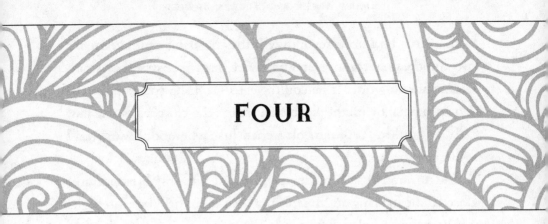

FOUR

Aros on the Docks

Aros crouched behind a tavern, concealed in shadow. He believed he had eluded his pursuers but wasn't willing to gamble his life on it. The guard would return within the hour, and he had to have an answer.

How had things gone so badly, so quickly? After last night's attempt to murder him, he had lurched from disaster to disaster. True, he had successfully avenged himself upon C'Vall, killing him in his own bedroom. Unfortunately, he had been discovered even as he fled the chamber where C'Vall's sword and skill had fallen before the barbarian's fury. Discovery and alarum led to another fight during which he had broken the heads of a pair of guards . . . and then fled before he could be overwhelmed.

But Aros had been recognized. His position as taxman was lost, and the only real option was to flee east to the desert or south on the morning tide. If he could get to sea, if he could make the right contacts, he might be able to escape the clutches of the law.

If he couldn't . . . his neck itched just where a noose would tighten.

There was a rustle in the alley behind him. He bristled, prepared to die fighting and free. If necessary. But he'd been so close!

Questions circled his mind like a cat chasing its flaming tail. Everything had been right, and now everything was wrong. The beast within him warred with the man. It was caught in a trap, but more important even than fighting its way out was finding the reason *why*.

The figure approaching him in the dark was more shadow than form, difficult to distinguish. "Who goes there?" Aros snarled.

"It's me!"

Aros recognized the voice—that was Teesha, the tavern wench from the Broken Skull, one of his favorite haunts. A saucy and well-turned wench, cute rather than beautiful but flexible and warm-hearted.

"What have you heard?" Aros asked.

Teesha had brought a bundle of rolls and a joint of beef. And . . . a map of the desert, bless her. He thanked her with a kiss and tore meat from the joint with his teeth, surprised to realize just how famished he was.

"There's talk," she said in a high, reedy voice, "that someone you cheated got their revenge."

Well, that was an easy call. "Man or woman?" he muttered. Angry husbands, cheated gamblers, jealous wenches, tax frauds brought to justice, men he had bested in arm wrestling, people he had robbed before taking the queen's shilling. Oh, the possibilities were endless.

"One of each, perhaps." She giggled. Her small, plump hand rested on his knee but began to climb higher. "Now, I've been a good girl for you, how about you paying me back a little?"

Aros shook his head. Teesha had always been a frisky lass, a quality he'd appreciated fully and frequently during his time in Quillia's capital. But it seemed unseemly at the moment, and he felt obliged to turn her down.

On the other hand, if he turned her down, wouldn't it be ungracious of him? And if he ever needed her help again, wouldn't it be less likely that she would . . . um . . . respond?

As her hand reached its target, he suddenly found himself having difficulty tasting his food. She was snuggling up close, and suddenly her mouth was on his, tongue questing as if she wanted to share his breakfast.

Oh well, what the hell—

There was always time for a knee trembler. *Waste not, want not.* The way things were going, it might well be his last opportunity for quite some time—

He lurched upright as she locked her legs around his waist, performing a perfectly adequate imitation of an octopus. Aros felt her hands fumbling for his belt, felt it go loose, and finally couldn't remember any of the carefully devised reasons this was a bad idea, the two of them clutching at each other, him hoisting her skirts up and . . .

Untied your sword belt—

The senses that were filled with the urgent, pungent awareness of Teesha suddenly watched him from another position, as if outside himself, seeing a pale slip of a girl entwined with a brown-skinned giant, naked from the waist down, his Aztec sword and belt down around his ankles. And the shadows around them were not empty.

His eyes snapped open, and suddenly there were two men in the alley, one with a sword, one with a knife. Her brothers Alf and Negron, co-owners of the Broken Skull, apparently out to earn a little extra collecting bounties.

Teesha buried her teeth in his shoulder. Her legs tightened around his waist, her fingers grasping handfuls of his black, straight hair. Mouth was buried against his neck, but she managed to scream, "Get him!"

Gods! He was dancing about in the alley, her two brothers clearly unimpressed with the sight of their sister half-naked and *in flagrante delicto.* They did seem unwilling to turn their sister into a pincushion, and he was able to use that to his advantage, using her as a shield as he stumbled back into the crates.

And fell, rolling, the hellcat still biting and scratching him, sharp little teeth worrying at his throat. Damn it, his reluctance to hurt a woman was costing him dearly. If a man had ridden him in such a manner, he might have simply grabbed a leg in each hand and made a wish. But he just couldn't . . . and that scrap of scruple would cost him his life if he wasn't careful.

He pushed with his legs, rolling over toward the sword. He managed to get his hand on it, but without the leverage necessary to slide Flaygod out of its scabbard. A sword nick on his right leg made him roar with pain. He finally abandoned his scruples, balled his fist and smacked Teesha on the side of the head hard enough to snap her face back and to the left, eyes crossed, barely conscious.

He rolled up as Negron stabbed at him and stepped on his scabbard, paradoxically providing the traction Aros needed to pull

Flaygod free. He drove the steel through Negron's shirt so quickly that his little piggy eyes popped out as much from astonishment as pain.

The other brother, the one with the knife backed up, screamed, "On him!"

And suddenly the early morning bristled with steel. Aros struggled to fight, not to trip over Teesha or run into Negron, who had collapsed to his knees and seemed to be trying to decide whether to simply die now or pull his intestines in and find a surgeon who would lie to him and take his money.

These city dwellers were slow and clumsy compared to the Aztec, but he knew from the sound of scurrying feet that Teesha and her brothers had brought enough help to seal his fate.

Kicking a barrel down the alley, he paused to gather up his breeches, slammed Flaygod back into its scabbard, and leapt for the edge of the roof above them.

One-handed (the other holding his pants), he swung himself up like one of the little monkeys in the jungles of his youth, far south of Quillia. Aros landed in a crouch.

A phalanx of patrol soldiers had been attracted by the commotion and were now headed this way. As the men in the alley below screamed in anger and pain, the crowd of soldiers decided to pursue.

Lovely.

Aros belted his pants and spun just in time to deflect a blade, clubbing a soldier down with his left. Damn it, damn it . . . *don't kill one of the queen's men if you don't have to.* Even if you were innocent, judges tended to have limited sympathy for anyone who dispatched officials.

Aros ran. Even as a boy, he had been fleetest and most agile.

This was why he had survived when his mother had been captured by the priests for nonpayment of taxes, her heart wrenched from her chest on a stone altar.

Damn the priests! First they'd taken his father, killed in a war to seek out victims for their thirsty god. Then they'd condemned his widowed mother simply for being poor. He would gladly have perished with her, but the frantic, doomed woman had wrung a promise from his lips. He'd sworn to stow away on a northern trade ship and try to build a life.

That had been very long ago. A lifetime ago. The small, nearly feral child named Aros had ripened over the years into a blooded warrior, a thief, a man of many lethal skills . . . and no home. He had made the mistake of thinking that Quillia might be a place to set roots.

Taxman had had a nice ring to it. Once upon a time.

He was not running randomly through the maze of roofs. His chance to make it out of the harbor seemed smaller by the moment, but he could still go the other way, east through the desert. He had allies who could smuggle him out of the city—

The lip of another roof was coming up fast. Aros's feet thumped the roof like the hands of a mad drummer, blurring . . . and he jumped. He leapt, the wind on his face, the void opening and then closing behind him as he hit the roof and rolled.

He heard other feet landing behind him—fewer, perhaps. His tactic had thinned them out. Behind him, a man screamed in shock and fear. Aros looked back over his shoulder and saw a soldier balancing wildly on one leg on the edge of the roof, waving his arms wildly—and then disappearing.

Ouch! Would he be blamed for whatever broken bones resulted from that? Best not to find out. Best to be certain that he wasn't captured.

Another roof edge. Almost twenty feet, Aros reckoned. He'd never jumped that far, but he felt loose and strong, juices up, confident that he could make it. And the men behind him would almost certainly give up. Aros increased his speed, closed his mind to all doubt, and jumped.

Sailing . . .

Freedom . . .

Aros hit the far roof in a joyous surge of triumphant laughter, rolling to his feet just in time for the roof of wood and mud brick to collapse beneath him.

He plunged down into a bedroom, where an astonished, pale, and naked man was being ridden by a busty woman old enough to be his mother. He only glimpsed them, however, because the floor beneath his falling feet gave way as well. Surrounded by a cascade of rotten boards and plaster dust, he plunged through into a tavern filled with soldiers.

They stared at him, and he at them, and then all dissolved into a milling chaos of fists and feet. While Aros defended himself with heroic strength and skill, the falling of his personal night was inevitable, and welcome when it finally pulled him from a world of pain.

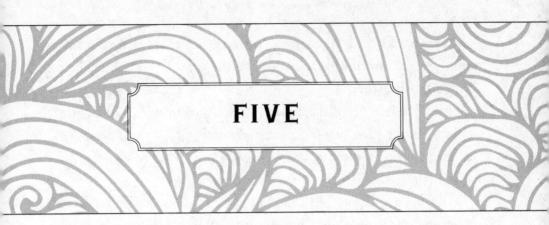

FIVE

The Proud Abyss

ONE MONTH LATER

Quillia's gold and crimson flag waved bravely against the ocean rain. The *Proud Abyss*, the royal fleet's most prized vessel, was a three-master riding high in the waves. Its prow was blessed with a mermaid statue with improbably blue eyes and blond hair, consecrated by priests to ferry the princess Tahlia safely to her destination and home once again. Ahead of them, the *Triton*. Behind, the *Domino*.

Tahlia leaned against the railing of the center ship, looking out at the rain-swept sea, mourning her life.

Zatch's wedding had been wonderful, for the fun of it, but also for the chance to see her cousin, whom she adored. With whom she had been raised, knowing that in days to come that relationship, fostered in childhood, would be the thread that bound their kingdoms together.

Her life had been like a clockwork toy, all jewels and tightly choreographed lessons, social engagements, travel . . . all designed to lead to the moment when she would be offered to the highest bidder in marriage.

No, it wasn't quite like that, but close enough. All of the royal privilege was merely preparation for her future role as royal wife: a jewel on the arm of a king or prince, a ravishing and limber bedmate, an advisor in matters of state.

And, most important, one of the anchors holding the kingdom of Quillia in the firmament. This was more important than ever after the death of her father. A widowed queen could be seen as weak, a potential opportunity for adventurous rulers who thought to pressure the kingdom by threats of war into more advantageous trade relations. Tribute. Gifts of land . . . or daughters.

That was what had happened to her cousin Zatch. The kingdom of Nandia had nibbled at Quillia's northern borders until the queen had agreed to release a disputed province and gift the dullard prince with one of Tahlia's beautiful cousins.

Only with trepidation had Tahlia traveled up the coast to the kingdom of Nandia. Captain Dinos had been a perfect host, even if his first mate, Chastain, made her skin crawl. Their ships were welcomed at harbor, and her cousin Zatch had greeted her warmly, sweeping her to a palace less imposing than her own, but of necessity more martial. Their neighboring kingdom of Shrike was not to be trifled with.

When she met the prince (And the oaf in question wasn't even the eldest! He would inherit lands and titles, but not a crown. And if the eldest had any doubts about his sibling's loyalty or ambitions, Tahlia hoped that Zatch would stay alert for poison . . .), she had been impressed by his manners if not his silhouette, which suggested he enjoyed food more than swordsmanship. She had been on the verge of mourning for her childhood friend, when she caught the brief, shielded glance between Zatch and the captain of the prince's guard, a handsome rogue with shoulders Atlas might have stood upon to lift the world.

Tahlia had hardly been able to control her curiosity until they were alone.

"Zatch!" she said, astonished by her cousin's boldness. "You aren't even married, and already taking liberties?"

Zatch had only grinned at her younger cousin. "Tahlia, you will learn the ways of the world. I have potions to prevent conception, so the royal line is secure. Second, because my husband is not in line for the throne—he has two other brothers who would ascend first—there is little concern about it. And third, the captain of the guard serves both the prince and princess. If you understand my meaning."

Zatch had thrown her head back and laughed raucously, as Tahlia gawked in astonishment.

So . . . perhaps she was naive. So . . . the marriages for which she and her cousins had been molded were often shams, with pleasure taken wherever it could be found.

Tahlia leaned against the railing, watching the waves wash up against the mermaid's painted eyes. So much beauty in the world, so many possibilities. And now she saw . . . so many fictions as well.

Unless she could marry for love.

"*Brill 'twith say honor,*" said a voice beside her.

"*Confir alth all tithing,*" she answered in ritual response. She smiled, wiping rain from her face. Even on a sea voyage, her faithful

Drasilljah was teaching her. In this case, the structure of ancient Lemur, the high language of the kingdom of Nandia.

"You did that deliberately," the princess pretended to pout. "You knew where my mind was straying."

Her nursemaid, the woman who had been with her since childhood, seemed to sense her mood. "Not your fate, child," the old woman said.

"And how do you know that?"

Drasilljah's kind mouth curled in a smile. "Not so powerful as I was in childhood," she said, and shook her head. "Raised by my weird sisters to be helpmate to a princess, trained in the powers and knowledge of the earth and the stones. The magic is in my blood. And then . . . the magic itself began to retreat. Nothing to be done."

She sighed. "But I know enough to see your fate, and it is not to be a plaything, or a bauble, or a beard."

"Then what is it?"

And here Drasilljah's face took on a more troubled aspect. "I am not sure," she said. "But if it were to be like your cousin, I would have felt a twinning of your paths. A doubling."

"What did you see in its stead?"

"Clouds." She looked up at the half-shrouded moon. "There is a darkness in my vision. At first I thought to blame the world, thought it was the action of some other sorcerer . . . but not now. It would take too much power to cloud my vision in such a fashion, so far from land, with such consistency. And while such power still exists in the world, it is difficult to believe anyone would expend it just to blind a graying old crow like me."

Tahlia hugged the crone. Drasilljah's shoulders were thinner, less padded than once they were, but Draz was still the same woman who had nurtured her in childhood, and it was incredibly comforting to have her close.

"So we don't know what the future will be. Only that it won't be *that*. There are suitors, of course. Some are even handsome." In truth, her only remaining suitors were actually of the very best families of the Eight Kingdoms, all wealthy, handsome, and powerful. Most were either brilliant or brave, and she imagined that, eventually, she would succumb to their blandishments and choose one. But . . .

"It will take more than handsome to make you happy. And more than power to keep the kingdom safe. Your mother will make the best match she can."

Tahlia ran her forefinger back and forth along the railing. "Must it be a prince?" she asked.

Drasilljah frowned. "Get that out of your head," she snapped. "That wizard is nothing but trouble."

Tahlia smiled. Neoloth was trouble—there was no question about it. But he was also courtly, and charming, and she found herself considering him favorably, especially compared with the clutch of dandified suitors who had descended upon her mother's kingdom drinking and eating up her substance like locusts, riding around the capital kingdom with their squads of bodyguards like clowns on parade at the circus.

Her choice of one of those egotistical young bravos or languid balladeers would end one phase of her life and begin another. New alliances. New resources. New trade agreements. All to produce, in years to come, a new brood of trading tokens to be married to seal future alliances.

She wasn't a human being. Peasants had it better, she thought. They could marry for love. Or at least lust.

Love . . .

Odd how, when she thought that word, her heart sped up, just a bit, and her skin felt the way she felt that time a picnic had been interrupted by a lightning storm, and she'd been much too close to an actual strike. The air hummed. And her skin did as well.

She remembered her cousin's face when she looked at the face of her paramour. That was not the face of the girl Tahlia had played dolls with in childhood; it was the face of a woman who knew more about her body than Tahlia did. A woman who knew what it was to be a *woman*.

Tahlia looked out across the ocean, dark but for slivers of moonlight dancing on the crescent waves. Restless, eternally in motion. Almost invisible. Like a woman's heart. Who did she want to take her to that distant land? In whose hands could she entrust her heart? Any of those rough or effete and pampered boys seeking fortune? Ah, some of them were pretty enough, but none of them bottled the lightning . . .

Draz had said something, quiet, but the softness itself had caught Tahlia's attention. "What? I didn't hear you."

"I said that the mermaid's eyes are open." The voice was cool, a little withdrawn. There was something in it.

Princess Tahlia looked over the side of the ship. The figurehead faced the sea ahead. How could Drasilljah see the eyes?

"I feel it," she said, answering the unspoken query.

"I thought the eyes were always open. In fact, when we came aboard, I saw that the statue's eyes were open."

Draz wagged her head. "Not the wooden eyes," she said. "The royal ships have figureheads carved from driftwood and blessed with the souls of Merfolk. We bond their spirits into the figureheads, and they give us protection."

"How do they do this wondrous thing?"

"Humans are not the only ones who work magic. We weird sisters have friends among the magical folk. When they age or sicken, if their lives cannot be saved, they sometimes benefit their clans by offering to bind their spirits into the carvings. Centaurs may become travel wagons. Weremice bond to household totems."

Tahlia nodded. She was actually a bit surprised that she'd never asked the question. "So the eyes . . ." She looked along the side of the ship and could see the back of the mermaid's head and part of the tail, but nothing of the face. It was not surprising that Drasilljah could, however. Drasilljah could do many things.

And right now Draz's tension was becoming alarm. Princess Tahlia looked up at the sky. Dark, long hours from dawn, rain clouds threaded with lightning, the distant roll of thunder mere echoes . . . but no hint of danger. What of the ocean? When the clouds parted enough for the moonlight to splash upon the waves, she could see nothing, but hers was not a sailor's practiced gaze, able to detect the masts of a pirate vessel bobbing at the horizon.

But still . . .

There . . . a patch of ocean to the north was silvered with moonlight. Nothing. Was she expecting a kraken?

"Look," Drasilljah pointed.

Tahlia tried to look along that finger, squinted, unsure if her eyes had adjusted to the darkness, or if she was merely imagining a hint of outline. There *did* seem to be something out there. At first she thought she was seeing a single wispy waterspout, then for a moment she wondered if she was seeing three such freaks of weather dancing on the waves.

No. Tiny streams, though. Like steam rising from a kettle's spout. And the crackling lightning revealed that the wisps seemed to issue from small black shapes upon the waves. The driving rain made it difficult to make out anything at all, but if she wasn't mistaken, between the first and second flashes, the objects had moved closer to the *Proud Abyss*.

That ruled out any kind of sailing vessels, she reckoned. The wind was blowing in the wrong direction.

Up in the crow's nest, First Mate Chastain whistled, pointing out "Starboard!" And the other sailors on late watch crowded to the right side of the ship, more curious than alarmed.

Tahlia clutched Drasilljah's hand. The woman she had known her entire life seemed . . . on point, like a hunting dog.

"What do you sense?" Tahlia asked. "Magic?"

"Not magic. No . . . yes, magic . . ." She shook her head. "I don't know. I've never felt anything quite like this before."

"Captain!" the old woman called. "Captain! On your guard!" Drasilljah turned toward the cabins. "I know not what this is, but I fear that only ill wind blows against the clouds. Come."

Tahlia caught one last glimpse before she followed her friend and protector. And that last glimpse revealed three small ships. It was difficult to establish size because of a lack of known objects with which to compare them. And they had no masts. She looked for oars in the water, but couldn't see them. They seemed to be on fire, although she could see no flame, and would have questioned its presence in this driving rain. But each roof emitted a thin, constant stream of smoke.

"Come!" Drasilljah tugged more urgently now. There was another puff of smoke from the closest vessel, which was now only two arrow flights away. Followed by a dull clap of thunder. Duller, perhaps. More localized, without that sense of everywhere-and-nowhere you had with the child of lightning, when fire was quenched in water.

Then the night exploded into flame.

Their trailing ship, the *Domino*, shuddered and lurched, as her amidships erupted like a volcano. Tahlia's eyes widened. Never had she seen such a thing. In the light of the spreading blaze (And *how* it spread! It was like a jellied layer of fire!) she glimpsed the smaller vessels riding the waves, now puffing burst after burst of fire into the night. The *Domino* erupted again and again, and the sailors crowded against the rails groaned in terror.

And then . . . the same thing happened just ahead of them. The *Triton's* side *burst*, wood arcing up into the sky, splinters and shards of singed wood rained down upon the deck of the *Proud Abyss*, still smoldering.

"Heaven preserve us! Demon fire!" the captain screamed. Then he called out: "Trim the sails! All passengers below deck!"

"What is happening?" Tahlia asked.

From the beginning of their voyage, Captain Dinos had been a fatherly figure. Now in this moment of trial he seemed to grow taller, even more protective. Tahlia was afraid for him, but also proud and reassured. "Whatever magic they use, they've not used it against us, Princess. I think they want you."

I think they want you.

The words reverberated in her head. Their meaning sank in more deeply. As she was pulled to her cabin, the ship lurched up and plunged down again, and at the apex she glimpsed one of the small ships, close enough now to make out the human shapes swarming the deck.

The pirate craft continued to belch fire. Then one of them exploded, like a pinecone in a bonfire, amid screams of dismay from its crew.

"Come on!" Drasilljah said, and hauled her into the cabin. Her nurse barricaded the door, and they sank back into the shadows, arms around each other.

Terrible things were happening above-decks. She heard shouts and then the shrill call of steel on steel. The *Proud Abyss* was being boarded. Screams and shouted orders. Captain Dinos's voice above the howling wind.

Then another scream, low with agony and wet against the rain. The captain's voice was stilled.

A pause, and then a banging at her door. "Open the door, Princess." The voice was like stone. "Open the door, and we swear you will come to no harm."

Drasilljah held her tight. *No.*

"Open the door. We know your nursemaid is with you. If you force us to break the door open, we'll kill her. If you open it yourself and offer no resistance, I promise no harm will come to her."

She looked at Drasilljah for guidance, and her nurse shook her head. *No.*

Tahlia thought frantically. This was nightmare. Whatever happened next, she knew those men could break down the door and take her. If there was any chance that Drasilljah could survive this, she would have to take it.

"I'll open the door," she said. Drasilljah pulled at her, silently begging, but Tahlia held her at arm's distance, suddenly transformed into the older of the two. "Whatever happens next," she said. "If I am to survive it, I will need you at my side."

The tears streamed from the old woman's eyes. It was not concern for herself that caused them; it was fear for her charge. Shame that she could not protect the girl she loved. Gratitude that that girl would think of her nursemaid before herself.

Tahlia opened the door, then shrank back.

The man at the door was the largest human being the princess had ever seen, a full head taller than the captain of her mother's guard. Part troll, perhaps. She had heard of such obscenities.

It snorted, its flat broad nostrils blowing hot air and wet drops at her, but she didn't flinch. It seized the meat of her upper arm like a wrestler grabbing a baby, and pulled her out onto the deck.

The man waiting there was smaller but more dangerous. He was broad and thick but moved with an odd fluidity, like a palace dancer. A sense of coiled, leashed potential. *This* was the power. This man. He was the one to deal with.

There was something else. Captain Dinos sprawled dead, curled on his side like a child. He had died protecting them.

But Chastain, the first mate, the man whose eyes she had felt crawling upon her from the first day . . . Chastain was alive. More than alive, Chastain stood at the side of the man she now assumed was the leader.

So, a traitor. She felt Drasilljah tense, heard a whispered curse.

"Not now," Tahlia whispered, and was relieved to feel Drasilljah relax away from the edge of the precipice.

"You are in charge here," she said to the leader. Not a question, a statement.

"Yes, I am," he said.

"Who are you?"

His smile was, considering the circumstances, rather kindly. "I hope you understand that the less you know of me, the more you can hope to eventually be returned to your mother safely."

She weighed his words. This man was not discourteous; he spoke well, with the enunciation of one who spent a great deal of time at some court, layered over a rougher tone. A military man, totally confident in his skills. Someone who had lived hard and fought his way to power. A man who lived by his guts. And yet . . . something about the delicacy of his phrasing, the excellent bones of his face suggested nobility. Perhaps even royalty.

Who was this man? Could his word be trusted?

She threw the dice. "I have your word that if I come with you without resistance, you will protect my life and that of my attendant?"

"Yes, you do," he said.

"There is one thing I must do before I leave this ship. Have I your permission?"

"We have not long, princess," he said.

"This will only take a moment."

He nodded agreement.

"Now," Tahlia whispered.

No one could have moved fast enough to stop what happened next. Drasilljah's hair comb was fashioned as a carved shell, but actually of painted steel, its edge as hard as metal and as sharp as broken glass. She whipped it across Chastain's throat so fast he hadn't even a chance to blink. His eyes opened wide, and he fell, gagging and clutching at the wound.

Tahlia held her breath. The next moment would tell the tale.

The leader watched Chastain die on the deck, his heels drumming against the wet.

He turned to Drasilljah and plucked the comb from her hand. "Nicely done," he said. "I loathe traitors."

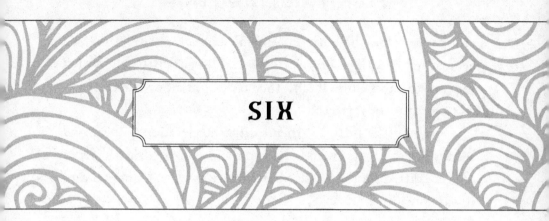

SIX

Bad News

Even before the guard arrived at his door, summoning him to the palace, Neoloth-Pteor knew that there was something terribly wrong. All night his sleep had been restless, filled with images of shadow creatures with bloody teeth.

His had been a shallow repose, a transparent state partway between ordinary sleep and wakefulness. "Wizard's Sleep" it was called, more efficient and effective than ordinary sleep, and one of the secrets of his power.

The knock at his door roused him in waves, thinning the line between sleep and wakefulness. "Sorcerer! You are needed!"

He rolled up, planted his feet on the floor, and stared at the wall. Neoloth could feel disaster looming, like a storm cloud crouching below the horizon, invisible but oppressive. It pressed against his head like a squeezing fist. The guards barely waited for him to dress himself, and they took him along the more direct corridor aboveground.

Climbing the hill gave them sufficient elevation to hear and see for miles. Lights twinkled down there. A dog barked sharply. Voices drifted on the wind. Something was wrong, and word of it was spreading.

The guards ushered him into the crown chamber. It seemed that the entire castle was awake. The queen sat rigidly upon her throne. Her eyes were red-rimmed, as if she had already been crying for hours. The smaller throne to her right, her daughter's throne, had never looked so empty.

Neoloth bowed deeply. "My queen," he said. "How may I serve you?"

"Conceal yourself in the private chamber," she said, voice urgent and strained. "Watch what occurs in the next hour. Advise me."

For the first time since he had been employed in Quillia, he reached out and took her hand. It was cool, and dry, and too thin, as if the substance between skin and bone were wasting away. She did not seem to consider his action a transgression and did not pull away from him.

"Go," she said, indicating a heavy red curtain behind the throne. He stepped quickly to conceal himself behind it, and found himself in a chamber just large enough for a single chair. A section of the curtain at face level was thinned enough for a man who pressed his face against it to see the throne room while remaining unseen to supplicants approaching the queen.

Neoloth waited.

The door at the far end of the outer chamber opened. Three

men were ushered in. They were tall and sun-darkened. They had spent time in the desert.

Mercenary sorcerers who would sell their arts to the highest bidder. One of them glanced directly at Neoloth's hiding place, as if he could see through the curtain. Then he looked away.

"Oh Great Queen. We bear greetings from the ruler of Shrike."

Yes. The kingdom north of Nandia, Princess Tahlia's destination. A closed kingdom ruled by a despot. They traded goods, of course, but only with the most stringent of oversight, and their citizens traveled abroad less frequently than those of any of the Eight Kingdoms.

Further, rumor had it that families never traveled together, wives and children acting as hostages against betrayal.

This was very, very bad indeed.

"Welcome to my kingdom, great ambassadors," the queen said. Her voice was so strong and regal. It was possible that only a liar as accomplished as Neoloth himself could have detected the tremor therein. "Upon your return, convey greetings to your great king. Tell me how I may serve you."

"We come seeking no service, Great Queen," the tallest of them said. "Rather, we seek to offer service."

"Service?" Her puzzlement seemed real.

"Yes. One of our trading vessels, bound for the southern kingdoms, encountered flotsam from one of your sailing ships, with sailors clinging to broken wood. Obeying the code of the sea, we rescued them and, upon hearing their tale and provenance, wish only to return them to safety."

"While I appreciate the rescue of our brave sailing men, I do not yet understand why my advisors considered this an emergency requiring my immediate personal attention."

"Your Royal Majesty. Upon interviewing the rescued sailors, we learned a fact that disturbed us deeply. A fact it would have been remiss not to bring to Your Majesty's attention. Those rescued claimed to have been sailors aboard three of Your Majesty's ships. They tell us that the flagship, the *Proud Abyss*, carried the royal daughter. Would these be considered facts?"

Neoloth could not see the queen's face, but he could visualize its sudden tightness. "Yes, it is true."

How it must have pained her to say this. What strength it required to keep the strain from her voice, Neoloth could only imagine. What he did know was that he was witnessing magic of a very different variety.

"Your Majesty, it is our sad duty to recount their tale."

"Or rather," said a shorter man, "allow the sailor to tell his own tale."

He clapped his hands again, and the door opened. Two small, dark Shriker types dragged in a man on a canvas travois. He looked dead but for a fitful, wet snore. A seventh man, face pale and clothes torn, shuffled into the room as if his feet were shackled.

"Oh mighty Queen," the man said, and he was shaking, afraid to meet her eyes.

"Rise," she said, as kindly as possible—again, Neoloth wondered where she found the strength. "Tell me what happened. Omit nothing."

"I'm Sanam. This is Glarios, but he cannot speak. He's been sleeping since they fished him out of the sea . . ." He told of an uneventful voyage, ending with, "We were returning from the wedding," he said, "and there was a storm."

"Your ship foundered in the storm?"

"No, Your Majesty. Our sailors were up to the mark. But in the midst of the storm, strange vessels appeared . . ."

And here the man's tale turned strange. Out of the storm came small fire-breathing vessels that attacked the three royal sailing ships. They carried no flags. No masts. Fire and thunder erupted in the midst of the rain. Sanam's ship, the *Domino*, groaned and sank in a chaos of shattered wood and screaming sailors. The next thing he knew, he was being plucked out of the sea by a ship flying under Shrike's flag. And there remained no trace of the *Proud Abyss*.

The queen cleared her throat. Her angular face had darkened, as if choking on her urge to scream curses and accusations at the man cowering before her. "Do you know what happened to the *Abyss*?"

"No, your majesty," he said, unable to meet her eyes. "Four were pulled out. Only me and Glarios are still alive."

"These . . . fires and explosions. Did you see such eruptions aboard the *Abyss*?"

The sailor hung his head in anguish. Such misery made it obvious to Neoloth that he was telling the truth as he saw it. On the other hand, there was something about the three men who had brought him. They were not sailors. Nor were they the usual ambassadors. Or soldiers. No. They were magic users of some kind, but they were either weak (no great surprise, in these milk-water days) or so powerful they could effectively shield themselves, even from the concealed Neoloth.

"No, Your Grace."

She nodded. "Is there anything else you wish to say?"

His eyes shifted. "No, Your Grace." *Later, perhaps.*

She nodded. "Please take these brave men to the healers, and to food and rest. I'll find a wizard as well and will come to you later." The sailors were led away, leaving the other three in the middle of the throne room.

For a long time no motion disturbed the room. The air was still. Silence reigned, as if the humans within, royals, nobles, advisors, and guards, were engaged in a test of wills to see who could longest refrain from speech.

"Have you more to tell me?" the queen asked. "Is there no word at all of my daughter? Has the ocean swallowed her entirely?"

"I do not believe that is the case," the tallest of the three ambassadors said. "We believe that these strange burning ships that throw fire are the same vessels who have attacked our own fleet. We seek them, but confess to surprise that they travel so far south. We seek them north of our own borders. We have agents among the Northfolk, and believe that, given time, we can learn what has happened."

"What is your belief?"

"I believe that the princess is alive and held by these men. They have raided ships before, seeking slaves, women, loot. While ruthless to men, they are not known to slaughter women. Rather, they hold them for ransom . . . or . . ." He paused significantly. "Keep them for themselves, if you understand the implications. We believe that we can find her, if she is where and with whom we believe her to be."

"The royal personage would appreciate any assistance you can offer. We will, of course, make our own inquiries."

"The sea leaves few traces, Your Majesty. We were fortunate to find witnesses at all."

That was certainly true. But better that these sailors had been swallowed by the waves if the smallest portion of their story proved untrue.

The tall man paused again. The silence thickened. This time, one of the queen's advisors seemed to recognize her distress and spoke in her stead. "We appreciate your return of our sailors. And any efforts you can make to recover our beloved princess. What can we offer you as a token of appreciation for your efforts?"

There it was. To maintain the pretense, the ambassadors could not ask for blackmail. It had to be offered.

The man bowed. "We wish only to continue making safe passage through your waters. That you allow us to conduct investigations and pursue our financial affairs as we see fit. In exchange, I believe we can promise that we will find and return the princess."

Neoloth reeled. The implied threat was more brazen than he would have believed.

There was more said, but after a relatively short exchange, the ambassadors retired from the room.

The next day was a whirlwind. Sanam the sailor was allowed to eat but not sleep. He was drilled endlessly on everything he had seen and heard. He said he had been treated well by the Shrikes. He bore no sign of coercion or magical control. Again and again he told the same story: A storm. Small steaming ships coming out of the night. Explosions. Sinking. Those steaming ships swarmed the *Abyss* instead of trying to take her down.

And that was the only consolation any of them had.

At midnight, the queen summoned Neoloth back to the throne room. "Great Mage," she said. An edge of desperation had crept into her voice. "What words of wisdom have you to offer?"

"This is like no magic I've ever heard of," Neoloth said, "and I thought I knew of every form of magic."

"My daughter?"

"It was a veiled threat, of course," he said. "They captured the princess and wish you not to interfere in their affairs."

"For what purpose?"

"I do not know," he replied honestly. "What I can say is that the very need to control us suggests that the princess yet lives. I would expect that in a moon or so, they will present a letter written by your daughter and supposedly smuggled out. It will contain information only she would know and will calm you."

He could see that she wanted terribly to believe what he was saying but was no fool. "And their ultimate purpose?"

"War, perhaps. They wish to be certain that you do not side with another kingdom against them."

"And they kidnapped Tahlia for this purpose. What can we do?"

"They perceive you as weak. They doubt you will launch an attack against them. After all, they merely returned two of your sailors and offered assistance. It would be difficult to get another of the kingdoms to stand with us on such meager evidence."

Despite her trappings of power, she seemed . . . diminished. Desperate. "Can you use your arts to find her? If so, your reward would be great."

A thought seemed to occur to her suddenly, and she raised her voice. "Send out the call," she said to an advisor. "To the princes who sought the hand of Tahlia in marriage. The royal or noble personage who returns my daughter to me wins my approval, and rich reward. He will wed her and inherit my kingdom. Send the word."

And so it was sent.

SEVEN

Wizard at Work

Reinforced by the talisman's powers, Neoloth-Pteor's scrying pool swirled, foaming into images of storm and sea so realistic they threatened to soak the room. He saw what the sailor saw, as the man had surrendered his mind to Neoloth's spells.

It was truth. All was as the wretched sailor had testified.

Vessels with neither mast nor sail, pouring smoke. Explosions like lightning striking dry trees but in the midst of the storm. *Drowning, gripping something as it banged against him, clinging, fainting.*

He tried other spells, other techniques to see if there was more information that could be extracted from the mind of this simple, honest man. He just didn't know enough.

And, failing that, were there other ways he could see into the future, determine what had happened, where the princess might be, and what might be done?

He tried everything he knew, and nothing worked. Twenty hours later, he was shaking and exhausted and frightened by the implications. Was a wizard blocking him? Or—

Wizards couldn't see into their own futures. If there was something *he* could do for the princess . . . it would not show in his scrying pool. Nothing to show for his work but this damned fog.

Shrike had once been an equal member of the Eight Kingdoms, but in recent years it had become more insular, less open to trade or cultural exchange. No one outside Shrike really seemed to know what was happening within it. Rather than respect or affection, the dominant emotion felt toward the northern kingdom was fear.

If they had kidnapped Tahlia, then minions of Shrike hadn't merely plucked her from the sea . . . they had actually strolled into her mother's throne room and announced their actions while maintaining plausible deniability. Which meant that they didn't merely want her life. Or a ransom. There was another game in play.

And the ambassadors had arrived in Quillia so openly that it was impossible for her citizens not to know.

This was a direct warning for Quillia to remain neutral. But neutral to what? Neoloth knew of no current events that might matter here and no ways that Quillia was involved in anything concerning Shrike. But this outrage might relate to something that would *become* known in the future.

Something huge. Something brewing in the heart of Shrike. No single kingdom could stand against the other seven king-doms. Quillia was one of the strongest . . . and Quillia had now been neutralized. What if Shrike had found ways to neutralize the others as well?

It was a game of chess played with invisible pieces, on a board of unknown dimensions, with unfathomed rules and objectives. The puzzle pieces chased themselves around and around in his head, whirling as if caught in a cyclone.

The princess had been kidnapped to retard response. He could assume that she had been taken by Shrike, but where exactly was she? An invasion would accomplish nothing and might kill the princess. What action could the queen take that would return her daughter?

Perhaps none. But, then, what could she do to protect her kingdom and her authority?

She could offer reward for the return of her daughter, and she had. That would free individual action, and that might work. Where a large-scale assault would almost certainly end in Tahlia's being murdered, it was just possible that smaller actions might suffice. And the queen had unleashed the fortune-seeking princes of seven countries to save her child.

Shrike had opened a door, and the queen had responded in kind. And whatever marched forth from that door might change their world with their struggles.

But with all of the storm and fury, all the war elephants clashing and rending the earth, all that might come . . .

It was possible, just possible, that a mouse could slip out of one door and through another.

Why had the queen brought him into the throne room and yet concealed him from sight? *She wanted him to know.* She was asking for him to take action.

Sleep, even Wizard's Sleep, eluded him. For the next two days, he exhaustively studied the kingdom of Shrike: its history, wealth, and powers. Its families and industries.

But it was in studying Shrike's military that he found the very first glimmer of hope.

He turned the idea around and around in his mind, trying to disprove it. And, instead, a second piece fell into place, so large and perfectly shaped it was almost as if it had all been predestined.

In fact, when he snapped out of his reverie and looked at the entirety of it, he almost forgot to breathe. Neoloth was overwhelmed with the perfection. The synchronicity.

All he needed now was to be certain that a certain barbarian had not yet been executed.

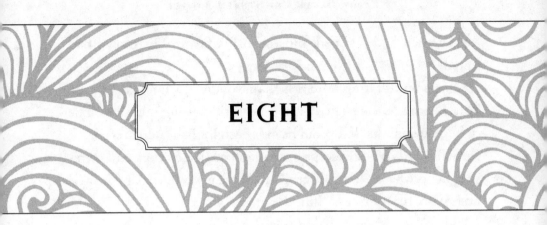

EIGHT

The Bargain

Chains, trials, testimony.

The last weeks had been filled with scowling faces and accusatory speeches. Aros had long experienced the ire with which people hold thieves, but the anger and hatred directed at a tax-man were a totally different standard. The strangling of C'Vall seemed a mere incident. It was amazing how many people came forward to accuse a chained man of perfidy. And, likewise, the number of people who seemed happy that he had been stripped of the trappings of authority, as they seemed to take unnatural pleasure from hauling him half-naked and chained before an unsympathetic judge.

His men had testified, mostly in his favor. The crowd had jeered.

It was humiliating. And if he had wondered who had betrayed him, he now knew that that had been the wrong question. The right question was, Why had he ever been foolish enough to think these bastards would accept him as an equal? Let alone fail to resent his power as tax collector? That they would not take their first opportunity to cast him down?

But Aros had never paid taxes.

Aros was languishing in his chains when the white-bearded jailer brought him his daily bowl of gruel. The ancient was a trustee, serving a life sentence for some crime he could no longer remember. Sometimes murder, sometimes theft, and once merely the seduction of a noble daughter. The story shifted with the phases of the moon.

"Pirates got the princess," he whispered as Aros sopped gruel in coarse bread and chewed.

That caught his attention, although he had never met or even seen her. "When?"

"I hear she was on her way back from her cousin's wedding."

"The ransom will be huge," he said. That was reflex: he would never touch it. "When did the news come?"

"Two days ago," the old man said.

"Pirates?"

The old man shrugged. "Don't know. But that's what I've heard. I think you're going to have other fish to fry soon. They're asking for death."

"I *fed* those people!" Aros shrugged his massive shoulders. Death came to all men. That didn't bother him as much as its manner. He'd hoped never to die on a gallows. Given half a chance, he would force the guardsman to give him a cleaner, swifter end.

So far he hadn't had the chance.

In the first hour after midnight, the door of his cell opened. "It stinks in here," said the man silhouetted in the door frame.

The light hurt Aros's eyes, and he shielded them with his arm. "Try shitting through a hole in the floor and see how you smell."

The man in the doorway cocked his head. "You are much as I remember you."

Aros squinted. "I know you? Come closer." Whoever this was, perhaps he could be lured within reach.

Aros had no friends in Quillia—he understood that now. Tor One-Eye had come once, bringing apples, but never since. If this fool had come to gloat, he would regret it. Briefly. Intensely.

He was studying Aros . . . perhaps his tattoos. "That's a nice seascape," the intruder said. "You must have jumped back pretty fast."

The seascape was a calm ocean, flat beneath a setting sun, in four colors—but tilted twenty degrees. It crossed his heart. Several small ships showed below the horizon.

"Not backward. I didn't have a sword," Aros said. "He got in one good slash right across my chest, and then I broke his knee and strangled him. Come, take a better look."

"This is fine. Are you ready to die?"

"We are born dying," Aros said. "Every warrior knows this."

"I was under the impression you were more of a thief than a warrior."

"One makes one's way in the world however one can," Aros

said. "Please, come closer. I still cannot see you. It is so dark in here."

The man stepped closer. Whatever he had to say, whatever offer he had to make, certainly nothing could be as satisfying as killing one more Quillian.

"So cold. So calm and certain," the stranger said. "You are the man I thought you were. No pleading or bribery or protestations of innocence."

The stranger balanced on the edge. Just another step. "If any of those would have made a difference," Aros growled, "I would have been happy to oblige. Are you saying they would? Please, come closer that I might see your face and know if you lie."

The man smiled. Where had Aros seen him before?

"I will come no closer," the man said. "I am not a fool."

"What are you? And why should I care? I am a man already dead."

"*Yesss.*" The single syllable was serpentine. He could easily imagine this creature slithering across sand on its belly. Come to taunt him? A torturer perhaps. Well, the bastard would gain no satisfaction here.

"How would you like to live?" the man said.

Aros felt something that he did not want to feel: *hope.* "Like a king. What nonsense is this?"

"Perhaps you have heard the uproar around you. In the streets. The kingdom is in peril."

"I had nothing to do with the disappearance of your princess," Aros said.

"Ah, yes. Your barbarian's code." He nodded. "I have to say that I have seen many things from you, but cruelty toward women was not one of them. Especially widows, I recall. I've often wondered if this had something to do with your past."

Who *was* this bastard? How the hell did he know so much?

"For instance, the Brothers of Blood were known to hold hostages, have they not?"

Aros felt his heart sink. The Brothers of Blood was his pirate crew, the tribe of brigands he'd captained for three years. He'd thought that his connection to them remained unknown. Certainly, it had never arisen in his trial. The judges had sentenced him to death without knowing all about his past. If they had known, they would have skinned him and rolled him in salt.

Best to say nothing. But . . . who was this man? Could he be lured another step closer? "You cannot connect me with that crew."

"Not without effort," the man said. "But what I *can* do . . . is set you free."

Aros felt it again, a tug at his leashed emotions. A hammer strike against the boulder he had rolled atop his hopes and dreams.

"In your time," the man said, "you have been many things. A thief, a pirate, a soldier, a . . . taxman." The hint of a smile. "I want to know if you can play one more role."

"What role is this?"

And now, for the first time, Aros had the sense that the man was revealing his actual feelings about . . . something.

"The princess Tahlia has been taken. We have good reason to believe that the nation of Shrike took her."

"Then go and get her. Quillia has an army."

"But where in Shrike is she?" Another hint of emotion. This man *cared*. Fascinating. "And where's the proof? If we invade and fail to find her, we will have started a war for no reason. Our relations with the Eight Kingdoms would crumble."

That made sense. In fact, unless his ears deceived him, this stranger had just spoken to him man to man, without the carefully judged obliqueness that had defined his speech until now.

There was something emotional. Something *personal*. Hope leapt within Aros. A man of high speech, with the power to enter his cell and speak to him privately. Yes, this was hope.

And hope killed.

"Go on," he said.

"Where armies cannot go, another approach might bear fruit." And now, for the first time, the stranger came closer. Now, if Aros whipped his chain up, he might be able to wrap it around the neck. A snap at that point would be satisfying beyond belief. But that would also destroy whatever small chance this represented.

And Aros knew that the stranger knew it. *Damn.*

"I asked about your ability to play a role," the stranger said. "And this is why I asked. Some say a minor prince, General Silith, is the most powerful man in the kingdom of Shrike. It is difficult to tell, because no one has seen the king for years. Some say this is due to fear of assassination. And others that he is already dead, and that Silith is Shrike's actual leader. Little is known of the general, except that he is a prince or half prince who had no hope of inheriting the throne. Instead of a life of leisure, he apparently chose the military path and has succeeded brilliantly. We know he is reputed to be one of the finest swordsmen in the world and a brilliant tactician as well. I see Sinjin Silith's hand in this kidnapping."

"You wish him killed?"

"No."

"What, then?"

"Fifteen years ago, his son Elio traveled with the son of a king of another of the Eight Kingdoms, as companion. The caravan was ambushed, the prince held for ransom. The general's son disappeared in the chaos and was not recovered when the ransom was paid. It is known that the general held his employers responsible and left to find his fortune elsewhere."

"Revenge?"

"Always a powerful motivator."

Damn it, now they were talking. Almost as if one of them were not covered in offal and crouching in chains.

"Is the boy dead?"

The man nodded. "Yes. But the general cannot be certain of this. He assumes it, yes. But his wife, Jade, has never given up hope. It is known that, as recently as last year, she paid for the testimony of a man who had encountered one of the original raiders, who spoke of desert tribes and a story she accepted as true."

"A mother's love," Aros said.

"And it is that mother who concerns us."

"Why?"

"Jade Silith is Azteca. She was offered to the general as part of his spoils of war, although it is said their bond has become one of love. The general is a huge man. Your size."

And there he stopped speaking.

Aros thought, and he suddenly saw it. "He's big, she's Azteca, and you are insane."

"You are about the age that Elio would be. Black hair, dark skin. You are a warrior, like his father. His mother is obsessed that the boy is still alive. Do you speak the language of the desert people?"

"A little. I fought a skirmish against them during the border wars."

"When was this?"

"Eight, nine years ago. I was a soldier."

"Well . . . that can be fixed. Yes."

"Tell me what you want."

"I want you to remake yourself as the general's missing son. To enter the kingdom with me, I as your servant. You must ingratiate yourself to the grieving mother and father. Allow them to celebrate your return. And during that process, I will find a chance to discover what I need."

"And if I do this? If I *can* do this?"

"If we do this and succeed, not only will you be free . . . but you will be wealthy, with the gratitude of the greatest queen in the Eight Kingdoms."

"Who are you," Aros said, suddenly without the need to ask. He knew.

"That is not important," the stranger said. This was no stranger. By the Feathered One, no stranger at all! "What is important is your oath. You are many things, but your people have a sacred pledge no righteous Aztec has ever broken. If you make that oath to me, I in turn will swear to set you free at the end of this."

The anger boiled within him. "You did this to me. You wanted my help and arranged for me to be here."

"I swear I had no such scheme," the man said. "Yes, I did put you here. No, it had nothing to do with the princess."

"The tomb?" The last time he had seen his old enemy, he had been sealed in a tomb infested with giant hungry arachnids.

"The tomb. I can see your scars. There's a spider bite under that setting sun. I bear their wounds as well."

Aros's lips curled in a smile. That, at least, was something.

He hated himself for not wringing the sorcerer's scrawny neck. But the desire for life had stirred within him, corrupting his resolve. But . . . he just couldn't help his worst enemy, damn it.

Could he?

"All right," he said. "By the Feathered One. I promise that if you free me, I will serve you until the princess is rescued or we discover it is impossible. But there is a condition: if you lie to me, even once . . . our deal is off."

"Agreed," the sorcerer said. "And if you disobey me or break your oath in any way . . . you are dead."

Aros thought about that and realized that he had nothing at all to lose. "Then in that case, Neoloth-Pteor, I'm your man."

NINE

In the Desert

For three days now, their tiny caravan had picked its way through sand and rock and rain-carved arroyos, through heat-shimmer mirages and past distant mountain ridges that resembled skeletal spines peeking through the earth in a dragon's graveyard.

Neoloth called to Aros, who rode a half length ahead. "You have passed this way?" he asked.

Aros nodded. Both wizard and barbarian rode brown stallions more spirited than the four packhorses following them, or the tiny, sure-footed mule carrying Fandy. "I was with the desert peoples south of here for half a year."

"Thieving, no doubt." Neoloth regretted saying it as soon as the words left his mouth. He just couldn't seem to stop himself from digging at his sun-bronzed companion. He noted the easy way Aros rode his horse, more centaur than soldier. The barbarian filled his leather tunic to perfection, arms swelling out of the diagonally cut sleeves. Neoloth realized that some of what he felt was anger . . . but another bit was pure jealousy.

Neoloth's elf Fandy rescued him from his thoughts. As he had for the last three days, the elf continued to drill Aros on his new assumed identity.

"What is your name?" he asked.

"Elio."

"What is your mother's name?" he asked.

"Jade," Aros said.

"And your father, General Silith?"

"Sinjin."

Fandy winced at the mangled accent. "Emphasis on the first syllable, please."

Aros looked as if he'd sucked a lemon. "*Sinjin*," he said.

Neoloth flinched. "And that . . . is not much better."

Aros's smile was just a little crooked, like the Aztec blade at his side. "Well, I tell you what. Why don't you use your magic and turn yourself into this lost waif of yours. I'm tired of your nonsense."

Neoloth shook his head. "That wouldn't work. I need you for a distraction while I do the searching."

Aros tried again, a bit of frustration creeping into his voice. "Then use it to make me sound like this Elio."

Neoloth laughed, and his elf laughed. And possibly Agatho-daemon, the constrictor nestled in the wicker basket on the third packhorse, laughed as well. But Neoloth wondered how convincing the mirth was. He didn't want to make another admission that he *couldn't do things like that. Not anymore.*

"We'll try it the other way," Neoloth said. "We'll say that you lost your memory."

Aros pulled to the left, moving his mount away from the edge of a ravine. Despite the fact that the afternoon air was dry and hot enough to turn grapes into raisins, it was clear that at times water still flowed across the surface. "My memory? That seems too convenient. How would that work?"

"I'm not sure." And he wasn't. But the more he considered the idea, born of necessity, the more he liked it. "We won't convince them you're General Silith's son. We'll do the opposite—make them convince *us.*"

He watched his captive colleague carefully. Aros chewed it over and then chuckled. The barbarian was grudgingly intrigued. "I'd like to see that," he admitted.

Neoloth allowed himself a smile. Calculated, of course, to help Aros forget that they weren't really an "us." "So would I," he said.

The sun was a hand closer to the western horizon by now, and the tension in their little group had progressed steadily. "You believe you can speak with this Chief Sky Mountain?"

"I hope so," Aros said. "I learned enough of their talk. I think."

The wizard kicked his mount's flanks, increasing speed slightly to even his stride with the barbarian's. "You're not sure. Let's hope we avoid them altogether or find them soon. The suspense is growing monotonous."

"Your monotony is just about over," Aros said, and flicked his head up and to the left. And then the right. "There they are."

Neoloth looked south and then north, across cactus and dry gulch to the ridges of mountains. If he squinted, he could make out a line of horsemen upon each ridge, pacing them.

Neoloth cursed quietly. "I . . . didn't see them."

Aros chuckled. "They saw us, and that's all that matters," he said. "They've been following us for the last hour."

Neoloth felt the anger boiling up inside him. "Why the hell didn't you say something?"

Aros's smile widened. What the hell did this bastard find amusing?

Fandy's nervous giggle floated up from behind them, and Neoloth realized that he had given Aros an unanticipated advantage in their little war of words and wills.

They continued riding east. Over the next two hours, the lines of native riders descended from the ridges and converged upon them, first flanking and then pulling ahead and around, finally facing them.

Aros raised his right hand, palm forward. The universal gesture of *I hold no weapon*. "I send greetings to Chief Sky Mountain," he said in their language.

"Tell him you bring greetings from our queen," Neoloth said, and Aros repeated the words in the tongue of the desert people.

"I am Great Elk." The bare-chested warrior did not change his expression. Their brown faces were streaked with paint; their hair, dressed with feathers. Their naked torsos looked hard and strong. Neoloth noted that the dust devils at their horse's sides swirled more slowly as they spoke but never seemed to dissipate. The horses themselves were a bit odd, watching with a greater level of attention than he was used to in ordinary mares and stallions. And, further, the heat shimmered around their flanks as if they were horse-shaped statues filled with molten metal. "Our treaties forbid your entry into our lands without parlay," he said.

Aros translated his words.

"We are here to parlay," Neoloth replied. "We did not hide ourselves and do not conceal our intentions now."

"What," the second warrior asked, "do you want of us?" His spear was tipped with blue and white feathers of some bird Neoloth didn't recognize. They rustled in the wind, which was strange, because he felt no wind.

"We seek the grave of one of our children," Neoloth said. "Slain by robbers," he added hastily. "Not at the hands of your people."

Great Elk's eyes narrowed as Aros translated the words. "When did this happen?"

"Almost twenty years ago," Neoloth said.

Great Elk nodded. "Evil men who hid in our lands. They were our enemies as well."

"What happened to them?" Aros asked on his own.

"We turned them into toads."

"Nice," Aros said. He turned to Neoloth. "You'd look good in green," he said, but declined to explain his comment.

"His convoy was hijacked," the wizard said. "For years we have not known if he lived or died. At last our seers found his burial place. Now we know he perished and wish to pay honor."

He paused as Aros translated. There was still no wind. The feathers twitched in still air.

"You seek only his bones?" Great Elk asked.

"Only his bones."

"Wait," he said. Great Elk pulled his people back. Their spears leaned against each other, and Neoloth thought he saw the tiny carved heads atop them moving slightly. Joining in the discussion, perhaps.

The warriors argued among themselves. Then Great Elk shook his head and returned to the wizard and the warrior. "You may pass. We give you three days. Honor your dead," he said. "And then . . . leave our lands."

"Thank you," Neoloth and Aros said.

For the first time, Great Elk smiled. The smile was cold. Then he spoke in Lemurian, the root language of Quillian, and a language Neoloth understood. "We are not fools. We know that you may be lying."

"Then why are you letting us through?" Aros asked, without bothering to translate.

Great Elk's smile deepened. "Because in these lands, lying brings its own pain."

The riders wheeled their horses about and left them.

"They spoke our language," Neoloth said.

Aros smiled. "Of course."

"And you knew that?" Behind him, Fandy was snickering again. Damn.

"I suspected."

Neoloth pondered Great Elk's last statement. " 'Its own pain.' What did they mean by that?"

"Nice to know you don't know everything," the barbarian said.

"I've *always* known that. I've spent my life as a student." Neoloth frowned, watching the desert men as their horses trotted away. The little dust devils followed obediently.

"Then it's nice to know you know you don't know."

Neoloth opened and closed his mouth. "I'm not sure how to answer that . . ."

Neoloth was fairly certain the barbarian was smirking, damn

it. In the old days, Neoloth would have rained lightning down on his head for such impudence. Perhaps before this was all over, an opportunity . . . and the means . . . would present themselves.

As night fell, Aros chose a campsite tucked comfortably into the lee of a ridge, reasonably clear of tumbleweed and scorpions.

"Fandy!" Neoloth called.

The little one hopped down off his mule at once. "Yes, sir?"

"Tie up our horses and gather firewood."

Aros called out. "Wizard? I'm not certain it's a good idea for Fandy to continue doing the work. Shouldn't you have some practice? As a servant, I mean."

Neoloth thought it over, and to his displeasure realized there was good sense in that idea. "Yes, damn you, I should. Fandy, I'll deal with the horses and gather what we can find to burn. Instruct me at need."

The little elf bowed elaborately. "As you wish."

Neoloth knew horses, and fire was easy. Presently Neoloth had a pot of pemmican and corn simmering over coals. Then he opened the basket on the second horse, extracting seven feet of sleepy serpent.

"*Hungrrrry,*" Agathodaemon whispered.

"Food soon." Neoloth stroked its head. Aros eyed him suspiciously. The barbarian didn't like snakes, especially talking ones. Neoloth enjoyed that.

"Not a bad spot," Neoloth said. "A bit of shelter from the wind."

"City dwellers," Aros sneered.

Neoloth draped his snake around his neck. "I've traveled hard before."

Aros leaned back against a rock, smiling. "I saw to that, at least twice."

Neoloth glared at him. Memories raced, and a sudden suspicion flared. "Did you poison my eagle?"

"Poison?" Aros stretched, yawning, and assumed an injured air. "Not poison. Never. Drugged, perhaps. I mean, the lockweed was right there. You may have this sense of the Great Gold Ones as mighty hunters of the sky, but they're really just vultures with pretty wings." He chuckled, as if with a pleasant memory. "Let's just say the sheep was right there, and an opportunity like that was too tempting to resist."

"As the shepherd said to the magistrate," Fandy chimed in.

Neoloth and Aros stared at him. Neoloth tried to repress his mirth but couldn't help it, roaring with laughter. Aros joined in, and their echoes rang across the darkened plain.

"So . . . ," Neoloth said. "You killed a ram and stuffed its belly with lockweed. Then, while I was in the tomb . . ."

"I offered your Gold One a snack," Aros said. "Which didn't take effect until you were cloudbound again. I had merely to follow you. Flying things tend to travel in a straight line. So do falling things, in fact. It wasn't difficult."

Neoloth pondered that for a time. "Well, yes. You almost killed me. I managed to guide his fall into a snowbank. Broke Sky King's neck, but I survived."

"You survived the yetis, too," Aros said.

Neoloth chuckled. "Barely."

Aros felt something at his feet and jumped up, waving his sword. "That damned snake climbed into my bedroll!"

"That's odd," Neoloth said, his tone measured. "Usually Agathodaemon's a much better judge of character. Even the simplest creatures can sense antipathy."

"I don't hate snakes." Aros glared. "Their meat is stringy but excellent."

"*Warrrm . . . ,*" Agathodaemon said.

Neoloth chuckled and raised his arms. "Come to me, my sweet." The snake slithered to him, coiled in his lap, and became still.

They lay quiet for a time. Neoloth seemed restless. Finally, he spoke. "I set the land-kraken on you."

Aros sat bolt upright. *"What?"*

"The matter of the liquid diamonds. Not something I'd think you'd forget."

Aros's mind raced. "The . . . land . . ." Then he sat up. "You *bastard!*" he said. "I still carry the scars. It's why I avoid cold weather." He rubbed his left elbow in memory.

Neoloth smiled. "That was me," he said. "You should be grateful."

"Grateful?" Aros roared. "Why in the hell?"

Neoloth shrugged. "I needed those diamonds. I had a fireworm in my gut, and the only remedy was to bribe her out of my body. I just couldn't let you get them. I was at my height of power then and could have just fried you with lightning."

Aros narrowed his eyes. "So why didn't you?"

Neoloth considered. Then he decided to tell the truth. "I . . . respected you. As an honorable adversary. Wanted to give you a fighting chance."

Aros stewed over this for a while and then grudgingly nodded. "Well, thank you. I look forward to returning the favor. As soon as possible." Then he lay back and pulled his blanket over his face.

The travelers were up, breakfasted, and traveling before morning sunlight crept across the desert.

Following an invisible map in Neoloth's head, they passed a cluster of boulders that seemed somehow out of place, as if they had been tumbled like a child's blocks. In addition, the stubbly trees were atilt, as if they had been torn up by the roots and jammed carelessly back into the earth.

"What is this?" Aros asked, uneasy now. His hands hovered around the hilt of his *Macuahuitl.*

"I'm not sure."

Aros hopped down off his horse and poked around. "The ground is hard here . . . but not too hard for footprints. What do you make of *this?*" He traced Flaygod's flat tip around an impression the size of a child's body. At first Neoloth thought it a sinkhole or a place where an oblong boulder had been rolled away. Then he spotted four smaller indentions above it.

Toes. A footprint.

"A mountain troll," Neoloth said.

"We're a long way from the mountains," Aros growled.

Fandy's large, soft eyes protruded. "Oh my. Oh my. We should be going."

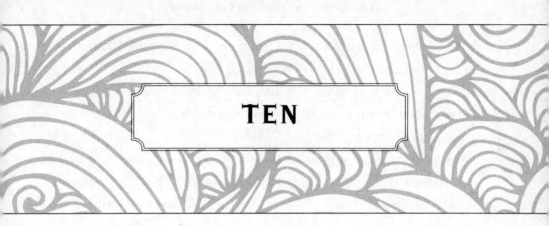

TEN

The Grave

Two hours before the sun buried itself in the western horizon, Aros asked, "Do you ever intend to tell me where we're going?"

"Almost there," Neoloth said. Draped around the wizard's neck, Agathodaemon flickered his tongue and hissed. The snake was content. Judging by the swelling in its belly, Neoloth had fed it, although Aros had not seen the moment of truth. Neoloth stroked his pet, perhaps as much to annoy Aros as anything else. "What, dearest? Where do we go?"

"This is ridiculous," Aros snarled.

"Shhh."

They traveled a bit farther and then Agathodaemon pulled

back. "Here," Neoloth said. The serpent slithered down from the horse's flank, curled around its leg, and then crawled across the ground to a heap of rocks Aros had missed on first glance. A cairn. Agathodaemon crawled all the way around the heap. And then coiled, forked tongue flicking. *"Heeeere."*

Aros frowned. "This is it? It's not even marked."

Neoloth had grown thoughtful. "No, it isn't." His face seemed longer, his mood heavy. "When I first considered this journey, I merely wished something I knew I'd find on the bones. But now . . ."

"How old are you?" Aros asked, looking down at Neoloth's slithering pet.

Neoloth's mouth creased in annoyance. "What difference does that make?"

"You still look the same as when I first saw you, ten years ago." He paused, shifting in the saddle. "Do I?"

"No," Neoloth said, still not grasping the issue. "You're thicker through the body. It's muscle, but probably better marbled than once it was."

Aros snorted and made an obscene suggestion. "Whatever. You've not changed. You are . . . living on a different scale. I don't think you understand. For you, a little more magic, a little more power, and you can stay young. The best that men like me can hope for is to stay alive. You don't understand. I doubt you ever will. But some part of you remembers, and the grave of a child moved you. Death such as this moves you. You are still human. Who knew?"

To that, Neoloth had no response. They unhorsed and removed rocks one by one and then dug with shovels from the packhorse. A few minutes of careful work uncovered a pitiful little bundle of oilskins.

Without a word, their motions had become less gross and eager and more delicate, as they might have if swaddling an infant. The wind whistled around them and then died down, as if even nature hushed her roar in the presence of tragedy.

Dark withered skin, and bird-like bones. For a moment, all sound was suspended, and they were alone with the pitifully small corpse of Elio Silith. A child who had been sent across the world as a bargaining chip, a tool to knit kingdoms together. The body was curled on its side, amid a scattering of toys: a top, a woven horse, and a ship carved in whale bone. And one item of value: a broad golden Aztec coin bearing the image of a handsome, hawk-nosed woman. A small hole had been drilled or punched at the top, and a rotted leather thong had passed through the hole. A necklace, perhaps.

"Strange," Aros said.

"What?"

"I wonder. It almost seems that the bandits loved him more than his own parents did. They left a gold coin with him."

"Perhaps to purchase his way into paradise," Neoloth said. "Jade is Azteca royalty. This image might be her mother."

The mood had changed suddenly, from a sense of celebration and discovery to something somber. The sun cast long, bleak shadows.

Neoloth examined the contents of the oilskin more carefully. "Look at this," the wizard said. "Could be natural causes. No obvious damage. Buried with his toys."

"Respect?"

"Possibly." He pointed to a bracelet. "That's a health talisman, made of herbs and such. They tried to heal him. Look at this."

He pulled out the horse, knotted patiently from twine. Aros pointed at the form of the neck. "Look at this knot around the neck," he said, holding it close. "A bowline. That's a sailor's knot."

"What does that mean?"

"That someone who had been to sea traveled with the boy," Aros said.

"Perhaps his guardians?"

"More likely the raiders themselves," Aros said. "They made him a toy."

Neoloth nodded, surprised at the sadness he felt. "Could be. I think they intended to ransom Elio. Then he sickened . . ."

"And they tried to make him well. They couldn't. He died. They buried him with respect."

The two of them were silent. Aros was the first to speak. "For most of us, this is all that remains. You wizards seek a way to cheat death His due." The wind gathered up his mane of black hair and then settled it again. "There is no way. I've lost track of the number of 'immortal' sorcerers Flaygod has sent to hell. 'I'll live forever!' they say. Right up until they squeal with their guts on the tip of my sword. They always look so surprised. Do you really think yourselves so superior to the rest of us?"

"Yes."

Aros's full lips curled in a smile. "At least you're honest," he said.

"Squeal?" Neoloth said. "They actually squeal?"

Aros smiled at him. "I look forward to demonstrating, one fine day."

"When our present business is concluded, of course."

"Indeed," Aros said. "When our present business is concluded."

Aros removed a small leather bag from his waist pouch, scattered a pinch of dust over the body, then squatted and chanted.

"What are you doing?" Fandy asked.

"It's a ritual my people use to pacify a soul. We use magic too,

Neoloth. He was just a boy," Aros said. "They used him like a token in some grand game. He was captured. We'll never know what happened to him before he died. They buried him in an unmarked grave. Now we're robbing his body . . . for what?"

A pause. Then, "For love," Neoloth said.

Aros stared at the wizard, as if wanting to believe. "If you're lying," he said, "I'll kill you."

"Fair enough."

As Aros studied the bones, Neoloth's fingers twisted as if possessed by individual life. "Sigils . . . awaken!"

The tattoos on the leathery flesh twitched, but that was all.

Aros squinted. "Ummm . . . what's wrong?"

Neoloth frowned. "There is resistance."

"Resistance?" Aros asked.

Neoloth gritted his teeth. "Sometimes . . . the spirit of the dead can resist if the living being would have resisted."

"I can't imagine why a boy wouldn't want an ancient wizard violating his corpse."

"I suppose you've a better idea?" Neoloth asked.

"Let's try honesty."

Aros knelt at the side of the shallow grave and gathered the bones into his arms. "I never knew you, Elio," he whispered. "You died alone . . . as I've been alone. I hope I'm wrong, that there was someone who cared for you. I don't know. I need to borrow something of you, in order to save a woman. I will need your mother and father to believe I am you. We have no wish to hurt them, only to rescue an innocent. I will do all I can to be fair to them. I wish your spirit no disrespect and know that you love them still."

Neoloth cleared his throat and then could think of nothing to say.

"If you will let me do this," Aros continued, "I will return your bones to your land of birth. Or allow you to remain at rest here. Tell me which you wish."

The wind stirred. And if he listened carefully, Neoloth would have sworn it moaned, *"Hooome."*

"Home," Aros said. "I have no home. I understand, and swear."

Aros turned to Neoloth, another thought coming to him. "Could we take his bones with us? After we are done, we could arrange for them to be delivered to his parents."

"That could be risky," Neoloth said. "Too risky."

"Then we can arrange for them to be told this location," he said. "I wish to keep my promise."

"That," Neoloth replied, "we can do."

The wind swirled and formed into a dust devil that hovered above the grave and then disappeared. The ink lines of the body wiggled.

Neoloth felt his own excitement building. "It's happening! Get ready!"

Agathodaemon wrapped itself around Aros, who had stripped to the breechclout. He was muscled like a circus acrobat, skin inscribed with arcane symbols and images. The barbarian groaned as his flesh crawled and the tattoos began to flex and stretch.

"Wizard!" Aros called. "I should have told you! Those tattoos: I had the woman work them over old scars! They're taking the scars with them!"

"Good. I knew," Neoloth said.

The tattoos and the scars beneath were crawling onto the bulge in the snake's belly. They sorted themselves, crescents and sea creatures and weird text, lumps and puckers and the long sword slash, crawling headward and tailward. Now they were lost in the patterning of Agathodaemon's markings.

Aros gaped, then turned to Neoloth. "What did your snake swallow?" The bulge was half the size of Fandy.

"You don't want to know," Neoloth said. "Really. Wait . . ." The tattoos on the withered corpse began to crawl. "Touch him. Quickly."

Aros set his hand on the corpse's chest. Markings flowed up Aros's arm and onto his body and then settled in appropriate locations. Chest: a sunburst in gold. Shoulder: a black star, like a flag Aros had seen once. Streaming up his arm, distorted into river lines, then crawling down his back: a young girl's face.

The wind died down. And then there was stillness. Aros looked down at himself, blowing like a bellows.

"How does it feel?" the wizard asked.

"I have no words," the warrior replied.

"That," the wizard said, "would be a nice change."

"Can we go now?" Fandy pled. "Please?"

"Yes," Neoloth said, and gathered his coat's collar more tightly around his throat. "I think it may be time."

They had set out their camp, eaten, and bedded down. Aros had barely closed his eyes when he detected Neoloth rolling out of his blanket and creeping away from them. The barbarian rose and followed silently.

Aros found the wizard around the bend of a rock. He had a small square of blanket spread on the ground. A small cylindrical object lay in the middle of the square. It was surrounded by something like a heat shimmer. The wizard gestured and chanted.

Aros watched until curiosity overwhelmed him. "What are you doing?"

Neoloth's head whipped around, and he snarled. "Go back! This is not for your eyes, Aztec."

"To hell with that," Aros growled. "Save your orders for Fandy. What are you doing? What is that?"

Neoloth looked as if he wanted to chew rocks and spit arrowheads. "I'm going to tell you a secret," he said. "The magic really is dwindling."

What kind of game was this? "I've seen magic."

"Think of gold in the ground, everywhere," Neoloth said. "As long as people only use a little of it, it lasts forever, or seems to. But build a huge city with artisans on every corner making gold jewelry and gold statues and gold ornaments and you deplete it rapidly."

"That's what magic is?" Aros asked. This was unexpected and fascinating. Oddly, he had never really wondered what magic was . . . only how it might help or harm him.

"Close enough," Neoloth said. "But out here"—he gestured at the desert plain—"where people have not plundered, magic remains."

"And because the great chief's people don't use as much of it as the cities . . ."

"I can borrow some, yes."

Aros considered. "And this device enables you to do this?"

"If I understand it properly, yes." Neoloth turned back to his work, while Aros watched.

After a time, the barbarian spoke again. "You know, when people say 'borrow' they generally mean something that they intend to return. Otherwise it is called 'stealing.'"

"The sort of distinction I'd expect you to be familiar with."

"Are you?"

"Very," Neoloth said.

Aros grunted. He sat for a while and watched, then finally

realized he was yawning restlessly and returned to his bedroll. He watched the play of lights, a bit like an electrical storm, just beyond their camp.

He examined his new tattoos with interest. Fandy watched him.

"This is a strange feeling."

Fandy scrambled closer. "How is it strange, Aros?"

"I've traveled. And sometimes I had my flesh paint-pricked to remind myself of a port . . . or a woman . . . or even an enemy."

"An enemy?" the elf asked.

Aros nodded. "Yes. I actually tattooed . . ."

He paused as Neoloth approached him, eyebrows arched in query.

Aros shrugged, changing his mind. "Never mind."

"No," Neoloth insisted. "Really."

Aros's eyes narrowed. *"No."*

He stood in the moonlight, looking at the new empty space on his flesh. "You took my scars," he said.

"Yes," Neoloth agreed. "Yes. Some of them."

Aros's voice lowered until it was nearly gravel. "I want them back."

"When we're finished," Neoloth replied. "But I have to ask . . . why?"

"Who am I without them?"

A thin thread of wind rustled the leaves. Neoloth sighed. "Who are any of us, without our memories?" He sat next to the fire, gazing into it.

"Aros," Fandy said.

"Yes?"

The elf's ears twitched, perhaps with the cold. "If you were not your history . . . who might you choose to be?"

That might have been the oddest question Aros had ever heard. "I don't know," he said. "Why would you even ask such a thing?"

"A prince?" Fandy offered.

Neoloth watched them both, silent.

"I don't know," he repeated.

"Then perhaps you know what you really want from all of this," Fandy said.

"A man without history has no future," Aros tried.

Now, at last, Neoloth spoke. "A man without history is not confined by it."

They both turned to look at the wizard. Aros felt both irritated and curious. "What are *you* running from?"

"Let's just say that I would like to stop running. And leave it at that."

Suddenly, Aros had an inkling. "The princess is your plan?"

"I wouldn't expect you to understand," Neoloth said, and turned over onto his side. And was snoring in suspiciously short order.

ELEVEN

The Troll

Neoloth awoke so quickly that he heard his own last snore. Awoke realizing that some instinct had functioned where conscious awareness had failed.

Something hunkered above them, a massive, vaguely man-shaped moon shadow. Larger than twenty men. "Who you?" the shadow said. A round-faced mountain with tree-trunk legs.

Across the ashes of the dying fire from Neoloth, Aros stirred. "Oh, blood and steel," he muttered. "I knew this would happen."

"I hurt," the ogre said.

"We haven't done anything to it," the barbarian whispered. "What is it talking about?"

"The beast is tied to the land," Neoloth whispered back.

"When I charged the talisman, I created a void. It feels that void like a gash."

"It's some kind of a watchdog?"

Before Neoloth could answer, the ogre swung at them. The arm was as massive as a log but thankfully slow enough that even the wizard could duck. Aros dodged even faster, drawing *Macuahuitl.* He darted in and slashed with the sawtooth edge, but the creature's shins were covered with matted hair so thick Flaygod couldn't reach flesh.

Aros screamed curses to his feathered god.

Neoloth grabbed the talisman, gripping it in both hands. "Death to the destroyer!"

Light boiled around the talisman, then lanced out at the ogre, who recoiled violently.

"Yes!" Aros screamed.

Then the talisman flickered, and the light died.

The ogre's arms hung at his sides, as limp as half-filled sausage skins. The beast shrugged and danced about until his saucer-like eyes strained from his rounded boulder of a head. His limbs trembled but would not obey him. His roar of frustration was disturbingly human.

Aros's head snapped around. "What in the hell is wrong with your damned magic?"

Neoloth looked at the talisman cylinder in dismay. "I guess it takes more time to charge than I thought."

"You didn't *know?*"

The ogre screamed and jumped up and down, flapping its arms around and around like a headless chicken. At last it seemed to grasp that its accustomed weapons had been rendered worthless and started trying to stomp his human targets. Horses and mule scattered, braying and neighing to wake the dead.

Aros avoided the huge feet at first. "The hell with this!" he screamed, and leapt to the attack.

The next minutes were a blur of jump and slash. Neoloth managed to generate flashes of light that dazzled without damaging. Dancing out of the way of the flapping arms in the bizarrely shadowed moonlight, Aros chopped away matted hair until Flaygod could slash the ogre's left ankle tendon. The creature bawled and fell to its knees. As if chopping a log, Aros hacked his sword down into the ogre's throat. Its roars died to screams. And then gurgles. And then it was silent.

Aros wiped blood from a bruised shoulder. "No wonder those desert dwellers believed the land would defend itself!"

"Oh, no . . . ," Neoloth said. The wizard's voice was flat. Sad.

And even without turning around, Aros knew what he would see.

The wizard stood over Fandy's crushed body, huddled next to the stone that had broken him.

"Is he?" The question felt stupid even before it left his lips.

"Yes," Neoloth said. "Dead."

"You're a sorcerer. Can't you?"

An odd menagerie of emotions crossed Neoloth's face. "It's what I've been trying to say. The magic is dying."

Aros grunted and sheathed his sword. "That leaves the world for me, I think. What can I do to hurry this miracle along?"

"I could give you good manners," Neoloth said. "That should eat the magic for miles around."

Aros laughed. Neoloth was right, damn him. Fandy had been a bit irritating but harmless. He didn't deserve squabbling at a time like this. The sight of the tiny crushed body sobered him.

"Let's give him a proper burial," he said. "And then . . ."

"What?"

"Let's charge up your damned talisman. I suspect we might need it."

"I think," Neoloth said, "that the ogre's death did that. I'll check . . ."

There was a saying Aros had heard about clouds and silver linings. Another about ill winds.

Neither felt worth a damn at the moment.

TWELVE

Warfroot

The coastal town of Warfroot was a warren of twisted salt-cured docks, dark alleys, and patchwork buildings that looked as if the next stout wind would sweep them into the bay. Aros and Neoloth reached it seven days after burying Fandy, and they had spoken little along the path. But now that they were actually walking the narrow, plank-paneled dockside alleys, the wizard was growing downright chatty. "All right," he said.

They'd left horses at a nearby stable, donned fashionably cowled tunics, and begun their search. After a quarter of an hour threading through darkened streets, Aros stopped them before a tavern called Sailor's Rest. The smell of stale beer and unwashed bodies rolled out in a cloud.

Neoloth asked, "I hope you know what you're doing. This is something of a dive."

"I think," Aros said, "that this place would need redecoration to qualify as a 'dive.'"

Neoloth glared at him. "You speak strangely for a barbarian."

"I'm foreign," Aros said, "not stupid. Come on."

The bar inside was noisy, raucous. The air shimmered with smoke and body heat. A swivel-hipped waitress approached them. She looked Aros up and down as if massaging him with her eyes. Neoloth, she barely noticed. "Roast lamb tonight, just got in new kegs. Table on the side." She pointed. "Be right with you."

Aros nodded at her, and the two men sat against the wall. Neoloth scanned the room, unimpressed. "Do you really think you can do this?"

The barbarian nodded. "I'm pretty sure. I don't know who's in harbor, but I'll see someone I knew from the old days." They drank their drinks slowly enough for him to inspect every face, but when nothing familiar presented itself, they went on their way.

They repeated the same behavior at two more taverns. Aros found no one that he knew. He changed approach and headed down to the docks. Early-morning fog enveloped them, clung to their coats and clothing. For the first time on their journey, Aros seemed a happy man, as if the ocean sounds were washing away the memory of Quillia's dungeons. Now, at last, the barbarian began to encounter a few old friends.

A pair of conversations led them to a slip at the northern end of the shipyard. "Who goes there?" a sailor called down from the deck of a triple-master.

"Ahoy, the *Pelican*," Aros called up.

"Who's asking?"

The barbarian seemed slightly reluctant to supply that information. "Kasha is the name. Is Golden Axe still the captain?"

The unseen sailor spit into the ocean. "He ain't been cap'n since he lost the ship a moon ago."

Aros's brow wrinkled, but Neoloth saw that his companion retained the ghost of a smile. "And how did he do that?"

"Gambling, of course."

What Neoloth had interpreted as a smile broadened. Aros said, "That sounds like the Gold I know. Who's first mate?"

"Dorgan. He ain't here neither."

"Where can we find Captain Gold?" Neoloth called up.

Now the shadow of a sailor's head appeared at the railing, peering down at them. "I think he's drinking himself to death in the Shark's Eye," he said. "If he ain't there, ask for Dorgan, the first mate. He's around."

"Thanks. I'll remember this."

"What now?" Neoloth asked.

Aros shrugged. "Let's try the Shark's Eye."

The Shark's Eye was a waterfront dive like those Neoloth and Aros had already investigated, a place it was wise to steer clear of, unless one was handy with fists and sword. As they entered, Aros looked around the bar, circling the room until he found a bear of a man sprawled sleeping across a table.

"And we have a winner," he said.

"Not according to your sailor friend," Neoloth sneered.

Aros pulled the sleeping man up. Rolls of fat jounced. "Ho! Goldie!"

The big man groaned. "Leave me alone. I got more money.

Take it and le'me alone." The man plopped back down on the table, thumping his head.

"This is just wonderful," Neoloth said.

Aros snarled. "Girl! Bring water!"

When it arrived, they dunked Gold's head in the bucket. He roared, sputtering as he came up, swinging. Aros ducked and caught his friend in a rear hug, avoiding flailing elbows. "What? What the hell? I'll kill you—" The barbarian released and spun him.

Gold's eyes widened. "Aros? What in the hell are *you* doing here?"

"I'm looking for passage on the *Pelican*."

Gold groaned and sank his head back into his arms. "You'll have to ask the new captain."

"What happened?"

Gold snorted. "The fates were against me."

Aros sat beside him. They made quite a picture: the sinewy barbarian and the corpulent captain.

"A month ago, I put Dorgan, my best man, against his in a wrasslin' match. I wagered everything. Including the *Pelican*."

"You lost?"

Gold nodded. "I don't know what happened. I thought for sure . . ."

"Did you know your ship is in port?" Neoloth asked.

Gold sank his head in his hands and groaned.

"And did you further know that Dorgan is now the first mate?"

Gold shook his head. "No, that's not possible. Captain Thorne always brings on his own crews."

Aros said nothing. Gold slowly raised his head. "Son of a sea turtle," he said, and then cursed more imaginatively. If a wizard had cursed thus, he might have obliterated the building. "They played me."

Neoloth nodded. "I'm afraid so."

Gold slammed his fist on the table, and the entire room shook. Suddenly, and at a moment, Neoloth saw a younger man inside the hulking shell. A man who might have adventured with Aros, once upon a long time ago. "I knew it. *I knew it!* That ape, that betrayer, that goat-eyed, beef-witted canker blossom!"

"Impressive," Neoloth admitted.

Aros smiled. "Would you like . . . revenge?"

The warehouse was packed from wall to battered wall with whooping brawny flesh. The smell of sweat and blood hung in the air until it drowned out the rotted smell of salt-warped boards. The audience was mostly sailors and their women, who were just as scarred and tough-looking.

"You can't use your magic in here?" Aros asked, and to Neoloth's satisfaction, the barbarian sounded just a bit nervous.

"I don't think so," Neoloth said. He pointed to the carved stone gargoyle over the door. It glared at them balefully. "Gambler's demon. Detects magic. We don't want it flapping its wings and squawking in here—we'd get torn to pieces if they thought we were cheating."

"Can't you beat it?"

"Given enough time, perhaps. But why are you worried? Since when are you afraid of a bone breaker?"

"Afraid might be too strong a word. Let's just say I don't mind a nice, unfair advantage."

The crowd roared with approval as two mountainous men

crashed against each other with a force that shook the room. Knuckles smashed into flesh, ripping skin and bruising bone.

Captain Thorne was a villainous-looking sea dog, perfectly cast for his role. Thin as a sword, with a hawk-sharp face. "Well. Isn't it the good Captain Gold?"

"And Captain Thorne," Gold said.

"*Admiral* Thorne now, thanks to you," Thorne grinned. "Come to lose another ship?" the slender man asked.

"Come to get my ship back."

Thorne roared as if that was one of the funniest things he'd ever heard. "That would require gettin' straight with the money-lenders. Take some heavy coin to balance your scales. Your pockets look a little light these days."

"I have money," Gold said. "Enough to wager on my man against your ape, at odds."

Thorne glanced at the smooth-limbed Aros. Aros without scars looked younger, more innocent. Whereas Thorne's champion looked like the ogre's shorter, knottier, uglier brother. Dorgan was almost a full head taller than Aros, and his skull looked thick enough to serve as an anvil.

Aros studiously avoided the big man's eyes. Thorne grinned. "You ready to die, Az?" An insulting term for "Azteca."

"Why don't you meet his eyes?" Gold said, nervous as well. "Dorgan will think you are afraid."

Aros raised an eyebrow. "And why should I care?"

Neoloth frowned. "I thought all you brawlers wanted to establish dominance. Control each other's minds."

"And why should I care what you think?"

"It's my gold," the wizard replied.

"It's my body," Aros said.

Neoloth couldn't argue with that. "That's true. And we need it whole. Try not to get it mangled."

"Your concern," Aros said, "is touching." Aros was seated on a table edge, busily wrapping his thick, scarred hands with leather straps.

"Like I said, it's my money."

The two of them were guided through a cheering crowd of drunken sailors. Aros gave the name "Kasha" to the rotund, bearded announcer: the opening gambit of their plan.

"All right, sea dogs," the announcer said. "We have a challenger! The savage son of the desert—Kasha!"

The crowd jeered as Aros raised his sinewy arms. A couple of the people in the crowd squinted as if wondering whether they recognized him, but his tattoos were different now, and their confusion was soon submerged in bloodlust.

"And in this corner, the champion of the Silver Skull and the *Pelican*, the bone breaker of the coast, Sailor Dorgan!"

The colossus lurched up out of the corner, raised his arms, and flexed his muscles. This took some time: there were a lot of them to flex.

"Large," Aros said.

Neoloth was beginning to feel a little worried. "Are you sure you can do this?"

Aros nodded. "You and that gargoyle just be sure this is fair. I'll deliver the victory."

Aros walked out onto the pit area. The crowd roared. Sailor Dorgan eyed his tattoos.

"Who are you?" the big man said. He was trying to growl, but his voice was almost child-like.

"Kasha," Aros said. "You know my name."

"I heard it," Dorgan replied.

"You'll remember it when we're done."

Dorgan snorted. "I don't remember every bone I've broken. You'll be forgotten with the rest."

Aros crouched on the far side of the ring. The crowd's roar diminished to silence in his mind. He dug his fingers into the sand and ran a handful between them. Closed his eyes.

He remembered. Aros floated away to the place he always sought when life and death were on the line.

His mother pulled from his hands . . .

Dragged away and up a pyramid, to execution.

Her loving heart ripped from her chest . . .

This, Aros had not seen. It was too far away, and he was running. But he had heard the shrieks, and blood was easy to imagine.

When Aros opened his eyes they were reddened. His face was beaded with sweat, his muscles tense and swollen. Neoloth was startled by the transformation.

Aros stood and turned. His head was lowered, his teeth clenched. The barbarian seemed as much animal as man. He glared at the man across the ring as if he wanted to eat him.

"All right, you bastards," the announcer said. "Anything goes except for bitin', eye gougin', and ball twistin'. Winning is by sub-mission, bein' thrown out of the ring, or gettin' knocked the hell out. Dyin' is just another word for losin'. Are you ready? Fight!"

The two men charged full out at each other. At the last in-stant, Aros ducked under the wild swing and heaved up. Sailor Dorgan flew through the air and smashed into the men standing at the ring's edge. They heaved him back into the ring, his feet never quite touching the ground. The crowd roared.

"Clever," Neoloth muttered.

The two men circled each other, arms milling. "Clever won't save little man," Dorgan growled.

Fists balled, the two men crashed together. Aros was faster, landing two punches for every one of Dorgan's. But Dorgan was a monster; no strike seemed to make any difference.

They gripped, fingers biting into each other's skin, ripping away and scraping as they twisted and pounded each other. Dorgan got a hold and threw Aros, who managed to land on his feet, keep hold of Dorgan's arm, and reverse the throw. Dorgan hit the ground so hard that the arena shook. Aros was on him like a terrier on a rat, kicking him before he could rise, then smashing him with a knee in the face.

Dorgan's teeth flew. He rolled and came up like thunder, flying at his man as rutting animals had since before men crawled out of the jungles. Fingers clawed for the Aztec's eyes. Aros screamed and smashed his way out of the trap, wiping blood from his face.

The Aztec snarled. "I thought this was just a *friendly* brawl," he said.

"The next bone that breaks is your neck," Dorgan said.

Aros looked around the ring and the crowd. Captain Thorne was smirking.

Dorgan attacked. Aros backpedaled. Dorgan hit him, and Aros rolled with it, turning a flip as his hand hit the sand, grabbing a handful. Continuing the somersault, he threw the sand into Dorgan's open eyes.

Dorgan flailed and backpedaled. Aros ran forward, crouched, and leapt up in a perfect dropkick, smashing Dorgan in the chest. The giant flew back out of the ring, smashing into the men at the edge—who threw him back again.

"What the hell!" Neoloth snarled. "Is every sailor in this damned place your shipmate?"

Thorne's grin widened.

Cheating, Neoloth thought. *Damn it, this man needs a lesson.* He looked back at the doorway. Up at the gargoyle. It was a fairly standard gambler's demon, charmed to awaken if any funny business went on. But it had been a *looong* time since there had been enough magic in this area to animate it. In fact . . .

It was possible that the gargoyle's stone heart had died. Or was so deeply asleep that a small spell could evade notice.

Aros was heaving for breath by now, as much with frustration as exhaustion. "What is it going to take to stop you?" he said to Dorgan.

The giant's answer was another charge, and by now Aros no longer seemed as fast and lithe as he had only minutes ago. Neoloth was starting to worry. Beside him, Captain Gold looked like he wanted to cry.

Dorgan closed with him again, clasped his arms around Aros's waist, and bent him backward. "Hear that sound? That's your back breaking."

Neoloth made a decision. Blood from this and previous bouts slicked the floor, directly under Dorgan's feet. Neoloth slipped his hand into the pouch at his waist and grasped the talisman. With his other hand he made a subtle gesture . . . and the blood beneath Dorgan's foot *froze*.

Dorgan's foot slipped. His *grip* slipped.

Aros twined his legs up and around like a monkey, clamping them around Dorgan's neck. His lower body against Dorgan's superior upper body. Dorgan tried to keep his grip on Aros's neck, but the position they were in was twisting him like a pretzel. Finally, Dorgan released his grip, tried to pull Aros's legs away. Flailed. Face reddened.

The crowd began to cheer: "*Kasha! Kasha!*"

Both men tumbled to the ground. Dorgan gasped and clutched, and his heels drummed against the ground . . . and then at last his massive body relaxed into unconsciousness.

Aros looked more dead than alive, as battered as driftwood. "And I hope that that . . . is that." He groaned.

Admiral Thorne sputtered, rage making his thin face even more skeletal. "I can't . . . I don't believe . . ."

Audience members were carrying Aros on their shoulders, chanting his assumed name for all to hear.

Excellent. Neoloth's tension headache was starting to ebb. "They seem a changeable lot," he said.

Gold radiated glee. "One thing sailors like is a fighting man," he said.

Thorne looked around the sand. Bent and fingered the blood, coming up with an ice crystal he crunched beneath his trembling fingers.

THIRTEEN

Boarding

Mist rolled in from the ocean like a thin layer of cotton. The ships in harbor rose and sank slowly on the swells of the morning tide. But even before the sun had finished rising, the mood was warm.

Captain Gold's smile grew broader by the moment. The rotund old moneylender who had engineered Admiral Thorne's coup was tearing up the contract, and the harbormaster soberly reviewed documents attesting to the fact that the *Pelican* was indeed once again in the possession of Captain Gold.

"And . . . your ship is yours again," the harbor master said.

"Thank you," Gold said. But as he said it, Thorne strode up, red-faced and furious. "I don't know what you did," he said. "Or how you did it. You can't cheat me."

"No. Cheating doesn't work. We know that, don't we?" Gold smiled at Thorne, and the smaller man snarled, spit, and stalked away.

"This ain't the last of it!"

"I hope not," Gold called after him. "Can always use another ship."

Sailors began to swarm over the *Pelican*. Somewhat to Neoloth's surprise, the bruised but massive Dorgan was among them. He stopped before the captain, unable to meet his eyes, scratching at the ground with his toe. "Cap'n Gold . . ."

Gold's smile vanished. "And what do you want, seaman?"

"Well, Cap'n, I know I done wrong, but I was lied to. Thorne told me I'd be captain. He only gave me first mate."

Gold shook his head in disbelief. "Dorgan, you traitorous bushwacker . . . you know you ain't got the brains Triton gave a kelp bed."

He punched Dorgan's huge chest, rubbed his bruised knuckles, and sighed. "But . . . damned if you aren't the strongest swabby I've ever seen. You have half your sea pay docked. But serve well, and all is forgiven."

The big man's eyes gleamed with hope. "You won't be disappointed, Cap'n!"

And he ran up the plank. He stopped and looked back at Aros. "You good, little man," he said. "Two out of three?"

Aros smiled, trying not to wince or touch his tender ribs. "Anytime." After Dorgan ran up, Aros wiped his hand across his forehead.

"What in the world are you doing?" Neoloth asked Gold.

"Oh, the big lug don't mean no harm. He's not too bright, and I yelled at him. Hurt his feelings. So he got back at me."

"Am I going to have trouble with him?" Aros asked. Visions of broken bones danced through his mind.

"Naw," Gold said. "He's strong as an ox, but he don't know the meaning of 'fear.'"

"Nor, I suspect, a wide variety of other nouns and adjectives," Neoloth said.

"You show me a man who'll climb the rigging in a storm, and I'll be willing to forgive *him* a few little foibles as well," Gold said.

"As you wish." Neoloth shrugged.

"Besides," Gold said, "I told Gretel I'd take care of him."

Aros squinted. "Who?"

"He's me sister's boy. Dumb as a stump but stronger'n hell, and fears nothin'," Captain Gold said, then cupped his hands to his mouth. "All aboard!"

FOURTEEN

All at Sea

The *Pelican*'s sails swelled with fair wind. Far off, on the horizon, storm clouds blossomed like toadstools to the north, but they continued to recede as their ship passed along, promising fair voyage.

Neoloth and Aros were making the best they could of the tiny, confined space Captain Gold had allotted them. They crouched together, studying a map of Quillia's capital. A badly outdated map, Neoloth was certain. "It begins now, Aros," he said. "The sailors on this ship will make port, and when they do will comment on what they see. Make no mistake: there are eyes upon us."

"I've played roles before," Aros grunted. He moved his arm; Agathodaemon was sliding toward it.

"And for your life, no doubt," Neoloth said. "But now we're playing for a life more precious than your own. The life of Tahlia. We don't know the game that is being played here."

Aros leaned back and began peeling an apple with his knife. "The snake needs to act like my pet, not yours."

"She already does. Just let her crawl on you."

Aros offered an arm, and Agathodaemon crawled along it, sniffing, rising toward his neck. Neoloth nodded, satisfied. "All right," he said. "Let's take a turn around the deck, try out our new roles."

"Bring Agathodaemon? Wait now—I'm giving orders here, aren't I? Agathodaemon stays here."

"Yes, sir."

"This," the thief said, grinning like a wolf, "I intend to enjoy."

The ship outside their cabin was alive with busy men. A working ship, especially one at sea, is always in the process of being torn apart by salt, wind, and water and is in constant repair by the crew.

Captain Gold was using his hand to shade his eyes against the glare, peering up into the rigging. "Dorgan, ye vast shirker! What see ye?"

The giant was up high enough to seem tiny at last. He hailed down. "All clear Cap'n!"

"Good morning, Captain!" Aros said cheerfully.

"All formal are we, today?" Then he remembered their role and fell into it. He eyed his passengers. "Ah, there's a game afoot, I know. And sooner or later, I'll reckon what it is."

"You owe us. Keep that big nose out of our business."

Gold scratched his balding head and grinned. "Arrrr. Is that any way to talk to an old friend? No harm. We all have our secrets, ay? Ay?" He nudged Aros hard with his elbow. Aros grunted but absorbed the blow with equanimity.

Instead of venting any irritation on the captain, he turned to Neoloth. "Fetch me water."

"Yes, sir," Neoloth said. He worked a pump on one of the water casks, drawing a cup of clear fluid. In truth, he was enjoying the journey more than he would have guessed. The sounds of the waves and rhythmic movement of the ship—even the smell of salt-cured boards—was somehow comforting.

Up above him, sailors were shimmying along a boom, singing as they mended a sail with black cross-stitching. The song was something scandalous about the romance of a shark and a mermaid. Neoloth hoped his ear was quick enough to remember it.

"Washelisk!" Aros roared. "My damned water!"

The thief was getting into his role. A bit too enthusiastically, perhaps, but at the moment, "Washelisk" was happy to settle for commitment. "Ah, yes sir!"

Neoloth brought the mug back to his "master," who downed it greedily. Gold watched them with a suspicious eye.

"Good," Aros said with an imperious sneer. "But next time"—he threw the rest of the water in Neoloth's face—"next time, when you're told what to do, you damned well hop to it!"

Neoloth fought his urge to use the talisman to turn the arrogant thief into a toad and bowed. "Yes, sir! I'm sorry, sir."

As he backed away, bowing and scraping, Captain Gold approached. "Not thirsty, *sir?*" The odd emphasis was a jest.

"Ah, don't have my sea legs yet. Feeling a bit chancy, and I thought the water would help. By the time this sluggard brought it, it was too late."

Was this role-playing? Actually, he did look a little brownish-green around the gills. Had Aros the pirate king always been a bit seasick? Gold had certainly never known that.

Gold decided there was enough truth here to matter. "I have just the thing," he said, then called out, "Steerman! Passenger taking the wheel!"

A raft of different emotions flickered across Aros's face, the last one a mixture of gratitude and concern. "Been a while."

Gold laughed. "Oh, just keep your eye on the east and steer us north. Feeling the wheel in your hands makes the waves feel . . . homey. Half-tamed. You'll remember fast."

Gold retreated from the scene, leaving Aros in control of the ship. After a minute, Neoloth humbly approached him.

"Was that imperious enough for you, Washelisk?" Aros said under his breath.

"You," Neoloth replied, "are enjoying this entirely too much."

"It's all in a good cause," he said reasonably. "Oop! Someone coming."

A sailor approached, winding a rope around his arm as he did, and Neoloth adjusted his body language to grovel a bit more. When the man passed, he drew closer. "Good, actually. But remember that the relationships are formalized, especially if the servant is not a bondsman. He has *chosen* to work with the master and could change his mind at any time, find a new employer. Losing a servant is a major hassle. Keep your manners unless something goes foul. Would you discharge me for a single error?"

"Depends on the mistake. Not for dawdling, right?"

"If not, don't threaten. If so, just do it and get me out of the house quick, before I decide to steal something on my way out of the door. If you swear, don't overdo it."

Aros cursed without heat. The feel of the wheel beneath his hands was beginning to sooth his gut. "So many rules."

"Perhaps I could find the right cloaking spell after all," Neoloth sneered. "Perhaps it's too much for you. Perhaps *I* should be the missing prince, and your heritage makes you more suitable as a servant than a master—"

As another sailor drew near, Aros gave Neoloth a backhanded slap across the mouth. Neoloth reeled back. His hands twisted as if about to perform an arcane gesture. Aros's hand slipped to the hilt of his sword.

"Be careful, wizard," he said. "There are limits." His eyes glittered. He fixed his eyes on the northern horizon. "Do you think I'm too stupid to recognize your hand in my downfall?"

Neoloth looked up at him, eyes blazing with both anger and curiosity. "Then . . . why?"

Aros laughed bitterly. "Do you think I wouldn't have done anything, *anything* to get out of that prison? And do you think that I won't find a way to take revenge?"

"If you try anything, you'll die . . . ," Neoloth began.

Aros's smile broadened. "Everyone dies, my fine wizard. *You* are the one for whom death holds terror. You are the one who sought to cheat death of his due. I'm a barbarian, remember? Don't you civilized men know we hold our lives cheaply? Didn't the implications of that occur to you?"

"But . . ." Neoloth's head was spinning.

"Why?" Aros asked. "Because we hold life cheap but freedom dear. Kill me now." He inhaled deeply. "And what happens? I die with the smell of the sea in my nose. The wind in my hair. And the happy knowledge that you'll be at the bottom of the ocean before my body is cool."

The wizard blinked. "What?"

Aros leaned close. "Where are you?" he asked. "Whose friends surround you? That is not solid ground beneath your feet. What law can protect you here? Yes, you have magic. But there are a thousand ways to die at sea. Care to wager on whether you can evade them all?"

Neoloth turned away, unwilling to let Aros see his eyes, which blazed. "I won't bet."

Aros gripped his arm. Despite the wizard's artificially maintained vigor, the barbarian's grip sank deep. He pulled Neoloth closer. "Then you will damned well show me respect. Or we can both die. Here. Or in Shrike, where again your life will be in my hands. Look in my eyes. Do I lie?"

Neoloth didn't need to look in Aros's eyes. And didn't need to look around to know that the sailors were laughing at him, thinking they were seeing a man of wealth and power abusing a helpless servant. And if he wasn't careful, they were right.

He swallowed his bile. This . . . was not the time or place. Later, after their mission was complete . . .

Yes. Later.

He said, "I don't need your eyes. The truth is in your voice."

Aros released his arm. Neoloth rubbed it, wincing as the circulation returned.

Aros turned the wheel this way and that, enjoying the day. "Please." All traces of his barbarous accent disappeared, and he spoke as one highborn. "Continue your discourse."

Neoloth steadied his voice. This man had depths he'd not expected. "If my service is pleasing to you, sometimes you thank me. 'Thank you' can also mean that you want me out of the room. You call me by my first name unless you're really angry, then use the whole name . . ."

Neoloth was looking straight out over the waves. Seething. He caught himself. This would not do. He had lost a beat, missed a step. Aros was now too much in control of the situation.

And, confound it, he was not the least bit comfortable with the extent of his dependency on the barbarian's oath and sense of honor.

FIFTEEN

Mers, Octopi, and Agathodaemon

The ship was at peace, and the men were stuffing their faces in the mess, Aros roaring wild songs with the best of them. "I beg your leave, sir," Neoloth said. Aros waved his hand at the wizard and he left, happy to emerge back in the air.

He spit over the rail, tasting blood. "Bastard," he said, and rubbed his mouth, imagining that he could still feel the impact of the Aztec's hand. "You'll pay for that."

The roar of the singing sailors rose above the sounds of wind and surf. Neoloth went up to the stern and looked down at the ship's silvery wake. Something was in it. Something with a luminescence all its own.

He stared down into the waters, and, as he did, he could finally make out a family of Merfolk following the ship.

They jigged and pranced in the water to the music wafting up from the mess. Dancing in the moonlight.

Neoloth watched them, a strange contentment stealing over his heart. "If such glory as this still exists in the world," he murmured, "perhaps all is not lost."

One of them rose up on his tail in the wake, then another, the wet blond hair dripping down over her breasts. Her smile was pure enticement. The sailors and Aros were singing of a tamed hurricane, and she sang, too.

Happy memories eased his foul mood. "Ah, my beauty. If this was another time and another place. I would show you such a mating dance. We would rejoice in the waves, you and I."

She canted her head questioningly, as if to say, *Why not now?*

"Why . . ." He laughed to himself. He shook his head. "I would seem stupid to you if I spoke the words."

Her eyes beckoned.

"I feel your pull, as of old. Feel what sailors have always felt, when you called to them. But another has my heart now. Another . . ."

He smiled. "Listen to me. I think I'm in love."

Almost as if she had been waiting for him to say those words, she smiled to him, fading back, the family capering on the waves. And as Aros's voice roared in the night, Neoloth did a few fancy jig steps on the forecastle, laughing at the world and at himself.

In the morning, the ship had docked at a small island. Aros and Neoloth disembarked. Neoloth carried the little oilskin-wrapped package beneath his arm. Agathodaemon was coiled around his neck.

Captain Gold stood at the head of the gangplank, looking down at them. "We'll have an hour or two here. Mind telling me what the play might be?"

Aros shrugged. "Magicians are a different breed," he said.

"I'll be back," Neoloth said. The wizard picked his way around the edge of the island. Aros accompanied him uneasily.

They found their way to a sheltered cove, out of sight of the ship.

"What now?" Aros said. Neoloth enjoyed the uncertainty in his voice.

"Now . . . we'll see what we see." From the little oilskin-wrapped package, he extracted the talisman and set it carefully on a flat rock at the edge of an outcropping. While the snake slithered about, Neoloth uncurled the papyrus and, reading, spoke under his breath.

Aros stood and stepped back. The rock vibrated, and the entire cove began to hum. "What are you doing?" he asked. And the trace of nervousness in that question was gratifying.

Neoloth shushed him. "Wait."

Nothing . . . and then the water rippled. Shapes crawled out of the little waves . . . not human, not even mammal, and hard to see. They flowed like hummingbird shadows. Aros had never seen an octopus, but this must be what they were. Several of them came crawling onto the sand, turning sand-colored as they came.

Agathodaemon regarded them. *Were they cousins to the serpent?* Aros wondered. There was a certain resemblance, a certain similarity of locomotion . . . suddenly he wished he had as much scroll learning as Neoloth.

But damned if he was going to ask the question.

"Thank you," Neoloth said, and bowed to one of the creatures, the biggest. "I bring greetings from your southern relations."

The octopus's beak didn't move. "We received your message. What is it you wish?"

The others crawled and pulsed. One of them confronted Neoloth's snake. They examined each other and then backed away. Colors ran across that one's flank, and Aros saw the shadow of a snake.

"I am Neoloth-Pteor," the wizard said with an incongruous little bow. "I travel to Shrike on business. I need to know what you know about them."

"I would not go there," the big one said.

"No!" the other agreed. "Not there." Those spoke up from the rocks, half in the wavelets. Aros could not see them clearly.

"Why not?" Aros asked, uninvited.

The cephalopod rippled, changed color, and then crept closer to Neoloth. "Who is this one?"

"One . . . who helps me," Neoloth said.

The octopus burbled and then continued. "When I was young, Shrike was a good place. The ships plied the sea and caught many fish, but the sailors respected the old gods and gave back a tenth of all they caught as offering."

"No more?"

"No more. Today the ships smell different. They smell like burning oil. They foul the water. They throb like living things and stink of pitch."

"What does that mean?" Neoloth asked.

"I do not know. But there is something else. Their ships travel far, and what they bring back does not smell like fish."

"What, then?" Aros asked.

"It smells like man."

"Cargo-hold passengers?"

The creature seemed to consider. "They dump the offal overboard. *That* smells like frightened human children. There is something else as well. The waters of their river are not good."

"A river that flows into the ocean?" Aros asked.

"Yes. It tastes of metal. They are using fire, inland."

Neoloth crouched down. "Can you go and find out what they are doing?"

The body of the octo-wizard turned blue and black. "Perhaps. If we wished to die. It is poison. It has killed fish. The waters are poison. We thought this was why they do not fish. There is little to fish. My people do not go there any longer. I have been poisoned. It will soon be my dying time."

"I am sorry to hear that," Aros said. "I wish you a good death." To Neoloth's surprise, he actually sounded sincere.

"One more thing. Have you seen this woman?" Neoloth produced an image of the princess.

"Who is she? Your mate?"

"She is a queen's daughter. Have you seen her?"

The octopus bubbled. "What happened to her?"

"She was kidnapped," he said. "We think she was taken to Shrike."

"How long ago?" it asked.

"Perhaps a moon. Have you seen her?"

"Possibly," the big one conceded. It whistled.

From the half-submerged rocks another octopus said, "A ship came into the harbor. One of their small, stinky ships came to it. Caught my attention. I went up to look. Two women were taken from the ship. Both wore masks. Smaller human's hair was gold."

"And the larger woman?"

It purpled. "We think it was a female. It is a little hard to tell humans apart."

"The larger one. The color of her hair?"

"Red. Coral red."

"That could be Drasilljah," Neoloth said. "It is possible. My friends, thank you so much. And if you could please speak with your friends and relations. It is critical that we find her."

Neoloth stood and stretched. He glanced back at the forested section of the island, seabirds whirling overhead. There was food and water here. And he knew what he had to do.

"I ask a favor of you," he said to the octopi.

"Another? You ask much."

"This is a small favor. I leave my companion Agathodaemon here. There is hunting for him here, and shelter. But I may not return from my quest. And if I don't . . . I ask that you come to visit him at the full moon, just so that he does not die of loneliness."

"This we can do, with pleasure," the octo-wizard replied.

The snake slithered about Neoloth's ankles, rubbing him like a cat. "I'll be back if I can," its master promised and scratched his head.

"*Please. Misssss you . . . ,*" Agathodaemon said.

On the way back to the ship, Aros watched his companion carefully. "I'll be damned," he said. "You really do have feelings."

Neoloth wanted to snarl at him but couldn't . . . and after he took a closer look at Aros's expression, he realized there was no mockery there. "He's been with me a long time." He shrugged.

"Well, then," Aros said. "Let's get your princess and get back here as soon as we can. If snakes can die of loneliness, it is a bigger, wider world than I ever would have thought."

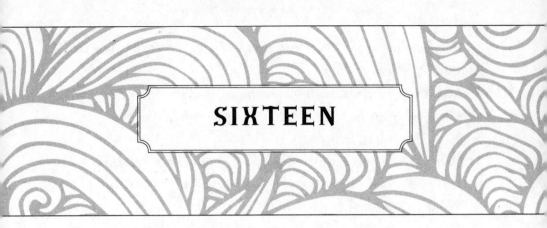

SIXTEEN

Ashore in Shrike

Aros and Neoloth slept, Aros's snore a steady burr, the wizard cocooned in silence. Neoloth slept in a servant's berth, a crowded thing, while Aros had the larger bed. Aros, nudged from a dream of carnivorous birds by a knock at the door, answered with a growl. "What the devil is it?"

Dorgan filled the doorway. "Cap'n Gold wants you."

"Well," Neoloth said. "What Captain Gold wants, Captain Gold gets."

Aros swung his feet down to the floor. "We'll be there in a moment."

Dorgan nodded and retreated.

"Remind me again," Neoloth said, "why I sleep in the inferior position."

Aros smiled. "Because in your infinite wisdom, you knew that any sailor who saw *me* folded up like a nightgown in that tiny bunk might well speak of it."

"Yes," the wizard grumbled. "That sounds like something I'd say."

"Who says I don't respect you?"

A few minutes later, Aros was rapping his scarred knuckles against the cabin door. "Requesting admittance, Cap'n."

"Granted," Gold said.

"What is the concern?" Neoloth asked as they entered.

"We enter Shrike Harbor tomorrow," Gold said. "Anything that remains to be done needs be done. If your plan fails, it won't be safe for me in Shrike for quite some time. Say . . . forever."

"It won't fail," Aros said.

"Timing the departure is likely to be a bit dicey," Gold observed, considering.

"It often is," Neoloth said. "You go about your business. We'll be in touch."

Gold drummed his fingers. "And if I have to leave?"

"Then we'll count on you being back in one moon. Otherwise . . . we'll make other arrangements."

Gold's fleshy lips curled in a smile. "Your story is fairly sound. At least, it's reasonable that I'd have been taken in by it."

"No one has ever accused you of keen perception," Aros said.

"Nor fine taste in friends."

"There's that. So we have our basic tale in place."

"The only one that I'd trust you to keep straight," Neoloth said to Aros. "You have no memory. But you have a few expensive things—perhaps things that might have been traded for the gems you had with you. And this—"

Neoloth handed him a belt buckle set with a gold coin—the coin from the child's grave, set against a silver frame.

"Well done," Aros said. "Excellent work. And your man will keep his mouth sealed?"

"He will," Gold said. "You say this was buried with him?"

"Yes. Which raises another set of questions," Aros said. "Why bury a valuable coin with him? We spoke of this in the desert."

Neoloth nodded. "It wouldn't seem to be an act of bandits, would it?"

"No . . . ," Aros said. "No. These waters might be deeper than we think."

"You have your choice of the garments I've . . . collected over the years."

Aros rummaged. "This. Hummm. And . . . this?"

"Your taste is less than impressive," Neoloth said. "Here. Let me help you. Even without a memory, a princeling is likely to make better choices than that . . ."

Captain Gold had been watching their efforts for the better part of an hour. "Do you really think you can transform this sow's ear into a silk purse?"

"We have to try. There is, however, a limit even to magic . . ."

Aros stepped out from behind the screen. He was wearing expensive robes. For a moment they were taken by surprise. Despite the rude garments that now lay at Aros's feet, the finery looked surprisingly regal on him. The sweep of his shoulders and narrow waist brought the clothes to life.

The air in the room seemed to have stilled. "My . . . now, that's a proper princeling."

"I have to admit . . . ," Neoloth began, and then caught himself.

"Yes?" Aros smiled.

"That you clean up adequately."

Aros snorted. "You can stick 'adequate' up your arse. Now this is more like it. I should have been dressing like this all along."

Neoloth rolled his eyes. "Father Set . . . what have I done?"

They entered Shrike Harbor the next day. Its lighthouse was a fantastic sculpture of a two-headed bird of prey, certainly one of the wonders of the world. One head looked out to the horizon; the other, back at the inner bay. A half-dozen small ships of unusual design patrolled the outskirts. No sails, no oars.

Aros pointed. "What . . . are those?"

Gold frowned. "Never seen their like."

One of the small ships pulled up alongside theirs. "Ahoy there! Prepare to receive boarders."

"Welcome aboard, good sirs," Gold said, smiling broadly.

"Do you know anything about those ships?" Aros asked Neoloth.

"I know that a sailor from the princess's fleet said that there were burning ships in the night."

"But what are they?" Aros said. "They move against the wind without oars. Have they dragons in their bellies?"

Neoloth seemed just as puzzled. "I don't know. Dragons are near extinct. This is some kind of magic I've not seen."

Lights shined up at them. Several men clambered up rope ladders. "I am Captain Nosturn," the first said. "A harbormaster of Shrike. Who is in charge here?"

"I am Captain Gold." Gold extended a hand. They shook.

"Your cargo?" Nosturn asked.

"Trade. Teas and fine woods. I've traded in Quillia before and have merchant contacts."

Nosturn nodded. "Take me to the hold."

Nosturn and Gold descended into the cargo hold. "Well stocked," Nosturn said after examining. "Are you saying that you are fulfilling contracts? I'd like to see them."

"No, sir," Gold said. "I'm saying that on previous voyages, I've spoken to merchants who said they needed certain things, and I thought that if I could supply them, a bit o' business might be done."

Aros straightened. "I would expect that the taxes on such transactions would be high . . ."

"And who might you be?" Nosturn asked.

"The name is Kasha."

"And you are?"

Gold stepped into the breech. "Just a passenger. Paid good gold to take him and his man to Shrike."

"And your business here?" Nosturn asked.

"I've heard that fighting men are valued in Shrike. And that the gambling palaces are second to none. Also, that the harbormaster is, upon occasion, allowed to collect taxes."

The harbormaster scanned him. "Have you been in Shrike before, sir?"

Aros hunched his shoulders ruefully. "I don't know."

"You don't . . . know?"

Aros laughed heartily. "No. I have no memory of anything before ten years ago. I woke up in the company of desert bandits, with nothing to identify me."

The harbormaster looked at the belt buckle. "And where did you get this?"

"Ah," Aros said. "I wore it as a bauble on a chain around my neck. Later we turned it into a belt buckle."

"It's a good stone."

"And carved like the harbor light of Shrike, I'd heard," Aros said. "I knew I wanted to visit here. In truth . . . at times I feel pulled. At any rate, it is my understanding that harbormasters can collect taxes upon occasion. Certainly there is some fee for expediting all of this trouble."

Nosturn smiled. "Well, for very special guests, all manner of things are possible."

Aros paused a moment and then drew a small sack from his pocket and handed it to Nosturn.

"Very generous, sir." Nosturn did a magic trick and made it disappear.

"And we ask that you make no mention of my master's arrival in Shrike, other than whatever proper channels you must go through to fulfill your obligations. We would like to keep . . . gossip and speculation to a minimum," Neoloth said.

Another coin changed hands. The man bowed and smiled. "I think that all is in order here," Nosturn said, and left.

Aros frowned. "I thought that the point was for rumors to get around."

Neoloth seemed satisfied with the results. "I have found that there is no faster way to spread a rumor than to pay someone to hide it. I think we have begun our arrival auspiciously. Captain! Take us to port."

Gold glowered at him. "I'll wait until yer master says the same."

Aros smiled broadly. "Captain," he said. "Take us in."

As the ship came into the dock, Aros and Neoloth watched from the rail. Neoloth was dead sober. "What do you see?" he asked.

"A harbor. Much like many others. Of course there are the boats."

Neoloth snorted. "I got a good, close look at the harbormaster's boat. Fire in its guts, and metal to hold it prisoner, but what for?"

"Magic."

"There are other things," Neoloth said. "The harbormaster, Nosturn. What was that thing he wore at his waist?"

Aros scratched his head. "I don't know. A little machine?"

"Yes. A little machine. But of what kind? *That* is the question. Do you know what it looked like to me?"

"I think I'm about to hear," Aros growled.

"A small cannon. A *hand* cannon."

Aros seemed doubtful. "I've seen them small enough to carry."

"On the back of a strong man, yes. But this—"

They heard a shrill sound, a whistle originating from somewhere in the city, and Neoloth's eyes picked out a chimney with steam gushing out the top.

"And I don't know what that is," Neoloth said. "What the purpose is, or how the sound was produced. Within a single hour, I've seen things, three things, I've never seen before. This place is a playground for a questing mind."

When they docked, Aros gathered his things and then shook Gold's hand. "Thank you, old friend," he said.

Dorgan seemed a bit downcast. "We wrestle again, little man?"

When my bones have healed, Aros thought. But what he said was, "Another time."

"Where to now, Master Kasha?" Neoloth asked.

"First, Washelisk, I think we find lodging."

And they strode down the gangplank together. Neoloth carried the bags until they found a porter.

The inn Gold had recommended was called the Boar's Head. It was sturdy, of old brick, with a substantial garden out back.

"This looks good," Aros said.

"A bit more upscale than your usual, I'd expect." Neoloth sniffed. To him, it was dreadful. One becomes accustomed to better things.

"Pay the man," Aros said.

The fat, greasy little innkeeper bowed. "Gentlemen! Gentlemen! Please enter and be welcome."

"Thank you," Aros said. "You see before you two weary travelers. We seek lodging and meals."

"You have come to just the right place!" the innkeeper said. "We are honored to accommodate gentlemen such as yourselves."

He took them up a stairway to a room with a view . . . of the castle.

Aros scanned the room. "Yes, I think that this will suit me well."

"Have you been to Shrike before?" the innkeeper asked.

"Never," Aros said. "From the harbor, I could see the castle. What is *that?*" He pointed at a series of low buildings arrayed before a black fence as tall as two men. The fence wound behind the palace and continued beyond his sight. It might well have abutted the shoreline, sealing off the city from . . . something beyond.

"Barracks," the innkeeper said. "The king likes to keep his men close."

Aros nodded soberly. "Very wise."

There was a black wall between the barracks and a rocky promontory. It had been reinforced. It looked as foreboding as a prison fortress for Titans.

He pointed. "And . . . what is that?"

"And that . . . is something best left to itself. Strangers need to learn not to ask certain questions." The man seemed ruffled that it had even come up.

He wiped his hands on his bloody shirt. "Now, then . . . Breakfast is at dawn, dinner at dusk. The room is twenty coppers a day, in advance."

"Pay the man," Aros said.

Neoloth did so, and the innkeeper left.

"So," Aros said, perching on a table's edge.

"So now we learn what we can," Neoloth said. "We will play it that Kasha is a gentleman of leisure, a soldier of fortune seeking adventure. You will sell your sword and skills."

By the time the morning sun had fully risen, Aros and Neoloth were out exploring the capital city. They saw children in windows, but not on the streets. Odd.

"Have you noticed that, as well?" Aros asked.

"Do you know what it reminds me of?" Neoloth said.

"Educate me."

"Some years back, there was a naval war, and the press-gangs were at work. The streets were clear of young men. I noticed that. The ways that people reacted . . . seemed similar."

They shopped until Neoloth and a hired servant were bending under a load . . . but wandering closer to that dark wall. It was constructed of something that looked like blackened bamboo. There was a pathway, well-grooved and roughly perpendicular, leading west to the harbor. They heard footsteps coming and followed the hired porter back into the shadows.

Around the corner came a string of miserable-looking wretches, half of them . . . children. Sobbing.

He watched the prisoners disappear through the gate like sheep herded to slaughter. "What is this?"

"Just slaves, sir," the hired man said. "It's safe now."

"They look new-captured," Aros growled. "I didn't see a slave market in the city. Some of those specimens look promising. Where could I find them?"

"Oh," their servant said. "They're for special use."

"By whom?"

"It is best not to ask, sir."

Neoloth looked at the wall and continued on.

Neoloth talked to everyone he could reach, including a scroll salesman, a weary pimp, and a gaggle of aging prostitutes. He bought drinks for rug merchants, one of whom had sold something to the castle on the hill. After hours, he wrangled an invitation to meet a man who traded in ancient scrolls and, through him, a group of scholars so pale and withered they might have been moles. Despite their obvious withdrawal from the world, they seemed to know everything and everyone and were open to wine and conversation.

Aros was walking down the street, the shadows of dusk reaching from every tavern and storefront. A strange metallic clanking sound reverberated behind him, as if a sack of base-metal coins were following him down the road.

He ducked into a doorway and drew his sword. The strange *"Ching! Ching!"* sound came closer. And then . . .

Aros's eyes widened. A man in a robe, an official of some kind, passed his doorway, huffing as his feet ran in circles. He was riding two wheels linked by a bar. How did he avoid falling over?

Aros replaced the sword in its sheath and watched, mystified, as the man leaned right and turned a corner instead of falling over. "What the feathered hell?"

Puzzled and troubled and slightly drunk, Neoloth found his way back to their rooms. Aros found him there hours later, drawing diagrams.

"What do you have there?"

"Just beginning to feel my way around," Neoloth said.

"Learning anything?"

Neoloth looked at him cannily. "We heard that a month ago a royal ship docked in the harbor and two masked female prisoners disembarked. They seem to have been taken to the Tower, which is the main prison block, protected by the army barracks."

Aros perked up at that. "Where?"

Neoloth stabbed a finger at the map. "Here."

"How do we find out if she's there?"

"We will," he said confidently.

"And if she is?"

Neoloth grinned at him. "We'll think of something. What have you learned?"

"People don't talk much to strangers. But I have the sense that most of these changes have happened in the last two years. There is a group called the 'Thousand.' Or maybe it's a place. Hard to tell, because you can't ask the same question twice without drawing attention. They seem to have gained power in the capital."

Neoloth nodded. "The king hasn't been seen for a year. Maybe more."

"I'd heard that, too. And there is something else."

He dropped a metal tube on the table.

Neoloth examined it. Glass at both ends, both rounded. "What is this?"

"You tell me."

Neoloth looked into it. Through it. Out the window, and saw the magnification.

"Spyglass," he murmured. "Never seen lenses so . . ." He examined them more carefully. "Look here."

Aros leaned in.

"See this tiny screw? I've never seen one that size. And the way the tube is sealed . . ."

Neoloth sat down and stared at it.

"What are you thinking?" Aros asked.

"More mysteries. The little ships. The small cannons."

Aros grunted. "You still think that is what those devices are?"

"Yes. They are worn like weapons. The men carrying them walk like giants."

The barbarian nodded. "Like master swordsmen, but without the discipline."

Neoloth smiled. "Well said. And this spyglass. Never seen anything as fine."

"I saw something as well," Aros said. "Some kind of machine that a man rode like a little horse. Two wheels, a bar between and a bar for steering. Very odd."

"I am beginning to suspect," Neoloth said, "that the oddities will only increase. Next week is a holiday of some kind. In it, the women of the kingdom lose their minds and engage in the kinds of foolishness generally reserved for men of a certain type."

"A certain type?"

"Yes, you know. Like you. It is all very entertaining, in a muscle-headed sort of way. I heard two things."

"And what are those?" Aros asked.

"One, that it was almost canceled this year. There was a general outcry."

"And the other?"

"That the general's wife, Jade, participates in a boat race."

"Ah!"

Neoloth smacked his hands down on the desk. "And tradition says that the winner is blessed of the gods and will receive a vision. It is a celebration of the wife of one of their deities. The near cancelation implies that worship has changed. Something has happened. Is happening."

"Yes," Aros agreed. "And it also suggests a possible approach, don't you think?"

The two men smiled at each other.

SEVENTEEN

The King

From the third-floor window of their bedroom, General Silith could see across the rows of empty taverns, shops, homes, and brothels to the shore. That was where the citizens were, in a vast crush of humanity as dense as the flotilla in the bay beyond. This was where his beloved wife, Jade, was preparing to go, and he just couldn't understand. Last year, a boat had capsized, and three women had drowned. Four years ago, it had been two losses. To Silith, the crowd below seemed a famished mob, and that was the most dangerous kind.

"Must you participate in this anachronism?" the general asked. "You don't even worship this petty god. It is unseemly in a woman so . . . mature."

"Mature" or not, Jade Silith was a dark-haired, dark-eyed beauty, even if her figure was fuller than it had been on their wedding day. She was still a delight to his heart. "Husband," she said. She stopped brushing her lustrous mane and frowned, lips in a playful pout. "Allow me a bit of fun in my declining years."

They laughed. Despite the fact that this was a hard man, there was affection between the two.

"General!" a soldier said, running up. "The king wishes to speak to you."

The general frowned. "Kindly tell him I'll be there shortly." He turned to his wife. "I suspect that he hasn't been drinking his teas."

"Husband," she whispered rigidly. "Be mindful."

His gaze grew distant. "Very soon, now, the time for caution will be past. Are you prepared?"

"Yes."

As she kissed him, he stroked her hair fondly.

"In all this bright and terrible world," he said. "There is only one thing I love."

"Once," she said, "there was more than one."

He held her. Kissed her again. "Come. Let us meet the people."

He led her out of the wing of the castle. It might be thought odd that the general lived there instead of in the barracks area. But if that was true, no one commented upon it in his presence.

"I give to you . . . Jade!"

She mounted the chariot's low step. The crowd cheered. Some of those cheers were encouraged by the soldiers.

General Silith turned to one of his men. "The usual arrangements have been made?"

"Yes, sir."

"Then let the games begin!"

Jade traveled along packed streets down to the docks. The other boatwomen smiled and bowed, dressed in identical blue uniforms that matched Jade's own boating dress.

Her female attendant bowed respectfully. "A good day for a race, mistress."

Jade smiled. "Oh, I'm quite certain that my husband has arranged for it to be anything but a race. But at my stage in life, I have to admit that I enjoy the fact that he bothers."

The assistant helped her onto the ship, coiling rope around her arm. "The general adores you."

"I grow tired of this charade," Jade said. "However entertaining it has been. I know the message: my husband loves me and wishes me peace. I will win this one last time and then retreat from the field."

The assistant paused. "If you win . . . will you ask the same question? The question you've—"

Jade cut her off. "Is there another?"

The crowd parted before General Silith's carriage and heeled behind it, a ship plowing through human waves. The horses pranced as the coachman brought them to a halt at the castle's side entrance. As soon as Silith disembarked, it pulled out toward one of the four stables.

As Silith entered, the guards clicked to attention up and down the corridor. They could not, he thought with a smile, have responded more briskly had he been the monarch himself.

His smile broadened but then flattened to a mere trace by the time he reached the throne room.

King Corinth hunched upon his grandfather's throne, a massive work of gem-encrusted gold and silver, intended to overawe supplicants, whatever their status or intent. Corinth was an old man, almost child-like against the massive throne. At first glance, he might have seemed imperious, but if you looked more closely there was a vagueness to his eyes, an unkempt bird's-nest quality to his hair that suggested something . . . a bit off. His advisors clustered on every side.

The general bowed deeply. "Your Majesty. How can I serve you?"

"General Silith," the king said, voice shaking. "Cousin. Good for you to come." He paused, then with a thin smile, said, "Bishop to king three."

"Knight to rook four, Your Majesty."

King Corinth chuckled. "Well played. Now to business. I know that you and your wife celebrate this holiday . . . religiously." The king chortled. "Yes, religiously. Oh, my, I made a joke!"

The room tittered with polite laughter.

The general's mouth curled upward, but his eyes were unchanged. "Yes, Your Majesty. You did indeed."

"Yes. Well . . . I wanted to speak with you because the accountants say that you have made several large withdrawals from the treasury and purchased . . ." He turned to the slight young man beside him.

"What was it he purchased?"

"Slaves, Your Majesty," the younger man said. "He purchased two boatloads of slaves, mostly natives captured in war by the Aztecs."

The king frowned. "Those fellows who tear the lungs out, aren't they?"

"Hearts, sir," the general said.

"Yes, of course. Hearts. Nasty."

He looked away a bit distracted and unfocused.

"Your Majesty?" General Silith nudged.

"Oh, yes! At any rate, I wished to know what this influx of labor represents. My minister of labor is concerned that it represents a threat to the honest working men of Shrike, and I wished to be certain this was not the case."

"Your Majesty," the general said, "it is not. Your previous minister of finance, regrettably ill, had no issue with the expenditures. These bondsmen do not threaten the honest working folk of Shrike and are merely helping us to build the workshops in which the Thousand can produce some of the luxuries Your Majesty enjoys."

To the side of the throne was an ornate clock with a broad, hand-painted face. In the momentary silence, it clicked and whirred merrily.

"Oh, yes, marvelous. Marvelous."

"Like this," the general said. He produced a cylinder of hard yellow material, the size of his forefinger. "It's a pen that never gets your fingers dirty. Look, the point pulls back when you do this—"

"Your Majesty," Minister Kang said. "Perhaps the general would be kind enough to explain more about the children."

The rotund minister and the general locked eyes. It was a war of wills, and Kang never blinked.

"The children?" the general asked.

"Yes. There are so many things afoot in the kingdom these

days. The general manages not only the army, but this . . . *spiritual* group as well."

Something about the way he said "spiritual" indicated that he considered it anything but.

"In addition, there are many new vessels in the fleet, new weapons in the army, all from the workshops hidden in the black forest. The secretive workshops."

"Secrets!" the king shrieked. "Secrets! The Thousand agreed to supply us with the fruits of their labors, but the conditions were too extreme! None of us get to see what they're . . . ah . . ."

Again his attention seemed to drift.

"Your Majesty?" Lord Kang's young assistant said politely.

"Oh, yes." His eyes refocused. "What was I saying?"

"I believe you were asking what they are doing in the black forest, Your Majesty."

General Silith stepped into the breech. "Since we gave them the land in the black forest, our army has lost not a skirmish. Our coffers are full. Our trade ships travel without fear of piracy. And all they ask is their privacy, Your Majesty. We can revoke our agreement, but all that will happen is that the Thousand will travel where they can work their wonders without interference."

"We have no wish to interfere with them," said Lord Kang. "But it is reasonable for us to wonder what is happening in the black forest . . . or even the Tower."

The two locked eyes again.

"Your Majesty," the general said. "I remind you that Your Majesty's sixtieth birthday is in but a month. The Thousand are preparing a wonderful celebration gift."

"A gift?"

"A wonderful gift. And if you can but wait until then, I promise that Your Majesty . . . and as many of his advisors as he wishes . . . will be free to travel into the forest and learn whatever he wishes to learn."

"My birthday, yes. I so love a surprise."

"I can promise you a wondrous one."

"Very well. Until my birthday. But then—"

"And then, Your Gracious Majesty, dear cousin," General Silith said, "All your curiosity will be satisfied."

The king's eyes sparkled. "That is wonderful, General Silith."

"And now, with Your Majesty's permission, there is a celebration to tend to. My wife, Jade, is competing once again."

The king nodded. "Well, please offer my wishes to your good lady wife."

"Thank you, Your Majesty."

He turned to leave. As he did, Lord Kang leaned closer to the king, jowls quivering. "Your Majesty, may I have a private word with the general?"

"Of course," the king said.

Lord Kang and the young scribe hurried after General Silith. "General!" Kang said, trying to match the general's long, effortless strides.

"Yes?" he said, continuing to glide toward the entrance.

"Can you wait a moment?" He panted. "I have difficulty talking and matching your stride at the same time."

The general gave that slight smile again. "My most sincere apologies, but I am late and wish to make up time. How can I help you?"

"We both know, General, that what happens in the black forest is more than merely providing shelter to some group of monks or magicians you saved on a whim."

The general glanced at him. "Oh? And what exactly do you think?"

"We have seen wonders emerge from the forest. Strange devices. Magic of a very different kind."

The general sniffed. "Magic has weakened in our world. This is the time of steel."

"But even there," Lord Kang said. "You clashed with pirates just a moon ago. And . . . destroyed them."

Silith's eyebrow arched. "Is that not a good thing?"

"More slaves enter the forest than leave. I have heard the word . . . necromancy."

"Have you?" Silith asked. "And what are you implying?"

The general had stopped. Lord Kang backed up. "Nothing. As yet. But there are whispers. If the king was himself . . ."

The general seemed shocked. "The king is not himself? What are you implying? And are you aware that such speech is seditious?"

They looked at each other coldly, and then Kang backed down. "I . . . meant no disrespect."

"See that you don't."

Lord Kang bowed and scraped his way away, eyes seething. The general waited in the empty hall. "Yes?"

Kang's assistant slipped out of the shadows. "My Lord. I don't mean to keep you from your duties. But you should know that I am responsible to my superiors, who will question everything I do and say."

"You are new, are you not?" the general mused.

"Yes," the assistant said. "I am Seff Janir. I came in after the unfortunate death of Seff Hesenshir."

"I see. And you are taking up where he left off? Counting every bean, being certain of every gold piece in its place. Admirable."

Seff Janir simpered. "Thank you, sir."

"It is important to be on the lookout for malfeasance, incompetency . . . and greed."

The assistant nodded. "Greed is always a problem, sir."

Silith's eyes were piercing. "Your predecessor certainly considered it so. A major sin, one he was quite mindful of in others. Have you ever observed that people tend to be more attentive to flaws in others than in themselves?"

"No, never. I am a humble accountant and just beginning down my road. I would appreciate any words of wisdom from a man such as yourself."

The general regarded him carefully. "You have reports to make, I presume."

"Yes."

"Good. Good. Many accounts will be placed in proper order, very soon. By, say, the king's birthday."

Seff Janir paused. "If there are temporary imbalances until that time, I'm quite certain it would be possible to . . . focus the light elsewhere."

"For a moon."

"Just a moon," the little man repeated. "After which, I assume, many things will have changed."

"Yes. And in the midst of change, those who provide service may be assured of position."

The assistant met his gaze squarely for the first time. "I would assume that the general prizes loyalty."

"And rewards it. And punishes the lack of it."

Seff Janir smiled. "It might be remarked that I had great loyalty to my predecessor, who mentored me. But none to Lord Kang, for instance."

"Those undeserving of loyalty might be discussed without concern for transgression. What becomes important . . . is truth."

"In that spirit, I thought you might wish to know that he has bribed a guard and intends to travel within the black forest very soon. Perhaps tonight."

The general mused. "That . . . is indeed a valuable thing to convey. I will not forget."

"Thank you, sir. Thank you," the accountant said, and backed away, bowing.

EIGHTEEN

The Race

E ven before the rising sun had set the bay to sparkling, the crowd had gathered on the sands and wharves. The titanic stone likeness of Shrike's two-headed avian goddess smiled down upon them from outside the harbor.

Almost two dozen sailboats bobbled for position on the waves.

A bearded, graying judge addressed them from a platform erected on a jetty lancing into the harbor like an accusing finger. "... And the first to circle the lighthouse and return wins the laurel and will be the guest of honor at the parade this evening!"

The crowd roared, chanted. "Jade! Jade!"

The boatwomen hauled ropes, set sails, caulked cracks, and waxed oars, singing and laughing with anticipation.

Jade's first mate grinned. "Listen to them! The crowd is with you!"

Jade nodded with satisfaction. "Let's make it a good day. There's a last time for everything."

The judge climbed down from his platform, which was itself composed of dried, aged timbers wrapped in oiled linens, an enormous torch.

The torch was lit!

The sailboats began their journey, canting their triangular sails to catch the wind.

A section of the crowd was marked off from the others by a line of armed men. In that group were red-robed monks and nuns, in a single file, chanting, eyes closed.

Deep in a crowd of cheering drunks, Aros and Neoloth watched the action in the bay with intense interest. Aros watched the boat-women. Neoloth was watching the monks.

"What do you think?"

Aros held the odd spyglass, twisting its beveled rim to adjust focus. It really was a miracle, like being reborn with an eagle's eye. "I think that I could have used these things, back in another life." He stopped. "Oh, you mean the sailors? They look very good."

"No, that's not what I meant," Neoloth said. "Look at the priests."

Aros trained his attention upon them. "Chanting. Hands folded."

Neoloth's eyes narrowed. "Look at the way they are folded."

Aros focused on their hands. They were folded in odd configurations. He shrugged. "What of it?"

"Those are Kryrick hand signs," Neoloth said. "Those haven't worked for many years."

"The magic went away?"

Neoloth nodded. "Yes."

"But if they did work, what would they accomplish?"

"Weather control, I think." Neoloth refocused the spyglass, moving from red robe to red robe. "Wind."

"So . . . if they had a source of magic . . . and knew these signs . . ."

"It could make a difference," Neoloth said.

"The rumors would be true."

Neoloth took the glass back, continued to scan the magic users. And then . . . held his breath. Most of these were strangers, unknown to him. But one strong feminine jawline and set of angular cheeks he recognized. "Shyena," he whispered. Her cowl concealed the spill of red hair as her robes concealed the lush form he knew so well, but it was Shyena. The Red Nun was here in Shrike.

As the boats left the harbor, Jade and the strong, sinewy woman at her side worked hard.

Even through the glass, Aros could see that much. "Well done," he murmured.

The sailboats reached the statue of the two-headed goddess and circled it. The other boats' sails seemed to be having trouble catching the wind. Neoloth smiled to himself.

"Very nicely done."

"What?"

"I thought they might control wind sprites, give the sails a boost. Or deny wind to the other boats. But that could be seen from shore: the sails would be fuller."

Aros humphed. "What, then?"

"The water," Neoloth said. "The current. They are creating a separate thread of current for the general's wife."

Aros was surprised. "You can see all that?"

Neoloth smiled. "Yes. What do you see?"

"That, if you're right, I think that General Silith loves his wife."

"Yes," Neoloth said. "Very good."

Jade worked the sails with her crew with ferocious enthusiasm. Born to leisure in one world, married into wealth and power in another, she had grown so soft that at times she barely recognized herself. This race, with the excitement, the sun and salt, the chafed hands and bruised bones, was the high point of her year.

The schooner smacked a wave, reared up out of the water, and then slammed back down.

All of her crew managed to hang on for dear life. Her nearest competitor fared more poorly, capsizing entirely.

Jade shrieked with delight, spared only a single glance back at the thrashing crew, and bent herself back to the glorious task at hand.

One of the other boats, with a different shape of sail, was pulling up next to her. And then . . . she pulled ahead just a little.

She paid no notice to anything but the water, the wind, the ropes and sails. None to the roar of the crowds as they drew ahead or crossed the line two seconds before the closest competitor.

After they slowed to an easier pace and were gliding back into the harbor, Jade's crew bowed to her. "My lady. You have triumphed again. Again, you can ask a boon of the goddess. Every year you have asked the same thing, with no answer. Perhaps . . . this year . . ."

She shook her head. "The heart wants what it wants, my friend."

And she went to her knees. Bowed. And prayed. Her crew watched respectfully. The wind was quiet, and then . . .

Something came crawling up over the edge of the boat.

A sailor pointed. "My lady!"

At first just a tentacle. Then several. Then the oddly human-looking eye of a sizable octopus appeared. Then its flank, spotted blue.

"Oh!" Jade said.

"What is it?" her lieutenant asked.

"It is a sign."

Brown on brown now, the side of the octopus showed a cartoon face, the face of a man in his thirties, square of jaw, handsome but a bit battered.

Jade was entranced. The octopus . . . posed?

She reached for the octopus. It turned away, quickly. Before it dropped into the water, Jade saw its other flank. That was blurry, but she could make out the flag symbol of the state of Hamnos.

"They say those creatures are sometimes magical," her first mate said. Clymnos nodded.

Crowds thronged the streets of Hamnos as the winners of various events paraded the avenue on platforms carried by costumed bearers. The crowds, perhaps somewhat encouraged by troops, cheered boisterously. Jade waved to the crowd, smiling, but she searched faces.

Something caught her eye: two men, apparently paying little attention to the show.

"Stop!" she called. "Stop the float!"

They did. She ran down from the chair of honor, into the press of cheering, inebriated humanity. She went this way and that, exultation slowly sliding into despair—

Then caught a glimpse of broad shoulders, walking away.

"There!" Jade screamed.

One of her bodyguards ran toward Aros and clapped his hand on the thief's shoulder.

A blur of motion, and the man was down, Aros's sword Flaygod at his throat.

"What the hell do you want from me?" Aros snarled. "Fool. You would rob me in broad daylight?"

The bodyguard raised a terrified hand to guard his throat. "No! No. My mistress seeks a word with you."

The Aztec sheathed his sword. "I have no words, nor time to offer them." He turned to go.

"Wait!" she called after him.

Aros turned. He looked down at the woman. She was brown, round, vibrant. Breathless. And, for a moment, he wavered. By the serpent, she reminded him of his mother!

He could think of nothing to say, and Neoloth jumped into the breech. "Can we help you, mistress?"

She didn't look at his angular servant, kept her eyes on Aros's face. "Who are you?"

"My name is Kasha," Aros said.

"Mine is Jade. May I . . . buy your dinner?"

Slowly, he nodded.

The tavern was a boisterous, rowdy scene, a little quieter near the corner where Jade and her bodyguards clustered around Aros and Neoloth. A tavern keeper was carving a major hunk of boar.

Aros tore into the meat with his powerful white teeth. "The meat is good." He drank deeply from his wine flagon and belched. "Now, lady . . . Jade. Suppose you tell me what this is all about?"

"How came you to our kingdom?" she asked, plump brown fingers folded.

Neoloth winced a bit, waiting for a faux pas.

"My man and I enjoy travel."

"But why Shrike? Have you been here before?"

Aros's teeth tore a chunk of meat that might have choked a lion. "I had of course heard of the mighty kingdom of Shrike, but never visited. Of late, I've had . . . dreams." He seemed to speak the last words reluctantly.

"What manner of dreams?"

"Of the fighting men of Shrike," he said. "I had heard that the general is the finest swordsman in the world, and skill at arms is something I appreciate."

"You thought to join our fighting forces?" she asked.

He nodded. "If the situation seems appropriate."

"What of your past? You are . . . Aztec?"

He nodded. "As you are, I believe, my lady."

She drew herself up. "Yes. I am. I was a princess of Azteca, won in battle and trade by my husband, a prince of Shrike."

Aros bowed while seated, an oddly formal gesture. "I pray he won your heart as well as your hand."

She smiled. "Yes," she said. "He did. Where are your people?"

The Aztec lowered his eyes. When he spoke, Neoloth was surprised by the pain in his voice. "In truth, I do not know. My first memories are of the desert people who raised me."

"And . . . did they tell you how you came among them?"

"I know that much. I was a slave. They purchased me from a merchant."

"And he?"

Aros shook his head. "He went his way."

She looked at his belt buckle. "Where did you get that buckle?"

He looked down. "From a gold coin. I think the merchant gave it to me."

"The man who sold you left you a gold coin?"

He shrugged. "I do not understand either. I had the sense that he sold me not for profit, but because he could not take care of me and wished me to have a good home. The story was that he haggled for my price . . . but then after he collected the money, gave me this gold coin to wear as a necklace."

"May I see it?" Jade asked.

Aros seemed a bit nonplussed, but in a good humor took it off. "When beautiful, titled ladies ask me to disrobe, it is rarely in public."

Neoloth winced. Was the fool making a pass at his own mother?

Jade was instantly embarrassed, flushed. "No, you don't understand."

She examined the belt buckle. "It is a popular fashion," she said, "to make jewelry out of coins. Nothing unique here. But . . . a long time ago, I gave a coin to someone."

"A coin like this one?"

"Much like," she replied.

She looked at his shirted chest, the spot where the tattoo would be, and Neoloth sensed that she was goosing up her courage to ask him about it . . . or ask him to show it, when there was a disturbance in the front of the tavern.

They turned around, and several bulky sword-wielding soldiers entered the tavern, flanking a man larger and more impressive than any of them.

"I seek my wife!" General Silith roared.

"Here, husband."

He kissed the top of her head, then scanned the table with open curiosity. "Well, there are many places to celebrate in our capital, but I didn't expect to find you here!"

"I didn't mean to worry you. I was just speaking to this young man here."

The general eyed Aros. "And who might you be?"

"My name is Kasha. I am of the Southern Desert people."

"That," Silith said, "is odd. I might have mistaken you for Azteca."

"I think it likely that such blood runs in my veins," he averred.

Silith humphed. "How came this young man to your attention, Jade?"

She stuttered a moment. "I . . . it had been a long time since I saw someone who seemed of my people, my husband. I hoped to speak words with him."

Silith turned back to Aros. He seemed barely to notice Neoloth existed at all. "And do you speak the language?"

"A bit, yes," Aros said. "But I don't remember where I learned it."

"Interesting. Is this your bondsman?"

"Yes," Aros said dismissively. "Washelisk has served me since my comrades and I spared his life."

"In war?"

"There are small wars everywhere," Aros said, smiling, one fighting man to another.

The general smiled back. "Yes. A merchant's life would be wasted on a man such as you. What brings you to Shrike?"

"I had heard that a good sword could find a home here."

"A home for a sword . . . with a bondsman." The general's eyes widened. "You see yourself as an officer."

"I have commanded men. I seek nothing more than a chance to prove my worth."

The general's smile hardened. "Do you now?"

Neoloth watched as Silith examined Aros boot to brow, that smile holding. And Aros seemed as sanguine. These two actually liked each other.

Was that a good or a bad thing?

"Well, then," Silith said. "Come to the barracks tomorrow morning, if you wish a test of your mettle. Prepare for bruises."

He stood. "Jade," he said. "Our carriage awaits."

They could now hear a clattering noise in the street. "Well. It has been good to speak to you, young man. I hope you will accept my husband's invitation."

"I would be honored," Aros said.

She turned away, took her husband's arm. Aros and Neoloth followed them out.

A wheeled conveyance half again the size of a carriage pulled up in the street outside. Steam drifted from its chimney. No horses pulled it, although a coachman drove.

The clientele goggled at the sight.

Aros and Neoloth watched, Aros stupified.

"What . . . is this vehicle?" Neoloth asked. "I've not seen its like."

"We have many wonders in Shrike," the general said. "Presently we shall share them with the world. You may wish to be a part of that gift."

His carriage pulled out and drove down the cobbled road. Other carriages, more standard with their horses, moved out of the way.

The general waited until they were down the road a piece and then turned to his wife. "And the real story here?"

She gave a secretive smile. "Perhaps," she said, "I have become an adventuress in my declining years."

The general held her hand warmly. "My heart is yours to hold, or break, as you wish."

She leaned her head against his shoulder. "Give me my little secret," she said. "Just for the night, a fantasy. But tomorrow, if Aros appears, make . . . swimming one of his tests."

Silith's eyebrows arched. "Why?"

"I wish to see him swim," she said, and from the set of her lips, he knew he would get no more from her.

"I will never understand women."

She leaned her head against his shoulder. "You should never try. Just . . . love us," she said.

Aros and Neoloth were walking back to their lodgings.

"Well," Aros said. "That was neatly done, I think. Or at least well begun."

"Well begun is half done. Your comment about disrobing.

Have you no sense of decency? The woman is your own mother? I don't know the customs where you—"

Aros glared at him.

"Do not. I had a reason for doing it, and that reason is what you just said."

Neoloth matched Aros's long stride, thinking.

"That anyone attempting to defraud the general, to impersonate his son, would not be stupid enough, tasteless enough, to make such an insinuating comment."

"Dawn comes late."

"I'm beginning to wonder whether I am dealing with a genius or a moron."

"Let me know when you've decided."

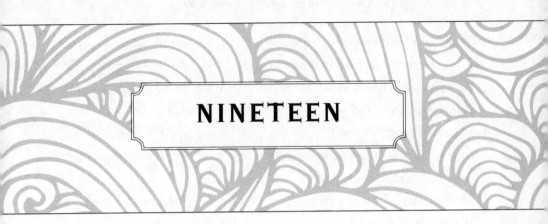

NINETEEN

Exercises

As the sunlight streamed in through the window, Neoloth awakened and dressed, determined to try his hand at a spell.

"The red robes were using magic," he muttered. "Perhaps there is mana in this place . . ."

He deployed a geomantic tool over a parchment map of Shrike. He gestured, he whispered, and . . . nothing. Dead sheepskin.

"Damnation."

He reluctantly took his talisman and leeched a bit of magic from it and then returned to the map. This time, he got indications, especially in the forbidden black forest . . . and the royal tower that abutted it.

He was not entirely displeased. "There is something," he said. "But the more important question is . . . how did the red robes do their magic? There is none in the ground here. Do they all have talismans? And if they do, how do they charge them?"

The Aztec was still sleeping. Let him sleep. He hated to admit it, but so far Aros was performing well. "You will have your own test today. Sleep well."

The streets were still dark as Neoloth slipped out of the inn. It was early morning, and the sun had yet to touch the flagstones and cobbles. A few early risers were already up and about. Bakers, road sweepers, a butcher.

Neoloth walked lanes narrow and broad seeking a sense of the capital, mapping the streets in his head.

A few servants lurked outside a morning pub near the outer gate of the palace. "G'morning to ye."

"G'morning. Oh, it's a good day to come, I think."

"I thought," Neoloth said, "that any tavern that serves the castle folks would be likely to have the very best."

The servant grinned. "And . . . ye thought right. Looking for a bit of breakfast?"

"That's just the thing."

"And your master be?"

He gritted his teeth. "My lord Kasha will be testing for the guard this day."

Another servant who had been eavesdropping suddenly perked up. "Really? Now, that be invitation only. He does that, and you're rolling in clover. I'd better buy you a cup today—and hope that you'll be rich enough to buy me breakfast tomorrow."

They were joined by a few others.

Neoloth was warming into his role. "My master fights for pleasure, not gold. We have plenty of coin. What say I buy drinks all around while we eat, and you tell me about the good people here-abouts . . . and maybe the lovely ladies, hey?"

The tavern teemed with serving wenches, cleaning folks, grooms, and the like filling their guts with porridge or, if lucky, a slice of last night's boar, still roasting over low coals.

"Tavern keeper!" Neoloth yelled. "Bring us a haunch to share with my friends."

The others clapped him on the back, in the manner of men everywhere who are offered a free meal. "It's a fine and generous man you are, sir Washelisk. I'm sure you and your master will do well here."

"What kind of people do well here?"

"Those with skills," one said.

"Those who know how to keep their noses clean and their mouths shut," another offered.

"Meaning?" Neoloth asked, trying not to seem too interested.

"Well . . . since the Thousand came. The Red Ones. We learn not to ask too many questions," the servant said, and seemed astonished at his own daring.

"Well . . . you let me know if I'm asking too many, but my master intends to rise here and wants to know all he can about where the power lies."

A buxom wench had pillowed her bosom against his arm. If her breath had not been a miasma of stale beer, the implied offer might have been tempting. "That's a sound idea."

"So . . . ," Neoloth went on. "The queen died three years ago."

"Tragic it was," she said. "But she'd fallen from her horse and broken her back. No one could save her, but the Red Nun kept her alive longer than anyone would have believed."

"Aye," another servant said. "And that was after the court doctors had given up. Probably that was the toehold that got them where they are today."

"Next to the true power," Neoloth said provocatively. "The king, hey?"

They looked at each other, as if nervous about speaking. "That . . . would be one way to look at it, yes."

There was a bit of reluctance to go further, and Neoloth smiled and withdrew.

On the flat dirt field at the front of the barracks, three dozen soldiers were engaged in various exercises and skill drills: throwing, lifting, jumping, grappling. A handful of stragglers . . . and Aros . . . stood separate from them, watching with the awareness that they might soon be asked to participate in the bruising games.

The general rode up and addressed a beefy NCO who had registered the newcomers.

"Good morning, Sergeant Fflogs."

The sergeant saluted sharply. "Morning, General. Congratulations on the wife's recent success."

The general smiled. "Becoming something of a tradition, isn't it?"

"That it is."

"What do you think of the recruits?" General Silith asked.

"The usual sad lot . . ." The sergeant frowned. "I noticed the Aztec. He's an odd one. He said he was invited? That true, sir?"

"It is," the general said.

"Explains why your lordship's out this morning. A relative?"

"Why do you say that?" the general asked.

Sergeant Fflogs scratched his head. "Well . . . he favors your lady wife a bit, that's all. Don't mind my saying, sir."

The general looked at Aros again. His wife, Jade, came up riding behind him.

"Good morning, Sergeant," she said.

"Morning, ma'am."

The sergeant looked at Jade and then at Aros and hid a bit of a smile. "What's on the agenda today, sir?"

"Let's give them a chance to strut. See what they can do."

"You heard the man!" the sergeant bawled. "Padded swords. Let's see what you're made of!"

The men were given padded swords and paired off. "This is not a blind brawl. You will listen to me. Here are the strokes: One! Two! Three . . ." As he counted them off, blocks and strikes were paired with blows and parries from complementary angles.

Jade rode up behind her husband.

"Jade. What brings you to the parade grounds?"

"I find myself interested in that young Aztec."

He raised an eyebrow. "Should I be jealous?"

"If I was going to betray our bed, I would have begun such nonsense long ago."

He chuckled. "You're not going to tell me, are you?"

"No," she said. "I'm not."

And she kissed his cheek. He laughed.

The training went on and on into the day. By afternoon, they were dragging. Enthusiasm had become fatigue.

"If you're afraid of a knock on the head, you're in the wrong profession!" Sergeant Fflogs said. "It's time to put this to use. Pair up! The ones still standing go on to the next test."

The men faced each other, and the general and his wife watched with interest. Aros downed his opponent with a feint and an ankle sweep.

The general pointed. "Sergeant Fflogs!" he called. "That man."

The sergeant looked where indicated. "The Aztec?"

The general nodded. "Yes. I want you to try him personally."

Sergeant Fflogs rolled his shoulders, producing a sound like crackling paper. "Yes, sir. Easy?"

The general dropped his voice almost to a whisper. "No. Hard."

The sergeant grinned like a wolf offered a lamb chop. "As you like it, sir."

He returned to the grounds. Several of the men were groaning on the sand, their conquerors panting over them.

Aros's partner was on his knees, groaning. They had missed the exchange. The partner, apparently, had not.

"Break!" the sergeant bawled. "The general wants a little demonstration match. You, Aztec. Your name?"

"Kasha," Aros said without hesitation.

"You seem pretty handy. You and me."

Aros nodded.

Sergeant Fflogs squared off with him. "Watch out for your head."

The sergeant swirled his padded sword in a fancy pattern. Aros watched him. Aros stabbed high, then low, then blocked high—

And kicked Sergeant Fflogs in the crotch, followed with a savage hooking punch to the head with the left hand. The NCO went down like a felled steer. Aros put his padded sword at the sergeant's throat.

The grounds were quiet. And then the men applauded.

Jade smiled. As did the general, who came down off his horse.

"Well done. Rules: stick with the sword. Otherwise, things may get a bit . . . unpleasant. For you."

"At your pleasure," Aros said.

The two men squared off. The swords touched. And then— an amazing blur of motion, forcing Aros to give way before a superior swordsman. His reflexes were cat-quick, and several times he would have contacted the general if not for the older man's brilliant efficiency of motion and flawless positioning. But the general was playing with him, and with a corkscrew motion, disarmed him. With the same motion, his sword ended at Aros's throat. "I'm dead," the Aztec said merrily.

A thin sheen of perspiration glistened on the general's lip. Aros had the distinct impression that he was unused to even *this* much competition. "Very well done, indeed. Sergeant!"

The sergeant rubbed his head but seemed to hold no rancor. A fighting man. "Yes, General."

"Horseback," the general said. "And then"—with a glance at Jade—"swimming."

In perfect formation, four men rolled past on double-wheeled devices of the same design he had seen two nights before. Their feet worked pedals driving thin chains around gears. Somehow, the devices stayed upright. The men wore metal tubes resembling horns with handles across their backs. What in the world?

"Keep your mind on your business," the general said.

For the next hours, the men were jumping, running, horseback riding. Aros was faster, stronger, simply better than the others. And Jade's pleasure was growing. The general was beginning to feel something as well.

"He rides like a centaur," the general murmured.

The wind caught Jade's hair. "Yes. Doesn't he."

By the time the sun was directly overhead, they had moved to the river. The men stripped down. Jade was watching very closely now, and General Silith was growing irritated. It was unseemly!

Aros was neck and neck with another man in a swim across the river but, on the return passage, exceeded him. Until now, Aros had worn a tunic, or his back had been to them (revealing only a small faded tattoo that might be a girl's face), or he had been in the water. But now . . .

As Aros turned, the general saw the tattoo on his upper chest. A sunburst in faded gold ink. Jade's eyes flew wide. The general's eyes narrowed.

"Hold!" he said. "Bring this man to my quarters."

"Yes, sir!" the sergeant said.

Aros continued to dry himself, long black hair streaming, his perfect body engraved with that tattoo . . .

While the general and his wife could do little but stare.

In the capital, the wizard Neoloth had made his way through the markets and byways, talking to people while in the guise of buying supplies. The Tower, an imposing structure at the edge of the barracks and the black forest, continued to draw his eye.

He returned to the rooms. A map of the capital was laid out.

He used the talisman to charge a little divining stone. He dangled it over the map until it began to bend toward the Tower.

Neoloth sprinkled powders in a circle on the floor, making a complex magical symbol. He carefully stepped into it, lay down, and closed his eyes . . .

He was viewing the capital from a killing height. Neoloth floated above the roofs, beak toward the Black Tower, gliding, gliding . . .

Then he was repelled by a sharp shock, as if the entire tower was protected by fire that burned fiercely, briefly. Neoloth *plunged helplessly toward the ground and smashed—*

Awakening, breathing hard, the wizard got shakily to his feet. He looked out the window at the Tower. "Someone has shielded you," he said. "Protected you well. I wonder why?"

TWENTY

Drasilljah

In the Tower, Drasilljah, the princess's woman, reeled against the wall, her mouth wide and straining in her angular face, uttering a silent scream.

The princess was aghast. "Drasilljah! Are you all right?"

Her faithful servingwoman shook her head. "Princess. I do not know. *Something* happened."

The princess made room on one of the room's two chairs for her friend. "Here. Sit down. What was it?"

"I do not know," Drasilljah said. "I was simply performing my daily meditations. Quieting my mind. I felt as if I was slipping into a dream, and in that dream . . . something familiar occurred."

"What?" the princess asked.

"I cannot say." She was bent over, sucking breath. "The memory worms away from me."

"Like a dream," the princess said. "Perhaps a dream?" She said this wistfully. Almost playfully, if there had been anything at all amusing about the situation. "Who was in this dream?"

"You will laugh at me," her lady said.

The princess laid her head on the older woman's shoulder. "Not I. Not you. Not ever."

Drasilljah kissed the smooth, troubled forehead. "Well . . . it was the magician."

The princess frowned. "What magician . . . Neoloth?"

"Yes."

The princess considered. "And what was he doing?"

"Searching for you," she smiled.

"Oh, Drasilljah . . ." The princess held her lady's cheeks in her hands and kissed them both. "Your powers might be strong, to reach all the way home to . . ."

Drasilljah grasped the princess's wrists. "Here. He's here."

"Here?" the princess said, eyes wide. "Oh, Neoloth! I knew it! I knew he would find me!"

"What do we do?" Drasilljah asked.

"If he is here in Shrike, surely he can find us within the Tower."

"I'm not sure," Drasilljah said. "There was contact . . . just for a moment. And then . . . nothing. We're cursed, I think."

"A barrier of some kind?"

"Yes," Drasilljah said. "Intelligent. Someone or something very powerful at work."

The princess mused. "You have said that you feel things. Different things, since we've been here."

"Yes, Princess. I don't know what to think of it. Let me try to describe. At home, I was confined to potions and mental tricks.

The magic is simply not as strong as it was in my grandmothers' time."

"Yes."

"It is as if the soil itself is depleted. But something else is happening here. I can feel it. In the woods behind the barrier, beyond the Black Tower. What they call the 'black forest.'"

"What are they doing?" the princess asked.

"Something that tears the soul. We are magic, at the core of us, the same magic that lived in the stars at the beginning of time. And this is why necromancy—the magic of death—is so strong. There is one thing that troubles me most deeply."

"And what is that?"

There was a pause, in which the Tower's hollow silences consumed them.

Then, "As we age, we lose this magic. The most powerful are the youngest."

"And you feel this power?" the princess asked.

"Yes, I do."

"And can you use it?"

"That is what my people do, Princess. The magic is in my blood. That . . . may be the one mistake they have made," Drasilljah said. "I think they are doing something . . . huge. Larger than my mind can hold. But they are drunken with their power and have begun to waste. To spill. Imagine that they have set an enormous blaze and grown careless of where the sparks fly. I . . . have been able to collect a few sparks."

The princess considered. "Then this is what you must do . . ."

The guards outside their door had been fully occupied for a time. Playing at dice.

"Ah!" one said, watching the knucklebones bounce off the wall. "I knew my luck would change. Hold on to your pay or your children will starve."

"As if you know your children," the second said. "Big talk. I'll have you for breakfast—"

Suddenly, a scream came from the dungeon.

"No, no!" It was the princess's high, sweet voice. "Back to the forest with you! In the name of all that's holy, NO!"

The guards looked at each other questioningly. "Be quiet down there!" one yelled.

There was a last groan of fear and pain . . . and then . . . nothing.

They stared at each other. "What in the world? Some kind of trick?"

No sound. Nothing.

They drew their swords and walked down the corridor, none too confidently.

"Princess Tahlia?" the taller asked.

"What is going on in the forest?" the shorter man whispered to his companion.

"That's not for such as us to know."

They reached the door. Looked in. Nothing. Empty.

The guard announced, "Princess Tahlia, I will now open the door."

The key turned. The door opened with a creak. The two guards stood looking through and in. Nothing. The cell was empty; the straw-covered floor, soaking under a puddle of blood. Shocked, they looked up at the ceiling. Nothing. Around the corner. Nothing.

Except . . .

A fragment of clothing against the far wall. A torn blouse. The guard approached it, picked it up. Rubbed his fingers on the red liquid smeared on it.

"Blood—" he began.

Behind him, the straw on the floor rose up in two large lumps, one behind each of the guards and then: *Thwack! Thwack!*

Both of them fell. *Thump.* The air *shimmered,* and the princess and Drasilljah appeared. Drasilljah staggered against the wall, gasping.

"Did you have to use so much blood?" the princess asked.

Drasilljah nodded weakly. "Even in a place like this, magic has its cost."

"I love you," Tahlia said, holding her old friend as tightly as she dared. "Come. Do you think you can follow your sense to Neoloth?"

"Yes. But first we have to get out of here."

"Come. Take the swords."

Each of them took a sword. Drasilljah was still wobbly.

"How many more times can you do that?" the princess asked.

Drasilljah's red-rimmed eyes told the story. "I hope it won't be needed even once."

Carefully, they made their way down the corridor. There was a room with sounds of laughter coming from it. They ducked under the door's barred window and kept going.

They wound down the stairway. The way was narrow and dark.

Neoloth wandered in the marketplace. He could feel it: something was calling to him. He looked at the Black Tower and took steps toward it . . . and then turned away. Not that direction at all. Something more than instinct was pulling him into the market . . .

The princess and Drasilljah were making their way along a balcony, staying within the shadows. But there was absolutely no way to pass the final stretch, leading to a door, without passing in plain sight.

"What now?" Drasilljah whispered.

"The Black Tower of Shrike was built by the same masons' guild that designed the tower in Quillia. And they had a trick. A secret exit and entrance to be used in emergencies by members of the royal family. The designs are similar aboveground. I think they may be similar belowground as well."

"Good. Lead me."

The princess replied. "We need to cover the distance between us and that wall. If I'm right, if the plans are sufficiently similar, the door is there."

"Are you sure?"

"No. But I don't know what else we can do. Can you . . . ? Just one more time?"

"Yes, my princess."

And she knelt and sliced her wrist. The blood poured out upon the ground, and Drasilljah murmured an incantation.

One slow inch at a time, the druid and the princess gained that odd camouflage, blending into the light and shadow.

Breathing shallowly, walking as if afraid to put their full weight upon the ground, they began to cross the gap.

In the dining hall below them, the guards ate boisterously. A few odd objects were splayed around the table, things the princess did not recognize: tubes, wheels, things that looked like miniature cannons. She yearned to inspect the objects more closely: something told her that there were answers here and possible tools that could ease their plight. No time. She moved on, praying thanks that Drasilljah's magic reduced visible signs of them to mere ripples against the wall.

Even to her own sight, her own arm was invisible unless she focused carefully. To see her friend and protector's face required even more concentration. The ripple would finally yield to focus, and like a suddenly dissolving mirage, a gasping, trembling woman appeared. Drasilljah smiled wanly and motioned her onward.

The druid was using up the last of her strength, using everything she had, possibly more than she could really afford, because they believed that there was the possibility of an ally just outside.

A voice from below: "Did you even take a good look at her? I'm telling you . . ."

"I don't know what they want that woman for, but she has meat on her bones, I'm telling you," the other said.

"Well, maybe after they're through with her . . ."

It seemed to take forever, but the two women finally reached the safety of the far wall. Tahlia's nervous fingers found the panel's hidden catch, and a door swung open. They slipped within, finding themselves in a dark tunnel.

Her fingers cast this way and that, finally finding a torch and a tiny leather pouch containing flint and steel. She struck them eight times before the sparks lit the oil-soaked torch, and they had light.

"How are you, Drasilljah?"

Her handmaiden gasped, straightening herself. "I'll be fine, if your wizard is really here."

"He's here. I can feel it. I know it."

"Then we'll be all right. I hope."

She stumbled, and the princess put her arm around her, helping her down the tunnel. The tunnel wound and twisted and then split.

"Which way?"

Drasilljah was woozier than she could possibly feel comfortable admitting. "This way, I think. What do you remember of the tunnels?"

"I used to hide and seek in them as a little girl. I knew them. I just have to hope that the plans are the same."

"We can both hope. It is rare that our youthful indiscretions come back to advantage, Princess. Let us consider this a good omen."

In the crowded marketplace beyond the Tower's walls, the wizard Neoloth was indeed nearby. He was bickering with an oil merchant over rare scents and unguents, but his attention was split. Several times in the last hour he had sensed . . . something. A presence. A faint voice, hovering just below the threshold of recognition.

Neoloth drifted further east, where he found a café next to a cutlery shop. He found an empty stool and sat down, unsure why he had been attracted to this spot.

A waiter approached. "Welcome to the Happy Orc. Today we have some excellent roast bison."

"Yes," the wizard said vaguely. "Yes. That will be fine."

From his seat, he could see the castle wall clearly. He looked around, uncertain. He was supposed to be here; he knew that. But . . . why?

In the tunnels, the princess and Drasilljah rested. Drasilljah's wounds had drained her.

"Did you hear that?" the princess said.

"What?"

"We're not down here by ourselves."

"That would have been too easy," Drasilljah sighed.

"Come on."

The tunnels were narrow and cramped and twisty. They heard a distant voice: "I see a light!"

"Damn!" the princess hissed, and put out her torch.

"What are you doing?" Drasilljah asked.

"I know the way. I'm sure. Do you trust me?"

"With my life."

The two women felt their way through the tunnels. A bit of glowing moss in the shape of an arrow gave them direction at a branching tunnel, and it was gratefully taken.

The voices were closer now. And then closer still.

The princess fell, and then got back up again.

"Here! Over here!"

They were tense, all was lost—the lights got closer . . . and then faded away, running into the distance. "Thank the gods," Drasilljah sighed.

"Here. Here it is."

A ladder. From above them, a tiny ray of light.

The waiter reappeared, lugging a platter with a cold joint of roast bison beef, and shook the table by depositing it in front of him. Neoloth jumped. His nerves were burning.

And then . . . Aros appeared. "I thought that I saw you!" the Aztec crowed, eyeing the fragrant platter.

"How did you find me?" the wizard said irritably.

"Pure accident. I was coming out of the parade grounds and

thought I noticed that loping gait of yours in the crowd. Meat looks good."

"Help yourself."

"Well, you are buying it with my money, after all."

Aros cut himself a huge wedge of meat and began to chatter. "You haven't asked me what happened today."

"Mmm."

"What happened. You know, how things went in the tryouts today."

Neoloth was distracted, not engaged. "Yes. Yes. What . . . um, what happened."

Aros was leaning close to Neoloth, chewing. "And you should have seen her gasp when she saw that sunflare tattoo! I have to admit that I didn't believe it would work, but, well, you know your stuff!"

"So . . . what now?"

"I am invited to their personal lodgings this evening. I think that it would be reasonable for me to bring my servant, don't you? And while they are having whatever conversation with me they wish to have—"

"There it is!" The princess climbed up the ladder. This led her to another tunnel, but here there was light . . . and sound. "We're under the street. Come."

"I'm . . . coming."

The princess and Drasilljah moved toward the light as swiftly as possible. As they came closer, it resolved into a doorway, and although the door was closed, they could hear voices and smell fresh bread and roast meat. A kitchen.

The princess and Drasilljah ran through the tunnel now and were almost to the camouflaged door when—

Soldiers broke out from either side and grabbed them. There was a moment when their struggling bodies slammed the door out of the wall and revealed their peril to the kitchen staff. But instead of helping, or even expressing shock, the cooks and serving boys just stared at them dully and then averted their eyes and returned to their labors.

While the princess and Drasilljah were dragged away, someone replaced the door.

A musician strummed his lute and sang of the mighty two-headed Shrike goddess as a second waiter brought bread and a jug of wine to Neoloth's table.

Aros grabbed at it and tore away a hunk of the loaf.

"Some kind of trouble in the kitchen?"

"The new boy dropped a tray," the man replied. "We'll beat him."

"The bread is hot."

Neoloth was looking back at the kitchen. The odd premonition had grown stronger . . . and then diminished. Now it was gone entirely. The wizard sighed and returned to his food.

The princess and Drasilljah were hauled back and away, through the tunnel, screaming and sobbing, all the way back to their cell. The door was slammed shut. They crouched in darkness.

"I am so sorry, so very sorry, my princess."

"No. You did all you could do."

For long hours they waited there in the darkness. Then there was a sound at the door and a scream from beyond. And a red-robed priestess stood there.

"Who are you?"

"Call me Shyena," the redhead said. "Some call me the Red Nun."

"You are . . . different."

"Yes. I am."

The princess pulled against her chain. Something about the Red Nun frightened her more than the silent, brutal males who had preceded her. "Where is the guard?"

"He is being disciplined," Shyena said. "He and the guards who were responsible for your safety."

A scream reverberated from down the hall.

"There are penalties in life for nonperformance."

The princess tried to draw herself up. "I have asked many times what is wanted from us."

"And no doubt received oblique and incomplete answers. Who are you?"

She had directed this question at Drasilljah, leaning close.

"Drasilljah," the handmaid answered.

"Perhaps you do not understand me," said the Red Nun. "Perhaps I should speak more clearly." She examined Drasilljah more closely. "You interest me. You have power. You used life magic to escape your cell. My underling should have felt this from you, known that you had such ability, and taken precautions. What you hear now is his . . . chastisement."

Another scream split the air. The Red Nun smiled.

"So . . . who are you, really?"

Drasilljah remained silent.

"You have a glamour about you," the Red Nun said mildly. "I think you have expended quite enough energy maintaining it, don't you?"

She smiled, and her left hand clutched a tiny cask pendant, while she gestured with her right. The air wavered as if with a heat shimmer, and Drasilljah's gray hair darkened to ochre, her wrinkled face filled in, and the shape beneath her dress developed curves and youthful heft.

The Red Nun laughed. "Well done. An old woman is better protection than a young one."

Drasilljah fumed without speaking.

"Good. Yes. You have spirit. That is good. I may yet find use for you."

"Never," the princess said.

Shyena grinned. "There are punishments. For disobedience. For incompetence. I cannot abide incompetence. Or insult. But resistance? I would expect nothing less from one of royal blood. But I believe that a demonstration is required. And this old-young woman of yours is the perfect canvas on which to paint my meaning."

Drasilljah moaned, and her hands flew to her face, covering her eyes. Crimson began oozing from between her fingers.

"You like blood magic, don't you?" Shyena purred. "I will show you what it really is."

Drasilljah slumped to the ground. The princess held her, sobbing. "Please. Stop. I'll do what you say. She is a druid. We've been together since we were children." Her voice broke. "She was only trying to protect me."

"And what were you trying to accomplish? No. No need to speak. Escape. But . . . why now? What motivated you?"

The princess knew she had to lie. "No one is coming to save us. No ransom. We made ourselves believe. We had to take control, or there was no hope at all."

"Yes," Shyena said. "Yes. No hope at all." Her gaze tracked from one of them to the other, and then she repeated more emphatically, "No hope at all."

She left them in each other's arms.

"I'm sorry. I'm so sorry," the princess said.

"I'm not," Drasilljah said between bloodied teeth. "We did what we had to do."

"How can she be so powerful? I thought such magic was gone from the world..."

"There are ways," Drasilljah said. "There are ways. And I think that she found them. And I think that if we cannot learn what she knows...we are going to die."

TWENTY-ONE

Jade

The gates of General Silith's palace opened for Aros and Neoloth and clanged shut behind them. The dwelling was fully half the size of the royal palace—an impressive mass of brick, iron, and glass.

Aros was dressed in his very best togs pilfered from Captain Gold's chest. "The invitation was a bit of a surprise," he said to the guard as they approached the front gate. "Are all military recruits asked to dine with the general?"

The soldier snapped to attention. "No, sir."

They walked on, through bushes trimmed into elephant shapes. "Sir?" Neoloth asked. "That augurs favorably."

"Doesn't it though."

They arrived at the front door. The doorman greeted them, took their assumed names, and then thunderously declared: "Announcing Kasha of the desert."

"And his manservant, Washelisk," Aros added.

He turned to the wizard, whose expression was suitably humble. Only a shift of his eyes suggested otherwise.

General Sinjin Silith met them in the hallway, striding toward them with the lazy confidence of a lion in his own lair.

"It is too kind of you to welcome us to your home."

General Sinjin Silith smiled. "Not at all. I was most impressed by your performance today. It is my belief that it is the personal relationships between a commander and his troops that make the difference in both war and peace."

"That sounds . . . promising."

The general slapped Aros on the shoulder. "Send your man to the kitchen. They will feed and care for him there. Giselle!"

A pretty maid appeared.

"Giselle, take this fellow," the general said. "Care for him."

"As you wish, sir."

Aros flicked his hand in the indicated direction. "Washelisk— you're in good hands."

Neoloth followed the maid's swaying hips as she sashayed out of the room.

"This way," the general said. With a touch on his elbow, General Silith guided Aros into a side chamber, where dozens of swords of different design, length, and culture were displayed in glass-fronted cases.

"War mementos?" Aros asked.

"Many of them. Others were gained by trade or were gifts. I don't have one like yours, however."

Aros's hand touched Flaygod, which hung low at his side. "No?"

"Would you care to sell it?"

"I won it in battle with one of my kinsmen," Aros said honestly. "He was a brave man, and I honor his death by carrying it. I would not dishonor him."

"A fine blade is won, not bought. Is that what you say?"

Aros shrugged.

"I can respect that. Of course, you can only win a sword if it fails its owner. Doesn't that bother you?"

"Flaygod did not fail its owner. Its owner failed Flaygod."

General Silith laughed and then led Aros through more of the house. As they walked, the general watched him carefully. "What do you think?"

"That this is a *man's* house."

The general's thin lips curled up at that answer. But Aros found he was shying away from dozens of expensive, fragile-seeming toys: ceramics, fabrics, little machines. Would an amnesiac prince feel so intimidated? He might.

They entered an expansive dining room, where Jade Silith awaited them at a surprisingly small and intimate table.

She rose as they entered. "Welcome. We decided to greet you in the personal dining room. There is another for guests and large gatherings. Do you mind?"

"This is wonderful." Aros gave a deep, formal bow. "You are being more than kind."

"Please be seated," the general said.

"Thank you."

Servants bustled about, serving. Aros enjoyed the food and wine. Jade glanced from Aros to the general, almost shyly. The general mouthed something to his wife that Aros couldn't decipher.

Aros stopped eating, looking from one of them to another and back again. After a moment the general began to eat, and then Jade, and then finally Aros followed suit.

"Please," Silith said. "Tell us more about yourself." Both Silith and his wife paused a moment, waiting for Aros to begin speaking.

"I've lived a variety of lives. But my earliest memories are of the Southern Desert people. Best I can guess, my parents died in the midst of some kind of journey, a pilgrimage perhaps. I was found by a kindly merchant and ultimately sold to the Chumash folk."

The general sliced his meat and lifted a chunk to his lips on a silver fork. "Sold by a merchant who left you a gold coin? Odd."

"Oh, yes. I've wondered. But I've no memory of any of it, so the trail is cold."

"No memory?"

"No. I'm told I had a head wound, and was in a fever when sold. I'm sure I was purchased at a bargain."

Jade laughed politely, then leaned forward. "The coin is Aztec. Did you travel there, try to find your parents or people?"

"Yes, once," he replied. "I was thought a spy and barely escaped with my life. I don't think I'm going to find many answers there."

He put his meat down. "You are Aztec," he said to the general's wife. "When did you leave?"

"Almost thirty years ago," she said. "I've not been back for two decades."

He nodded, chewing. "I think that the heart rippers have taken hold. It may not be the place you remember."

"There was a time when the sacrifice made the fields and

wombs fertile. And perhaps another time when the priests took that power for themselves. That would be a great pity. But I promise you: you come from a great people."

Aros grunted. "I did see the pyramids. I'm not sure I'd ever seen anything so wondrous. But . . . so much *death*."

Jade's smile was the sort she might have offered a child. "Death and birth are two sides of the same thing. Both have power."

"Please pardon me for saying, Madam Silith, but I'm sure that's easier to see from a palace than from the fields."

That quieted the table for a moment, and Aros began to worry if he had pushed too far.

But Jade spoke again. "What if you had come from the palace, Kasha? What if it had been your responsibility to be certain that everything flows smoothly, that order is maintained, that the people prosper. Could you have had the strength to stamp out a few individual grains, that the crop might flourish?"

"I don't know," he said. "I'm a simple man. I can only imagine that I came from simple folk. I live; I fight; one day I will die."

She set her fork down, looking stricken. "And that is all?"

"I don't know what more there is," he replied. "I am content."

"There is more than contentment in life. There is closeness. Hope. Ambition." She paused. "Family."

"I am happy for you that you have known such things. I come to offer my sword. Perhaps helping to protect your dream might make mine more of a reality."

"And what is your dream, Kasha?"

He considered. "I would find my own kingdom one day. A place to fight for, worth dying for. A woman to be my queen. Comrades to battle at my side." He sighed. "I have spent my entire life with no one to trust. It grows . . . weary."

"How old were you when you were sold?" the general asked.

He chewed. "I'm not sure. Not yet a man. Perhaps . . . fifteen summers. All I remember before that was following a wagon. Selling goods. Fighting bandits. A city, somewhere. Deserts. Little more."

Jade seemed to have forgotten her food. "No mother. No father. No love. Nothing but travail, all your life." She paused. "What must you think of a mother and father who would take you into such a situation? Or leave you in such?"

Aros chose his next words most carefully. "I think they were probably peddlers, doing the best they could. Died protecting me and would have done more if they could."

"You think they're dead?"

"Yes. Otherwise, I believe they never would have stopped looking for me. Never. I feel it in my heart. My mother loved me."

Jade stifled a sound. Aros pretended not to notice, silently calling himself a bastard. The general's face was as hard as a sack of walnuts.

"Do you . . . ," Jade Silith said, voice muffled, "remember anything of her at all?"

Aros scowled. "You'll laugh."

"No, we won't," she promised.

"Sometimes I have dreams. I dream of a woman who is very beautiful. Something like the image on the coin. The Aztec women are unmatched, and I would think that my mother was as beautiful as one of their princesses. I imagine that she tucked me into bed. Sang to me." He paused, then added, "Loved me."

He scowled some more, as if challenging them to mock him. The general was speechless.

"Anyway," he said, and stretched. "Enough of this talk. A warrior doesn't lose himself in thoughts of yesterday. Now is what matters, eh? Now, and tomorrow. And if now, right now, I can pledge my sword and help you make your tomorrow better, perhaps there is a place for me, hey?"

Jade looked at her husband imploringly.

"Yes," the general said slowly. "I think there is a place for a man like you. A man just like you."

"A future here?"

Silith nodded. "A future. You have sought a home. Shrike could be that home."

Aros sipped and then put his cup down. "I have told you of me. And my dreams. Would it be too much to ask you of yours?"

The general nodded. "I was a younger child of a minor wife of the last king of Shrike. I knew I had a destiny and that it was not waiting for a throne that would never be mine. So I roused an army and took it to the south, where I aided an Aztec king, Toutezequatyl, put down an uprising and incursion from his southern neighbors. Created the trade alliances we enjoy to this day and won my beautiful Jade as a wife. This was my beginning."

Aros toasted him. "That would be another man's lifetime career. And now you have wealth, and power, and position?"

"And hope of more."

Aros's left eyebrow arched. "More? You are a great man. The greatest swordsman I have ever seen. I was fortunate to taste your skill without dying. And of royal blood. And with a woman such as this at your side. And even a man like you . . . wants more."

"And?"

"And I would not be so foolish as to think I could understand the mind and heart of such a man upon so brief an acquaintance."

The general seemed pleased by that answer. "You have never had schooling?"

"Only what I could learn along the way."

"You will pardon me for saying," the general said, "but I have to wonder what you might have been, had you been given such preparation. Clearly, you . . . come of fine stock. Fine stock. Well. This is a portentous evening. You come at a time of great . . . potential, Kasha. This is what I say to you: train hard. Show us who you are. I would enjoy playing swords with you again."

"I would enjoy that, too," Aros said.

The general stood. "And now . . . I must bid you good evening. My wife and I have business to attend to."

Aros paused for a moment and then stood as well. "It has been my pleasure. General? Lady Jade? I bid you good evening."

He rose and left, the slightest of smiles on his face.

The general filled a flagon of wine and went to stand by the roaring fire. He looked into it, scowling.

"Oh, husband . . . ," she said, pulling at his arm.

"No."

"How can you say that? How can you doubt? That was the coin I gave him. The one with the picture of my mother on it. How did he come by it?"

"I don't know."

"He is the right age. He has my nose. He has your eyes. He has the tattoos! How can you doubt?"

The general snarled at her. "Any man can get a tattoo!"

"The coin?"

"I don't know, damn you! Damn it . . ." His massive fist struck the wall next to the window. The glass cracked.

"Husband," she whispered.

He held out a flat palm, pushing her away. "Leave me alone."

She ignored him, came closer. "What is it?"

"What he said," the general's voice was roughened by emotion.

"That his parents loved him. Would never have stopped looking for him."

"Sinjin . . ."

He turned and looked at his wife. "We should never have stopped looking for him. Never."

Aros and Neoloth headed away from the castle. Aros was swaggering just a bit.

"So . . . ?" Neoloth asked.

"I could get used to castle food. And maybe I will."

Neoloth said, "They fed me well enough, too. The general eats mostly meat; his wife likes bread and vegetables and honey flavors, according to the head cook. Both like chilies. They were slow to talk, so I told them stories and listened to their remarks. They wanted to know about you."

"You held to our tale?"

"I embellished a bit. You get seasick. When drinking you turn harsh to your servants—but I left out details, so they may think that's just me. They started to tell me of a servant the general killed but stopped each other. Truly, I learned little. You?"

"I think I'm hired. As for finding my parents, maybe."

Neoloth smiled.

TWENTY-TWO

Lord Kang

It seemed to Aros that the sun had been beating down on them from directly overhead since dawn, and the orb deliberately and maliciously refused to set. Through the running, fighting, wrestling, archery—all of it—he was glad that it was still not as fierce an orb as that which blazed in southern lands.

In the distance, behind a wall sectioning off another part of the grounds, came explosions, varying between deep and low or sharp and fast. With them came cheers and laughter from the men who were preparing themselves, practicing with tools Aros had never dreamed of and seen only in flashes.

Despite his growing relationship with the general, there were places he was not as yet welcome. Sights that were not for his eyes. What were these strange devices? From whence had they appeared? He didn't know but reckoned that the answers were behind the wall that sealed the mountain pass behind the castle. Before this affair was over, he intended to see what was behind the wall.

He wasn't certain he would survive the experience.

Despite the fact that it had been a hard day, the men had been buzzing for the last hour with the notion that the king himself was due to inspect the troops. His Majesty was rarely seen outside the castle anymore, and it was a cause of speculation.

There was a disturbance at the gate to the training ground, and a line of horses entered. In the midst were two huge men, bodyguards no doubt, flanking an aged man in silvered armor, his gray-streaked beard flagging. For all his years, the man seemed to Aros an odd combination of alert and somehow intoxicated. He sat horse beautifully, like someone trained from infancy, but swayed a bit out of rhythm with the jouncing.

Odd.

The general rode out to meet the king, bowing from horseback. "Your Majesty honors us."

Silith received the faintest of royal smiles in return. "Well, General—you will be leading our forces out for another border skirmish." He leaned closer to the general. "I believe you will be using your fascinating toys against these mountain people. Is that right?"

"Yes, Your Majesty."

"Oh my, would that I could accompany you!" He stroked his beard, combing it with his fingers. "You know, when I was a lad, my father sent me out on patrol with his troops. He thought it would be good for my character."

"I'd say he was a wise and prudent man, Your Majesty."

"Ah! Weeks in the saddle, under the sun! The adventure, and the . . . the . . ." He suddenly grew vague, as if struggling to remember where he was or what he was doing there.

"Your Majesty," the general whispered. "You wish to inspect the troops."

The king's withered forefinger lanced into the air. "The troops! Yes!"

"Troops! Gather in formation!"

The men, tired as they might have been, ran to take formation and stood at attention.

"A fine body of men, General," the king said vaguely. "And these are the new soldiers?"

"Yes, Sire."

The king waved his hand in their general direction, as if in a half-remembered ritual. "Well. You are all members of the royal army of Shrike. Be proud! Fight well! We depend upon you."

The men gave a rather unconvincing cheer, glancing at one another with shared doubt.

The king rode past them, nodding as if conferring blessing.

The general directed his attention toward Aros. "And . . . this man, Sire."

The king managed to focus on the Aztec, for a moment genuinely interested. "And who might he be?"

"He is Kasha, of the Southern Desert," the general said.

"A dusky rogue, isn't he?" He smiled. "Well, we must make allowances mustn't we?" His smile grew sly. "They make handsome women, hey? I hear that they'll do—"

"My wife is Aztec, Your Majesty." Silith's expression was unchanged, but his voice had tightened.

"Oh, well then. You already know that." The king changed tacks and subjects as if his brain was on a pivot. He turned to Aros. "Why came you here, sir?"

Aros snapped to stricter attention. "To serve Your Majesty. To kill his enemies and protect the realm!"

King Corinth nodded happy agreement. "Well spoken, sir! Oh! Very good, very good."

The general leaned closer to the king's ear. "I recommend this man for a commission."

"Do you now? Oh. That is unusual. Blooded is he?"

The general shook his head. "Not yet. But I have reason to believe he has great potential."

The king examined Aros from forehead to fetlock, noting every curve of muscle and bone as if examining livestock. "Well . . . bring him back to me after he has distinguished himself in the killing." He laughed, a sound that threatened to turn into a giggle. "After all, what good is a killer who has not killed, eh? Eh?"

Aros inclined his head. "I've killed, Your Majesty, but not in your service."

King Corinth nodded and wheeled his horse around. As he passed Silith, he quietly said, "Queen's pawn takes pawn."

"Castle," the general replied. The king squinted, then continued on.

The general watched as the king rode stiffly away. When he was beyond earshot, the general said, "Our glorious monarch."

"There are questions," Aros said, "it is probably best not to ask."

The general met his eyes squarely. "My wife is correct. There *is* a mind in there."

"Opinions vary," Aros said.

The general chuckled. "Well. You will have your opportunity to test your mettle soon. *Too* soon if you don't train hard. See that you do."

"Yes, General."

"Kasha," he said. "You are intelligent enough to know that you have attracted my attention. Mine . . . and my wife's."

"Yes, sir." He paused, suddenly uncomfortable. Could Jade have recounted his rather rude conversational gambit to her husband? "I hope you don't think . . ."

The general waved Aros's troubling thought away. "Jade and I have known each other for a great many years. I hope you are not suggesting that she might be disloyal to my bed."

"Sir. No sir," the Aztec stuttered.

The general glared at him and then roared with laughter. "I'm long past the phase of life concerned with petty jealousy. But even were I not, my wife has never given me the slightest reason for concern."

Aros felt huge relief. "I'm sure, sir."

"This is an opportunity, not a gift. Nothing is foredestined here. You are merely being given an opportunity to demonstrate your capacities. Do not presume."

"No, sir."

"But make no mistake . . . for the right man . . . this is indeed the right time. Are you the right man?"

"I prefer actions to conjecture."

The general smiled. "The right man would indeed speak thus. Carry on."

Aros felt troubled indeed as the general rode away. *What's the matter with me?* he thought. Something about that man disturbed him. Much to his surprise, he found that he actually liked the general.

And that might prove troublesome.

The shadows fell long and sharp across the kingdom of Shrike, and although there was no obvious reason to do so, it seemed that the citizens fled indoors with the sinking of the sun.

Neoloth was uncertain whether this was a good or bad thing, whether he was disadvantaged by the lack of crowds to blend into or comforted by the lack of prying eyes to follow him.

He was at the easternmost edge of the kingdom, had worked his way behind the castle and royal grounds to where the Great Wall sealed off the mountain gap, protecting whatever secrets lay beyond.

"They'll put guards in the mountain passes," he whispered to himself. "I could approach from the rear by circling around a hundred miles, but..." But, in short, he had no taste for that.

Footsteps signaled approaching strangers, potential risk. He pushed himself back into shadow as three men approached and entered a different shadow. One was small and somewhat effete; one, hulking; and one, furtive as a rat in a kitchen.

The furtive one began examining the wall. Searching for something in the brick and wood lattice. "What have we here?" Neoloth whispered. "Others upon the same mission?"

Gliding from shadow to shadow, using techniques learned partly from Agathodaemon, he approached close enough to overhear their conversation.

"You swear," said the delicate one, "that no one knows of this?"

"Indeed, Your Highness," the rodential one replied. "You may trust the triple S."

"What is that?"

"We have a saying: 'In Shrike, silver buys silence.'"

A purse changed hands. The slender one spoke imperiously. "And if you betray me, gold guarantees a grave. I need to see what the general has done with the freedom and riches the king has offered. And also . . ."

"Yes, m'lord?"

"I wish to see this fabulous workshop that has produced so many miracles. The riding machines. The hand cannons. The dragon mouths that vomit fire. I cannot explain these things and wish to understand."

"Chron wants to see, too," the enormous man at his side said.

"As you wish, Lord Kang," Rat Face said, "but I believe the answers wait within."

The little group tapped their way along the wall. One tap yielded a slightly different sound, and the lackey perked up. "Here! Here sir. This is the doorway I spoke of. The builders constructed it as a safeguard."

"Against what?" Lord Kang, the man with the money, said.

"Trust is scarce in Shrike, sir. In case the wall was used to confine the builders themselves."

He performed some manipulations, and a section of the wall opened before them. Beveled edges, a thick door no higher than a normal man. Neoloth could see nothing but dimness beyond. Rat Man darted through. Money Man strolled. The big man had to stoop to get through, and then the wall closed.

Neoloth crept up into the shadow that had consumed them. Carefully, he tested various pressures and taps against the wall until he found a plate that provided a different sound. He pushed, and it yielded, and then sprang back.

All right, then that hadn't been the method. What had Rat

Man done? He pushed and then slid the slab a few inches to the side and felt a latch come undone.

Now it opened.

"Ingenious," he murmured, and entered.

The tunnel was cooler than the outside air, as if the rock itself had absorbed the day's heat. It was perhaps twenty feet long, narrow and sufficiently low-ceilinged to force him to crouch. By the time he was out the other side, his back was beginning to ache.

Very carefully, he pushed at the slab of rock that sealed the far end, and for a horrible moment was certain that he had been mousetrapped, caught in this trap, he and Aros had—

The door opened. He was able to peek out and see that the three men had almost disappeared across a narrow courtyard into a series of low buildings, barracks perhaps. A nicely maintained road ran through and beyond the buildings, into a single yellow light that didn't flicker. Magic? The glow outlined the rough stone surfaces of a cavern's mouth and, dimly, the road.

First, his quarry. As soon as they were swallowed by rectangular shadows, Neoloth followed. He caught up just in time to hear the tail end of their conversation. "What is this?" Lord Kang was saying.

"I know only that guards and slaves are quartered here."

That wide, straight path began between the apparent barracks buildings and ran into the mountain, through thickly spaced trees and into the yellow glare. Neoloth moved from shadow to shadow, pausing each time to listen for sounds: breathing, footsteps, anything. By the time he left the shadow of the last barracks, he was certain of two things: no one was following him, but someone was indeed following the nobleman. Someone large, who moved very well.

Still, he was able to get close enough to hear, knowing that he was witnessing a personal disaster in the making. This . . . was not going to be pretty.

He could guess why the wall had been built: not just to keep people out, but to keep them from seeing . . . this. The lighted cavern was irresistible: nobody could see that and turn away and return home. The three he followed were on their bellies, hidden in the shadow of the cavern wall, creeping toward . . . a big angular building just outside the cavern on the left.

What he could see inside the cavern mouth was just a handful of tents and a scattering of . . . hmm? Some of these carelessly piled items looked like what he'd been seeing in town: two-wheelers, fire tubes—and some looked like a great deal of fishermen's net. And some was just weird.

Neoloth-Pteor removed his talisman from the pouch at his back and held it toward the structure. It tingled, more powerfully than it had in the desert lands. There was magic here, more than should exist in this age, but tightly focused. Now he turned his talisman into the cavern itself and felt . . . nothing.

He crept closer, entranced.

The nobleman and his giant bodyguard Chron were entranced as well, so focused on the angular building that they didn't notice the man coming up behind them. Neoloth saw him, though, and fell back into the cloaking darkness.

"There—what in God's name is that?"

The lackey seemed genuinely shocked. "I do not know. When last I came here, it wasn't there."

They followed the shadow, followed stealthily by a single figure. Neoloth followed *him*. As they grew closer, Neoloth could hear terrible, low moans. Not the screams and cries themselves, but as if the screams themselves were being siphoned away, leaving the undertones only.

His bones bled at the sound.

The air stank of torn flesh and burning metal.

Lord Kang shuddered. "What in the name of . . ."

The lackey shrank back; courage fled. "Sir, I don't believe this is safe. I don't think we should be here."

"If you want the rest of your wages . . . ," Kang began.

The lackey shrugged off the hand on his shoulder. "Of what use is silver or gold if I can't survive to spend it!"

A snarl: "Then go back! I go on. Chron will protect me." The big man flexed his shoulders. "Go, coward."

"Go on, then. Good luck to you, sir! Good luck!"

And he turned back. Neoloth melted into the tree line as the man scrambled past. And scrambled past the other figure. He heard an "urk" below him and looked down with his dark-adjusted eyes to see two men grab the rat, take him silently to the ground.

Had he, Neoloth, been seen?

It was too late: he was committed now. No way out but up.

He heard a thin scream, a voice. A foreign voice, speaking some barbaric tongue. Mayan? The desert people? A plea. A throat-shredding shriek of agony.

And then . . . silence. And then the hiss of a machine. More moaning and pleading.

Lord Kang hunched low, paralyzed by that scream. His hulking bodyguard was on the dirt . . . but Neoloth saw him rise up and peer into a window too high for a normal man. Lord Kang spoke. The big man spoke. Panicky whispers too low to be heard.

And then . . . the other shadow moved in on him.

The massive Chron whirled and lunged, and there was a moment when it seemed that the smaller shadow would be cloven in twain. There was no apparent move to block. But the cleaving sword missed. Just . . . missed.

The answering thrust did not. Chron sagged and wrapped himself around himself, and Lord Kang squealed, backing away.

The other man stepped out of the shadow. Of course it was the general. Neoloth felt uneasy: he had just witnessed magic of a kind. This man was more dangerous than he had anticipated.

"Unhand me!"

"Lord Kang." Those were Silith's deep, cool tones. "How good to see you."

Kang struggled to no effect, a mouse in the claws of a cat. "You have no right . . ."

"To satisfy your curiosity about our little venture? I had assumed this is why you came. Am I mistaken?"

Kang's desperation was wrenching. What had the man seen? "I . . . I . . . I've changed my mind."

"No, no. Please. Allow me. You have expended such great efforts already. Never mind what's happening in the Octagon. That's of no interest. But what you're about to see is beyond even *my* guessing."

Now the general pushed him toward the cavern. Kang's fingernails scraped at the Octagon wall, and he howled for help, screamed for assistance, but there was none. He looked back at the gashed corpse of his bodyguard with total, paralyzing terror.

Neoloth watched General Silith lead Kang into the cavern until he had passed under the great yellow light. After that, they were difficult to see.

He had a suicidal, almost irresistible urge to see what was happening in the odd building. Not the cavern, not yet, but what had the big man seen just before he died? It required all his self-control to back up, flowing from shadow to shadow, aware that he was in terrible danger without knowing the precise nature of it.

He made it down to the barracks buildings. Everything seemed abandoned . . . then he heard voices and footsteps: approaching soldiers.

He backed into a shadow and put his hand on the talisman. A small jolt might well give him the camouflage he needed to—

Then a hand reached out from behind him, covering his mouth to prevent a scream, and hauled him back and into darkness.

TWENTY-THREE

Shyena

C ome with me," a woman's voice said, and to his amazement, Neoloth recognized it at once.

Shyena, the Red Nun. He had seen her at the race, near the docks. And now she was saving him.

What was her game?

They were both silent as she led him away from the Octagon, through a network of shadows and two secret doors, and to a flat, dark building, quite unprepossessing. Once they were through the door, he was dazzled by the opulent draperies and furnishings.

She took him down a side hall and through another door, and then they were in her private quarters.

Shyena threw her hood back, revealing the beautiful, angular features he had seen through the tricky spyglass.

The Red Nun lit a candle, then doffed her cloak. Finally, she spoke. "So. I was correct. It is Neoloth-Pteor. I thought so. Was puzzled only by the way you followed that barbarian around like a lap dog. What is your interest here?"

"Interest?" he asked.

"Do not seek to play me for a fool. Don't you realize that I can raise my voice and you will be torn apart?"

He smiled without humor. "And why don't you?"

"Perhaps I will."

He studied her. "No, I don't think so."

She slid around the table toward him, approaching more directly. The air in the room shifted, and suddenly he caught her scent. It was not entirely perfume, or soap.

"You think my memory of your skills in the boudoir will silence my tongue? That perhaps I will find better use for it than betrayal?"

Shyena's face was very close.

"No," Neoloth said.

When she spoke again, her voice was extraordinarily intimate. "What, then?"

"I think you need to know who I have told of you. And what my intentions are, and whether they conflict with yours."

She smiled, pleased by his acumen. "You have lost nothing of your vision, wizard. Come. Drink with me."

Neoloth looked at the wine flagons, suspicious.

Shyena laughed. "You may choose the flagon," she said. "You may choose the wine bottle. And remember—killing you accomplishes nothing if you have spoken of me in the wrong quarters."

"That . . . is truth," Neoloth said. "We are equally exposed, I think."

He poured both glasses, and they sat on the divan, eyeing each other. "You were waiting for me."

"Yes."

"You've known I was here for quite a while."

"Yes. Since the sail race."

"I saw you," he said.

She smiled. "I felt you see me."

He shook his head. "Proximity sense?"

"Attention sense," Shyena replied.

"I . . . never saw that in you."

"I know how to keep my secrets," she said. "Knowing when someone is focused on me has kept me alive and helped me rise here."

"I'm sure," he said. "So this is your place, and these are your people. And this is your work."

The Red Nun narrowed her eyes. "Are you judging me?"

Neoloth paused. A tense moment. He gestured to the east. "Necromancy."

"Yes."

"You are doing something to create these strange machines."

She shook her head, but smiled.

"Something. Not creating. But . . . obtaining?"

She nodded.

"From another land. From the spirit realm . . . They are made in fairy workshops."

Her smile was only a faint curl . . . but told him he was on the wrong track. "You lack imagination."

He pondered.

"They are not of this land. But not of another land. They are not made by fairies, or spirits, but by men. But not our men. You like riddles?"

He frowned and then stared at her.

Then took a deep breath and tried again. "What could be done with unlimited mana, gained by slaughtering men, women, and children—"

The Red Nun recoiled, raising a hand, her long sharpened fingernails like claws. "No! Not children. I have limited influence with the Ten, but was able to confine them to prisoners of war and adult slaves. No children."

When Shyena next looked at him, her eyes blazed. He couldn't look away.

"You, above all others, should know me better than that."

"So . . . you have not forgotten?"

"Who could?" she said, allowing her voice and face to soften. "How could you even wonder?"

"And with that memory burning bright, as bright as the houses aflame, you serve the man who killed your family?"

She glared at him.

"No," he said. "And that is why you did not betray me."

"And you. Following that ignorant barbarian like a dog. Pretending to be a servant. You serve the queen of Quillia."

"How do you know this?"

She smiled again. "The Ten has their own secrets and sources."

"So," Neoloth said. "You know."

She nodded. "Yours is a mission of rescue."

"And yours," he said, "one of vengeance."

"You think you know revenge? Did you ever have anyone you cared about, Neoloth? Ever? I had everything taken from me, by the very man who now seeks the power to rule the world. I will bring him low; I swear it. And if you will help me . . . I will help you."

"And if I don't? Or can't?"

Her eyes were blazing cold. "Do not stand between me and my vengeance. I swear that if you do, I will destroy you."

Neoloth nodded. "We are both vulnerable here. We each have secrets. My goals do not conflict with yours . . . even if they are not in alignment."

"You seek the princess. I need her to complete our spell."

"And I cannot let you destroy or corrupt her."

The Red Nun matched him stare for stare. "Then we are at an impasse. Each of us can destroy the other. Neither of us will help the other. We do not trust. I don't know what you want here, but, whatever your purpose, you have made a mistake."

Neoloth's mind buzzed. This moment could totally make or break his entire mission. Finally, he spoke. "What if there was a way?"

Her expression was guarded. "To what?"

"For us to trust each other. To know each other's mind."

Now, for the first time, her expression seemed . . . pleased. "You don't mean . . ."

"The Yellow Rose. Yes."

Her posture changed. Became some odd mixture of tart and priestess. Her smile was cynical. "I thought you were in love."

"Love is love," he said. "Business is business."

TWENTY-FOUR

The Yellow Rose

The candles were freshly lit, incense curling from the scented sticks to ghost-dance around the shadowed room. They had drawn a magical circle on the floor, candles burning, and she mounted him in seated position, tightly intertwined. They gazed deeply into each other's eyes, timing their breaths to synchronize with each other.

At first it was just penetration and envelopment, but then they began to experience a variety of powerful shifts, the room around them melting, and Neoloth saw the girl within the woman.

He saw things, memories from her past: The village that burned. The lost parents. The vow of vengeance. Becoming a courtesan. The day she became the mistress of a great wizard, where first she met Neoloth. And, finally, her ceremony of Becoming, when she stepped into her power and joined the Thousand. One focused decision at a time, working her way up to being one of the Ten.

His mind exploded with her memories.

The sun was just shining through the window as the two of them lay sprawled on the beam floor, their bodies intertwined.

Shyena's breath was wine and honey. "You . . . ," she began, but could not complete the thought. "That was magic."

He chuckled, low in his throat. "We are magicians, after all."

More chuckling from both. Then she grew more serious. "So," she said. "You do love her."

"Yes, I do."

"And you are willing to die in your quest."

He hesitated, then answered. "Yes." And was surprised to realize that he meant it.

"My silence is as yours, things being equal . . . which of course they never are." Her smile was wan, and her naked hips withdrew an inch. "We interfere not with each other's plans. But I need more, because your interests are directly opposed to mine . . . unless you have something to add."

"I'm still trying to believe . . . the cavern . . . we never knew any of that, ever. Let me think." He thought, while she watched his face. "If I have the princess . . . it weakens your plans."

"Unless?"

"Unless there is a way that a living princess advantages you."

"And how might that be?"

"If the Thousand, or their leaders the Ten, accomplish their aims, this world changes. Magic becomes a shadow. In that world, what have you really won?"

She thought. "Power. Revenge."

"What if you could have all three? Power, revenge . . . *and* magic?"

She frowned. "How?"

"If the general dies, you have your revenge. Need you kill him yourself?" He thought he saw a touch of hunger in her eyes.

"I thought to, as there is no one I trust enough to have engaged as an assassin."

He smiled. "I may have just the man. And if he dies and the princess disappears . . . what then?"

"When the truth is learned? War between Quillia and Shrike?"

"And?"

"Shrike will use its new weapons and win."

"Unless the other seven kingdoms rise against her," Neoloth said.

"And Shrike will be destroyed, at great cost to the kingdoms." Her face darkened. "There is no joy in that thought. Most of the dead are blameless."

"Unless . . ." He paused, feeling the tension. "Unless the princess was found to have been captured by bandits and returned by Shrike."

The breath caught in Shyena's throat. "Even if you agreed to such a thing, how could we be certain the princess herself would. She knows where she is. And who has her. Make no mistake."

Neoloth felt more confidence now. He had her. "It is in the princess's interests to see peace. If the cavern were destroyed or blocked and the general destroyed . . . where then does that leave you?"

"In a power vacuum," she mused. "In need of allies." She raised an eyebrow in implied question.

"While I will be the consort of the next queen of Quillia, a man deep in your debt. I wish to live my life in peace, would have no reason to betray an ally. In fact...I believe that you would find me, and the princess, to be extraordinarily grateful to you."

The distance between them vanished in warmth and softness. "Would you, now?"

"You came to Shrike seeking vengeance and power."

She nodded.

"I can provide both—not in the form you sought, but in a manner that should satisfy your appetites. The general dead. The Ten vanquished. A power vacuum. The gratitude of the greatest kingdom of the Eight in support of your ambitions. What poor magic remains in this world would still be the most powerful force."

"I can be certain of this, precisely how?"

They smiled at each other. Neoloth felt his loins tingling again. Magic was a wonderful thing. "Our first ceremony brought us close enough to dream. It seems another may be needed to complete the deal."

"The princess for the general. Your assassin, my knowledge. We...share. You and I, Neoloth...we are two of a kind. It is a shame..."

"Yes. But we have this moment. And any moment, lived deeply enough, is all the time that there is..."

As their bodies cooled again, Neoloth rolled onto his back, sighing. "Under what circumstances can I trust you?"

"Only those in which I may have my revenge. Stand in my way, and I will destroy you, even at the cost of my own life."

Neoloth smiled. "But destroying yourself will prevent you from accomplishing your aims."

"But my willingness to die is the only thing that will neutralize you, my old lover."

"What if there was another way. Another way to destroy him."

"And his aims. The Ten have opened the door to the future."

Neoloth nodded. "I *never* saw that coming."

The Red Nun seemed thoughtful. "They cannot see that, in time, what they do will destroy them. They see only the power that can be gained now, not what our descendants will lose if magic is no longer primary in the world."

"So . . . ," Neoloth asked, "if the general *and* the tunnels were destroyed . . . you would not mourn."

"With you, I might survive this." She fidgeted, and he intuited that they were closer to some truth. "And that is not something I had dreamed of. I thought to die with him."

She turned on her side and softly began to cry.

"Why do you cry?" Neoloth asked, gently.

"When we joined, I saw," she said.

"What did you see?"

"You speak the truth. You are willing to die for her. You . . . love her."

"Yes," Neoloth admitted. "Yes, I do. Why do you cry?"

"Because we could do this. You and I. A man like you. Willing to do what you have been willing to do for your love."

"And the power, Shyena," he said. "Please, don't paint me as a saint."

She smiled at him wanly. "So wise. So foolish."

He flinched. "What do you mean?"

"I saw into your heart, Neoloth. I know what you are afraid to say to yourself."

She rolled over and caressed his face. "I will be damned. You are a good man, after all. But can a good man sacrifice a friend?"

"Aros is not my friend."

"Then what is he to you?"

Neoloth considered. "I suppose that as long as he keeps his word and does as he has agreed . . . he is an ally."

"So . . . you will task him with killing the general. And if he refuses?"

"Why would he?"

Her expression hardened. "I must *know* he will."

Neoloth's eyebrows drew together. "It is important?"

"More than you know," she said.

"Then I promise you, I will convince him," Neoloth swore. "But . . . why is it so urgent?"

"Because if I can't trust you, your man is dead."

"Dead?" Neoloth asked. "When?"

"I would say three days from now," the Red Nun said.

"What are you saying?"

"The general dies in three days, and Aros with him."

Neoloth frowned. "Ah. You set up a game?"

She tensed, considering, and then sighed. "The Ten," she said. "He grows too powerful. When he takes the kingdom, he will turn on us. So . . . now that he has served his function, we have arranged an . . . incident."

"Where is he now? I saw him only hours ago."

"But with the dawn, he took his men on patrol. By now, long gone. He and all with him will die. Including your ally. Would that disturb you?"

He thought of the abuse he had suffered at Aros's hands . . .

but also that the man had kept his word and displayed considerable wit, nerve, and . . . even charm.

"Yes," Neoloth said, amazed to hear the words from his mouth. "I would be disturbed."

"I understand. Well . . . if I can trust you, if you promise that the general will die . . . I will tell you how to save your man and help you free your precious princess."

TWENTY-FIVE

Bad Ground

For three days the column of soldiers and tarp-covered, horse-drawn wagons had raised dust through the mountain trails and now along the plains beyond.

General Silith clenched his teeth and whistled, drawing the attention of an officer. "Keep them steady."

"Yes, sir," the man replied.

The general rode back in the column to where Aros rode. The Aztec's long black hair swayed as he looked side to side, alert.

"What do you think?"

"I think," Aros said, "that we are in enemy territory."

The general chuckled. "And why do you think this?"

Aros gestured behind them. "I saw a burned wagon and simple graves. Someone buried someone quickly, then moved on."

"Hmmm. And what does that say to you?"

"An ambush," Aros said. "But the attackers were not strong . . . just deadly."

"And why do you say that?"

"Because they left someone behind alive enough to bury the dead."

The general roared with laughter. "An interesting mind. Keep it active."

"Yes, sir."

The general rode off, galloping like a centaur. Aros watched him, again feeling more genuine admiration than seemed appropriate . . . or comfortable.

That night, as the previous three nights, the men were camped beneath the stars. Sentries posted. Aros sat at the campfire with some of the other men, laughing, drinking, and joking.

"—so I told her: then don't do that with your legs, if they weren't made to bend that way!"

The men erupted with laughter.

Aros laughed as loudly as any of them and added his own bawdy embellishments to the story. Sergeant Fflogs approached.

"Kasha!" Fflogs said. "You are on watch. Eyes worn open. The cost for falling asleep on watch in a war zone is death."

Aros watched the man's nostrils flare, recognizing, not for the first time, that there was real anger and personal animus on display. He concealed his amusement. "I suppose I'll just have to stay awake."

"See that you do." Fflogs paused. "I can't imagine why, but the general has taken an interest in you."

"He's a great man."

"That he is." The sergeant gazed up at the sun, a red ball heading for the horizon. "See that you don't abuse it. It won't save you, you know. He's had favorites before."

"I don't need saving," Aros said.

The sergeant's heavy lips curled in a smile. Not a pleasant expression. "We all need a little saving, from time to time."

The sergeant stalked away.

Aros looked out over the mountainous territory around them. The night was chilly. He heard footsteps approaching and recognized them without turning. "Making rounds, General?"

"Yes. Also remembering what you said about the small raiding party. That could be true. Or it could be a deliberate misdirection. Or nothing at all."

Aros chuckled. "A suspicious man."

"One of the reasons," the general said, "that I'm still alive. What have you seen?"

Aros shrugged. "Nothing alarming. Quiet."

"Isn't this the moment when you say, 'Too quiet'?"

They laughed. It felt good.

"No. Glad for the quiet. Be happy to crawl back into my bedroll in three hours."

The general grunted, looked up at the moon. It was bloody. "One good thing about a general patrol is that we can get more sleep."

Aros managed to bow while seated. "For which I am grateful. General?"

"Yes?"

"Surely you do not need to be out here with us on a standard patrol."

"This border has been disputed for generations. There has been some activity here lately. I think to acquire . . . prisoners."

That caught the Aztec's attention. "For interrogation? As slaves?"

"Yes," the general said.

There was a *keep your nose out of this* quality to the single syllable, a sharpness that had been lacking from previous conversation. Aros nodded.

"I don't mean to question you, sir. Just wondering . . ."

"Why do I do what I do?"

Aros nodded. "Yes."

A metallic laugh in return. "Why do you do what *you* do?"

"To survive," he said. "And find entertainment, sometimes. Is there more?"

"Survival is for animals. Men were meant to lead or follow a leader."

Aros nodded. "It is what men do."

There was silence between the two of them for a few moments, companionable and deep. Then the general placed his hands upon his thighs and levered himself heavily to his feet. "Stay alert."

And the general continued on his rounds.

For three days, through spell and trance, Neoloth had struggled to reach Aros. But even as he did, he wasn't certain what his purpose should be.

"What would you do, barbarian, were you in my place?" he whispered. "Would you betray me? Damn you. I know what you would say: that what I do is not the issue. It is who you have committed to being. And so . . . although I know you are waiting for a chance to betray me."

For two days he had attempted lesser spells. But if the Red Nun's information was accurate, he was running out of time. Aros was running out of time. And, ultimately, the question was not, What would Aros do? The question was, What would he, Neoloth, do?

What would a man worthy of marrying a princess do?

He created another circle, then cradled the talisman in his hands. It buzzed, crackling with energy. He slipped into sleep again.

Aros slept. It was three o'clock in the morning. His eyes snapped open. He looked both ways, startled, the remnants of an evil dream slipping away like an oil slick. Something was very wrong.

No sound outside him save the usual night murmurings. But . . . that sense that there was danger could not be removed. He rolled out of his blanket and strapped on his sword.

He headed to the perimeter, drawing the attention of the guard. "Who goes there?"

"Kasha, second company."

"Advance and be recognized." He relaxed when he saw the familiar face. "Ah, it is you, Aztec."

"What is to be seen?"

"Nothing."

The rain was falling lightly. The night was very dark. "Nothing is out there."

"Nothing."

"Nothing," Aros repeated doubtfully. "Where is the sergeant's tent?"

"You would do well not to awaken him," the guard said.

"And you," Aros replied, "would do well to remain on guard."

He peered out into the night. The damned clouds blocked stars and moon. He hurried to the sergeant.

Fflogs was snoring like a sick bear. Aros shook him. "Wake up, damn it."

The sergeant groaned and then snapped up to sitting. "What the hell do you want? What time is it?"

"Time to get your sword."

"What? Is it an attack?" A moment of respect and concern amid the disdain.

"I think so, yes."

Fflogs shook his head. "You think? Are you suffering from nerves?"

"We are going to be attacked," Aros said, as positively as he could manage.

"We are *going* to be? Are you a coward?" He groaned and rolled over. "Let me sleep, damn it."

"Sergeant, you should wake."

"And I don't know what kind of game you're playing with the general, but let him sleep."

"What if I'm right?" Aros asked.

Fflogs groaned and peered back over his shoulder. "I'd be more concerned about what happens if you're wrong."

"You aren't me."

"Your funeral," the sergeant said.

And without further words, Aros headed to General Silith's tent.

The general made no sound at all as he slept. Aros stood well back. "General Silith. I need to speak with you."

"Who?"

"It is Kasha."

Silith rose to hands and knees, and then stood. "What is the hour?"

"The hour of our death, if we aren't careful."

"We are under attack?"

"Unless you city folk use a different word, yes."

The general buckled on his sword. "And if you are wrong?"

"You would punish one who seeks to keep you alive?"

Silith grinned. "Are you a gambling man?"

"If the wager is right."

The general nodded. "If you're right . . . you live, and get your promotion."

"And if I lose? If there is no attack?"

The general looked at the weapon at Aros's side. Flaygod. "Your sword."

"Excuse me?"

"I want your sword for my wall. I'd rather not kill you for it. Don't worry. I'll find you a perfectly good Shrike blade."

"Agreed."

The general clambered out.

The sky was dark with rain clouds. There was no moon overhead. When they reached Sergeant Fflogs, he was leaning back against a boulder, drowsing, but not asleep.

Fflogs jerked himself awake. "General!"

"As you were," Silith growled. "What's the word?"

"Nothing, sir."

Aros faced the breeze, turned slowly, and then looked back out into the rain. He himself was uncertain of the source of his intuition. Only that it was overwhelmingly powerful. He decided on a partial lie. "I smelled something."

The general seemed doubtful. "You . . . smell something? In the rain?"

"Smelled. Earlier. Before the rain started."

"Explain."

Aros's brows furrowed. "I've smelled something like it before."

"And when was this?"

"The Southern Desert. There had been a series of wars with the Mayans come north, seeking empire."

The General frowned. "The Mayans smelled in this way?"

"No," Aros said. "They smelled like men. But the plain where we met had seen blood before, many times. So much death . . . so many dead men, over generations. Something came and started . . . feeding."

The general stared at him.

"The animals got used to it. Eating us. And not just animals. Cannibals who lived in the mountains above the plain. Most times, they hunted in the mountain, but after a battle they came down and carried away the dead. We hunted them once, found the salted flesh of our comrades. Wiped them out, such as we could find."

"Gods!"

"No gods. Not in that damned place. But what I remember most was the smell. And what a man eats comes out in his sweat. In his shit. You can smell it."

"Is that right?"

Aros said, "You said that many battles have been fought here. For generations. What is under this ground?"

The general's eyes widened. "Caves. I think . . . Corporal! Lanterns!"

Aros didn't know the word. He didn't know the reality either. Lights sprang up among the men, and they didn't flicker. They weren't afire.

The weird torches cast their glow out into the rain. They could see nothing out across the desert, but men roused each other and armed themselves.

"Sir?" Sergeant Fflogs said. "You believe this?"

"I believe that the cost if he's right is more than the cost of losing a bit of sleep," Silith replied.

The strange light of the box torches projected out into the rain but, despite their magic, was conquered by the rain. Then . . . lightning. And in the crackle of lightning Aros saw something that froze his blood. Hundreds of crawling *things* swarming out of tunnels in the ground. Humping across the plain toward them.

Once, Aros had broken open a log infested with termites. Had been repelled by the pale, pasty little things squirming to evade the light. If those things had been increased in size until they rivaled men and been given two legs and two arms and heads with sightless milky eyes, they might have resembled the horde coming for them.

To his credit, the general didn't miss a moment. "On your marks! Prepare the cannon!"

The men responded at once. They threw tarps off the devices they had been hauling. Tubes as long as canoes, mounted on wagons.

Before they could get everything in place, an ungodly howl rose from all around them.

"Sir!" Sergeant Fflogs screamed against the wind. "We don't have time!"

"If we don't have time, then we'll have blood. On your guard!"

The first wave hit their lines, and the battle began. Aros wielded a sword like a demon; the general fought beside him. "Too many of them!"

The grubs carried swords made of bone—but harder and

stronger, like bones dipped in steel—and spears, also made of bone. They were dressed in human skins, explaining the resemblance to men. Beneath those skins was flesh more alien, and coming to the distance for sword strokes just made it clearer that the soldiers were not fighting cannibals. Cannibals eat the flesh of their own species. These things had never been men at all.

Aros perceived a pattern in their attack, something that he did not understand: the things were coming for Silith. More than their dreadful attentions to the other men, they sought the general. Once, twice, three times.

The line seemed to be breaking—

BOOM!

Cannons fired into the mass of grubs, shattering the line. They swarmed back, and then in again . . .

BOOM!

And then tubes bundled together like straws fired, pop-pop-pop, ripping the ranks.

"I don't know what those weapons are," Aros yelled above the din, "but I'm glad they're on our side!"

The cannons roared again, jolting the wagons backward, and the ground under them buckled.

Then one of the cannons *exploded*; the barrel shattered as if a bomb had burst in its guts. Amid a rain of fire and hail of torn steel, the soldiers were thrown screaming to the earth, stunned.

They were recovering, their brother soldiers protecting them. Then—

Cracks ran along the sodden earth as the ground collapsed, and men plunged screaming into the dark. General Silith watched the chaos for a moment too long, and the very ground beneath his feet dropped away.

"What in nine hells——?"

"General!" Aros screamed. He could see down into the hole. Despite the murk, he could tell that the men had fallen ten feet down, perhaps, to a ledge of rock, a tunnel beneath the surface. Silith lay stunned, and grubs squirmed toward him, away from other men who had fallen through the crust.

General Silith's men hesitated, frozen with terror. A few climbed on crumbling dirt.

And not entirely knowing what he was doing, Aros jumped down into the collapsed ground, as the general was swarmed by grubs.

Aros got Silith to his feet, the grubs clawing at him until they pulled his cloak off. There were too many of them; they would be slaughtered . . .

And then the strangest thing happened. The grubs were ripping and tearing and fighting over Silith's coat, almost ignoring Silith and Aros. Aros had never seen anything quite like that.

Ropes were dangled down from the surface, and Aros helped the dazed Silith step into a knotted loop at the end, and he was hauled up. Aros climbed as rapidly as he ever had, and a moment later was at the surface.

The sun was rising in the east, and as its rays stretched across the land, the grubs fled, vanished into their holes and back into the darkness. They had what they wanted: the cloak was shredded and gone.

"General, sir!" Sergeant Fflogs yelled. "Are you alive? We saw the ground open and swallow you."

The general glowered at him, struck the sergeant to the ground. "Yes! And the only one of you miserable bastards who went after me is Kasha."

"Sir, I wasn't close enough!"

The general's eyes were like coals. "Corporal, give the sergeant your sword."

Fflogs's eyes flew wide. "General, what——"

The general was like ice. "When Kasha and I came upon you this evening, you were asleep."

The sergeant was stricken. "Sir! No! It . . . don't you remember?"

The general turned to Aros. "Kasha. You remember, don't you?"

Aros didn't know what to say. The sergeant's face was twisted in a silent plea. "Maybe . . . maybe he'd closed his eyes for a moment."

The general drew his blood-crusted sword. A little more would mean little. "Then let him close them permanently."

The sergeant recoiled, mouth working without producing sound.

Aros raised his hand. "I said . . . *maybe*. I came upon him first, general . . . and I believe his eyes were open. It was a blink."

"A blink?" Silith asked.

Aros nodded, holding his eyes. "A very long, slow . . . blink."

In spite of his mood, the corners of Silith's mouth flickered up and then flattened again. "I see. I owe a favor to the man who saved my life. Is this the favor you seek?"

Desperation lived in Fflogs's face. He was a man who needed a favor and knew he had no right to ask.

"He was awake, sir. I ask no favor. Just . . . justice for a good man."

Silence, as the entire camp watched. "I see. Strike the camp! We head home."

The soldiers were a thinner, shorter line than they had been just a day before. But blooded warriors all.

The general pulled his horse beside Aros. "Last night," he said.

"A hell of a night."

"Could have been my last one," the general said.

"Close call."

"Yes. Very. That cannon exploded. Someone will be held responsible for that."

"I'm sure, sir. Don't sweat the small stuff."

The general's eyebrows jumped. "Compared to what?"

"Your cloak. Did you notice the way the grubs came at you? And then, when you shed it, how they went after the cloak?"

Silith shook his head. "You're right. I must be getting old. I was so dazed I really didn't think about that." He closed his eyes for a moment. "Yes. Almost as if it was pulling them."

"As if there was something they wanted in it. Or something that angered them."

"There are lures that hunters use," Silith said. "The musk of certain animals attracts them."

"Something they can smell that you did not."

Silith hunched in his saddle. "Yes. Almost as if someone had deliberately scented my cloak. I wonder," he said, with a side gaze at Aros. "Who would do such a thing?"

"Great men have great enemies, sir."

Silith nodded. "Much to think on. You have a very good head, Aztec. I want it close to me."

"Whatever you wish, sir."

Silith was silent for a quarter mile, lost in thought before he spoke again. "Last night, when the sergeant was on the spot. I had the impression he's made things hard on you. Why did you testify for him?"

"And against you, I assume you mean."

"Some could see it that way," the general said.

Aros fought for the right words. "I am new here. I don't know how things are done, or what history there is that would motivate your lordship. Maybe I don't know the customs hereabouts, and folks sleep standing up. I can only say what I saw."

"Some would say you were impertinent," the general said.

Aros snorted. "But, sir, if they said that, do you know what I'd say?"

A muscle the size of half a walnut twitched at the corner of Silith's jaw. "What would you say?"

"I'd say that I don't know what that word means, sir. Me being a simple man and all."

The general stared at him . . . and then roared with laughter and kicked the sides of his horse. As he did, he called back over his shoulder: "You keep your sword for now, Outlander. But I'll get it, one way or the other!"

It seemed that Aros would never be alone. The sergeant rode up next. "Aztec!" Fflogs roared.

"Yes?"

The sergeant shook his head. "I've ridden you pretty hard."

Aros laughed. "This is the army, not a damn nursery."

The sergeant nodded approvingly. "No. No it's not."

Aros rode along. The other men grunted approval, and one handed him a canteen to share. It was beer. He grinned and drank deeply.

I could get used to this, Aros said to himself. *I truly could.*

TWENTY-SIX

The One

Shyena the Red Nun stepped down from her carriage and presented her papers to the guard at the gate in the Great Wall. Her face alone should have been sufficient, but the general was taking no chances, and neither were the Hundred, let alone the Ten.

Or . . . the One. She shuddered at the thought of facing him, kept her fear locked deep inside herself, walked with purpose and poise, her red robe trailing lightly behind her, her eyes focused directly ahead, arms folded into her sleeves.

The wall Neoloth had crawled through was thick, as if designed to keep in some enormous beast. The lies that had been told to the population of the capital city had been convincing, she supposed, and it had required over a year just to create the skeleton, let alone the time required to fill it with cement.

The thousand-year spell had begun.

From around the world, the mages had come, drawn by the One, and the Ten, to be part of the Hundred who would rule the Thousand . . .

A pyramid and the One who ruled them all were terrifying to her, and she could not let that show, because fear would open the door to her heart, and once the One was in her, the One would know who had betrayed them.

Shyena's carriage passed the shops, the training grounds where the Thousand, recruited from Shrike's armies and artisans, worked, built, and trained with the anomalies. That was what these strange devices were called. The anomalies.

The king knew a bit about what was going on here, but the senile old fool couldn't possibly know precisely what was happening. Even she could barely hold the reality in her mind, and there were times she awakened in the middle of the night sweating even if the night was cold. What were they doing? Could such a colossal action take place without risking the sanity of reality itself? What price would they pay, would the world pay, if they were making a mistake?

What price this final victory? Her mind swam.

Her carriage paused before the round red building, and she dismounted. Other carriages, as well as several of the odd two-wheeled balancing vehicles, were parked around the building, and she heard the voices within even before she entered. The hall was designed so that it might hold the Hundred, with semicircular rows of seats facing a raised dais. On this day the Hundred only numbered sixty-one.

She was one of the last to arrive, and the others turned to watch her as she entered. In terms of power and authority, Shyena was positioned in the Hundred's bottom half, but due to her beauty and mystery, she was of interest to those among the highest.

The Red Nun took her seat. Folded her hands and waited. Two more arrived and took their seats.

Two acolytes closed and bolted the door.

The lamps were dimmed, and a glowing glass cast a circle of light on the dais. The smell of incense, cinnamon, and blood filled the room.

And then a voice floated out of the corners of the room, from everywhere and nowhere, all at once. "Our time is here," the voice said. It was neither male nor female, and she shuddered.

The One.

A cloaked figure moved from the shadows. Had it been there previously, unnoticed? She wasn't sure, but it was possible. Hiding in plain sight. Watching them, unsensed.

Her flesh crawled.

The form was bulky, with wide hips and shoulders, thickness in the middle. The arms of the robe were swollen with muscle, the chest doubled with enormous breasts.

When the One reached the dais, the One threw back the cowl to reveal a face that was both strongly masculine and beautifully feminine, depending on the angles from which it was perceived. Long black hair, painted mouth, eyes lined with highlights. Strong cheekbones, full lips with the tip of a pink tongue darting to moisten them.

The One. "Belot" was all the name the Red Nun knew. She had the impression that once Belot had been either male or female and that some magic had been employed to change the body and mind. Why? No one knew. Some said Belot was a woman who had wished the strength of a man. Others that Belot was a man who had desired to bear children, that the acolytes that accompanied Belot everywhere were those offspring, and that Belot had had them without the intercession of another male. Had impregnated herself.

No one knew. Or dared to ask. Belot was the most powerful sorcerer known to walk the earth, and Belot's word was law.

"Our time is here," Belot repeated. "That time for which we have worked so long, suffered so much is here. I wish to acknowledge the works, the very good works from our brothers and sisters of the Guild. It is they, and their descendants, who have accomplished this. You are strong in the Way."

The room broke into murmurs. The Guild was all-important, its members lives extended to twice the norm. It would be their task to keep the Spell going through the years. The decades. The long centuries. For the moment, the cave was blocked by a long, conspicuous wall. Gates were there to support the traffic that carried explorers in, anomalies out. When this work was done, the wall would disappear; the cave wall would be partly blocked, then hidden.

She did not understand all that was being done. Knew that it required the lives of slaves and captives to drive the energies that pierced time. Children to do the seeking; but why children? She knew that slowly, the aperture between this world and that to come was growing wider. And what would happen as it did? Shrike would have weapons no other kingdom could match, and it would take the lead in the world. And as the tunnels lengthened? *Was* there a far end?

She could not even imagine. But with a sinking feeling in her gut, she suspected that Neoloth was right: of what use is magic in a world in which every cobbler can create a miracle?

"We bring you here," Belot said, "because one of our greatest allies wishes to speak with us, feels that we can assist him in resolving a conundrum. I wish each and every one of you to listen closely and help to the limit of your capacity."

The Red Nun kept her face calm, even as she felt alarm, as the general strode up to the podium.

An ally, not a member. A magic user, but not a magician. She realized she was in a dual trap. The general would be scanning the audience to see what guilt might surface on their faces.

But Belot would be doing the same, and for different reasons.

"As some of you may have heard," the general began, "four days ago, on a mission to push back the forces who have ambushed settlers, on the plains to our east, my men were set upon by cannibals. There is no better word for it."

Murmurs swept the room in waves. General Silith raised his hand. The hand fell down to touch the bandage at the side of his face.

"We survived. Conquered, but only because we held them off until dawn. This bare fact is not what I wish to bring to your attention."

Belot's voice rolled, its range immense. "What, my friend, is your purpose? And might I say that we are all profoundly grateful that our friend and ally was delivered from death."

Silith smiled. It looked like a slit carved in a bronze mask. "Thank you. The thing I wish to bring to your attention is that the cannibals sought me out for special attention. In the attack, my cloak was ripped from my body, and, when it was, they attacked *that*." He paused. "There are scents hunters use to attract prey. I have done this myself: secretions of musk glands and so forth. And I was reminded of nothing so much as this when they tore into my cloak."

Belot steepled her hands. "And were you able to retrieve this cloak?"

"No, I'm afraid not." Silith's eyes shone.

"That is a pity," Belot said. "Were we able to examine it, much might be determined."

"Yes," Silith agreed. "Much." He paused, leaving the implication hanging.

"So . . ." Belot went on. "Let us assume that something, some trick, some stratagem was employed to attract these creatures to you. What do you infer from this?"

"That it was not a simple attack. That it was an attempted assassination. Someone knew where we were traveling, knew of the existence of these creatures, and saw it as an opportunity to remove me from some battle plan."

"And who would wish to do such a thing?"

"I haven't thought that far," Silith said.

Belot's templed fingers absorbed her attention for a long moment, and then she looked up. "I think that, considering the mundane nature of the trap, we can assume that the conspirators did not have access to magic."

Silith said, "Ah. Continue."

"What remains is the general's rivals in the military, or perhaps courtiers jealous of his burgeoning influence."

The general's eyes shifted sideways without his head turning. "I come to you in the belief that we share the same goals, that our partnership, which has come so far, serves purposes dear to us all. That there might be one of this august body who may know a fact that helps me determine the truth of what has happened."

No one moved or spoke. The Red Nun held her breath, kept her face calm. She dared not use a glamour to control her appearance: Belot would be watching.

Belot would know that something had happened. Might well know that Silith had been somehow warned. And if he knew that, he might know he had been betrayed. Two men searching a single audience for a betrayer.

But amid sixty men and women seeking to conceal their thoughts and feelings, she was merely one more. Without focusing her eyes on Belot, she could see the One scanning them, and Belot's eyes did not linger upon her.

"Know for a certainty," said Silith, "that I will discover who did this, who is responsible. And that when I do, I hope my allies, yourselves, would be among those most eager for justice to be done. It is, I believe, in all our interests."

He scanned them. "Twelve years ago, your leader Belot came to me and told me of the Thousand Year Spell. That if a secure place could be found, where men might labor in secret for generations, a miracle could be achieved. That Shrike was positioned perfectly so that hidden caves within the mountains might be secured more firmly with magic and armed force to turn away prying eyes, and that with the power of Shrike, magic could be extracted from slaves and captives to create a bridge to the future, one maintained by generation after generation, even after the magic dies in the rest of the world. That we, on *this* end, could make it work."

Appreciative murmuring followed. Nodding heads.

"And it has. As we have worked to maintain and widen it, future generations of the Hundred have kept faith with us and held open the tunnels. The farthest caverns are too narrow for any but children to reach the miracles of further time. I could not have predicted the results. Trifles at first. But then . . . lights without fire. Cannon that can be carried by a single soldier. Boats that run on burning wood and boiling water rather than wind, or rowers. Trivia: tiny tubes that project lines of light, the most marvelous cat toy imaginable. Miracles."

"And more to come," Belot reminded them.

"Yes, and more to come. But as our plans approach fruition, it is important to remember how much we still need each other. It would be a grave error to assume that the partnership that has brought us so far can now be discarded."

"Unwise indeed, General."

Silith examined their faces, searching for guilt, or guile. His eyes met hers, and she had the sense that he lingered for an extra moment, but it might have been her imagination. Then he looked on.

And at the same time, of course, Belot was watching them as well. Looking for something different.

Finally, the general nodded. "As you know, certain things have begun to accelerate. Our time is now. I would suggest that each of you look at the brother or sister to your left and right. Know that they might be the weak link in the chain. And keep your eyes on them."

He nodded and left the dais. Belot returned. "An excellent notion. I make the same suggestion. That each of you look to the right and left. Know that the secrets of the Hundred are for us"— she inclined her head graciously toward the general—"and our allies, of course. And that any who share those secrets, for whatever cause, are risking all our lives."

There were varied other bits of business to be handled, but much was communication, information, or instructions to be passed down the line to the Thousand. And then the formal meeting was called, and questions or requests taken. And then the meeting was dismissed.

The Red Nun was exiting the building when one of the acolytes approached her, a youth whose sallow face was sunken deep in his cowl's shadows. "Belot wishes a word to you."

She nodded, hoping that he could not hear the way her heartbeat raced. That would not do at all.

The Octagon was built upon a maze of corridors, such that only those who lived within it truly knew all its secrets. It must be deliberate: the confusion of one led within, the implied helplessness once you had taken too many twists and turns in the corridors adding to the confusion and eventual submission. With every step, her sense of helplessness increased.

Torches had led the way only months before. Now there were gas lamps, fed by pipes concealed within the walls. She wondered what she would see the next time she entered. The changes were happening more rapidly now.

The acolyte walked tall, as well he might. He knew that his path ahead was secure. Was not every strange machine that flowed back along the time stream evidence that the Thousand had succeeded? That they were stretching their hands forward into the future? That nothing had stopped their growth? That, in time, they may well have inherited the earth itself?

He walked like a conqueror, and that was what he might well be.

The tunnel went down and down. This was, she knew, their plan: an underground world that might be concealed from prying eyes, something that could last a thousand years, or ten thousand, however long it took to fulfill their aims.

She was taken to an office hollowed out of the stone. The

gaslights were accompanied by other, stranger devices, glowing glass bulbs hooked to boxes sprouting wires. The light flickered but was bright enough to test the eyes, and she could not understand what she was looking at. Magic?

"I called you here, Shyena, for a very special reason," Belot said.

"I am here to serve you," the Red Nun replied.

"And this is good. The reason is your ambition."

"My . . . ambition?" she asked, trying to keep the stress from closing her throat.

"Yes. I know that you would seek to be one of the Ten. Is this not true?"

She nodded slowly. Where was this leading?

"You are fortunate," Belot said, "in that you are intelligent and ambitious enough to seek membership in the Ten, without the skill or power necessary to have betrayed me."

She hoped that she kept the anger from her face, but at the same time realized that Belot had spoken a simple truth: she could not have pierced the veil of distance, reached the general in any way, by herself.

"How and why do you believe the general was alerted?"

Belot interlaced her disturbingly long and tapered fingers. "We do not have direct sources. As you can imagine, the nature of the trap we set made it difficult to place spies among the troops. All were expendable. So those who survived are not easily convinced to share knowledge. The lure was placed in the general's cloak, and his scouts were . . . urged to encourage the general to camp on the old battlegrounds."

"And did any of your pawns survive?"

"We believe that one did, yes. And that he is being questioned as we speak." Belot waved a dismissive hand. "The inquiries will lead nowhere."

"And how do you believe the betrayal was effected?"

"We are not certain. Certainly, if it had been a mundane effect, a message or a messenger arriving before that night, the camp would never have been made there. Perhaps a messenger arrived late. So it is possible that a fool spoke to the wrong person. We are investigating that as we speak."

She knew what that meant: torture followed by murder.

"And the other option?"

"That there was a magical communication of some kind. Perhaps directly to the general. Perhaps to one of his men, a magic user we had not identified."

"That would make the communication more efficient. Require less mana."

Belot watched her carefully, but the Red Nun kept her emotions under control. Belot did not suspect her. Perhaps wished her as an ally. After all, she was ambitious, but weak.

Grim humor to be found in that irony. Too weak to be a threat, but powerful enough to be an enemy.

Belot was smiling at her, and the Red Nun had another, terrible thought. A trap. It was all a trap. Be very, very careful.

The Red Nun was very careful for the rest of the day and the next. But she noticed something: one at a time, at least a dozen other members of the Hundred had been summoned before Belot and questioned and probably recruited to the purpose of determining who and how their plans had been foiled.

And she decided, after much thought, that she was safe. Not even Belot could watch everyone. Or have enough trusted acolytes to watch everyone, with others watching the watchmen. And so a day later, she took a deep breath and traveled to the Tower. She had been there before, and there was nothing unusual about it, but she felt as if every eye was upon her.

The Red Nun had always hated the prison. It smelled like fear and pain and death. And whereas she could handle all of that, it also smelled of burned blood, a smell that reminded her of another place, another time, and people who once had loved her.

There were three levels aboveground and a dungeon below the ground. The people there were standard-issue criminals: thieves, murderers, general scoundrels.

But they were not of interest to the woman who called herself the Red Nun. She had left such things behind long ago.

And on the ground level was an armory, where tools were made, some of them of standard design, and others strange things in new designs she had never seen. That no one had ever seen.

The cries, moans, and screams echoed even in the quiet. She could close her ears to it, but it still reverberated in her bones. And what she felt the most was that she was a part of this. Her quest for revenge didn't change the fact that she had and was collaborating with evil.

She was evil. Evil had entered her heart, and she had yielded, and for that, she felt . . . what?

For so long she had sealed away her emotions, sealed away everything in her heart except the urge for vengeance. And an unexpected side effect of her session with Neoloth was the opening of her heart.

What had happened? Was it that he had opened his own heart, and by linking to him, that softness had infected her? Or was it just the knowledge that Neoloth had seen what she was.

She had spent the last day going about her business, fulfilling her functions, controlling her emotions tightly, trying not to feel what was welling up within her.

Praying that no one saw what was behind her eyes. That would be lethal.

She approached the guards. "It is time," she said. And they merely nodded to her. One of the Hundred came every day, on the same mission. There was nothing surprising about her trip, although she had to be certain that it was not out of the ordinary.

The guard passed her to the kitchen, and there she received a tray of food. She inspected: slices of beef, bread, a piece of fruit. A serving girl carried a second tray.

Together they walked up the narrow stairs to the top of the Tower, past another guard, to the corridor where the princess and her attendant were confined.

After the escape attempt, they were no longer in the same cell. The serving girl gave her tray to the attendant for Drasilljah, but the Red Nun served the princess directly.

"Princess Tahlia," she said. "Dinner."

There was a stirring within the cell. The guard opened the door, and the Witch entered.

The cell was almost bare, strewn with straw with a simple cot against a wall. A chamber pot. No window.

The princess lay on the cot, her face turned toward the wall. When she finally turned back, the Red Nun caught her breath.

Tahlia's expression was haughty, but anyone could see that the girl was close to cracking. That she was using all of her will to maintain a facade of strength and spirit. Shyena didn't want to see this. But once she did, the urge to comfort welled up in her.

And she had to repress it so that the guard would not detect anything.

"It is time to eat," she said. The princess was fed only twice a day, so the hunger was real.

The girl watched the Red Nun through slitted eyes as she ate. "Is Drasilljah eating?"

"Yes. It is not our intent to starve either of you."

"No, I don't think it is."

"You will see that we merely wish you to be our ambassador to your great country."

The princess mopped gravy up with her bread, wolfed it down. "Only a while ago, you weren't even admitting I was in Shrike. The story has changed."

"Yes," the Witch said. "There are always mysteries. Those of diplomacy are above me. I merely wish you to return to your home unmolested."

The princess's eyes touched hers with a moment of inquiry. As the Witch had suspected, the others who served her used different language.

When the princess's eyes met hers, the Witch shifted to look back at the meat.

"It would be good for you to cooperate," she said. "That would go better for everyone."

"I will not write your letter," she said. "I will not lie to my mother."

"In time, I hope you will see that truth is a tricky thing. Do not let a scrap of paper stand between you and freedom."

A scrap of paper. A statement that the princess had been rescued from pirates by the forces of Shrike and would be soon returned.

Of course she would. The Red Nun stood, straightened her robe, and left the cell.

The princess ate slowly as the door closed. The Red Nun had been . . . different this time. It was an oddness, and she didn't know quite what to think of it, or even what precisely had triggered that reaction. But . . . there it was.

Of course, if she wrote the note, the kingdom of Shrike would be absolved of responsibility in her kidnapping precisely as long as the princess was kept separate from her mother. At that instant, the charade would end, and war begin.

What, then, was the purpose? The letter was her death warrant: the instant she signed it, she was dead, and a sad message would reach her mother that pirates, or disease, or a storm had taken the princess.

But certainly they knew she would make that connection. They were not intending to starve her to try to make her sign it. What then was the purpose?

There would seem to be no purpose, unless the entire thing was a bluff. A stall. Something to distract her attention from what was really going on, the actual intent. Meanwhile, they were keeping her in excellent health. Giving her hope. Had not mistreated her.

Why did she remember stories about the fatted calf . . . ?

And why had the Red Nun's eyes shifted again and again, looking at the meat? It was just a chunk of steak, two chunks, actually, a decent amount. She hoped Drasilljah had had as much—

She poked at the steak, and there, hidden under the gravy, was a folded slip of waxed paper.

She chewed more slowly, shifting her eyes to see if she was being watched. No, no one at the door. She set the tray down and walked carefully to the door, as if about to request a favor. No one there.

Back to the tray. There was no knife; she was expected to use her teeth. She peeled the folded bit of paper apart and unrolled it. In a cramped hand, she read the following words:

A friend is nearby. Remember a conversation on the balcony with one who could not admit he loves you. Have hope.

A friend? A conversation on a balcony? The princess blinked, trying to clear her mind. It had been horrible, being separated from Drasilljah. She hadn't realized how much she needed her old friend.

Her hands shook. Was this even real? And if it was . . .

Neoloth-Pteor. That was the friend.

The Red Nun had passed a message from Neoloth-Pteor? Did that even make sense, considering what had happened, all that had happened and been done?

And if it did make sense . . .

Have hope.

Then there was help nearby. The only reason she might write their letter for them was hopelessness. Under no circumstances would this note be given to her by someone who believed it would induce her to write and sign.

What if she was wrong? Make it: "Help is near. Go ahead, write the note. It doesn't matter . . ."

But if not. If no one reacted that way. If there was no increased pressure . . . then arguably she now had two allies: Neoloth and whoever had passed her the note.

If the Red Nun herself had passed it, if she had an ally *that* powerful . . .

Then, for the first time in weeks, she felt a shred of hope.

The princess pressed her hands against the wall. There were limits to imagination. She did not know what was happening to Drasilljah in the cell next to her. She wanted to communicate with her, reach out . . .

There is hope.

Was it even her old friend in the next cell? Drasilljah might be dead, or in another part of the prison. Anything was possible. She had to keep this to herself.

She ate, with more appetite than she had felt in a very long time. It was a terrible, wonderful meal.

TWENTY-SEVEN

Mijista Wile

Aros guided Jade Silith's steam coach, enjoying the wind in his face and the smiles and expressions of admiration from the people they passed.

"Do you see the way they look at you?" she asked.

"Perhaps they are looking at you. The general's wife, the winner of the Goddess Day race . . ."

Her laugh was musical. In a younger woman, he would have thought it flirtatious. This was different. He knew what to call it but couldn't quite bring himself to do so.

"No, Kasha. My husband is loved and feared. And it is said that you jumped down into the tunnel to save him. Those who hate him hate you. Those who love him . . . love you."

She touched his hand gently. A mother's touch, he thought.

He had been touched many times in many different ways over the course of his life. But to his horror, he couldn't remember a single touch from his mother. He imagined that it would feel . . . something like this.

Everything had been different since he jumped down into the tunnels. The general had taken him into his inner circle and begun training him for better things. Personally.

Jade Silith had begun to request his presence as personal bodyguard at functions. He understood what this meant—he was being introduced to society, without direct claims of lineage.

The general's men welcomed him. He was known. And that made him just a little more uncomfortable, because while bonding with the general was a positive thing, maintaining a high profile was not necessarily a good idea. What if he was recognized by someone who could contradict his stated history? That could be a great deal worse than embarrassing.

That could be . . .

Well, he could imagine all the disastrous scenarios he wanted. But none of that would change the moment: he traveled at the side of a gracious woman who believed he had saved the husband she loved. Son or not, he had arrived.

"Where are we going?" he asked again. He had asked that question since the previous day, when she had requested his presence for a luncheon meeting.

She just smiled mysteriously. They were on the northern edge of the sprawling city, where a series of villas carved into cliffs rose above the waves. Their coach traveled up a narrow, winding road that invited disaster to a clumsy coachman. Aros was troubled little by heights, and Jade enjoyed the ride tremendously, laughing.

"I feel so alive," she said, and looked at him with dewy eyes.

"You bring something out in me, Kasha." The gentleness in her eyes, combined with an odd mischief, gave him a momentarily uncomfortable reaction. If he had misread her reaction, if she was taking him to some kind of hideaway with the intent to . . .

His mind couldn't even quite wrap around that, but in the next moment he was convinced he was wrong. But there was something here, something secretive, and delicious . . .

What in the world?

The coach pulled up to the gate of one of the largest estates. They were at the back, with the villa built so that a front window looked out upon the crashing waves below. An impressive amount of work, certainly. Who could live here?

The coach came to a stop, and the two of them sat. Aros waited until his curiosity was overwhelming.

"What . . . do we do now?" he asked.

That mischievous smile grew wider. "Now you get out," she said. "I will be back to get you this evening."

He opened his mouth, closed it again. Had no slightest idea what this was about, but nothing about her manner or words suggested danger of any kind. Deep amusement, yes. But . . .

What was expected of him? Obedience, he supposed.

Aros nodded and stepped down from the carriage.

The carriage slid away—no horses, no sound but for a faint hiss—leaving Aros at the door.

That door was a huge slab of some heavy, dark wood that Aros didn't recognize. In the middle of it was a massive brass knocker, which he lifted and slammed down twice. The door might have been a bell or some other object designed to amplify vibration: it boomed, startling him.

After a pause, the door opened. A liveried servant, pale and bald and thin and aged, answered the door.

"You are Kasha? Then you are on time, sir," the man said, and Aros repressed the urge to ask, On time for what? He stepped inside.

The hall within was long and masculine, with trophies and reminders of military campaigns and travels to foreign lands.

"The end of the hall, sir." The servant gestured with a long thin arm.

Halfway down the hall was a painting of a man with a broad, strong face; gray mustache and hair; and a commanding air. A candle burned before the picture in a golden dish, a wick floating in an aromatic oil.

"My husband," a voice said behind him. "He was a great man."

Aros turned. A slender woman stood at the end of the hall, holding a burning taper to a candlestick. The hall grew less dim. "As his widow, I've been offered the privilege of the new light globes, but I admit that I don't understand how they work and prefer the old ways."

She approached him, swaying beneath a transparent oversheath and a dark, clinging dress beneath. Her face was heart-shaped and lovely, her eyes wide and dark. She looked like a thorough-bred racehorse, in the sense that her skin was perfect, the fires within her burning brightly. She seemed both curious and filled with doubt.

"Madam?" he asked. "I'm afraid you have me at a disadvantage."

"Yes, I imagine I do." She turned languidly, either a natural motion or one practiced to perfection. She walked toward a distant light, and when he followed her, he scented a perfumed trail behind her.

By the serpent! What was this! His neck itched with danger, but at the same time he could not take his eyes off the swaying hips. She was perfectly made up and presented. The servant was nowhere in sight. She had been careful to inform him that her husband was dead.

What did this woman of means have in mind?

She led him to a window overlooking the waves. If he had been prone to vertigo, both the company and the view might have unmanned him.

She sat looking at him speculatively. The servant appeared and served them wine, allowing him to choose his cup first.

They sat in low chairs, facing each other, and she was playing a game, waiting for him to speak.

He hated the fact that he was motivated to speak first. "Who are you, and what is it you wish of me?"

"I am the wife of Major Sepphus," she said. "And before I married, my name was Mijista Wile. Does that name mean anything to you?"

He searched his memory. What did he know of Shrike's nobility and wealthy folk? Had he heard the name Mijista? Or Wile? The second name rang a very distant bell, but he could make nothing of the connection.

"I'm afraid not," he said. "And regret that. M'lady does not seem someone it would be possible to forget."

She smiled, and a bit of the lady of the manor affect dissolved. "Yes. That would be the correct answer, no matter what the truth."

His brows beetled. "What truth are you seeking? I've done some traveling, learned some secrets."

"It is said you have no memory of your life as a child. Is that true?"

He nodded.

She frowned a bit. "Do you know the customs of Shrike? Or the Eight Kingdoms?"

"Some," he said.

"I refer specifically to the betrothal customs among the wealthy and powerful. Children are game pieces, to be married or betrothed to the advantage of their families. Children are sometimes promised before birth."

He scoffed, taking another drink. The wine was excellent! "And they have no choice in the matter? And they call me barbaric. Is that what happened with your husband? You were promised to an older man in exchange for political advantage?"

A darkness crossed her face. A private pain, perhaps, and he regretted what he had said. "Yes. But, as often happens, I grew to love him."

"How long were you married . . . and what happened to him?"

"For nine years. We married when I was sixteen years. He died in battle for our king three years ago."

"I'm sorry."

She studied him. "I might have been married even earlier, but I could not. I was in mourning."

"In mourning . . . for what?"

"For the one I had been betrothed to in childhood. He disappeared when he was ten years old. I was eleven."

The alarm began to creep up his neck.

"What . . . happened to him?"

"We do not know. He was traveling to visit a cousin, and the caravan was attacked, according to a survivor. No sign was ever found."

"I see." He set the wine down. The last thing in the world he needed at this moment was clouded senses. "And who," he asked, already knowing the answer, "was the intended?"

She was watching him so very carefully. "He was the son of General Silith and his wife, Jade. Elio Silith."

"And when were you betrothed?"

"At birth. His, not mine."

"I would assume that you had some say in your eventual husband, as you were older at the time. I regret having to say this, but it may have been a blessing."

Something about his answer pleased her. "That is so very much like what Elio would have said."

"Or so you remember him. It was long ago."

"Memory is a tricky thing," she conceded. "But I believe I can trust my heart."

They spoke on for a time, of life and the politics of Shrike, and the sea, which she loved. And at all times, at every moment, he was aware that there was a conversation going on beneath the conversation. *Who are you?*

And at last, he began to wonder.

He remembered his youth in Azteca, but not his mother's face. Remembered little of his wanderings before he found the sea.

Which made it easy to turn his memories to the purpose at hand.

She listened, with a wit and wisdom in her words and smiles, her small gestures that he found calming, noting at every moment that somehow the room continued to grow smaller and more intimate. "It is a strange thing," she said. "We know each other, know ourselves, largely by the people around us. They reinforce our memories, our identities. And ultimately they can create memory that didn't exist, just by telling us things again and again."

What, then, was he to make of that? He didn't remember. He had no companions, no family to tell him. Anything was possible . . . except of course for any tattoos that had been placed in childhood.

No, damn it, not even that. Hadn't he seen Neoloth remove

one set of tattoos and replace them with another? It would be absurd to think him the only mage with such ability.

Anything was . . .

The sun was nearing the horizon, the shadows long and deep. Somehow, Mijista Wile had drawn closer to him. So close that he could scent the wine upon her breath.

"What do you think of me?" she asked boldly, and as she said it Mijista made a presentation of herself. Her hair, her eyes—all seemed to glow.

"You are the very essence of a noblewoman," he said honestly, and for the first time in his life, he wished he was another man. A man who had been born to such a station. Because nothing in him wanted to lie to this woman, and he had already told so many.

"And you have a politician's tongue," she said. But while there was mockery in those words, there was also a hint of something else. Some challenge.

"Would you do me a favor?" Mijista asked, every word warm and wafting on a warm, moist breeze.

"Of course," he answered.

"The boy I remember was my betrothed. And before he left, he showed me the tattoo that had been graven in his skin. It hurt terribly, he said. But he was very brave."

She stood. "I also traveled, as the highborn do, between the Eight Kingdoms. And I also received such a tattoo. If you would care to see it, first show me yours."

He took a deep breath. For what purpose had Jade Silith brought him to this house? Was this a trap? And yet . . . at no time had he claimed to be this or that person. True, they had manipulated the . . .

His brain wasn't working properly. As he was thinking, he was also standing up and, in standing, had already begun the unbuttoning, the shedding, there in the light from the setting sun. Until his chest was bare, and with it the tattoos that had once been upon the boy they had found in an unmarked grave.

Yes, the boy. He, Aros, could not be other than he was: a thief, a mercenary, a man of no consequence in the world. His momentary fantasy dispelled and . . .

She was touching him. Her fingers tracing their way across his chest. "Turn," she said, and did the same thing along his back. "Strange," she said. "The images are familiar. But . . . not so large as I would have expected."

"I can't see my own back."

"If you are the boy I remember—"

"I never claimed to be."

She looked at him carefully. "No," she said. "You never claimed to be. But here you are, in Shrike. In the chariot of the most powerful woman in the kingdom. Who brought you to me. What do you think of this?"

"I think that m'lady makes more of it than I do."

"Yes. Well spoken. You are not the boy I knew," she said. His heart raced. Then she said, "But you are the man he would have grown to be."

Her lips pressed against his and then withdrew.

Eyes half-lidded, she took a half step backward.

And then showed him the tattoo on her back, as he had displayed his own. Faded blue, it covered most of her upper back: a dark, ten-year-old boy with an infectious smile.

TWENTY-EIGHT

Assassin

The carriage returned for Aros at dawn. Jade Silith was not in it.

Again, the coachman had no horses to manage and steered the steaming device with a lever that stuck through the floor, with a great wheel not too dissimilar to the wheel of a sailing ship.

"Where to, sir?"

Sir? Aros could think of precious few times in his life that he had ever been addressed in such a fashion, and fewer still when it was said without irony or hope of immediate reward.

Sir.

"To the Boar's Head Inn," he replied. The coach began to wind along the narrow path, and in the darkness of early morning, it somehow seemed more sure-footed. Or . . . perhaps he was just less concerned, more relaxed.

He felt happy.

And it wasn't just the spectacular evening that Mijista Wile had afforded him. Not just the things she had said, or done, or what had happened since he'd returned from the desert.

It was the fact that everything before the desert had been artifice. But what had happened there, fighting beside the general and leaping down into the cavern to save him . . . Neoloth's trickery had had no part in that. That had been no fraud, no plan, no act. He had jumped into darkness to save a man he admired.

And that man had responded by promoting him. His wife had responded with the gratitude any loving wife might feel. Introducing him to society and then . . . to his former fiancée.

NO! Not his. The boy who had died in the desert, and been laid in his grave. Whose tattoos they had stolen.

Unless . . . for some reason he did not understand, those tattoos had been transferred from one boy to another. As if . . .

Well, but that way lay insanity.

But what was happening to him was insane. The general didn't care who he was—he cared that Aros had saved his life, at the risk of his own.

The general's wife didn't care. Oh, it was clear that she toyed with the notion that he was her son . . . but her mother's heart was ready to accept him regardless.

And what of Mijista Wile? Certainly part of what had happened between them could be considered a very intimate inspection of his tattoos. Madam Silith had known Mijista Wile was a lusty widow and could be trusted to report back. And what would be said? That the tattoos were there; yes, they were. But weren't quite right. Too small. Skewed, perhaps.

He had never claimed to be their son. In a world in which tattoos could be moved from one body to another or duplicated or removed . . . who knew what was possible?

He had pleasured the widow; and she, him. There had been no artifice about that, either. And the memory of her clutchings, and gaspings, and rising heat, and cooling kisses had been as real as anything in this world or the next.

He felt it. There was a place for him in this kingdom. In this place. And that was something he had never known before, in all his life, and all his wanderings.

Sunlight was creeping across the rooftops by the time he returned to their lodgings. There was a barracks berth for him, of course, but no one would question his return to the lodgings he shared with his manservant.

The very manservant waiting for Aros when he strode through the door.

Neoloth had been up for some time, apparently, working on a scroll. Aros wondered if another scroll may have been on the table just moments before, if a hasty substitution had been made when footsteps were heard on the stair.

"Ah, the hero returns," Neoloth said, and his smile was not exactly a comforting thing. "It has been some time. I'd begun to wonder if you were coming back."

"I keep my word," the Aztec growled.

"So I have seen, and I appreciate that. In return, I can tell you that our purpose here grows sharp."

"Eh?" Aros felt a wave of fatigue flowing over him. It had been . . . a strenuous evening. Mijista Wile was quite a woman. He wondered if she would be available again that evening . . .

"Listen to me," Neoloth said sharply, drawing his attention back. "The stars are aligning to our purpose. I know where the princess is. I have an ally who can help her escape."

"Ally?"

Neoloth nodded. "The same who helped me reach into your dream."

Aros rubbed his head. "That was strange. It felt as if you were walking into my head. You and someone else."

"Never mind that."

"Who was she? Another magician?"

Neoloth's expression was a stone wall. *Do not ask. I will not say.*

Aros shrugged. "All right. You saved my life. I won't ask how. What now?"

"Now," Neoloth said, "you kill the general."

Of all the things that Neoloth might have said, that was the last he had wanted to hear. "W-what? I think you had better spell that out for me."

Neoloth sat next to him, exuding a sort of avuncular ease that felt positively serpentine. "I made an arrangement to save the princess. It involves the death of General Silith."

"Why?"

"Because Silith was involved in a massacre some time ago, and my . . . ally wishes revenge. My ally can get the princess out of prison. We will have to get her to the ship, and away. That will require a distraction. I believe that freeing the captives would create enough chaos to—"

"Wait," Aros said, holding his hands up. "Wait just a moment. Slow down. I never agreed to be an assassin. This is supposed to be a rescue mission."

"It seems to me that you were perfectly happy to play the assassin on Catal Island, some time ago."

Aros's eyebrows furrowed. "That was different."

"How?"

"I didn't know him."

"Oh, so that makes the difference? You've discovered morality?"

Aros slammed his fist on the table. "Do not speak to me as if I am some servant of yours, wizard. You can take my life, but you cannot take my honor. Silith has done me no wrong. In fact, he has treated me better than anyone ever has. *Ever*. His wife has treated me like a son. You tread very carefully here: do not think I will simply obey you if you snap your fingers."

Neoloth ground his teeth. "You understand that, in order for us to complete our mission, I must have allies. There are costs to that. All I had to do was remain silent, and you and your precious general would have died. At great cost, I reached out to you, saved your life. I could have completed my mission without you. So . . . you owe General Silith. What do you owe me?"

Aros groaned. There was no escaping the logic. He had promised to free the princess. Neoloth had, in warning him, proved himself a worthy ally. He hadn't had to do that. Aros would never have known. Even if he had survived, he would never have suspected the wizard had any part in it.

What did he owe Neoloth? What did he owe General Silith?

By the serpent! He had never had to deal with a quandary like this one!

He had saved the general's life. Would he now take it?

He sighed. "I have no answer for you. I appreciate that you saved my life. It is true that I am in your debt, a greater debt than I owe the general. With that truth upon the table, can you see my dilemma?"

Neoloth nodded. The barbarian was in a hard place. The laws of hospitality were engaged the moment he took wine, meat, and bread in the general's house. Not to mention the promotions. And . . . he was not blind to the degree to which the barbarian was growing to admire the general.

He had not anticipated that Aros's pretending to be a son might blossom into the real emotions of being a son.

This was as delicate a moment as Neoloth had ever navigated. The future of his entire venture was being decided now, in this room, beneath this guttering candle. "All right, Aros," Neoloth said. "Allow us to postpone our decision. Will that suffice?"

The barbarian nodded gratefully.

"What are your plans? I'll have to work around them. Are you near to learning anything?"

"I don't have your background," Aros said. "I'm seeing things *you* might understand, if you saw enough. I've seen something like miniature volcanic explosions set off with little tubes, or inside big iron or bronze tubes, or tubes hung over a man's back. We'd be up against those in any assault, or maybe we could use them ourselves."

"I trust the magic I know and my allies. If I were to kill the general, would you be bound—"

"No. Feel free; I won't hold a grudge. But he's no lightweight. And someone else is trying to kill him, too."

TWENTY~NINE

Messages

Neoloth rented a horse and rode out beyond the city limits to the stony beaches south of the capital of Shrike, beyond the sight of the great statue in her harbor.

The last days had brought both joy and new problems. He had to believe that, overall, things were going his way, that the new challenges actually resulted from an embarrassment of riches. New allies, new problems.

In a week, he had gone from having no idea where the princess might be found to knowing exactly where she was and how she could be obtained . . . if he could fulfill his side of a deal. General Silith had to die. And that he could do, even if the barbarian was not his instrument.

If he understood the Red Nun correctly, Silith was allied with the Hundred but not formally one of them. Why had he not joined? Because he was not a magic user . . . although he was willing to use magic to suit his aims. Perhaps he did not wish to be formally ranked less than the One, whom the Red Nun addressed only in hushed, awed tones.

What was the way forward, then? Aros would not assassinate the general. The Aztec would not feel obliged to avenge his death, so long as he was not involved in it. Barbarians were practical if nothing else.

How? Neoloth had killed before . . . but never like this.

Well. First things first.

Last night he'd used the talisman to call upon the other allies he needed. But he could not send specific information in such a way: a time and location were the most he could manage, and by the time he reached Smuggler's Cove, he was drawing his cloak tightly across his shoulders and shivering with the cold and wet.

The moon was shielded behind dark clouds. When it shone through, it seemed unnaturally huge and silvery, like a bright, pockmarked coin.

Neoloth unseated from his horse and stepped out to the edge of the wave, spreading his cloak and placing the talisman upon it, smoothing out the ruffles carefully with his hands.

Then he sat and began to chant his spells.

In a meditating state, he chanted. Far into the night, until just before the sun would have come creeping up from behind him, he saw the wakes and knew that his spells had been answered.

Two Merfolk had answered his call. If they had young, they had doubtless been told to remain concealed.

The male was bearded, the breasts of the female bare and beautiful, rounded and full in the waning light.

"You call, wizard. Who are you to use the secret signs of the Merfolk?"

"One who is a friend to M'thrilli of the southern waters," he said. "We have traded often, to mutual benefit. I bring tokens of friendship."

Neoloth waded out into the water and offered this newcomer four spearheads, upon a folded leather square. The merman took them, and examined them, eyes glittering.

"This is good," he said. "And what is it you wish of me?"

"Just one thing," he said. "To get this parchment to M'thrilli. It is of importance to your people. I ask this favor, as an old friend to your people. If you can make this happen, it serves you well, and I will not forget the service."

The merman extended a hand and Neoloth slipped a folded paper into it. On it were writings in the Mer-language, and others in the language of the Eight Kingdoms.

The merman handed the paper to his bride, and she read them. "I speak and read the human tongue," she said, speaking for the first time. "I know what you ask. There is danger."

"Yes. But you must know that what Shrike plans is the end to all magic. It is to both our good that you do as I ask."

She read them again. "And all you wish is that we get this to M'thrilli. It may take days."

That was true, and Neoloth cursed under his breath. Time was of the essence.

Then she smiled. "Is it true what they say? That upon a time you danced with our people?"

"Yes," he said. "They were the best days of my life."

"Tell me of this time," she said.

He closed his eyes. And began to speak of a time when a younger man, a more powerful man, fancied himself master of air and water and land. And fell in love with a mermaid, and for a glorious time had been her mate.

Another world, another life. A time when it seemed all things were possible for one such as he. And when he spoke of her, Pha-shere, he found the emotion rising in his voice and realized that he was not pretending. That he had loved.

As now he loved.

Why was it so easy for him to forget his own emotions?

By the time Aros returned to their lodgings, the sun was alive along the alleyways. He fully expected to meet Neoloth in his cups, but the room was empty.

Where was the wizard? And . . . what was the next step? He would not kill the general. But if Neoloth attacked him . . .

How would he respond?

Certainly, he need not help!

He sighed. Things were so much more complicated these days that it almost made his head hurt.

His thoughts were interrupted by a knock on the door. It couldn't be Neoloth. The wizard would have simply entered, ser-vile on the outside, imperious once inside. Aros thought the change was amusing and enjoyed watching it.

But it wasn't Neoloth at the door. It was a boy of perhaps four-teen years, with a pale and narrow face, who wore a quasi-military uniform. He handed Aros an envelope. "From Jade Silith, sir."

Aros nodded. He waited for the boy to leave, then opened the envelope.

To Captain Kasha

You are cordially invited to the birthday celebration hunt of General Sinjin Silith.

He gazed at it, aware that he was beginning to smile so widely that it would have been embarrassing in public.

The door opened again, and this time Neoloth walked in. As expected, his posture changed the moment he was in the room.

"Things are going well," Neoloth said.

"Very," Aros replied. Without being certain why, he concealed the invitation. "Where have you been?"

"Planning," Neoloth said. He was keeping something to himself, but that wasn't surprising. Each of them had secrets. "And you?"

Aros grinned. "Let's say I've made a friend," he said. "And leave it at that."

Neoloth was angling for something, Aros was certain, but he wasn't sure what.

"I know that our transportation will be back in harbor in a week, at the next moon," the wizard said. "Our plans need to be complete by then."

"Complete." That meant the princess rescued, and their escape in hand. "That means very careful timing," Aros said. "Escape will be difficult once the alarm goes up."

"We'll need a distraction. I have something in mind," he said.

"What?"

Neoloth smiled. "When the time is ready, you will know."

So. Trust was running thin. That reinforced his sense that it would be wise to keep his own secrets to himself.

Neoloth was straightening his side of the room. It seemed to Aros that he was somewhat odd about it, repeating the same movements in a pattern. In entirely too casual a voice, the wizard asked, "What are your plans tomorrow?"

"Was there something you needed me to do?"

"If I did?"

"I would have to find an excuse to my officers," Aros said, lying automatically. "There is a training ride to the northern border. I'm expected to lead the men."

Neoloth seemed to consider, then turned, suddenly seeming lighter. "Ah! That's right, you've been promoted. The responsibilities of office. I should have news for you upon return."

Aros nodded. "Good. I'm ready to get the hell out of here." He yawned. "And now . . . it was a very long and active evening. I need sleep before I report to the barracks."

He sighed and rolled onto his bed, covering himself with a blanket and turning to the wall. He was asleep within moments.

Neoloth watched his companion, feeling a vague twinge of guilt. Should he have told Aros of his plans? No. He had saved the Aztec's life and nearly destroyed his newfound alliance in the process. But all would be well. For the first time, he could actually see the means of bringing this affair to a satisfactory conclusion.

If he could get the princess to the harbor and away before the alarm was raised.

If he could break the princess out of her prison.

If the Red Nun's information was accurate, and she was not playing some *other* twisted game.

And most important . . . if the general's upcoming birthday could be made his last.

THIRTY

The Birthday Party

South of the Great Wall was a path of hills far kinder to travelers and day walkers than the harsh and foreboding mountains. This was where the general's caravan headed, on horse and carriage and an odd machine that spat steam.

"I don't understand these things," Aros said, "but I might get used to them."

Jade Silith said, "They are amusing. I'm not sure our horses are in danger of losing employment, but it is comfortable."

The general rode his horse next to the little steam engine. "I love horseflesh," he said, laughing. "But I have to admit that they can be fractious. I do believe the traffic will all flow more naturally when everything moves by motor."

"Motor." Aros would remember the new word, for Neoloth's sake.

Jade had recruited him as her driver for the day, and he was enjoying it. "I still don't understand how it works. Is there a small dragon or demon in that iron container?"

Silith shook his head. "No, I think not. But I'd be lying if I said I knew all about it."

"How does Shrike have such things?" Aros asked. "I thought that I'd traveled far, and I've never seen anything like what you have here. These strange things that fart steam. The wheeled vehicles that pedal. The steaming ships in your harbor. And the cannons your men carry." He shook his head. "What wonders! How did you come to possess them? Why don't others have them?"

"There are secrets," the general said.

"Oh, Sinjin," his wife laughed. "You and your secrets. I was asking him just those things myself, and he gave me this carriage as a gift." She leaned closer to Aros, and whispered: "I think that the idea was that I stop asking questions."

"Did it work?" he asked, looking from her to the general.

"For a while. He tells me just a little while longer, and all my questions will be answered."

"Can I have such a carriage?" Aros asked.

"You can have much, much more," Silith replied.

"How much more?"

"I think you're advancing just fine," he replied. "All things in time."

All morning, the caravan wound up the mountainside, until they were high above the ocean. Aros helped the general's wife from the wagon and looked down into the waves.

"Quite a drop," he said. The waves crashed together below.

Pools and tides and swirling foam. Few large rocks, but it was still a sobering sight.

Servants were setting up a pavilion beneath which the general's party would sup and enjoy the sight of the sun sinking toward the horizon.

"When I was a boy," Silith said, "I loved coming up here."

"What's on the other side of the mountain?" Aros asked.

"The section behind the Great Wall," he said.

"And when will I see this sight?"

"Soon," Silith said. "Have patience."

"Was that easy for you?"

Silith laughed. "What do you think?"

Although Aros had been introduced to the general's friends and family as a bodyguard, there was no mistaking the beam of pride on Jade's face whenever she gazed upon him, to the point where the family was whispering about her. No doubt their first thought was something unwholesome: that she had taken a young lover. Silith's approval of Aros complicated things, he supposed, but then these civilized folks had ways beyond his understanding. He was, after all, a simple man, with simple tastes and appetites.

Mijista Wile sat next to Jade, providing enough private conversation that the expressions of the other women were filled with steamy speculation. Aros felt the back of his neck burn as the men enjoyed the afternoon with races and archery games.

No matter what the game, the general was the winner. At padded swords, no one even came close. No two of them matched him, but when Aros joined forces with another officer, they were at last able to extend him a bit, before he booted the officer in the gut and trapped Aros's blade down, elbowing him in the chest to disarm him. The general roared with laughter, flipped the mock sword up on the toe of his boot, and flipped it into the air.

He caught it, spinning, by the hilt, and handed it back.

"Your Aztec blade, Flaygod. I would try it."

Aros had doffed that blade in exchange for a more traditional but padded weapon for the play. A practice session with live blades required the utmost skill and trust between competitors.

The audience murmured: clearly they understood this. And more: it was to be a clash of very different weapon styles. This . . . would be fascinating, for all involved.

Aros walked to his seat at the pavilion and picked up his belt and Flaygod's sheath. Extracted it and weighed it in his hand.

"Tell you what," the general said. "I'll wager a gold purse against Flaygod that I can disarm you within ten strokes."

Aros squinted at him. "No, thank you. My needs are few."

Silith smiled. "I'll use my left hand. That should give you enough advantage."

Aros stood on the far side of a combat circle they had drawn in the ground for their games. He leaned on Flaygod and grinned at the general. "I'm a simple man, General. My needs are few."

Silith nodded, and the witnesses, who had begun to gather more closely, standing and sitting on the grass next to the cliff, laughed and leaned forward in anticipation.

Ah, well, might as well get this over with.

There was no question that Flaygod was a superb melee weapon, and intimidating to most. It wouldn't be to Silith, and a pointed weapon had advantages against one that depended on momentum. On the other hand, the design might work well for a man with greater speed and sufficient strength. Silith had far greater skill and was almost certainly stronger. But Flaygod actually made better use of strength than the sword. And Aros believed that, if skill was removed from the equation, he was actually faster.

Of course, skill wasn't removed from the equation . . .

He smiled. "Shall we begin?"

The general had barely said "yes" when Aros charged him, in quasi-berserker mode, trusting that the general's very skill would give him an advantage. The general would not want to injure him . . . too badly. And that meant that if he attacked full-out, Silith would have to use some of his skill just to keep the engagement safe. It was Aros's job to only *appear* to go berserk, because if there was an opening . . . if his ferocity did achieve its objective—

He would have to be careful to reserve enough control to prevent injury.

As the initial assault unfolded, the general's back was to the cliff, and as Aros adjusted his charge, the sun coming from the east was in Aros's eyes.

Those things combined to create a moment's disconcertion, a moment when, if Aros had been totally committed, the third clash of club upon sword could have ended in an upstroke that might have ripped away scalp.

Instead, it grazed Silith's hair, close enough that the audience groaned with appreciation. His club came down on the sword near the handle, and only a clever twist by the general kept it from being shivered out of his hand.

Aros groaned. That was all he had, and he knew that this next part would be no fun at all. The general grinned at him. "That . . . was very good. Try this."

And then Aros's illusion that he was in any way faster than the general dissolved in a blur of steel. Silith's blade was here, there, everywhere at once. With some bare part of his mind Aros realized he was being paid a singular honor: Silith had been almost embarrassed, and this was a reassertion of dominance. Twice he could have disarmed Aros, but continued to blaze to demonstrate his supreme skill, keeping the Aztec on his toes: *here, there, high, low, left, right* . . .

Never had he seen such a display. Only at the last moment did he realize that he had been too preoccupied with the leaping steel dart. He had been circled around until his back was to the cliff.

Silith paused, grinning, breathing a little heavy as Aros looked back over his shoulder at the waves below. It looked like a *looong* way.

Aros dropped Flaygod to the ground. He was covered with sweat, heaving for breath . . . but for some reason he was uncertain of, he was pretending, just a bit. He wasn't as tired as he was acting. And he had a glimmer of insight: if, and *if* was a nasty word, he had been able to keep the fight going another minute or two, Silith might very well have become fatigued.

Silith roared with appreciation. "And that was the most fun I've had in moons, young man. You are a righteous challenge!" He put his arm around Aros's shoulders as they applauded.

The food had been cooked in pits, bread and meat and corn and desserts of iced fruits, and there was plenty, and it was a feast such as Aros had rarely known.

Mijista Wile's hand was on his knee much of the feast. Her slanted gaze told him that she anticipated the night beyond as much as she did the meal itself. He liked that.

One at a time, the guests stood and said great things about a great man. At first he thought that this was reserved for those who had known him longest and best, but then realized that there was a pattern to the seating. He was not under the far awning with the guards and servants. He was here, with family and friends.

Somehow, he hadn't let himself understand fully what the meaning of that was until he realized that all eyes were upon him, and that he was expected to say something.

Suddenly unsure of himself, he rose to his feet. His throat seemed to close. What was he supposed to . . . ?

"Go ahead," Mijista whispered to him.

He nodded. "I came to Shrike," he said. And laughed, because he noticed that a black shrike had landed on the grass before them, seemed to be watching them. It was a sign, he decided.

"I came here with nothing but my manservant and was welcomed into your hearts. Madam Silith and the general have been more than kind to a poor wanderer, giving me opportunities and connections I could not have found in a lifetime. Because they were willing to look beyond the surface."

Damn it, he was starting to choke up. He didn't want that, was embarrassed by it, but the faces gazing at him, and the beautiful woman at his side who reached up to take his hand . . . the face of Madam Silith, with tears sparkling in her eyes, and that of the general himself, his broad face carved with a warm smile . . .

He felt like utter shit.

And he felt at home. He raised his cup. "To the greatest swordsman, the greatest soldier"—he nodded to Madam Silith—"the greatest husband, and the greatest man I've ever known. Happy birthday, General Silith!" And they applauded as he sat back down.

"That was very good," Madam Silith said, leaning over.

"You are too kind," he said.

"No. Not really. If I had been more kind . . ." She stopped herself, her voice suddenly choked.

But he knew what she had not said, what she wanted to say: "If I had thought of my son, instead of politics, I would not have sent you away. This would be your family."

As if she knew he was reading her thoughts, without moving her lips, she went on. "But thank the gods, there are some mistakes that can be remedied."

He did not ask her what she meant. He knew, and she knew that he did.

And there it was.

And if only he hadn't been about to betray them both, his whole world could have begun here and now.

There were three shrikes on the grass now, looking at him. Laughing, no doubt.

THIRTY-ONE

The Birds

After the meal, there was music and dancing. Aros was nimble enough but knew none of the court dances that the king and his court knew so well. The old man was spryer than he looked and seemed to enjoy the outing fully.

Aros's feet tangled about one another as he attempted the complex patterns of the various court dances. By the serpent! He preferred the simple quicksteps of the desert folk to these ankle twisters!

But Mijista Wile got him up when they played a more sprightly tune than what had induced the king and his lady to click their heels. The queen had died years before, and the king's mistress was certainly not destined for the throne. She was a big, handsome woman who supported him inconspicuously during the dance . . . or did she? Now he was guiding her. Stronger than he looked.

But it was the general and his lady who captured the day. Their affection and mutual regard was so clear and strong that it overshadowed all else. Whatever else was true about General Silith, he and his wife moved as one creature, a thing of grace.

Even the birds seemed to appreciate the day (since the time he had begun dancing, the shrikes seemed to have multiplied, until the trees around them were heavy with black feathers).

As sunset approached, the servants began to pack up the equipment. The king had already made his apologies and returned to the palace, and the rest of them were feeling that they had had a very good, full day . . . especially the Aztec wandering among them.

The steam carriage was hot and ready to go as he swung up on it, Mijista Wile at his side. He looked back at the trees. "Are they always like that?" he asked.

The trees were heavy with the birds now, like fruit trees burdened until the branches bow low. Thousands of small, bright, beady shrike eyes watched them, enough eyes to suck some of the joy from the day.

Aros's skin was crawling. They needed to be out of here. On their way. The king and his train were already well down the road.

The caravan proceeded with a sense of haste that was at odds with the leisurely way they had arrived. Birds were perched on the rocks, on the branches, and now, as the sun began to set, they wheeled in the sky itself.

Aros was just about to speak when he heard something, one tone that was low and high at the same time, soft and loud. Almost as if it was coming from inside his head rather than from an exterior source. It was unnerving . . .

It had an immediate effect. The birds attacked.

In their thousands, they swarmed, attacking every human being on that narrow trail and then converging on the general's carriage itself.

Silith had thrown himself over Jade as the shrikes attacked, wave after wave of feathered death, beaks and tiny claws tearing. Thousands darkened the sky. Individually, or even in dozens, they might not have been more than a nuisance.

Aros and the bodyguards did what they could to shield their charges, as the general roared and Madam Silith screamed. Man after man plunged off the edge of the roadway. "Back up the path!" Silith called, his face shrouded with his cloak as the birds dove mercilessly at his eyes and face.

Another scream, and another man plunged off the edge of the cliff, howling as he plummeted onto the rocks.

"Back up, back to the top!" the general screamed. The steam car was the most covered conveyance, and several piled in, while other guests fled down the mountain. Aros guarded his eyes as birds pecked at his arms, but he was able to note that the guests were pursued with less vigor.

This was deliberate. Conscious. A targeted attack.

The birds were after the general, and the rest of them were simply collateral damage. The general's party was almost obscured, and Silith's very attempt to protect his wife was placing her at risk.

Aros dropped out of the carriage so he could swing his *Macuahuitl*. His cloak wrapped around his face, he ran up the trail after the others. By the time he reached the top, the birds were wheeling and diving. Two more guests had fallen and were crawling toward the side of the mountain, birds pecking and clawing at them. The ground was littered with corpses, human and feathered.

With arm and cloak shading his eyes, he managed to spot where they had gone, an opening shaded by a clump of bushes.

"General!" Aros screamed, running faster, and as he neared the wall, the birds swarmed him more ferociously. He was blind by the time he staggered into the bushes.

They were just birds, just damned birds. This was a hell of a way to die . . .

A brawny arm snaked out of the bushes and dragged him back. The bushes were pushed aside to make room for him, and then tumbled back into place.

Aros lay on his belly, huffing for breath and shaking. Just birds. Birds, damn it!

He rolled over. The general was holding a torch: real fire. He looked at Aros with sympathy, his face torn and bleeding, but somehow managing to smile. "Perhaps they just wanted to wish me a happy birthday," he said.

Madam Silith clung to him, blood running down her leg, Mijista Wile improvising a bandage.

"What is happening?" Madam Silith asked.

"It's a repeat of what happened in the desert," the general said.

"Search yourself," Aros said, and held the torch for the general as he patted himself down. Shadow flickered back in the tunnel. It stretched back farther than the light. "What is this place?" he asked.

"When we were building . . . certain things," the general said. He had already removed his cloak and was searching pockets and weapons pouches. "We made a connection to a system of caves and explored them."

"Why?"

The general looked at him carefully and seemed to be mulling a decision. "The Hundred have a project which must remain se-cret . . . for longer than you would believe. This tunnel was one of the means by which it might one day be discovered. So the tunnel must be sealed, eventually. I knew it of old, and in fact it was in investigating it that I found the location for the party."

"Coincidence."

The general had finished looking through his clothing. He was bruised and cut, and he limped. "I don't see anything," he said.

The brush they had piled into the tunnel opening shook as wave after wave of birds thundered into it. They were crawling through, breaking their wings on the branches. Chittered, until Mijista Wile clapped her hands over her ears and screamed, "Make them stop! Make them stop, please!"

"It's that damned hunting lure again," Aros said.

"Then if I strip?"

"It's too late," Aros said. "It's all over you now. They'll kill you no matter what."

Madam Silith clung to her husband. "What are we going to do?" she asked.

Silith stood up, bleeding, leaning back against the wall. "I can lead them away. You'll survive."

Seven words to say good-bye.

Given the general's enormous vitality, in an hour he might have recuperated enough to be able to do it, but in the current condition there was no chance. None.

Unless.

"Give your clothing to me," Aros said.

"What are you doing?" Silith was hurrying, stripping off his clothing.

"Here. Mijista, love, take the water. Mix it with earth and smear the general with mud. Dampen the scent."

"What are you going to do?"

"I'm going to lead them away," Aros said. Would Neoloth rage if Aros saved the general again? Ah, well.

Mijista clung to him, eyes pleading. "You can't. They'll kill you."

"They have to catch me first," he replied, wishing he felt as confident as he sounded.

A few more birds managed to wiggle their way through the briars. The servants thrashed and stomped at them in desperation.

"I'll draw them out," he told the servant. General Silith's brow still oozed blood into his eyes, so much so that it almost blinded him.

"Boy," he said to Aros. "You are the biggest fool I've ever met. Either that or . . ." He couldn't finish the sentence.

"Say it," Madam Silith said. "Say it, damn you. He's about to die for you. At least you can acknowledge him."

Silith sighed. "Either that . . . or you are my son."

Aros laughed. Damn, that felt good. "Let's save the family stuff for later."

Silith doffed his shirt, displaying his massively muscled upper body. An older warrior he was, but still impressive in every way.

Aros took the shirt, breathed in it . . . and was unable to smell anything but General Silith's sweat and blood. Then . . . far down at the base of the grime was a different smell, something that seemed rather like a sweetness, vaguely decayed, perhaps something that wouldn't be detected unless one was looking for it.

Oddly, he was relieved. At least this wasn't Neoloth's work. He'd been afraid to think that thought.

"Do you smell anything?" Silith asked.

"Not quite the same as with the cannibal worms," Aros said. "Who laid your clothes out for you today?"

"Someone I'm going to have a very hard conversation with. When we're through this."

Madam Silith embraced him while the servants screamed at the blockade, waving their torches to drive the shrikes back.

Aros donned the clothes. Mijista Wile kissed him deeply. "Come back," she said.

"Good plan," he replied, and then turned toward the opening.

"Peel a corner!" he called. This would be brutal. He covered his face, except for his eyes, and pulled his hands down inside Silith's cloak so that nothing was visible.

"Stop. I know a way out. Halt, boy!"

When Aros turned to look at him, there was an expression on Silith's face he had not before seen. Fear? Silith examined the men and women crowded into the passage, eyes filled with strong emotion. But . . . what?

"You would do this thing?" Silith asked him, and his black eyes searched Aros's face deeply. "For me and my family. You would give yourself?"

Aros shivered. "I might get away with diving off the cliff. Doff the clothes. Swim." Miss the rocks? Was it even possible? And if he did, would the birds kill him even in the water? As frenzied as they were?

And what amazed him was that he knew there was a part of him that did not care.

"Yes," he said, meeting Silith's gaze with cold control of the fear he felt boiling within him.

Jade Silith brushed his cheek with the back of her hand as Mijista wrapped her arms around him.

And then both of them looked at Silith, as if hoping for a miracle.

Silith sighed deeply. "I believe you," he said. "And that is why I cannot let you do it."

The birds chittered behind them. Starving. Angry. "Take that off," he said. "Slather yourself with mud: wash as much of the smell off you as you can. And then . . . I will show you something. But"—his voice rose to reach the servants and soldiers—"you must swear not to reveal what I show you, to anyone. Do all of you so swear?"

They nodded, mumbled. Aros had no idea what was about to unfold but recognized the voice of command when he heard it. He stripped off the clothes and slathered mud over his body. Mijista helped, and, although her hands were brisk and businesslike, she found time and opportunity for a few lingering touches.

When he kissed Mijista, Madam Silith smiled through her own pain.

General Silith had taken his torch down the cave and was examining the rock face. Aros stood at his side, striving to see what he saw. Nothing but the end of the cave.

"Here," Silith said. "Strike here, with Flaygod." He indicated the rock.

"What?"

"Strike!" the general roared, and Aros struck overhand with both arms. Once, twice, three times, and on the fourth he felt the rock shudder oddly, and was heartened, and on the fifth it crumbled.

The rock had not been natural rock at all, but something else, fibrous stuff that resembled stone but was less sturdy.

Now they tore at it with their fists. The lower corner of the rock wall crumbled, leaving a space wide enough for a man to crawl through, and this the general did, on hands and knees. "Hand me the torch!" he called back.

Aros handed the torch through the hole and then, growing impatient, crawled after him.

He stood on the far side, next to the general. The torch cast light for twenty feet or more, but then darkness swallowed the illumination. Behind him came a servant, who helped Jade through, then Mijista. Then more.

"What is this?" Aros whispered.

"When I was a boy," Silith said, "I knew every inch of these tunnels. It was part of why I knew the plan could work."

"What plan?" Aros asked, mystified even more.

Silith's face was grim, his gaze a self-crucifixion. "You will see. They didn't tell me everything, but I have spies. Shrike help me, you will see."

They pulled others through the hole. Sixteen had crawled through before they heard screams on the far side, and the fluttering of wings: the birds had pecked their way through the makeshift barrier.

The last servant tried to crawl through the hole. His face was a mask of blood, eye sockets crimsoned. He screamed: "Go! Go!" He shuddered, balling himself up, perhaps to minimize the amount of skin exposed to the birds, perhaps to plug the hole.

The birds were devouring him alive.

"As he wished," Silith called. "Fill the hole!"

And they did, piling rocks to cover what was left of the body, and then the hole.

The sixteen survivors panted, faces pale and strained in the light of their flickering torches.

Aros brought up the rear. "This way," Silith called back.

"Husband," Jade asked. "Who did this? Who sealed up this tunnel? What is this all about?"

"I did," he said. "With the help of those who tried to kill me.

For the second time. Hang on to each other; don't get separated. My spies tell me we'll see things that aren't there."

She seemed about to ask him another question, but he waved it away. "There will be a time for questions later. Now . . . watch your step."

He showed them the edge of the trail, leaned over into a pit deep enough that the torchlight ended in midnight. He nudged a rock over the side with his toe, and it fell for two long breaths. They all stuck closer to the wall after that.

THIRTY-TWO

Tunnels Branching

P ut out the torches." Silith put his own out. "There are explorers all through here. We don't want to be seen. There
will be a kind of light."

Now Aros's hands had to serve as his eyes.

Silith talked, his voice a little blurred by cave echoes. "The cavern runs from a wide mouth into channels that fission out like
tributaries of a river. It may have been *formed* by an underground
river. When witches within the Hundred talked of a river of time,
it seemed to fit what I knew of the cavern."

There was light . . . was that light? Or a flickering in Aros's
brain? He saw blocky, glassy shapes reaching high, lined with

rectangular arrays of lighted dots. His hands told him where the cave walls were, and they didn't match this oddness.

The general called, "Stay together. What do you see? Great buildings? Heek! Watch it through here; there's a flash of light."

For Aros the flash came several steps later. It burned through his closed eyelids for just a moment. When he saw again it was a fiery cloud, shaped like a toadstool. Gone now. Stumps of enormous buildings.

The general called, "I'm turning us around. We took the wrong direction, into one of the futures."

"Dear? *One* of the futures?" Jade was losing her emotional balance. The birds hadn't done that to her, but this did.

"The Hundred were able to turn the cavern system into a map of time," Silith said. "There are many futures. I never dared walk these paths myself, but I listen. The less likely futures pinch off. Getting into these worlds, getting magical stuff out of a future, requires spells I don't know."

Aros said, "A spell must be working here." He wasn't touching rock with his left hand. This was a smooth surface, curved metal. A cleverly shaped handle. Pull, reach inside . . . leather . . . buttons and twisty things . . . a sudden cannonade of light.

"Leave it, Kasha. Don't lose touch," the general said.

Here was a building, seen by night, that ran up and up and . . . "I heard of this. It goes up to reach the stars," Silith said. "A cable. One of the Hundred tried to tell me how it hangs from itself, from the sky, but I didn't understand. I know where we are, though. We turn here."

Aros considered silence, but then he'd never know. "Why did you need slaves?"

"Sacrifice powers their magic," Silith said.

Aros said, "There were children among the captives I saw."

Jade said, "Dearest?" on a rising note.

"No! No, dear. No, Kasha. No children are sacrificed. The children are needed for the exploring."

Aros said nothing.

"Turn here and I'll show you. Feel how the rock converges? This one's short. To get farther into this future, you need to be small, a child or a dwarf."

"I'm small," said Zunsher, one of the younger soldiers. "I can . . . here, I'm holding something the size of a man. A barrel, weird to the touch, like a big pisspot, from the smell. Squeeze past that and . . ." The voice trailed off.

Jade asked, "Why did Kasha see *more* children? When do the Hundred have enough?"

"I asked. They get lost," the general said. "Or they run, when they find a future they desire. Freeman Zunsher, where are you?"

Nothing.

They went up and down and around through chambers and caverns, and past running water that flowed in streams and cascades and constantly moistened the air and filled the chambers with echoes. Aros had never been in caverns like these, with sawtooth daggers projecting from the ceiling to gouge a scalp. Bats, disturbed by their passage, flew above them.

Mijista Wile had dropped back to his side and took his arm, as much for affection as comfort. "I'm glad you're with us," she said. "And I think that Jade and the general feel much the same."

"I'm glad you're not here without me."

"Really?"

"Woman, you must have noticed that I'm not allergic to your company. How can we not share these wonders?" What they saw was not the cave but a line of messages glowing in weird colors, every message different, running on both sides of a wide, flat, glistening wet stone path. The cavern followed for a bit, then veered away.

She laughed and snuggled closer to him, and in the cool air of the cave, he noticed more than ever her warmth.

He asked, "Can you see the opportunities?"

"To see the future? But there must be many wrong futures."

"Even those must hold miracles. And we're being led past them. These wizards are looting time, and killing to do it."

Silith called, "I've finally put us in the main trunk, going back into the past. This'll get us home. We may have to fight."

The troop followed a curve, following Silith. Aros's questing hands found—"Hold up a breath, General?"

"Yes, but keep talking, Kasha."

"It's too narrow for my shoulders, but I can get my head— Hello. It's a melee. Or looting after a battle." In a glare of wizard's light, Aros was looking at an array of random wealth and a swarm of strangely garbed folk grabbing at it all, sometimes fighting over it, clothing, tools, dishware, silverware. A nine-year-old girl was staring solemnly at Aros. Her arms clutched a silver flagon with a lid and a cord trailing down from it. Her clothes were familiar, Quillian garb.

Aros gestured to her. "Come, girl. Come with us."

She shook her head. Turned and walked away. "She's escaping, General," Mijista called. "Maybe she'll find . . ." She trailed off.

The general moved on, and they followed.

"I was saying that you have been accepted," Mijista said. "By me . . . by Jade, and now the general. But I can feel that you aren't comfortable with it. And that makes me wonder why."

"Everyone seems to believe that I'm this prince," he said, finally, realizing the source of his discomfort. "What if I'm not? What if I'm just a wanderer?"

"Maybe you're selling us short," Mijista said. "Perhaps we see clearly. Perhaps we see who you are now, not what you might have been years ago. Did you not consider that?"

Aros nodded in the dark. "I'd considered it, yes . . ."

"You saved General Silith. Were willing to die to protect us. Does it not occur to you that those things, in themselves, would earn affection?"

Aros wanted to grumble, to say *wait, not me, not ever me* . . .

But could not. Here, in this place below the earth, perhaps outside the earth, they didn't care. And if they didn't, why couldn't he accept the gift of their regard?

The line came to a halt. He looked ahead and saw that the general had raised his hand: *stop.*

Aros squeezed Mijista's arm and made his way along the line, noticing how tired and frightened they seemed. The path had widened. Thirteen, there were only thirteen now. Near panic.

When he reached the general, the larger man said, "We are near the main cavern. You will come with me?" Aros noted the question. And, clearly, the general was uncomfortable about something. In a lesser man, he might have been seeing fear or guilt.

Silith went to his wife, Jade, who was clearly near exhaustion and trembling. "I'll be back."

"Are you taking Kasha with you?" she asked, looking anxiously from one of them to the other in the glow of timelight.

"Yes."

"Good," she said. And then she looked at Aros. "Keep him safe."

"Yes, ma'am."

She kissed Silith. And then, impulsively, kissed Aros as well. He felt dizzy.

The background light, the timelight, had faded almost to nothing.

Together, Aros and the general crept forward. At first they sidled along a wall and then moved down to all fours as the ceiling dropped. He had no idea how the general was finding his way through the gloom, but he never seemed to hesitate.

Then there was a glimmer ahead, and a shimmering radiance that grew brighter and wider, expanding as they approached. Silith stopped, and a moment later the great man's hand was on his shoulder. "This I've seen," he said.

Wizard light lit the cavern mouth. Not far within was what looked like a heap of wire netting covering something Aros did recognize: a stone altar of a type used across many of the southeastern lands. He looked for bloodstains but saw none.

Aros asked, "Did you see it used?"

"No. They wanted me intimidated, not terrified."

Aros was about to ask another question when he heard a scream. Seeking its source, he saw a man, muscular and stripped to the waist, dragged into the mouth of the cave, toward the netting.

The man was struggling, and if his arms had not been tied behind him and his feet shackled, Aros would have given him an excellent chance against the pair dragging him to the altar.

The netting stood up. It wobbled into the shape of a spherical cage, five-sided outlines with the altar in the center. Aros remembered something from his past and said, "Pentagrams. It's all pentagrams."

"Does that matter?"

"I don't know. Wizards like pentagrams. Are you moved to interfere, sir?"

"Not yet," the general whispered.

They chained the half-naked victim to the altar, which was of polished stone, with shackles positioned for a spread-eagle victim. They attached each wrist to an iron cuff. He managed to wrench an arm free and smash his fist into a captor's face before the arm was grappled down and anchored.

He tossed himself back and forth, heaving against the shackles, until his wrists bled with the effort and his lips were frothed.

Aros was simultaneously fascinated and horrified. Lights began to dance around the sacrificial platform, and, as Aros watched, the victim's skin began to glow . . . and then bubble. Aros watched him evaporate, skin and muscle and then organs, until there was nothing left but the skeleton.

But, hideously, the skeleton was still alive, the bones still moved on their own accord, thrashing as if in pain, still somehow sensate.

Aros and the general slid back from the edge.

"What is that?" Aros said.

"It's the power that shapes the time tunnels," the general said.

How long have you known about this? he wondered but asked instead, "Who are those people?"

"They are the ones who tried to kill me. Again." His eyes burned. "I swore never to reveal this secret, but everything has changed now. Everything." He looked at Aros directly. "What happens next depends on you, young man."

"Me?"

"Yes. I am about to go against everything I have committed to for the last decade. When my son was taken from me, I swore revenge. I was filled with hatred for everything in the world except my good lady wife. I never thought anything could fill that void."

"I think I understand."

"I think you do. But you more than understand. Suddenly, you are here. And you have saved my life, twice. And saved the life of my wife and my friends."

"General . . . ," Aros said. "I have never claimed to be your son."

"My wife thinks you are, and Mijista is falling in love with you. You never claimed to be my son. But that doesn't mean we weren't intended to think so." He gripped Aros's arm. "I ask you one question, and one question only, man to man. No lies, no games. I think you owe me that much."

"And more," Aros said.

The general nodded. For a moment there was no general and lieutenant. There was no elder and younger. Not even false father and faux son.

There were just two men, knowing that some things could not be known and prepared to settle for those that could be, as men have done since the beginning of time.

"Did you know about the attack on my family?" he asked, urgently.

Without hesitation, Aros replied, "On my life and honor, I did not."

The general stared into him, holding his wrist as if taking his pulse, as if some force within him was trying to crawl into Aros to see the world through his eyes. The intensity of the gaze so strong it had an impact like a physical blow. He barely wanted to blink.

Then . . . the focus receded, and there in the dim light from below, Aros saw an old man, a man who had made too many mistakes, and one whose judgment of himself was almost too heavy to bear.

"You . . . would have died for me."

"I saw a trick," Aros said. "Something I might get away with. I wanted you and your family to live and saw a way to make it happen."

The general shook his head. "I see in you what Jade sees," he said. "The rest doesn't matter."

He smiled. "And that means that nothing that has happened until now matters. But what happens now matters very much indeed." His smile grew broader and colder. "I think Flaygod has work to do."

THIRTY-THREE

The Tower

The night had grown cold, and as Neoloth walked the deserted streets with Shyena the Red Nun, he was very aware of every sound, every sight. Not just because these were things that might influence their plan's successful outcome, but because things could go very wrong indeed. This might be the very last night of his life.

In that case . . . perhaps it was time to appreciate the stars and the moon. The faint salt-ocean tang. The sounds of carts and tradesmen in the early morning, preparing for the day.

So many things, so little time. And he wondered if he had given them enough time and emphasis. Whether his striving for power, at all costs, had been the actions of a foolish man.

Here he was, rescuing a princess. The woman at his side was strong and useful and sensual, and she would take him as a mate.

Together, they would make quite a pair, capable of achieving . . . things undreamed.

But not for a moment had he seriously considered changing his path. Princess Tahlia ruled his heart, and he could only wonder about that. He had played a role, until the role had become him.

Shyena took him through the trade section of the city. "As you know, the royal family has secret escape tunnels built into the residence. There are also secret tunnels connecting the Tower to the outside, in case the family was ever captured and jailed there in war."

"Stranger things have happened."

She pulled them into shadow and watched a tavern across the road. It was dark. "I was fairly certain that it would be abandoned at this hour."

Neoloth recognized the Happy Orc. He'd eaten there. "I know this place."

"You think so?" She grinned at him and then hurried them across the street.

The front door was locked, but she produced a key and solved that problem swiftly. Neoloth slipped in.

The room had a smell of tallow and sour fat, with a trace of dried vomit and beer. The previous evening's revels must have been riotous. She led him through the dark room to the kitchen, where a single kitchen boy was curled in the corner on a makeshift bed, asleep.

She studied the boy for a moment and then they continued on. In the back of the shop, she tapped on the floor in a variety of spots until rewarded by a hollow "thump."

The Red Nun bent and pressed the tip of a stiletto into a seam between two stones and levered one up. A loop of leather thong was anchored to a wooden panel beneath. When she pulled that, a ladder was exposed, leading down into darkness.

Neoloth felt the hair on the back of his neck burning. This was a hidden pathway to his princess? He had eaten in this tavern! He had been so close, had actually had an intuitive sense that something about this place was important . . . but had not followed his hunch. Anger boiled his blood.

The wizard followed her down into darkness. The tunnels beneath were dank and night-cold, the walls marked with bits of glowing fungus.

The Red Nun had brought with her one of the odd, small torches that seemed to make light without heat. She had shuttered its opening lens to make a narrower beam, and this was what carried them through the darkness.

He could do little save follow. She seemed to have a sense of where she was going, turning this way and that in the semidark until the tunnel began to rise. They followed the incline for perhaps a quarter of an hour, and then the tunnel came to an end.

"Shhh," she said, and very cautiously opened the door. The room beyond was a weapons' repository. Coals glowed dully in a fireplace. The room was deserted.

"Come," she said. She led them to a narrow staircase that wound up the wall a level, then to another stair leading into the Tower. Before they exited on that level, she stopped them and flattened against the wall.

"Now," she said.

Neoloth opened a vial he had spent the last days preparing. It was filled with a yellow powder, and when he spilled it on the floor, he was careful not to inhale. He stroked a long tube against his talisman and then blew into the powder.

It puffed into the air in a little cloud, but neither dispersed nor settled back down. It was almost invisible in the darkness, but his eyes, darkness-adjusted, could see it slip around the corner like a large, vague caterpillar.

And now he heard the snoring sound. Near.. The snores were interrupted by a strangled sound and then stopped. No sound at all.

The Red Nun peeked around the corner and nodded with satisfaction.

When Neoloth joined her, the guard was very dead, yellowish powder clotted under his nose. She slipped his keys off their ring. They tiptoed down the hall. Several cells on that floor, and Shyena peered into each before coming to the one she sought.

She opened the door. "Princess?" Shyena called. There was a single figure on the straw, asleep, and it stirred . . .

And was revealed as a young woman Neoloth had never seen. "Who are you?"

"Why, Drasilljah. You're with *her*?" The woman suddenly remembered something and concentrated. For an instant, her face flickered and became older, riven with wrinkles, and Neoloth was gob-smacked.

"That . . . is impressive," he admitted once he managed to untangle his tongue. "We'll discuss spells later. Where is the princess?"

Drasilljah clutched his forearms. "Oh, sir! The princess was right. You did come for her. For us. I'm so sorry: you're too late. But you're with her?"

He felt an icy hand on his neck. "No, she's with me. Too late?"

"Yes. They took her away at dusk. There was nothing I could do."

He looked at the Red Nun. "It could be true," she said. "But she may still be alive. If they wish to use her royal blood in a ceremony, they will wait for dawn."

"We have time, then," he said. "We can get to her."

"It is behind the wall," Shyena said. "And in the tunnels. We will need help. Where is your barbarian?"

"I would guess him abed with his new paramour," he said. "We can find him, I think. A simple locator spell should suffice. I tagged him."

Neoloth sank to the floor and held the talisman. It glowed a bit, and then the glow diminished, its power nearly drained. But when he came out of the spell, his eyes were wide.

"He's already in the tunnels," he said.

"How is that possible?" Drasilljah asked, astonished.

"Because he's Aros. If ever there was a spoiler, that is the man."

Something had happened outside, something like a lightning strike. It momentarily shook the ground and lit up the sky outside the little window. Brass horns and screams, and suddenly the floor beneath them vibrated. The Tower was coming to life.

"What in the world?"

Shyena was staring out the window at the end of the corridor. Neoloth and Drasilljah were confused. "What? Who?" A fireball rose high, crested over the enormous wall in back of the capital.

"Aros," he said.

THIRTY-FOUR

Escape

Aros and the general descended upon the guards like avenging demons. There were five of the unfortunates, and they stood no chance at all. The suddenness, violence, and efficiency of the two warriors were part of the problem, and the shock of seeing the general attacking them did the rest.

By the time the guards fully appreciated what was happening, swords were in their gullets and guts, and the uneven rock floor was slippery with their blood.

As his second man dropped, Aros spun to help the general, just in time to see two men attack him from opposite sides. With dazzling footwork, Silith eased between the two and sliced like a man peeling an apple, a long continuous cut that somehow wound between the two men, killing them both with a single stroke.

Aros wiped Flaygod on the gashed body of his second victim. A sense of satisfaction in a job well done and a sense of relief in surviving warred with an odd curiosity. "General," he asked, an ugly thought stirring in his mind, "weren't these your men?"

"No," he said. "Once they were, but they volunteered to work with the Hundred."

"Didn't they think they were . . . ," he started to say, *working for you?* But he saw the haunted expression on Silith's face and thought that silence might be his best option.

"Get the others," the general said, voice flat. Aros didn't argue. He seemed to be getting better at following orders these days.

Aros sprinted up the steep incline of the narrow path carved into the rock face of the cave leading up to the narrow tunnel, crawled back through, and rejoined the others. Jade and Mijista smothered him with kisses and hugs when he told them all was well, and on hands and knees led them through the low passage until they emerged in the cavern.

They walked almost to the cavern mouth and stopped. Eyes went wide as they saw what abutted the mouth of the cave: an artificial wall, a building of some kind backing into it. At the edge of the wall was a mound of bones.

The mound was as tall as two men. Hundreds, perhaps over a thousand, corpses' worth of bones. Aros had never seen such a thing and had been so focused on fighting that he hadn't noticed it even though it had been in plain sight. Human bones.

And coming out of the building, led by the general, were dozens of captives, shivering and terrified, in chains. Slaves, he supposed, most of them. And captives of war—a third of them had the manner of fighting men. Even in the shadow of this horror, they still carried themselves with what he recognized as pride.

And then, coming last from the building . . . You had to look at her. She was calm in the midst of chaos. Bright, alert, ready. Her clothing was filthy, tattered, and hardly regal, but as he came closer he could see that they had been fashioned from excellent cloth. Her bearing was royal, and even though he could see the fear in her face, in her eyes, the set of her lips was strong and determined.

Jade Silith's eyes went from the princess to her husband and back again. And it actually pained Aros to see the changes her face went through: from curiosity to astonishment to comprehension and then . . . to grief.

"What is this?" she asked her husband. "What is all of this? Where have you brought us?" Before he could answer, she turned to the princess.

"Are you Tahlia?" she asked. "I believe I saw a drawing of Your Highness once, and I have heard that you had been captured."

"I am Tahlia, princess of Quillia. And if you can return me to my . . . my . . . country, my mother . . ."

"We can do that," Jade said.

Trembling, Tahlia gathered herself to search Madam Silith's eyes, seeking treachery.

Aros spoke. "I am with Neoloth-Pteor," he said. "Princess Tahlia, I—"

"You?" An Azteca warrior? She wasn't quite buying it. "But where is Neoloth? Wait. What of Drasilljah? My—"

Aros didn't look at Silith. "Neoloth must be trying to rescue you. He'll get Drasilljah, if she's still in the Tower. I hope to meet him later."

She collapsed. All of the strength that had sustained her had drained out at the first kind word or ray of hope.

"Husband," Jade said, and there was something in her voice that Aros had never heard before, from anyone, some combination of emotions that were painful to hear. "The people who tried to kill us. The . . . the Hundred? They kidnapped the princess for their . . . sacrifices. And . . . you rescued her?"

There it was. She knew. Somehow, drawing on things said over the years of their marriage, she'd guessed at more deaths than an Aztec royal could face.

The others, including Mijista, were hovering around the princess or trying to succor the freed victims . . .

Jade knew. But she was asking him to lie to her.

And he would not. Could not. He took her hands in his and stroked her smooth skin with his thumbs. "I was part of this thing."

Her face looked like it was about to crack or melt, and suddenly in the cold and alien light of the crystal tube, she looked old in a way she never had before. Her lip trembled.

"Our son—" he began.

She slapped him, hard.

His face did not turn away. "I was so filled with hate and anger from what happened to our son—"

She slapped him again.

He continued. "I wanted revenge."

"You . . . ," she said, voice swollen with indignation and disbelief. "You would know the pain that I suffered at the loss of our child and give that exact same pain to another woman? And to other children. This is how you honor me? Honor our dead?"

Aros felt more embarrassed than anything else. This was not a discussion he wanted to be a part of, in any way.

"But Kasha made me realize what I did. Made me see. I have been wrong."

"Wrong? Is that how you describe the destruction of everything we've ever been to each other, to the world? Wrong?"

"I'm sorry," he said, and cast his eyes down.

Jade Silith looked around them. At the mountain of bones. The wretched victims. Her anger faded, and with it her strength, and she collapsed against Mijista.

Mijista held her, glancing from the sagging woman to her husband, to the wall of bones and the stunned and newly freed victims to General Silith and back again.

"What do you plan to do now?" she asked.

Silith paused, thinking. Aros thought that he might have remained silent forever had Madam Silith not come out of her trance and looked at him. Their surviving guests. The rescued victims.

"What the hell," he whispered. "They tried to kill me twice. I've slaughtered the men who guarded this tunnel."

"Why?" Jade asked. Aros could tell that she was hoping for an answer that would let her love this man . . . and, more important, trust him.

"They would kill any of you who knew of this. I intended to sneak you out and let them wonder. It won't work. They'll know it was me once they know I survived. I have no allies there. All I have is my family, and I don't even know if I have that."

Princess Tahlia was trying to follow. She asked, looking first at Aros and then the general, "What was this all about?"

Silith said, "To use their magic to open a door to the future and, from that future, to bring weapons that would control the present. Destroy any army that stood against us. And . . . destroy magic itself."

"That's what we were dying for?" Tahlia demanded.

Silith tried to meet his wife's gaze and could not, but he spoke to her. "Yes. Princess, you were a twofold target. Your mother could be controlled with threats, and your royal blood would open the aperture much further. I was insane with grief and rage, and my soul is lost." When he looked at them, there was a pain in his eyes that Aros had rarely seen. "Then I saw you, Kasha. My son, come to life."

Aros started to speak, and the general shushed him. "Neoloth? Your servant? Never mind, I don't want to know more. I ask you for one thing: if I do all I can to undo the hell I have wrought, will you do what you can to protect my wife and guests . . . ?" He smiled at Mijista. "I believe I can trust you to protect my son's would-be bride." The smile hardened. "Do I have your word you will protect the princess?"

Aros fumbled for words. "General, Princess, that word is already given. I . . . she will need to be returned home."

"I believe you are a man of resource," the general said. *No more lies.*

"I will. I so swear, by the Feathered Serpent."

The general nodded. He turned to the captives, who were no longer quite so dazed. "Men!" he called. "Many of you were captured in war. You may not see your homes again. But if you are fighting men, then you can die as warriors instead of sheep. You can fight beside me, and if we win this day, I swear you will be returned to your homes and compensated for the wrongs done to you. And that effort will help the helpless among you, those who cannot fight but were caught up in this terrible thing. So I ask you . . . who fights with me?"

The former captives looked from one to the other, and, one at a time, their arms rose with hands clenched into fists.

"You know what it was like to fight against me," he said. "Now, let us learn what it is to fight together!"

They drummed their chests with their fists, perhaps wary of making too much noise.

"Kasha. The army on this side of the wall is loyal to the Hundred, I'm afraid," he said. "If I can reach my men in the royal barracks, we are saved. But that will require a distraction."

"What do you have in mind?" Aros said, beginning to guess.

"There is the abomination I helped to create," Silith said, waving into the cavern mouth. "And there"—he pointed to wooden crates—"are some of the marvels that were sent back to us. Come."

With the general's help, Aros pried open one of the boxes. It was filled with sawdust and paper-wrapped tubes that looked like candles. He reached out for one.

"Be careful," the general cautioned him. "They have great power."

"What are they?"

"Some sort of strange magic," the general replied. "Little volcanoes. We take a little silver stick—" There was a smaller bundle within the box, and it contained multiple metallic sticks the length of his thumb and not much wider than a nail. The general pushed one into the top of one of the candles. Coiled at the side of the box was a reel of red cord. The general used his knife to cut off a length of it and stuck it down the hole made by the silver stick.

"When I light this, the stick goes 'bang'; then the candle goes 'bang.' You can bundle these together to make a larger 'bang.'"

"I think that might be a very good idea," Aros said.

They worked together for a half hour, grouping boxes of the candles around the base of the main tunnel, then setting several sticks into candles and cords to the sticks.

Long cords.

"These are our lifelines," Silith said. "We must be out of the compound by the time the fuse burns down, or we die. Listen to me!" He raised his voice to a scream.

"There are women and children here. And those who cannot fight. We will have to make our way through the barrier before the candles explode."

"Through the gates? Are they not heavily guarded?" Jade asked.

"There is another way," Silith said.

The prisoners had been held in the rear of the Octagon, and Silith had had to kill only two guards to free them. Aros followed his lead, the fighting men they had freed before and behind, scavenging weapons from the dead as they went.

They encountered scant resistance, and Silith and Aros met it stride for stride. In the moments they had been together, testing each other's skills or fighting in tandem, Aros was learning something different, something new about the art of the sword and combat itself.

Aros's sword was like his arm, obeying his commands instantly. But Silith seemed to be *one* with his sword. His mind and heart were within it, transforming it into an intelligent thing that seemed to have a mind of its own, such that the men who came against him were like cattle presenting themselves for the slaughter. He blended with them, found openings, as water flows through an open hand, leaving death in his wake.

How had such a man made himself a part of such evil? Aros tried not to wonder what some other person would think of the less savory parts of his own past.

Not only had Aros never seen its like, but Silith seemed to inspire him to find that place within himself, such that by the time they reached the outer door, a trail of gashed corpses behind them, both men panting now, he realized he had been transformed by the experience.

"What now?" he asked. "What do we do?"

Silith looked down the hill at the barracks. It had not awakened: their butcher's work had been sufficiently quiet. It seemed that a building constructed to stifle the screams of the damned could also serve to suppress those of the dying.

"Follow me," he said.

Moving from shadow to shadow, Silith led the captives to a section of the wall and probed to find a hidden door. "Through here," he whispered. "You take the front."

"And on the other side?"

"Make your way to my home," Silith said. "Get Jade and Mijista there, and the Quillian princess. It is secure. And get the princess back to her home, whatever it takes."

Aros knew exactly what he needed to do to accomplish that. But what of the others who had accompanied them?

"On the other side of the Great Wall will be those who try to kill you." The fighting men among the prisoners were bloodied now, their stolen swords slicked with gore, their eyes those of rabid wolves. They had no love for the man who had captured them, did not know why he had suddenly become their benefactor, and in time they might very well turn against him. But for now, they were his.

"You will fight through the city," he told them, the call of command still in his voice. "And cut your way to the harbor. Take a ship. Some of you are sailors?"

They nodded.

"Then, good luck." He opened the passageway, and they began to crawl through.

Jade threw her arms around her husband's neck. "What of you?" she asked. "What is your intention?"

"I have business," he said, "with the wizard who tried to kill you. And I will have satisfaction."

Her eyes widened with alarm. "No! Please! Come with us!"

She kissed him, and he drank deeply of her lips. "Know, my darling, that for all my sins, I have loved you more than anything in this life."

He gripped Aros's hand, locking eyes with him. "Fight beside a man, and you know him," he said. "You may or may not be my son . . . but you are my brother. Take care of her. See the princess home."

"That I will do."

And now, at last, a smile curled Silith's lips. "And Mijista would make a good wife—"

Behind them, the sky lit with blue flame, and the earth shook with a ghastly roar. Flame and smoke gushed from the cave, laced with lightning, and then the mountainside collapsed.

"Go!" he whispered fiercely as the entire compound awakened, men crying alarum.

Aros ushered the last of them into the tunnel and closed the door behind him.

THIRTY-FIVE

Changing Faces

General Sinjin Silith was in a killing mood. He flowed from shadow to shadow like a wraith and watched with savage satisfaction as the compound boiled with screaming, running men.

When he encountered a soldier, he let the man run by if possible. But every member of the Hundred, every red robe, he slew without mercy before they could mumble their spells or point their wands. He was almost surprised at how easy it was. Most of their magic must have been invested in the time tunnel, with little remaining for their personal safety.

Bad planning.

He entered the round red building, the compound wherein the

Hundred found strength. And here he encountered the most fanatical guards. Four of them surrounded him.

"General Silith," the largest of them said. "In the name of the One, we are forced to ask for your life."

"Take it if you can," he growled. Silith reversed his sword and stabbed the man behind him, then leapt to grab him. With his left arm, he used the man as a shield, twisting him this way and that to take the sword blows that would have fallen upon his own body, until the human shield was a red ruin and the men who had stood at his side lay bleeding on the ground like broken dolls.

Silith panted, his great chest rising and falling as the killing passion rose within him.

One last thing to do. Kill Belot, the One. He'd seen this male-female apparition several times in his life. He didn't know enough of Belot, and he knew it, but how hard could it be to kill?

He stalked that narrow, dark hallway back to the living quarters of the man-woman he wished to kill. Threw open an impressively massive metal door and stopped in shock. He was looking at himself.

A little too far away. He'd have to charge.

"General Silith," the apparition said. "Good for you to come to me."

Silith laughed. "More tricks. Looking like me won't help your skill."

"No," the apparition said. "But when you're dead, I'll take yours." Then, before Silith could speak, the One raised his hand. There was something like a small hand cannon in it, and there was a flash of fire and a roar, and General Silith felt a terrible blow in his chest.

Right through the bronze armor.

He tried to raise his sword, but to his surprise all the strength seemed to have drained from his limbs. He tried to speak, but his lips couldn't seem to fit around his thoughts. And then . . . darkness.

His very last thoughts were, *Jade, my love. I am so sorry.*

And, *Kasha, be careful.*

THIRTY~SIX

Sanctuary

Aros and the women moved through the streets of Shrike as panic blossomed around them. They were noticed—a big dark warrior guarding three royal women with a weirdly shaped, massive sword—but never accosted.

The freed captives had spread in all directions, seeking to blend with the population. He wished them well, but the fighting men were setting fires and stirring chaos, distractions as the alarms went up, and the odd blue-white lights crackled behind the barricade.

Princess Tahlia seemed to be rising from a stupor. "I never asked. Who are you? Where is Neoloth?"

"I don't know," Aros replied. "But I know where he will be waiting for us. I'm Aros, but call me Kasha."

"Where, then?"

They were moving fast down a narrow, morning-dark street. Footfalls from the other direction, a row of guards, as there was another explosion from the direction of the barricade. Fire raged, and the entire capital seemed to be awakening.

"It's best you not know yet, Princess," he said. "You're moving well. Not like a prisoner."

"I exercised. Stretched. Drasilljah made me, until they separated us. Where are we headed now?"

"To the palace," he said. "It is the only place Jade and Mijista will be safe now."

There was little more talk, but lots of sinking back into shadows and careful silence. They would have been accosted by now, he thought, if Flaygod had seemed an ordinary sword. Aros was just too weird.

Jade was taking the lead now. "I know a way into the palace," she confided as a phalanx of men ran along the boulevard. Somewhere, a man screamed in mortal terror. The armed prisoners were making an attack on the Tower, perhaps seeking to free more allies. He wished them well.

Jade led them to a house butted against the wall around the palace and knocked.

There was a pause, and a hidden slit in the wall—not the door itself—opened. "Madam Silith!" The eyes opened wide. "What is your need?"

"To see the king," she said. "And sanctuary for my friends. There is danger tonight. My husband fights for the crown."

The slit closed and then the door opened, and they were ushered in. This kingdom, Aros thought, seemed riddled with passages. Did no one trust anyone here?

The seven of them were ushered through the house and then down into the basement. One of the walls was pushed aside to reveal a tunnel, and they were ushered along it by a doughy woman who looked as if she had not slept in a month. After a few minutes along the panel, they rose up into another room, through the back door of a cupboard stocked with bags of flour and hanging sides of beef.

The woman opened the outer door and issued them into a small kitchen, perhaps one serving the servants' quarters.

The servants seemed nervous, which was easy to understand considering the noises outside: chaos in the streets; shouting; and, even as he stopped to hear it, the sound of another explosion.

The freed prisoners were keeping their word.

They were ushered through another hall into a well-appointed waiting room, with enough chairs for most of them to sit. "Wait here," the doughy woman said, and left them.

Aros stood, hand on Flaygod's hilt, uncomfortable in the extreme. The last weeks had taken him to places in the world, and within his own heart, that he had never visited, nor thought to.

Jade Silith held his arm, seated, as if afraid that she would slip away into a shark-ridden sea if she lost it for a moment. Mijista held his other arm, and Tahlia watched him closely. In some way he had become a center of strength in the room for all of them.

Damn. Wasn't *this* a strange development!

Princess Tahlia was on Madam Silith's other side. She was in a strange land, surrounded by danger. She had no solid reason to trust any of them. But Jade Silith's obvious sorrow and quiet dignity spoke volumes.

The door opened, and two guards entered the room. "Come with us," they said. One cast a glance at Aros's sword but did not attempt to take it away from him, which was very good for the guard.

They traveled down another corridor, but the appointments were becoming lush now, and he could feel that they were heading deeper into the castle.

They emerged in the throne room. The king sat on his throne, a phalanx of guards on either side of them. Most of them were halted behind a hemp rope, but Jade Silith and Princess Tahlia were beckoned forward.

King Corinth was swathed in a fine robe, but Aros had the sense that he had awakened recently and not had time or interest in donning his usual garb. "Madam Silith," he said, "do you have information for me on . . . on . . ." A robed advisor whispered in his ear. "Ah, yes. The nature of these disturbances? Riots."

"Your Majesty," Jade said. "My husband has uncovered a terrible plot against the crown and is even now risking his life to expose and end the traitors. We ask for sanctuary."

"Yes, yes. Of course. And . . . who is this?"

"She is the Princess Tahlia—"

"May I speak, Your Majesty?" the princess asked.

The king seemed a little taken aback. "Why, yes, of course."

"I am Princess Tahlia of Quillia."

"What are you doing here, my child?"

"My ship was attacked by pirates, and my lady servant and I kidnapped. We were brought here and held in a tower, where terrible things happened that I will not trouble Your Majesty with. Until this night, I had assumed that these things were an act of war against Quillia, but now I see that Your Majesty knew nothing of it, that it was the action of some traitors who have deceived

Your Majesty. It is a tale of magic and horror, my lord, and I am grateful to find safe harbor."

Now Aros saw in the princess what Neoloth had seen. Despite her appearance, humbled by starvation and deprivation, her clothes and hair a ratty bird's nest, there was a natural gentility and power within her that called to him. This was a remarkable young woman. He believed that Neoloth could indeed genuinely love her.

Or she could be a wonderful path to power. Wizards, after all . . .

"What would you have me do, my child?" the king asked.

"Return me to my mother," she said. "If you can do that, I will promise that no actions will be taken against your kingdom. Rather, it will be a symbol of faith and trust—"

"Hold!" a voice called behind them, and striding into the throne room came . . .

General Silith.

Jade almost collapsed with relief the instant she saw him, and Mijista also seemed ready to weep with joy. He was scarred and bleeding but still a towering figure. Jade ran to him, and he embraced her.

"Sire!" Silith said. "I have terrible news for you. There has indeed been a conspiracy of vipers under your very heel, involving members of your loyal corps, the Hundred."

"Indeed?"

"Yes. But, at great cost, the traitors have been killed, and soon peace will be restored." He smiled at the princess. "Princess! I am so glad to see that you are well. Come with me, and we will see you safely home—"

But as he spoke, Jade Silith's face had tightened. She drew back from him, face slack, and then angry.

"You are not Sinjin," she said. "This is not my husband!"

The room grew quiet. Silent. The guards fingering their weapons, while the troops who had followed Silith in the chamber fingered theirs.

"My dear," Silith said. "I'm afraid that the night's affairs have strained your mind. Please forgive her, Your Majesty—"

Jade had torn herself away completely and stood back glaring at the man at her side.

"You are not . . . my husband."

Silith made a placating gesture to the king. "Please, Your Majesty. Understand that the stress of her recent brush with death has unbalanced my wife."

"I understand," the king said. Aros watched the tableau with fascination, unable to speak. What did he think?

"Is something wrong with Madam Silith?" Aros whispered. "It is the general!"

Mijista stiffened. "I trust a woman to know her husband."

"But how . . . ?"

"There are magics," Mijista snapped. "I have heard of such things. This one is called *glamour*."

There was something in her voice that made Aros look at her again. She was as intent as he, but he noted that her hand had tightened on his arm.

"I too have seen such things," the princess said. She seemed to be coming out of her trance. "My lady in waiting can do this."

The king watched them all. "Ah, well, General . . . knight to queen four. Mate."

General Silith flinched, and then relaxed. "Well played, Your Majesty."

The king's eyes glittered. "You know . . . for some time I've known that all of you have considered me a fool. That there was something . . . were things going on in my kingdom that were not of my making. There was little I could do about it, because the power of the priesthood and the military seemed to have been aligned and turned against me."

He appeared to have regained his full stature. "But I believe that Madam Silith is correct. You are not the general. I believe you are Belot and do not know the small games that we play. And if you are imitating the general, then he attempted to move against you and failed. The plot has splintered. And this would be a very good time indeed to become my father's son once again."

There was a slyness in the king's eye that glittered, a sense of power that Aros had not seen before but suddenly recognized. A man who knew his throne was precarious, that his enemies were too powerful to confront directly, and that only if he played the doddering fool could his life be secure.

"This is the wizard, Belot! Seize this creature!" he said to his guard, who hesitated.

"Silith" swept his sword out of its scabbard. For all the speed and smoothness of that draw, Aros knew in that moment that it was not the general.

But the general's men did not see, did not notice. They were entranced by the situation. "On them!" the impostor snarled.

"By the serpent!" Aros snarled and drew his sword. And for a moment he was terribly tempted to dive forward and engage.

Retreat felt like swallowing fire. "Ladies, behind me," he said, and he watched to be sure they'd done that before he began to back away.

The One's grin was a bit wrong. He hadn't noticed what was happening behind him. He laughed, not quite like the general. "No? No fight left?"

"Silith would have known I have promises to keep. Behind you, wizard."

Belot sneered, then looked anyway.

Half of Silith's troops were dropping back, lowering their weapons. More followed. An officer shouted, "General Silith or no, I stand with my king!"

"Guards, attack! Take them, you cowards!" the Silith figure commanded. More dropped back.

Belot lashed out. Two men fell. Silith's remaining troops parted in martial order, leaving him a wide path. The One ran lightly from the throne room, and a score of troops followed.

THIRTY-SEVEN

Shadows

The city burned around them. Somehow, and Neolith was uncertain when it had happened, the fight had shifted. It was not between the escaped sacrificial subjects and the city guard. Now the conflict was between the king's loyal guard and the general's remaining troops.

In the time that they had crept through the streets heading south toward the bay, violence had erupted, and Neoloth figured that he knew who and what was responsible for freeing these victims turned warriors. He saw Aros's handiwork in this.

Aros. His heart ached. Everything had exploded now, and he had no idea how to fix it, where the princess was, or even if she was still alive. There was only one man who could conceivably bring it all together, and that was a man whom he had betrayed. Neoloth had helped the Red Nun get the lure into the general's clothing again, even after massive security had been implemented. One of Shyena's best potions, buttressed by power from the talisman. He hadn't known Aros would be at the party: the Aztec had lied! But if Aros thought he had been betrayed, who knew what he might do?

And yet . . . and yet . . . So much chaos and confusion, and that was the Aztec's specialty. He had been with the general's family. The time tunnel had been attacked. Prisoners freed. Tahlia had been one of the prisoners . . .

He could search for the princess and miss his ship . . . if the message had reached Captain Gold, and Gold had responded. There was no certainty here. All he could do was head for the bay . . .

"Where are we going?" Drasilljah asked.

"To the South Bay," the Red Nun replied.

The chaos seemed to be spreading. A thug rose up out of the shadows and challenged them. "Who the hell are you!"

He turned and yelled to people that they couldn't see. "Over here! I think we have—"

The Red Nun blew a handful of powders into the man's face, and he fell back, twitching violently.

Good. Neoloth wasn't certain how much charge remained within his talisman: he had taxed it greatly since the last recharging. There was just no way of telling how much remained.

They were safe in the darkness for the moment but would have to move, and move soon, if they were to have any chance at all of making their ship. Still—

"Wait," he said. "We need to see."

"I have a spell," Drasilljah said. "But not the power to use it. I am sorry."

"You protected the princess," he said. "You have no reason to apologize." Something occurred to him. "What if we made the spell together?" He glanced at the Red Nun.

"We . . . joined to share power," he said. "Is it possible that Drasilljah and I can do the same?"

A cynical smile crossed Shyena's lovely face. "My favorite spell. I doubt that that ceremony can be duplicated in this time and place," she said. "But I think I can form a conduit between the two of you. Together, perhaps."

They linked hands, both Drasilljah and Neoloth holding the edges of the talisman.

As Drasilljah and the Red Nun watched, his shadow began to grow. It thinned and stretched and slithered out of the alley, and eventually detached from his body and became a thing unto itself.

Neoloth sank back against the wall and, with eyes closed, became one with his shadow, seeing what it saw as it moved through the streets.

There . . . a barricade.

There . . . soldiers.

The other way. He slid back and went to the left. The further it stretched, the more it hurt. He couldn't breathe.

But he could *see.* Soldiers on the odd wheeled vehicles to the left, nothing to the right.

They ran together, following the twisting shadow, and then reeled the shade back into their bodies, took a moment to breathe, and began again.

Again and again they stopped, rested, and then extended their shadows.

From Neoloth's perspective, it was a strange thing . . . he felt somehow flattened, extended, as if the world had expelled color and devolved to shades of gray, as he stretched around corners and up walls.

The last barrier was a building on the outskirts of town, and here there was a barricade of soldiers who were beating an escaped prisoner with clubs as the shadow watched.

No way around the soldiers, and if they waited longer, the sun would be up, and they would be more exposed.

They had to move, and *now*. He and the Red Nun might have been capable of climbing over the building and lowering themselves on the other side. Aros would have scrambled up like a spider, with no problem at all.

Neoloth cursed under his breath. The three magic users knew there was nothing to do but move forward. Right through the blockade.

A diminished tingle told him the talisman was almost exhausted. The charge stored up in the desert was a distant memory. But there was another source, if he had to tap it. The idea sent fear through him, but . . .

If he had to, he would.

One step at a time, the three emerged from the alley, now cloaked in their mutual shadow. If a particularly focused and sharp-eyed individual were to stop and look directly at them, he might notice the change in light and shape of the shadows, but the battle was raging at the barricade, the escaped prisoners desperately struggling with the guards.

One step at a time. Cloaked in shadow, they were like some primitive jellyfish, the organs within barely visible through the clear flesh. If the guards stopped and stared . . .

"Here," Shyena whispered. They had reached the barricade on the road, a series of spiked wheels blocking the way.

It was possible to climb up through them, but it was hard. Once Shyena slipped and was gouged by a spike. She howled in pain—

And one of the guards, just administering a coup de grâce to a wounded prisoner, turned.

They froze on the barricade, afraid to move. Neoloth wasn't certain but suspected that the talisman required less energy to cloak a stationary object than a moving one.

The guard wiped blood out of his eyes (apparently, the escaped prisoner had managed to get in his own blows) and flicked the blood off his sword and approached the barricade.

To Neoloth the world looked like it might have from within a sandstorm, dimness filled with dark, swirling clouds. Clearly, to the guard, something was vaguely visible, unclear . . . but he snatched up one of those odd, flameless torches and shined it over them.

Suddenly, his eyes widened, and he opened his mouth, "Hey!"

Then his eyes went even wider, and he fell to the ground, an arrow in the back of his neck. With a scream, another trio of escaping prisoners fell upon the guards, and while they were busy, Neoloth and his companions scrambled the rest of the way up the barricade and were gone.

The sandstorm image had cleared just as the guard's eyes widened. The talisman might be useful again in the future, but for now it was almost dead.

They fled south along a narrow path and then reached a dock, already busy with morning fishermen. The fishermen's gaze slid over the three, and then back at the smoke rising from the city, and then to their nets and oars. He noticed that the boats were all the standard sailers or rowers. None of the new, odd steam vessels. That might have explained their lack of interest. More than most, they may have understood that something was happening in the world and wished to stay out of its way.

So, after arraying their clothing carefully, they walked the dock's stinking planks until coming down the other side and heading off around a rock-strewn path between two tumbled masses of boulders, to a bay on the far side.

And there, for the first time, Neoloth was able to draw a breath, because Captain Gold's triple-masted ship was anchored, and a rowboat awaited.

Gold's giant nephew Dorgan stood balancing in the boat, looking anxiously up at the smoke curling into the air from the direction of the city. When he saw them, he seemed infinitely relieved. "Where is Kasha?" he asked.

"Coming," Neoloth said, with all the hope he had ever felt in his voice.

"We have to go," the giant said. "Uncle says we miss the tide if we don't. And maybe soldiers come."

"We have to wait, please," Drasilljah said.

"Who you?" the giant said, eyes roaming over her with obvious relish. She pulled her cloak tighter. "Wizard? Can you make tide?"

She shook her head.

"We wait five minutes," he said.

But five became ten, and ten fifteen, and every time the giant began to draw up the anchor, Drasilljah showed him a little more leg, and he relented.

Then, at the last moment, when they had to leave . . .

A horse came riding up along the beach, and on its back was Aros. And behind him, clinging with desperate strength, was the princess.

THIRTY-EIGHT

Debts

A s sun rose over the coastal mountains, Captain Gold's *Pelican* was out to sea, bobbing on the morning tide, sails filled with wind.

Neoloth stood on the quarter deck, looking down at the main deck, where Aros, Captain Gold, and Dorgan were commiserating, planning, reconnecting, perhaps celebrating their escape.

Aros looked up at the wizard and waved his arm in lazy salute, smiling. He waved back, nodding.

There would be time for discussion. Tales to be told. But now . . .

Neoloth knocked on the cabin door. Drasilljah opened it, young now, plain and winded, but proud. She looked at Neoloth shyly. "The princess is resting," she said. "But . . . I think she would like very much to see you."

"Yes, I would," Tahlia called to them. She was sitting on a couch at the side of the room, swathed in robes, her hair disarrayed and wet, perhaps from a bath.

She was exhausted, trembling. For weeks, terribly long weeks, she had kept her terror under control, but the last days had been beyond her limit. All those skeletons. She would have been one of them, and who would ever have known which? It lived in her viscera, that memory.

She'd tried to save them. Had done her best and failed.

Those candy princes who spouted poetry and spoke of love were useless, as were the muscle-bound adventurers who thought jousting and hunting prowess would stir her heart. Aros had seemed one of those.

Two things had sustained her. One was Drasilljah, stalwart and true through the very worst. There was no way she could repay her maidservant, but she would surely try.

And the other . . . Neoloth-Pteor, the court magician. Mysterious, not quite to be trusted . . . but somehow, under it all, she had known there lurked a heart, and that it was hers. And where that had always amused her, knowing that she would be traded for advantage to a prince of another kingdom, there had always been a part of her that had wondered.

How different would each of us have to have been?

And here they were in a cabin on the *Pelican,* heading back to Quillia, and safety, because of this man. What must she look like? To herself, in the mirror (and Gold had given her the captain's cabin—was there any way to repay him, as well?) she was wan, and the bruises on her cheek and arms darkened her.

But she was not in the mood for cosmetics. She had been hustled aboard the *Pelican* with time only for a brief and formal greeting with the wizard before Drasilljah and Gold had taken her to the cabin in a thunderous rustle of canvas.

It was time for more.

"Leave us," she said, surprised at the huskiness in her voice. Was that deprivation or emotion?

Drasilljah retired from the room without protest.

The candles flickered in the light wind sighing through the portal, and the creaking timbers spoke of the endless rolling and washing of the ocean carrying her to safety.

"Neoloth," she said. "You have done great service to my queen mother, and to Quillia." A quick, soft smile. "And to me."

"That reason," Neoloth said, "was more important to me, by far, than the others."

She nodded carefully, watching his face. "May I ask you a question? Several questions, actually."

"Of course. Anything."

"And you will answer honestly, to the best of your ability."

"I swear. Truth or silence."

She smiled. A good answer. "Very well, then. The Red Nun. She was my jailor. And now she seems to be an ally. How did this happen?" She paused, feeling for the right words. "Can she be trusted?"

"You would not be free without her, Princess. She joined the Hundred to gain revenge against General Silith, who destroyed her childhood village. I convinced her that helping you was her best way to bring this to pass, and from that moment on she was an ally, and trustworthy, as long as Silith remains dead. We have Aros's word for that."

She looked carefully at his bearded face, and knew that there was more to the story. *Wizard's secrets.* She had seen so much by now that she was not at all certain that she would want to know.

"I see. Well, the proof is in the fact that I am free. When we reach Quillia, she will be treated very well indeed." She paused. "Now, who is this man Aros? He seems quite remarkable. I am to understand that in the effort to rescue me he impersonated this general's missing son?"

Neoloth laughed. "Yes, that was the plan."

"A dear friend and ally to you?"

"Ha," he said. "I arranged for him to be arrested. I rescued him from execution, placing him in my debt. He was forced to play the role."

Her eyes widened. "Well . . . who was he?"

"An enemy," he said. "The worst . . . or best . . . I ever had." He gave her a brief history of their contentions. "It seemed perfectly reasonable to render him to the hangman when I had the opportunity. And equally reasonable to consider a man of his resource and capacity the perfect ally in arranging your release."

"And has he fulfilled his obligations to you?"

Neoloth sighed. "More than. He has demonstrated an intelligence, courage, and honesty which quite frankly make me reconsider everything I thought I knew of him."

She smiled, delighted. "Excellent. You are my subject?"

"Loyally and to the death."

"Then you will immediately free him from bondage. When we return to Quillia, he will be offered a high commission in my mother's army; you may depend upon it."

His expression was one of humorous satisfaction. "What a strange place the world is, Tahlia."

"Indeed. And I assume this ship and its sailors are friends of yours?"

"Of Aros," he said. "And they also have performed with honor."

She shook her head. "Rogues, with a code of honor. I think that something must be done for them, as well."

"As you wish."

"And now we come to the last and most important questions." She rose and inspected one of the candles. Its fire wavered in the breeze. She needed a moment to collect her thoughts.

"What does it concern, Princess?"

"You, my fine wizard. You placed your life and soul in jeopardy for me. You have been the greatest imaginable servant to my mother and the kingdom. What reward do you seek?"

His eyes shifted away from hers in a way that told her everything she needed to know. Her formal, imperious manner dissolved. She crossed the cabin and took his hands in hers.

"Tell me," she said softly. "Speak your truth."

"Princess . . ." He wet his lips. And then sighed. "I stand before you a man who has worn many masks. Played many roles. I have done evil things, but I dare to hope that . . . that I . . ." Words seemed to fail him.

"That you are not an evil man?"

His red-rimmed eyes could barely meet hers. "Yes." He said, voice husky, "That I am not an evil man. I thought that I did what I did to gain your mother's favor. To gain . . . *your* favor. But now, seeing you free, knowing that somehow a lifetime of subterfuge and living in the shadows made me the man I needed to be to free you . . . I wonder about all of it. Wonder if it might be possible that I did those things to be ready for this moment. And that, this moment having come, I might not be able to give those things up. To be a new . . . a new . . ."

And again words failed him.

"A wizard worthy of a princess?" she said softly.

He could not speak. And then he could. "No. A man worthy of a good woman."

She felt a great smile spreading across her face. "These are things to be spoken of again," she said. "When we are safe. I can tell you that no one has ever done more for me. No one has ever been so worthy of my trust. My faith . . ."

She touched his lips softly with hers. A butterfly kiss, and his eyes widened.

"My love," she said, just a whisper.

"Thank you, my princess," he said in a husky voice. "I will leave you now: there is much to do. I am sure you are tired and need rest."

He raised her hands and kissed them, then turned and left.

Princess Tahlia lay on her bed, the captain's bed, thinking. How strange. In that moment, she knew Neoloth could have had more than a kiss. But he had not even attempted to deepen it. Her rescuer, her savior, had either not understood the depth of her gratitude . . . or his emotions were exactly what he had described.

THIRTY-NINE

Tattoos

Neoloth found Aros on the quarterdeck, looking out over the waves. There was no land to be seen on any side, just the waves and the sun and the wheeling, "skawing" gray and white gulls above them and the clouds and the constant hauling of ropes, painting of planks, and burnishing of brass that make up life on any sailing ship.

Aros grunted as Neoloth came to stand next to him. The wizard hoped that the Aztec might speak first, but he didn't, and after a time he was forced to step into the silence.

"We won," Neoloth said.

"That we have," Aros agreed.

"I . . . you . . ." Gods! Why was this so hard? "You kept your oath to me," Neoloth said.

"You expected otherwise?"

Behind him, the sailors broke out in song, and Shyena was dancing to the tune, entertaining them with her quicksilver foot-work and dizzying hips.

"A comely wench," Aros said. "I've watched the way she looks at you. You could have her, you know."

Neoloth suspected that the barbarian's keen senses saw more than Neoloth was comfortable admitting. He said, "She is not who I wanted."

Neoloth stood gazing at the waves, hearing the whooping and hollering of the men behind them and the sound of the Red Nun's quick, light steps and knew that he was a different man than he who had begun this journey.

And when he looked up into the face of the sun-bronzed barbarian with the hair cut squarely across his forehead, there was laughter in his eyes.

Suddenly, Neoloth swelled in anger. "What the hell are you laughing at?"

"A wizard in love. Who would have thought?"

Neoloth toyed with bluster but ultimately began to laugh himself, and the two of them stood at the rail and guffawed, all of the tension of the last weeks ebbing out of them like a poison.

And by the time they were done, Neoloth was nodding, as much to himself as the barbarian at his side.

"Well," he said. "Regardless of why you did what you did . . ." Neoloth extracted the talisman from its case. "Very little power remaining," he said. "Just enough, I think, to do this."

He put one hand on Aros's chest, and the other held the talis-man, which in the early-evening light began to glow.

The barbarian flinched at first and then relaxed, eyes rolling up as a wave of bluish light rolled through his body. The sculpted chest visible through his open shirt trembled and . . . crawling around his side and toward the light came three tattoos.

"Wait," Aros said. "I accept the breaking of the spell . . . but the girl . . . I've grown rather fond of." He paused. "And so has someone else. Leave them in place."

"As you wish," Neoloth said, and the tattoos crawled back into place and were still. "The curse is gone. The other tattoos, the scars, they are with Agathodaemon."

Aros's eyes remained closed. He sighed, deeply, like a man laying down a great burden. Then he opened them and looked at Neoloth with curiosity. "I'd wondered," he said.

"Wondered what?"

"If you would keep your word. After all, if I wasn't under your curse, what would keep me from killing you?"

"Why would you do that?"

Aros's eyes were as hard as glass. "Because you put me in that dungeon to begin with and then used that to force me to do your will."

Flaygod, Aros's sword, was close to hand. The barbarian could seize it, and in an impulsive moment take Neoloth's head off. And then ransom the princess or . . .

But on a day such as this, Neoloth decided not to worry about such things. "Well," he said. "What's a little coercion between friends?"

Aros's hand froze, and his eyes narrowed, as if wondering if the wizard was mocking him, and then his eyes softened. And he laughed.

"What the hell," he said.

"Yes," Neoloth said. What the hell. Then suddenly his eyes widened. "I completely forgot about Agathodaemon!"

"The snake?"

The wizard groaned. "After we deliver the princess, I'll have to go back, unless . . ."

"Don't look at me," Aros said. "I don't like snakes."

Neoloth shook his head silently, and together they watched the waves, the moon dancing upon them, as the *Pelican* slid south toward Quillia.

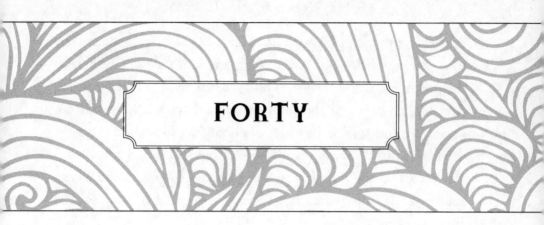

FORTY

Into the Storm

It was just before dawn on the third day that it happened. The intervening days had been happy ones aboard the *Pelican*, with hard work for the sailors, but much sleep and rest time for Princess Tahlia, who ventured from her cabin only after a day and a half of deep, healing sleep. She tended to wander about the ship, greeting the sailors with a slightly sleepy, almost embarrassed expression, nothing regal about her.

She inquired after their health and well-being and showed great curiosity in their work such that, by the end of the second day, she was greatly admired and even loved by the crew, who proclaimed that if all princesses were made of the same stuff, the world would be a better place indeed.

She spent much time with Drasilljah, but also with Shyena, she who was called the Red Nun, asking questions about Shrike and the people in it, and how she and Neoloth had come to help her. And if she suspected that both witch and wizard were skirting some of her questions, she had the delicacy not to probe too deeply.

By the third day the mood aboard the *Pelican* had lifted considerably, and she found herself crying and singing and dancing spontaneously, as if finally believing that she had escaped the clutches of her captors.

Aros was enjoying himself, becoming more familiar with the *Pelican*, remembering his freebooter days, and wondering what it might be like to be a privateer in the service of the Quillian queen. From poop to bowsprit he explored the craft, familiarizing himself with everything about it and climbing up in the rigging, sometimes just hanging there, much to the sailors' amusement. He was more nimble than the rest by a wide margin, save for a tiny man named Nimbett, who was an absolute monkey on the lines. And stronger than any two of them with the exception of Dorgan.

Captain Gold was tolerant and amused by his explorations, and Aros used his time to roam and learn and entertain himself and the others.

Hanging there in the rigging, he would look at the sky and the sea, each in the other's place, and think back over his life and wonder about the life to come. Where would he go now? And what of his choices were determined by whatever it was he had been until this point?

What in a man's future was the meaning of his past? In Shrike, he had told a lie about his past. It had been a lie, hadn't it? He did know who and what he was, didn't he?

If he didn't know who he had been . . . what did that mean about who he might become?

His head hurt. Such questions were for philosophers, not simple fighting men. Better get those tattoos back. Find the snake again.

And then he noticed something strange. Lines of smudge dropping down from the sky . . .

He curled up, grabbed the rope, and hung suspended there, thirty feet above the deck, looking out at the horizon. On it, he saw three lines of smoke, rising from the waves.

Fire on the sea.

Heart thundering, he went hand over hand to the foremast and stood on the crow's nest gazing back at the horizon. Not three columns of smoke . . . five. Eight. More.

"Ahoy, mates!" he called out. "We have trouble coming up behind!"

The crew crowded around the forecastle, using their telescope or keen eyes to see what he saw.

A flotilla of the damned Shrike burning ships coming up behind them. At the horizon now, but not far enough.

There was little doubt that their sails had been seen.

He climbed down and joined the men who were packed along the rail, eyes shaded.

Captain Gold looked pensive. "They'll catch us," he said.

"You're sure of that?"

The big man nodded his head. Fingers nervously braided his beard. He was a courageous man, but every man has his limits, and the things Aros had told him of, and hinted of, had unnerved the captain. "Aye. I've seen them keep up with me, even at full sail. This is a poor wind."

"How long do we have?"

Gold looked up at the billowing canvas rectangles. "We have an east wind. Reckon I can set the sails to catch enough to make a good pace, but it's no contest. I'd say they'll catch us by nightfall." His face was grave. "Aye, and then there'll be hell to pay."

"Can we make harbor?"

"We're a day away from Ween's Mask, and that's just a beach. I'm afraid we're on our own, boyo." He raised his voice high. "All right, lads! We're going to make a run of it, and then we'll make a fight of it, and we may not live through this one, but I'll be damned if we'll go down without spilling some Shrike blood!"

Princess Tahlia looked up at him. "If they catch us . . ." Her face looked ashen. "What if I go back quietly. Surely not all of you have to die."

The wizard had found his way beside them now. "We need to be realistic," he said.

The Red Nun had long since stopped dancing. "We destroyed the time tunnels," she said. "If we reach Quillia and tell our story, she will raise the kingdoms against Shrike, and there will be a war she cannot win."

"What do we do?" the princess asked.

"Prayer might be a good idea. The sea has held mana longer than the land."

All that day they ran, and ran, and the ships behind them began to close the distance, such that through the telescopes they could make out a few details. They could not, as yet, see men on the deck, but that would happen soon. And soon after that they would be in firing range.

"No sail ships," Aros noted. "These steam farters are all with the Hundred."

And that was the most likely outcome here—not capture, but death. The *Pelican* had to go down. A single survivor reaching a friendly ear could doom Shrike, or at the very least the plans of the Hundred. Neoloth had no idea what had happened in the kingdom since he had left, but he knew that witnesses would make it impossible for the truth to be contained.

If it could, and the time tunnel could be reopened . . . the plan could go forward. But only if no one knew. If the other seven kingdoms were not raised up against them.

Aros stood on the poop deck, gazing out at the southern horizon. His eyes caught against the dark clouds, a flash of lightning.

Captain Gold stood at his side. Aros knew that his old friend had to feel tense. No coward, he was realist enough to know that capture meant death to all involved.

"Looks like a storm," Aros said.

"That it does," Gold replied.

"Those steam engines . . . ," Neoloth began. "What is the advantage of such devices?"

Gold stroked his beard. "One can keep moving no matter the wind. It takes real skill to use sails to catch the wind as God intended."

"Aye," Neoloth said. "And that's what I was thinking. The real advantage of a hand cannon is that it negates a lifetime of sword craft."

Aros fingered Flaygod. It was true, and in his less reasonable moments, he considered it bloody unfair.

"What's your point?"

"That if steam, and all these machines make experience less important, how much more likely is it that they will be used by . . . inexperienced people?"

"Much." Gold's bushy eyebrows narrowed.

"And what is the most important thing in a storm?"

"To ride her. To know when to strike the sails, when to drop anchor or turn the ship to take a wave head-on rather than broadside."

Neoloth's voice lowered. "And what teaches a man to do such things?"

Gold smiled. "Experience," he said.

Then Gold raised his voice. "Ahoy, mates! Oars in the water, sails at full! Throw everything overboard we don't need to fight!"

"The food, Cap'n?" one of his men said.

"Aye. We're just two days out of Quillia, and we won't starve before we get there. Everything over the side!"

The men fell to, heaving furniture and gear over the side. Oars extruded from belowdecks, and the men broke their backs straining in rhythm, digging at the waves.

"Will we make it?" the princess asked. "Is there any magic that can help?"

"I think we're about out of magic," Neoloth said. Looked to Drasilljah and the Red Nun.

"I'm stripped," the Red Nun said. "In these magic-poor times, I'm surprised to have done what we have."

Captain Gold fingered his beard. "Here's what I say," he said. "Before those ships reach firing distance, the water will be no sea of glass. And then we'll see what kind of captains they have."

The sun had disappeared behind the clouds, and the sea itself grown angry before the first cannons blazed behind them.

Aros ran back to the forecastle and used the spyglass. The ships were clearly visible, and if the light had been better, he could have made out the men on the deck. The steam farters were powerful, but not faster than a good sail under a capable captain—if the wind was right.

But the wind was starting to shift and blow against them, slowing their progress despite the backbreaking labor of the oarsmen.

"What do you think?" he asked.

"We won't make it," Gold said soberly. "Unless . . ." Something had occurred to him, and he trained his spyglass south.

"Yes. The wind has shifted. We're slowing, but the storm is coming our way."

"Damned good," Aros said. "At the very least, I'm hoping we can force these bastards to close quarters."

"It's a fleet of the damned ships," Gold said. "We're probably outnumbered at least ten to one."

"I don't give a damn," he said. "If I die, I die, but I don't want to just be blown out of the water."

"They'll want to cripple us and come on board to be sure they've got the princess," Gold said, and spit overboard. "That's one small blessing."

"Probably want to torture me, as well," Aros said, philosophically.

"My kind of men," Gold said, and slapped his shoulder.

The cannon rang again.

The *Pelican* had two cannon positions in her stern and was capable of making a reply. As Gold had thought, their range seemed better. But although, at Gold's command, the cannon roared, they missed . . . and then hit one of the steamers, and the men cheered as it burst amidships, was consumed in flame.

"We must have hit the powder magazine!" Gold cried. "That's givin' it to 'em, boys!"

Initial enthusiasm gave way to disappointment when the next three shots hit nothing but water, and then a shot from the steamers smashed through the gallery at the *Pelican*'s stern.

Some of the men screamed in pain and anger. Never fear, Aros noted. Whatever else might be said of them, these were stout rascals.

The princess stood with Neoloth, his arm around her, protecting her from the wind . . . and then the rain. It fell in cold drops at first, and then in sheets, and the men cheered.

They were in the storm. The waves roughened and then became walls of water slamming into them . . . and into the steamers as well.

"How are they handling the waves?" Aros asked.

Gold's eyes narrowed. "Better than I'd hoped, but I'll wager not as well as they'd wish. I think they're getting water down the pipe, and that will trouble the fires driving the damned things."

The oars fought against the steam engines after the *Pelican* struck her sails. If they hadn't, the wind would have driven them right into their enemy's arms.

Another fusillade from both sides. They hit another ship, which began to burn. The men cheered . . .

Then, with a stroke of lightning, the cheers died, because on the northern horizon were at least a dozen more of the steam ships.

"By the Feathered One," Aros breathed. There was no way they could fight half that many ships. The courage and will were bleeding out of the men as he watched.

And then . . .

From behind them a roar of cannon, and with despair Captain Gold pivoted. "Damnation!" he screamed against the wind and the crashing waves. "How in hell did they get behind us?"

It was Princess Tahlia who ran back to the forecastle, looking out into the darkness, her eyes widening as, from the spray and the darkness, emerged the silhouettes of a vast armada.

Sailing ships, not steamers.

"It's the fleet!" she screamed, sobbing in relief and joy. "It's my mother's fleet!"

And it was, breaking from the mist beneath a hollow moon, the Quillian fleet heading north.

Neoloth's desperate message to the queen had gone through.

FORTY ONE

Boarding

In an instant, the game had changed. The steamers ceased to concentrate their fire on the *Pelican* and began to array for battle against the Quillian fleet. Although they were outmatched in size and cannon, they outnumbered the fleet two to one and were far more mobile.

The steamers rose and fell on the crashing waves that now sent floods of water and deafening noise onto the deck of the *Pelican*.

Pelican sped forward as if its heart was buoyed by the arrival of allies. The first of the Quillian ships closed around her, blocking her from the first line of steamers.

Aros, Gold, Tahlia, the Red Nun, and Drasilljah stood at the poop, watching the battle rage. The Quillian fleet had the gun power to defeat the smaller boats . . . if only they would stand still. But steamers could maneuver against the wind with a baffling facility, their plumes of steam rising up through the rain, the smaller vessels rising and falling on the swells, which the Quillian ships had never prepared for.

The roar of cannon was deafening, and the smell of the smoke, even in the drenching rain, hung over them in a pall.

The entire Quillian fleet was not here, as those aboard the *Pelican* had originally thought. It was six ships against twenty smaller ones and two larger ships, and through the telescope, Neoloth watched the bow of the flagship and saw General Silith's massive shape on the bow, surrounded by officers.

Neoloth handed the glass to Aros, and he focused in turn. "That's not Silith," he said. "But this is the Shrike navy, and I'm betting most of these men think that it's him."

One of the Quillian ships was burning now, foundering, having taken cannonade after cannonade. As they watched, it began to break in two, sailors leaping overboard into the maelstrom, most quickly sucked down.

"Oh my God," Tahlia whispered. "We can't win."

And then . . . something happened. Out of the blackness of the ocean something horrible came. An eight-foot writhing tentacle grasped one of the sailors, but instead of pulling him down, it lifted him *up* and placed him on the deck of the *Pelican*.

Something was happening to one of the steamers. It began spinning in a circle, as if its rudder had been broken or bent. Another of the steamers began to founder, its bow dipping down until the sailors screamed, and the water flooded its boiler so that the steam died.

Neoloth watched carefully, eyes narrowed, water pouring down his face from the rain, and he pointed. "There!"

They saw a finny tail shape on the waves, swiftly diving out of sight.

"Merfolk!" he cried. The Merfolk and their allies had arrived.

And, almost overwhelmed with relief as he was, he understood what this meant. The magical folk, driven to the ocean's depths or to the desert barrens to survive, understood that this was the last stand for all of them. If the magicians of the Hundred had their way, they would bring devices from the future more powerful than magic, draining the magic from the world in the process. They would control everything, and everyone.

Magic might already be a dying form, a dead art. But this would accelerate it. Here and now, in the ocean north of Quillia, they had decided to take their stand.

There were shapes in the ocean that he had never seen, and hoped never to see again. Monsters and monstrous shapes that were not fish or land animals or men but squiddy things with parrot beaks and arms that reached out to the decks and lifted men up to rend them apart.

So exposed, the cannon could find them, and the steamers had more, had the ability to gush fire in the rain, a harmless weapon against waterlogged ships but searing to flesh, even flesh so strange as this.

They could hear the screams, smell charred meat when the wind shifted to their direction.

Even with the magical folk, the battle seemed too even. And then . . . it was not even anymore.

Shrike's flagship bore forward, and now when they saw it more clearly, saw that the bow was reinforced with metal, some kind of cutting arrangement, such that as it came forward it struck one of the Quillian vessels amidships. With a grinding crash, the ship split, wood splinters cascading in all directions as the ship died.

It was coming directly at them. Coming straight for them.

"To your cabin, Princess!" Gold screamed.

"I'll miss it all! Drasilljah, no!"

A cannon's roar exploded wood splinters across the deck, and Neoloth felt it pluck at him and was dazed.

"Drop anchor!" Gold screamed, and they heard the chain whir as the anchor was released. It struck bottom, and the chain slacked, then tautened. The *Pelican* began to swing sideways, so that the flagship could not strike her solidly.

But grappling hooks attached to thick brown ropes were cast down from the higher deck, piercing the *Pelican*'s sides.

Men jumped down from the higher deck onto their ship, brandishing swords and shoulder pipes, and the battle was on.

Now, at last, Aros had something to do other than watch the carnage. Snarling, he threw himself into the fray, Flaygod in one hand and Captain Gold's good strong Quillian steel in the other. Shrike's men came in waves, but the *Pelican*'s crew had been wound like springs, running all day from their foe, and now that the enemies were before them, the crew was eager to come to close quarters and do real damage.

The storm thundered down on the desperate struggle, the waves crashing against the bow, shaking it repeatedly under the black clouds, the lightning above and the flash of steel below creating a nightmarish situation where the enemy was only clearly visible for moments at a time. But in those moments, the cleaving of skulls and lopping of limbs, the screams as men were blasted at close range by the shoulder cannons were terrifying.

And now there was another crash that shook them all, as one of the Quillian fleet smashed into the enemy vessel from the far side, and it was boarded in turn. Clearly, everyone understood that this vessel, the *Pelican*, was the key to all of it. This was where the fight would end. Most of the ships were heading toward them, tying on with grapnels such that the maze of steamers and sail ships, of rope and chains and hooks, the swarms of Shrikian and Quillian sailors swarming along the lines toward them made, in the middle of the storm, something like a floating island peopled by men and ruled by madness.

Aros noted that Neoloth, the Red Nun, and Drasilljah were on the quarterdeck before the princess's room, barring passage. Lights swirled up there, and men who tried to approach were skewered by lightning that rocked the ship. A storm must make lightning easy for wizards.

Even granting that, Aros was confused. This was mighty magic. From whence could such power be drawn? Then three men came at him, and he was forced to wipe the water and blood out of his face, set his feet, and fight.

His Quillian steel wrought havoc, but it was Flaygod that cut the widest swath. Aros cleared the deck around him, smashing bones and caving skulls as much as cutting flesh. With the deck around him cleared for a moment, he put the sword between his teeth, slammed Flaygod into its scabbard, and climbed the rigging, seeking a better view of what was happening.

There was a balance, precarious now, between the forces of Quillia and those of Shrike and the mermen and their allies, now battling across the decks and in the ocean, cannon, swords, and tentacles all taking their share of lives below him.

He saw Captain Gold battling in the forecastle next to his nephew Dorgan, who was flinging men around like dolls. Not much of a swordsman, yet the giant was worth three of the others in sheer ferocity.

"For the princess!" men cried. "For Shrike!" others answered, and the uniforms mingled so that, often, men seemed not to know who was a brother and who an enemy until they were face-to-face, close enough to see the style of sword.

And then . . . Aros saw General Silith.

Silith was dead, of course. It had to be the wizard Neoloth had spoken of, Belot. But watching him, even if a double, cutting his (her? its?) way through the troops made his heart sink. Double or not, the wizard had the general's style, as if taking his visage allowed him to access that skill. He was heading toward Neoloth, and the princess.

Aros dove into the fray, landing on the slick deck in three-point balance, snarling defiance into the rain. "Time for you to die," he called.

The false general cocked his head, shaking blood and water from his weapon. "You must be the Aztec I've heard of," he said.

"I am."

"Good," Belot said. The wizard's voice was a strange blend of Silith's baritone and a deeply musical woman's contralto. He'd never heard the like. "You have caused me trouble, but nothing I cannot undo, after all of you are dead. The war has merely started early."

"And there's nothing here that steel cannot undo," Aros said. "Look out for your head."

And with that Aros came at him.

There was something that he had learned from his battle with the general—that battle ferocity alone was not enough, that somehow there had to be a part of you watching the fight as it unfolded, like an angel above or demon below. That was the gift that Silith had given him. And from that perspective, Aros knew that the wizard had all of Silith's technique. Every stroke, block, and piece of footwork. His thrusts and parries were almost as fast, his arm almost as strong. If Aros had not sparred with the real general and then battled beside him, he would have been dead in seconds.

Aros compensated by moving backward, giving way while probing for flaws. There were none, and for a moment he felt despair.

Then it dawned on him that the wizard was predictable.

Aros could see his every next move. He had Silith's moves, his skill, but not his spontaneous ability to combine them in new and disorienting ways. The instant intuitive *creativity* was missing.

And that lack of instant adaptation gave Aros time to adjust. He noticed something else: the wizard was not as strong as Silith had been. Magic and knowledge hadn't quite compensated for a lifetime of wielding that sword, with all the strength and endurance that implied. Regardless of the wizard's powers, Aros's exertions were beginning to stress it. Its eyes were not quite human now. They were empty holes, deep as the chasm between sanity and madness. The mouth a thin line, like a sword slash in wet flesh. In the flashes of light, he saw things, things that chilled him.

It was Silith. It was not.

It was a man. It was a woman. Mere flashes. The lightning revealed such things for moments only, and then the night concealed them again.

"I took his skill," it hissed. "Sucked it from his marrow as he died. As I will take yours." But, Aros wondered, was it speaking to him? Or to itself? Was it quite as confident as it wanted him to believe?

Lightning crashed overhead, and that awful glare again revealed a face that was both male and female and larger than either a normal man's or woman's. Not human at all.

But this time, the men around them saw the horror and fell back, screaming, "That ain't the general!" And the murmur ran through them, and they backed away from the men they had been hacking.

"General Silith is dead!" the thing screamed above the roar of the wind. "I, Belot, the One, am in command!"

"I ain't fightin' for no wizard!" one of the men screamed. "Hold up! I fight for king and general!"

There were screams of shared agreement, and the thing in the general's costume struck the sailor down. He groaned and sank, his brains spilled onto the deck.

The men around him grumbled, retreating, swords high but refusing to fight.

"I am in charge!" Belot shrieked. "I am greater than any general, any king, and I—"

And in that moment's distraction, Aros stabbed him through the side ribs, pierced the creature's heart. Not a particularly honorable thing to do, he knew.

But, after all, he was a barbarian.

FORTY-TWO

Waging Peace

Belot, the creature who had masqueraded as General Silith, slid to the deck. The male-female form wasted away as well, revealing something beneath that was part squid, part ape. Something that might have thrived on an earlier, less sane world.

And then . . . it melted away as well, as if its true form was nothing appropriate for this world.

"What was it?" Captain Gold asked, as his surgeon bandaged his arm.

"One of the old ones," Neoloth said. "We used to pray to them." Aros turned and looked at his companion. There was something wrong with the wizard. He seemed . . . *old*.

The Shrike sailors seemed uncertain. Their commander was the first to speak. "What now? We sailed thinking we had been commanded by our general. If we stop fighting you now . . . what happens?"

There was general murmuring from both sets of combatants. What indeed? Wars had begun over events far more trivial than the kidnapping of a princess or an assault on a royal fleet.

"I can tell you what will happen," Tahlia said. "I am Princess Tahlia, of Quillia." She was dressed in a rough cotton robe, not a crown, but she managed to make it regal.

"Princess," the admiral said. In genuflecting rows, the sailors of the Quillian navy went to one knee before her.

She extended her hand to the admiral, and, after a moment's pause, he took it and kissed the back.

"What will you tell your mother, Princess Tahlia? Whither do we go from here?"

"Home," the princess said. "There has been enough death this day. I will tell my mother that I was stolen by the Hundred, by a monster which imitated the form of the general and others to foment war. And that the good people of Shrike, once they became aware of this abomination, freed me and fought with me against this evil, and assisted in returning me home. Further, I will say that the good people of Shrike wish nothing but kinship with Quillia and that your act of kindness and fealty to your rightful king can and should be considered the first act in a new and better relationship between Shrike and the other seven kingdoms. By this act, you have earned my friendship and undying gratitude of the queen of Quillia."

And Aros knew that in that statement she meant not merely

her mother, but the woman she would be, for this was the first act of a woman who deserved the title *queen* in every way.

The lines were untied, the damaged ships evaluated, sailors returned to their vessels. Once war is begun, it is difficult to put those dogs back in the kennel, but every sailor there knew that the future of their nations depended on courtesy and caution for the next hours. By the time the lines were untied, the damaged ships evaluated, the sailors returned to their vessels and the Shrike vessels headed north, all were ready to breathe a sigh of relief.

The sailors marveled at the magical creatures that danced on the waves around them as the storm died down and calm returned to the waters.

Aros had watched Neoloth. Something had happened to the man he now considered . . . if not a friend, then certainly a companion. An ally who understood him entirely too well.

"Help me," Neoloth whispered, and Aros assisted him to his feet. The princess was being transferred to the flagship of the Quillian navy, which fortunately had not sustained great damage.

"Will you come with me?" the princess asked. She must have noticed that there was something amiss with Neoloth. His complexion had gone pasty, and streaks of white ran in his hair.

"No, no," he said. "I'll be on soon. I promise." He managed to wink at her. "More spells to be done, first. Gratitude to our helpers."

She didn't seem to believe him totally, but there was little she could say. She and Drasilljah walked the gangplank over to the other ship, and with a final look back over her shoulder, disappeared onto the deck. The plank was struck, and slowly, ponderously, the great ship began to turn, its oars stroking the water until its sails could catch the wind and power her home.

And then Neoloth collapsed.

The escape and subsequent battle had taken all of the old wizard's strength.

Aros bent over him. "By the serpent!" he said. "Your hair! Your face!"

Neoloth reached up a trembling hand to clasp Aros's arm. The wizard's hand was knobbed and wrinkled. "Well, it was worth it."

"Worth what?" Aros asked.

"I've used spells to keep me young, so that the last bit of magic was in me. I gave it up to work with the Red Nun and Drasilljah to protect Tahlia."

"How . . . old are you?" Aros asked. And there was a tenderness in the Aztec's eyes that he thought never to see. How strange, for such a thing at the very end of life.

"Too old to count birthdays." He laughed. A wheezing sound.

The world whirled and faded, and when it returned the Red Nun stood beside him.

"What can I do?" she asked.

"There is nothing," he sighed, exhaling as if he no longer had the strength to keep breath in his body. "I paid the price for victory, and I'm satisfied with what I purchased."

Aros held the wizard's hand. Neoloth could see it withering even as he watched. What was he now? He couldn't even remember his years, but they had to be more than . . .

His mind was growing dim. How strange to be here now, surrounded by these people in the last moments of his long and strange life.

Captain Gold appeared in his wavering vision. Looked at him with concern, but his face was . . . strange. "Aros," he said. "Bring the wizard to the side of the ship."

"Why?" the Aztec asked.

"He's asked for."

Without another word, Aros slid his arms under Neoloth, as gently and easily as lifting a baby, carried him to the side, and propped him up.

Neoloth could feel it. He was a feather. He was positioned so that he could look down over the side of the ship, and down there in the waves danced the Merfolk.

M'thrilli and his family.

"Neoloth," the merman said. "We have won."

"Yes." He barely recognized his own voice.

"The victory was dearly won, I see."

"No man lives forever," Neoloth said. "I think that . . . perhaps . . . I finally found something worth dying for."

Aros shook his head. "That means that, after all this time, you found something worth living for."

Neoloth laughed at the absurdity of it, and before he knew what had happened, the others were laughing as well. He laughed and laughed until the tears streamed down his face.

How old was he, Neoloth? He didn't even know. Old enough to die here now, beneath the stars, on this ship. Having saved his love, destroyed the greatest threat the world had ever seen . . .

And found a friend in a former enemy. What a strange life. What a strange, strange . . .

M'thrilli smiled to him. Beside him, his woman whispered something in his ear, and he nodded. "You have been a great friend to the sea folk," he said. "And I think we would like to show you something. Come."

Neoloth was too weak to argue. One place to die was the same as another.

"Good-bye, Aros," he whispered. "Go and find the life you deserve," he said. And then slipped over the side and into the welcoming arms of the sea.

FORTY-THREE

Undersea

After he entered the water, Neoloth never completely knew what was dream and what was reality.

He was only semiconscious when he struck the water. He remembered being held above the water, and something slipped over his head by the pod of Merfolk, some sort of membrane like the external skin of a jellyfish. He could barely breathe through it, and then, when they pulled him down below the waves and he was being dragged through the water, he could *still* barely breathe.

But . . . to his wonderment, he could breathe.

In all his life, Neoloth had seen so many wonders, had created so many that he thought he could no longer be amazed.

He was wrong.

They took him down into the depths, out into the deeps. He could barely think or feel anything, so overwhelmed with the very fact of being where he was that he drifted into a kind of trance.

It was dark, darker than night. And then . . . it was not. There was something up ahead, a reef, he thought. It was not a building, or a city, in any sense he had ever known. This was something different. If the creatures of the sea, the things that were of magic, were as those on the surface, not all of them could live together. Some, such as the leviathans and the great tentacled things that had fought beside them, were clearly no part of this . . . world.

But there were so many creatures, things he had never seen. Melds of fish and man or horse or lion, beasts that seemed more plant than fish or animal. Things that were translucent, with other creatures living within them.

And the reef, a sort of living complex of small creatures creating structures for larger creatures. And it glowed. He could *feel* it.

This was a place of almost unimaginable magic, as such wonders might have existed when the world was young. Men and gods had squandered mana on the surface, but here the sea denizens had invested it more elegantly. Here diamonds flamed in heaps and acres uncounted, and the magical bestiary swarmed peacefully, living together as men so seldom managed to do on dry land.

Neoloth thought, "What is this?"

And his thought was heard. Or perhaps he spoke and was unaware he was speaking, so dream-like was it all. M'thrilli said, *It is not a place for men.*

Why did you bring me here? I am a man.

Today you are not, the merman thought to him. *Today, you are a friend.*

In and out of consciousness Neoloth flowed; down and down and down they took him into a place beneath the sea—and within himself, which he had never found or suspected.

You are very near to death.

Let me go.

Do you love? Does Neoloth-Pteor love?

Yes, I love.

Then do you not wish to live?

I cannot live. I can feel that something is dissolved within me.

Yes. You can no longer use those spells. You have gone too far.

Then let me go.

But there is one last gift we can give you. But it is a final gift, and you would have to accept a normal life and age as other men do.

To cry underwater would seem impossible, but he knew it was happening. Was there even a chance for a life with Tahlia? To even have a chance?

They were giving him that opportunity, in a moment when he feared he had nothing at all. "Yes," he said. And he felt as if his skin was peeling away, as if he was a pearl, revealing layers. All of the men he had been, all of the lands he had traveled. So many memories dissolving, until some essential grain of sand, some irritation in the core of the pearl, was revealed.

What was it? What had begun his path toward damnation, that path that had been disrupted in the oddest way. By love. The Red Nun had begun her path to vengeance after a disaster . . .

Just as Neoloth had been cast from his home by violence . . .

Neoloth, in a land far away, had had a mother and a father in a life so distant that he had not remembered their names and faces for years. Common folk they had been, living common lives. He recalled that childhood, lived simply and warmly. No disasters. No catastrophes.

Just normal enough for him to feel . . .

I want more.

That was how he had begun. That was all it had taken.

I want more.

And if he had more, then what? He'd had treasure enough for three kingdoms, adventures enough for a dozen men, knowledge to surpass a university of scholars.

How much is enough? Had he ever had more than what he'd felt just kissing Tahlia's hand? Had he ever had as much as his parents, in their common lives, with their simple love for each other and their children?

How much is enough?

And something called out from him. *One life, one love is enough. And a thousand lives without something meaningful is not.*

He made his choice.

And, really, it was no choice at all.

FORTY-FOUR

Exit the Taxman

When Neoloth woke, he was being hauled up from the waves in a bosun's chair. He looked back down into the water and saw glowing eyes and faint figures of magical creatures as they sank back into the deep, sadness and profound thanks mingling as he realized that he would never see them again.

By the time he stepped up onto the *Pelican*'s deck, he knew that something was different within him. He felt stronger, more solid than he had in decades.

Friends and comrades were waiting.

"Your face," Aros said.

Neoloth felt his cheeks and nose, exploring a foreign territory. It was strange to him. A younger man's face. What . . . ?

He stumbled to the captain's cabin, still redolent of her scent, the bed still rumpled from when she had last slept there. And above a chest of trinkets, something used to adorn Captain Gold's daily costumes. A mirror. And in it Neoloth saw something he had not seen in a lifetime.

The younger man, but a different man, as if he had forgotten the toll his life had taken from him, the weight on his soul.

He laughed and laughed, as if it was the first time in a long, excellent life. And perhaps it was.

Three days later, they touched port. Aros had waited on the deck from before dawn, thinking about the man Neoloth seemed to have become so swiftly and completely, and he knew what was about to happen, even if he didn't know why.

Neoloth started down the gangplank, then paused and turned. "We're here," he said. "You're free. More than free. I believe that there are certain honors and riches that are yours now. What was your previous occupation other than thief and rogue?"

"Taxman," Aros said. "Does that meet the standard?"

"We can do better."

Aros smiled. "Well, I think I'll keep those honors on account," he said. "I know that you're about to make a play for a princess. That's not something I want to watch."

"What? Is that such an unlikely thing?"

The Aztec chuckled in reply. "No more likely than a barbarian who has half the royal households in Shrike indebted, invested, or in bed. You . . . keep the reward money for me."

"I can do that."

"Oh, I think there will be many . . . interesting conversations between Shrike and Quillia. And a lot of ways for a person willing to position himself properly."

"A man who sees an opportunity."

"Well . . . I haven't been in love in a while."

"Better late than never."

There was something uncomfortable in that silence, something that neither of them wanted to discuss. Neoloth spoke first.

"In another life," he said. "I think . . ."

"Yes," Aros said. "But let's keep this between ourselves. We have reputations to uphold."

The two men extended and shook hands. "I have enough friends," Aros said. "What a great man needs is an enemy of quality."

"Do you aspire to greatness?"

"Who better?"

Neoloth left the ship, walking down the gangplank with the stride of a man in his thirties, something different than he had ever been. A mortal man, just a man of wisdom and knowledge, who loved a princess.

Shyena the Red Nun leaned against the rail beside Aros wearing a crimson sheath dress she had constructed in their days at sea. It clung to her curves. "You don't hate him, do you?"

"No," Aros said, eyes gliding over her body. "Not anymore."

"He framed you, you know."

"Of course he did. But he also trusted me."

"Yes. And once warned you and saved your life."

"That . . . was strange," Aros said. "He sent me a dream that saved my life. He has powers."

"That one he needed a little help with." Her smile was mischievous. Seductive. "I'm not completely without my own resource."

"How exactly did you help him?" Aros asked, beginning to wonder.

"It's a long trip back to Shrike," she said. "I could tell you . . . or I could show you."

Aros felt his smile grow wide, and warm. "It *is* a long trip."

She had contrived to angle her hip against his, a warm, heavy, luscious weight. "And this noble who waits for you in Shrike. I have heard she is a good woman."

"She is," Aros said. "Very. But, as you said, Mijista is in Shrike."

Aros did not know what was ahead for him. What was behind was strange enough. Today was where he had to live.

The Red Nun looked back at him over her shoulder as she reached the cabin door.

He was just a simple fighting man. Why would he care about magic?

"Well," Captain Gold asked, chuckling. His friend had appeared behind him without a sound. Their recent success in battle had put a twinkle in his eye, like the old days. The whole world seemed new. "What are you waiting for, laddie?"

"Nothing," he said, and slapped Gold's shoulder. "Absolutely nothing at all. How many days back to Shrike?"

"Six, maybe seven."

Aros nodded and stepped to the cabin's threshold. He turned and grinned like a shark.

"Make it eight," Aros said, and closed the door behind him.